About The Author

Steve Berry is the *New York Times* bestselling author of *The Emperor's Tomb*, *The Paris Vendetta*, *The Charlemagne Pursuit*, *The Venetian Betrayal*, *The Alexandria Link*, *The Templar Legacy*, *The Third Secret*, *The Romanov Prophecy*, *The Amber Room*, and the short stories 'The Balkan Escape' and 'The Devil's Gold'. His books have been translated into forty languages and sold in fifty-one countries. He lives in the historic city of St. Augustine, Florida, and is working on his next novel. He and his wife, Elizabeth, have founded History Matters, a nonprofit organization dedicated to preserving our heritage. To learn more about Steve Berry and the foundation, visit www.steveberry.org.

Also by Steve Berry

NOVELS

The Amber Room
The Romanov Prophecy
The Third Secret
The Templar Legacy
The Alexandria Link
The Venetian Betrayal
The Charlemagne Pursuit
The Paris Vendetta
The Emperor's Tomb

E-BOOKS

'The Balkan Escape'
'The Devil's Gold'

THE JEFFERSON KEY

STEVE BERRY

HODDER

First published in Great Britain in 2011 by Hodder & Stoughton
An Hachette UK company

First published in paperback in 2011

1

Published by arrangement with Ballantine Books, an imprint of
Random House Publishing Group, a division of Random House, Inc.

A CIP catalogue record for this title is available from the British Library.

B Format Paperback ISBN 978 1 444 70940 7
A Format Paperback ISBN 978 1 444 73897 1

Typeset by Hewer Text UK Ltd, Edinburgh

Printed and bound by CPI Group (UK) Ltd, Croydon, CR0 4YY

Hodder & Stoughton policy is to use papers that are natural,
renewable and recyclable products and made from wood grown
in sustainable forests. The logging and manufacturing processes
are expected to conform to the environmental regulations
of the country of origin.

Hodder & Stoughton Ltd
338 Euston Road
London NW1 3BH

www.hodder.co.uk

For Zachary and Alex,
The next generation

Acknowledgments

To Gina Centrello, Libby McQuire, Kim Hovey, Cindy Murray, Carole Lowenstein, Quinne Rogers, Matt Schwartz, and everyone in Promotions and Sales – a heartfelt and sincere thanks.

To my agent and friend, Pam Ahearn – I offer another bow of deep appreciation.

To Mark Tavani, for pushing to the limit.

And to Simon Lipskar, thanks for your wisdom and guidance.

A few special mentions: a bow to the great novelist and friend, Katherine Neville, for opening doors at Monticello; the wonderful folks at Monticello who were most helpful; the great professionals at the Library of Virginia, who assisted with the Andrew Jackson research; Meryl Moss and her terrific publicity staff; Esther Garver and Jessica Johns, who continue to keep Steve Berry Enterprises working; Simon Gardner, from the Grand Hyatt, for providing fascinating insights on both the hotel and New York; Dr. Joe Murad, our chauffeur and tour guide in Bath; Kim Hovey, who offered some excellent on-site observations and photographs of Mahone Bay; and, as always, little would be accomplished without Elizabeth – wife, mother, friend, editor, and critic. Quite the real deal.

This book is for our grandsons, Zachary and Alex.

To them, I'm Papa Steve.

For me, they're both quite special.

The Congress shall have Power to ... grant Letters of Marque and Reprisal, and make Rules concerning Captures on Land and Water ...

- CONSTITUTION OF THE UNITED STATES,
Article 1, section 8

Privateers are the nursery for pirates.

- CAPTAIN CHARLES JOHNSON (1724)

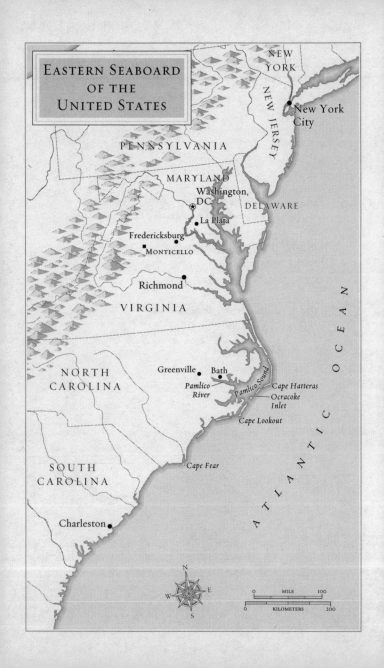

EASTERN SEABOARD
OF THE
UNITED STATES

NEW YORK

NEW JERSEY

New York City

PENNSYLVANIA

MARYLAND

Washington, DC

DELAWARE

La Plata

Fredericksburg

MONTICELLO

Richmond

VIRGINIA

NORTH CAROLINA

Greenville   Bath

Pamlico River

Pamlico Sound

Cape Hatteras

Ocracoke Inlet

Cape Lookout

SOUTH CAROLINA

Cape Fear

Charleston

ATLANTIC OCEAN

N
W   E
S

0   MILE   100

0   KILOMETERS   200

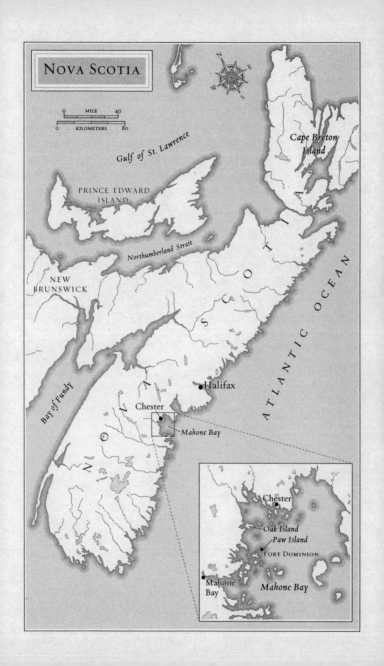

Prologue

Washington, DC
January 30, 1835
11:00 AM

President Andrew Jackson faced the gun aimed at his chest. A strange sight but not altogether unfamiliar, not for a man who'd spent nearly his entire life fighting wars. He was leaving the Capitol Rotunda, walking toward the East Portico, his somber mood matching the day's weather. His Treasury secretary, Levi Woodbury, steadied him, as did his trusted walking cane. Winter had been harsh this year, especially on a gaunt, sixty-seven-year-old body – his muscles were unusually stiff, his lungs perpetually congested.

He'd ventured from the White House only to say goodbye to a former friend – Warren Davis of South Carolina, elected twice to Congress, once as an ally, a Jacksonian Democrat, the other as a Nullifier. His enemy, the former vice president John C. Calhoun, had concocted the Nullifier Party, its members actually believing that states could choose what federal laws they wanted to obey. *The devil's work* was how he'd described such foolishness. There'd be no country if the Nullifiers had their way – which, he supposed, was their entire intent. Thankfully, the Constitution spoke of a unified government, not a loose league where everyone could do as they pleased.

People, not states, were paramount.

He hadn't planned to attend the funeral, but thought better yesterday. No matter their political disagreements he'd liked Warren Davis, so he'd tolerated the chaplain's depressing sermon – *life is uncertain, particularly for the aged* – then filed past the open casket, muttered a prayer, and descended to the Rotunda.

The throng of onlookers was impressive.

Hundreds had come to glimpse him. He'd missed the attention. When in a crowd he felt as a father surrounded by his children, happy in their affection, loving them as a dutiful parent. And there was much to be proud of. He'd just completed the impossible – paying off the national debt, satisfied in full during the 58th year of the republic – in the 6th year of his presidency, and several in the crowd hollered their approval. Upstairs, one of his cabinet secretaries had told him that the spectators had braved the cold mainly to see Old Hickory.

He'd smiled at the reference to his toughness, but was suspicious of the compliment.

He knew many were worried that he might break with precedent and seek a third term, among them members of his own party, some of whom harbored presidential ambitions of their own. Enemies seemed everywhere, especially here, in the Capitol, where southern representatives were becoming increasingly bold and northern legislators arrogant.

Keeping some semblance of order had become difficult, even for his strong hand.

And worse, of late he'd found himself losing interest in politics.

All the major battles seemed behind him.

Only two more years were left in office and then his career would be over. That was why he'd been coy about the possibility of a third term. If nothing else, the prospect of him running again kept his enemies at bay.

In fact, he harbored no intentions of another term. He would retire to Nashville. Home to Tennessee and his beloved Hermitage.

But first there was the matter of the gun.

The well-dressed stranger pointing the single-shot brass pistol had emerged from the onlookers, his face covered in a thick black beard. As a general Jackson had defeated British, Spanish, and Indian armies. As a duelist he'd once killed in the name of honor. He was afraid of no man. Certainly not this fool, whose pale lips quivered, like the hand aiming the gun.

The young man pressed the trigger.

The hammer snapped.

Its percussion cap detonated.

A bang echoed off the Rotunda's stone walls. But no spark ignited the powder in the barrel.

Misfire.

The assailant seemed shocked.

Jackson knew what had happened. Cold, damp air. He'd fought many a battle in the rain and knew the importance of keeping powder dry.

Anger rushed through him.

He gripped his walking cane with both hands, like a spear, and charged his attacker.

The young man tossed the gun away.

A second brass pistol appeared, its barrel now only inches from Jackson's chest.

The gunman pressed the trigger.

Another retort from the percussion cap, but no spark.

A second misfire.

Before his cane could jab the assailant's gut, Woodbury grabbed his arm, his secretary of the navy the other. A man in uniform leaped on the gunman, as did several members of Congress, one of them Davy Crockett from Tennessee.

'Let me go,' Jackson cried. 'Let me at him. I know where he comes from.'

But the two men did not relinquish their grip.

The assassin's hands flailed above a sea of heads, then the man was toppled to the floor.

'Let me go,' Jackson said again. 'I can protect myself.'

Police appeared and the man was jerked to his feet. Crockett handed him over to the officers and proclaimed, 'I wanted to see the damnedest villain in this world and now I have.'

The gunman babbled something about being the king of England and having more money once Jackson was dead.

'We must leave,' Woodbury whispered to him. 'That man is obviously insane.'

He did not want to hear that excuse. 'No insanity. There was a plot and that man was a tool.'

'Come, sir,' his secretary of the Treasury said, leading him out into the misty morning and a waiting carriage.

Jackson complied.

But his mind churned.

He agreed with what Richard Wilde, a congressman from Georgia, had once told him. *Rumor, with her hundred tongues, gives at least as many tales.* He hoped so. He'd faced that assassin without a hint of fear. Even two guns had not deterred him. Everyone present would attest to his courage.

And, thanks to God almighty, providence had guarded him.

He truly did seem destined to raise the country's glory and maintain the cause of the people.

He stepped into the carriage. Woodbury followed him inside, and the horses advanced through the rain. He no longer felt cold, or old, or tired. Strength surged through him. Like last time. Two years ago. During a steamboat excursion to Fredericksburg. A disturbed former naval officer, whom he'd fired, had bloodied his face registering the first physical assault on an American president. After, he'd declined to press charges and vetoed his aides' advice that a military guard surround him at all times. The press already labeled him a king, his White House a court. He would not provide further grist for that mill.

Now someone had actually tried to kill him.

Another first for an American president.

Assassination.

More an act, he thought, that belonged to Europe and ancient Rome. Usually employed against despots, monarchs, and aristocrats, not popularly elected leaders.

He glared at Woodbury. 'I know who ordered this. They have not the courage to face me. Instead, they send a crazy man to do their bidding.'

'Who are you referring to?'

'Traitors,' was all he offered.

And there'd be hell to pay.

PART ONE

I

O ne mistake was not enough for Cotton Malone.
 He made two.

Error number one was being on the fifteenth floor of the Grand Hyatt hotel. The request had come from his old boss Stephanie Nelle, through an email sent two days ago. She needed to see him, in New York, on Saturday. Apparently, the subject matter was something they could discuss only in person. And apparently, it was important. He'd tried to call anyway, phoning Magellan Billet headquarters in Atlanta, but was told by her assistant, 'She's been out of the office for six days now on DNC.'

He knew better than to ask where.

DNC. Do Not Contact.

That meant don't call me, I'll call you.

He'd been there before himself – the agent in the field, deciding when best to report in. That status, though, was a bit unusual for the head of the Magellan Billet. Stephanie was responsible for all twelve of the department's covert operatives. Her task was to supervise. For her to be DNC meant that something extraordinary had attracted her attention.

He and Cassiopeia Vitt had decided to make a New York weekend of the trip, with dinner and a show after he discovered what Stephanie wanted. They'd flown from Copenhagen yesterday and checked into the St. Regis, a few blocks north of where he now stood. Cassiopeia chose the accommodations and, since she was also paying for them, he hadn't protested. Plus, it was hard to argue with regal ambience, breathtaking views, and a suite larger than his apartment in Denmark.

He'd replied to Stephanie's email and told her where he was staying. After breakfast this morning, a key card for the Grand Hyatt had been waiting at the St. Regis' front desk along with a room number and a note.

PLEASE MEET ME AT EXACTLY 6:15 THIS EVENING

He'd wondered about the word *exactly,* but realized his former boss suffered from an incurable case of obsessive behavior, which made her both a good administrator and aggravating. But he also knew she would not have contacted him if it wasn't truly important.

He inserted the key card, noting and ignoring the DO NOT DISTURB sign.

The indicator light on the door's electronic lock switched to green and the latch released.

The interior was spacious, with a king-sized bed covered in plush purple pillows. A work area was provided at an oak-top desk with an ergonomic chair. The room occupied a corner, two windows facing East 42nd Street, the other offering views west toward 5th Avenue. The rest of the décor was what would be expected from a high-class, Midtown Manhattan hotel.

Except for two things.

His gaze locked on the first: some sort of contraption, fashioned from what appeared to be aluminum struts, bolted together like an Erector Set. It stood before one of the front windows, left of the bed, facing outward. Atop the sturdy metal support sat a rectangular box, perhaps two feet by three, it too made of dull aluminum, its sides bolted together and centered on the window. More girders extended to the walls, front and back, one set on the floor, another braced a couple of feet above, seemingly anchoring the unit in place.

Was this what Stephanie meant when she'd said *important*?

A short barrel poked from the front of the box. There seemed no way to search its interior, short of unbolting the sides. Sets of gears adorned both the box and the frame. Chains ran the length of the supports, as if the whole thing was designed to move.

He reached for the second anomaly.

An envelope. Sealed. With his name on it.

He glanced at his watch. 6:17 PM.

Where was Stephanie?

He heard the shrill of sirens from outside.

With the envelope in hand, he stepped to one of the room's windows and glanced down fourteen stories. East 42nd Street was devoid of cars. Traffic had been cordoned off. He'd noticed the police outside when he'd arrived a few minutes ago.

Something was happening.

He knew the reputation of Cipriani across the street. He'd been inside before and recalled its marble columns, inlaid floors, and crystal chandeliers – a former bank, built in Italian Renaissance style, leased out for elite social gatherings. Just such an event seemed to be happening this evening, important enough to stop traffic, clear the sidewalks, and command the presence of half a dozen of New York City's finest, who stood before the elegant entrance.

Two police cars approached from the west, lights flashing, followed by an oversized black Cadillac DTS. Another New York City police car trailed. Two pennants rose from either side of the Cadillac's hood. One an American flag, the other the presidential standard.

Only one person rode in that car.

President Danny Daniels.

The motorcade wheeled to the curb before Cipriani. Doors opened. Three Secret Service agents sprang from the car, studied the surroundings, then signaled. Danny Daniels emerged, his tall, broad frame sheathed by a dark suit, white shirt, and powder-blue tie.

Malone heard whirring.

His gaze found the source.

The contraption had come to life.

Two retorts banged and the window on the other side of the room shattered, glass plunging downward to the sidewalk far below. Cool air rushed inside, as did the sounds of a pulsating city. Gears spun and the device telescoped through the now empty window frame.

He glanced down.

The window's shattering had attracted the Secret Service's attention. Heads were now angled up, toward the Grand Hyatt.

Everything happened in a matter of a few seconds.

Window gone. Device out. Then—

Rat-tat-tat.

Shots were fired at the president of the United States.

Agents smothered Daniels to the sidewalk.

Malone stuffed the envelope into his pocket and raced across the room, grabbing hold of the aluminum frame, trying to dislodge the device.

But it would not budge.

He searched for and spotted no power cords. The thing, apparently a remote-controlled, high-powered weapon, kept firing. He saw agents trying to maneuver their charge back to the car. He knew that once Daniels was inside, armor plating would provide protection.

The device spit out more rounds.

He dove out the window, balancing himself on the frame, and grabbed hold of the aluminum box. If he could yank it from side to side, or up and down, at least he could deflect its aim.

He managed to force the barrel left, but motors inside quickly compensated.

Below, with incoming fire momentarily deflected, agents stuffed Daniels back into the car, which wheeled away. Three men remained, along with the policemen who'd been waiting at Cipriani.

Guns were drawn.

His second mistake now became evident.

They started firing.

At him.

2

Quentin Hale could think of few things better than slicing through white-foamed crests under a towering glide of sail. If seawater could actually be a part of someone's blood, that was surely the case with him.

Sloops had been the ocean workhorses of the 17th and 18th centuries. Small, single-masted, their spread of sails had made them quick and maneuverable. Shallow drafts and fast lines only added to their suitability. Most carried around seventy-five men and fourteen cannons. His modern incarnation was larger, 280 feet, and instead of wood the latest composite materials made her light and sleek. No cannons weighed down this beauty. Instead, she was delightful to the eye, soothing to the soul – a bluewater vessel built for comfort and loaded with toys. Twelve guests could enjoy her luxury cabins and sixteen were employed as crew, many of them descendants of those who'd served Hales since the American Revolution.

'Why are you doing this?' his victim screamed. 'Why, Quentin?'

Hale stared at the man lying on the deck, shackled in heavy chains and encapsulated in a gibbet – a cage constructed of flat bars of iron, three inches in breadth. A rounded portion enclosed the chest and head, while the thighs and legs were barred within separate enclosures. Centuries ago the cages were made to fit the victim, but this one was more off the rack. Not a muscle could move besides the man's head and jaw, and he'd purposely not been gagged.

'Are you insane?' the man yelled. 'What you're doing is murder.'

Hale took offense to that charge. 'Killing a traitor is not murder.'

The chained man, as had his father and grandfather before him, kept the Hale family ledger. He was an accountant who lived in coastal Virginia on an exquisite estate. Hale Enterprises, Ltd., spanned the globe and required the attention of nearly three hundred employees. Many accountants were on the corporate payroll, but this man worked outside that bureaucracy, answerable only to Hale.

'I swear to you, Quentin,' the man screamed. 'I gave them only the barest information.'

'Your life depends on that being true.' He allowed his words to carry a measure of hope. He wanted this man to talk. He must be sure.

'They came to me with subpoenas. They already knew the answers to their questions. They told me if I didn't cooperate I'd go to jail and lose everything I had.'

The accountant started crying.

Again.

They were the Internal Revenue Service. Agents from the criminal enforcement division who'd descended one morning on Hale Enterprises. They'd also appeared at eight banks around the country, demanding account information on both the corporation and Hale. All the American banks complied. No surprise. Few laws guaranteed privacy. Which was why those accounts were supported by a meticulous paper trail. That was not the case with foreign banks, especially the Swiss, where financial privacy had long been a national obsession.

'They knew about the UBS accounts,' his accountant hollered over the wind and sea. 'I only discussed those with them. No more. I swear. Only those.'

He stared past the rail at the churning sea. His victim lay on the aft deck, near the Jacuzzi and dip pool, out of sight from any passing boaters, but they'd been sailing for the better part of the morning and, so far, had spotted no one.

'What was I to do?' his accountant begged. 'The bank caved.'

United Bank of Switzerland had indeed yielded to American pressure and finally, for the first time, allowed more than fifty thousand accounts to be subject to foreign subpoenas. Of course, threats of criminal prosecution to the bank's U.S. executives had made that decision easy. And what his accountant said was true. He'd checked. Only UBS records had been seized. No accounts in the other seven countries had been touched.

'I had no choice. For God's sake, Quentin. What did you want me to do?'

'I wanted you to keep to the Articles.'

From the sloop's crew to his house staff to the estate keepers to himself, the Articles were what bound them together.

'You swore an oath and gave your word,' he called out from the railing. 'You signed them.'

Which was meant to ensure loyalty. Occasionally, though, violations occurred and were dealt with. Like today.

He glanced out again at the blue-gray water. *Adventure* had caught a stiff southeastern breeze. They were fifty miles offshore, headed south, back from Virginia. The DynaRig system was performing perfectly. Fifteen square sails formed the modern version of the once-square rigger, the difference being that now the yards did not swing around a fixed mast. Instead, they were permanently attached, the masts rotating with the wind. No crewmen had to brave the heights and release the rigging. Technology stored the sails inside the mast and unfurled them by electric motor in less than six minutes. Computers controlled every angle, keeping the sails full.

He savored the salt air and cleared his brain.

'Tell me this,' he called out.

'Anything, Quentin. Just get me out of this cage.'

'The ledger. Did you speak of that?'

The man's head shook. 'Not a word. Nothing. They seized UBS records and never mentioned the ledger.'

'Is it safe?'

'Where we keep it. Always. Just you and me. We're the only ones who know.'

He believed him. Not a word had so far been mentioned of the ledger, which relieved some of his anxiety.

But not all.

The storms he was about to face would be far worse than the squall he spotted brewing off to the east. The entire weight of the U.S. intelligence community, along with the Internal Revenue Service and the Justice Department, was bearing down upon him. Not unlike what his ancestors had faced when kings, queens, and presidents dispatched whole navies to hunt down the sloops and hang their captains.

He turned back to the pitiful man in the iron cage and stepped close.

'Please, Quentin. I'm begging you. Don't do this.' The voice was racked by sobs. 'I've never asked about the business. Never cared. I just kept the ledger. Like my dad. And his. I never touched a penny that wasn't mine. We never have.'

No, his family hadn't.

But Article 6 was clear.

If any Man shall violate the Company as a Whole he shall be shot.

Never had the Commonwealth faced something this threatening. If only he could find the key and solve the cipher. That would end it all and make what he was about to do unnecessary. Unfortunately, a captain's duty sometimes entailed ordering unpleasant things.

He gestured and three men hoisted the gibbet, hauling it toward the railing.

The bound man screamed, 'Don't do this, please. I thought I knew you. I thought we were friends. Why are you acting like some damn pirate?'

The three men hesitated a moment, waiting for his signal.

He nodded.

The cage was tossed overboard and the sea devoured the offering.

The crew returned to their posts.

He stood alone on the deck, his face washed by the breeze, and considered the man's final insult.

Acting like some damn pirate.

Sea monsters, hellhounds, robbers, opposers, corsairs, buccaneers, violators of all laws human and divine, devils incarnate, children of the wicked one.

All labels for pirates.

Was he one of them?

'If that's what they think of me,' he whispered, 'then why not?'

3

New York City

Jonathan Wyatt watched the scene unfold. He sat alone at a window table in the Grand Hyatt's New York Central restaurant, a glass-atrium eatery that offered an unobstructed view of East 42nd Street two stories below. He'd caught the moment when traffic was stopped, the sidewalks cleared, and the presidential motorcade arrived at Cipriani. He'd heard a bang from above, then the crash of glass to the sidewalk. When shots started he knew that the device had begun working.

He'd chosen this table with care and noticed that two men nearby had done the same. Secret Service agents, who'd commandeered the far end of the restaurant, assuming a position at the windows, their view of the scene below also unimpaired. Both men were wired with radios and the serving staff had intentionally seated no one near them.

He knew their operating procedure.

Presidential security relied on a controlled-perimeter mentality, usually three layers starting with counter snipers on adjacent rooftops, ending with agents standing within a few feet of their charge. Bringing a president into the congestion of a place like New York City posed extraordinary challenges. Buildings everywhere, each a sea of windows, topped by open roofs. The Grand Hyatt seemed a perfect example. Twenty-plus stories and two towers of glass walls.

Down on the street agents reacted to the shots, leaping onto Danny Daniels, implementing another time-honored practice – 'cover and evacuate.' Of course, the automated weapon had been positioned high enough to shoot over any vehicles, and he watched policemen and the remaining agents dive left and right, trying to avoid the rounds.

Had Daniels been hit? Hard to say.

He watched as the two agents, standing fifty feet away, reacted to the melee, doing their job, acting as eyes and ears, clearly frustrated they were so far away. He knew the men on the street carried radios with earpieces. They'd all been trained. Unfortunately, reality rarely resembled scenarios enacted at an instructional facility. This was a perfect example. An automated, remote-controlled weapon directed by closed-circuit TV? Bet they hadn't seen that one before.

Thirty other patrons filled the restaurant, and everyone's attention was directed toward the street.

More retorts echoed off the buildings.

The president was shoved back into his limousine.

Cadillac One – or as the Secret Service referred to it, the Beast – sported military-grade armor, five inches thick, and wheels fitted to run even on dead flat tires. Three hundred thousand dollars of General Motors ingenuity. He knew that, since Dallas in 1963, the car was always flown to wherever the president required ground transportation. It had arrived by military transport three hours ago at JFK, waiting on the tarmac for Air Force One to touch down. Breaking with procedure, no other vehicles had been flown in. Usually several support cars came along.

He cut a glance at the two antsy agents, who held their position.

Not to worry, he thought. *Soon you'll both join the fray.*

He returned his attention to his dinner, a delicious Cobb salad. His stomach bubbled with anxiety. He'd waited a long time for this. *Camp by the riverside*. Advice he'd received years ago – and as true as ever. If you waited by the river long enough, eventually your enemies would float by.

He savored another tangy bite of salad and washed it down with a sweet red wine. A pleasant aftertaste of fruit and wood lingered. He supposed he should show some interest in what was happening, but no one was paying him the slightest attention. And why would they? The president of the United States was under fire and the shocked people around him had a ringside seat. Several of them would shortly find themselves on CNN or Fox News, becoming, for a few precious moments, celebrities. They should actually thank him for the opportunity.

The two agents' voices rose.

He glanced out the window as Cadillac One roared from the curb.

The defenders in front of Cipriani sprang to their feet, pointing upward, toward the Grand Hyatt.

Guns appeared.

Aims were steadied.

Shots were fired.

He smiled.

Cotton Malone had apparently done exactly what Wyatt thought he would do.

Too bad for Malone things were about to get worse.

Malone heard bullets ping off glass panels to his left and right. The aluminum bronco he straddled was still firing. He yanked the mechanism again, but internal gears whirled the gun barrel back toward its target.

He should retreat inside.

Daniels was in the car and about to speed away. Calling out would be useless. No one would hear him over the gunshots and the discordant wail of New York's street opera.

Another window exploded, this one at the opposite corner of the Grand Hyatt, a hundred feet away from where he was perched.

Another aluminum box extended out into the evening.

He immediately noticed that its barrel was wider than the one he was trying to tame. This was no rifle. Some type of mortar or rocket launcher.

The agents and police firing at him spotted the newcomer and directed their attention toward that threat. Instantly he realized that whoever had planted these devices had counted on Daniels being herded back into the car and driven away. He'd wondered about the accuracy of some remote-controlled, automated rifle – how good could it be? – but saw now that hitting anything didn't matter. The idea had been to drive the target into something that could be more easily acquired.

Like an oversized black Cadillac.

He knew the presidential limousine bore armor plating. But could it withstand a rocket attack from a few hundred feet away? And what type of warhead was the projectile equipped with?

Agents and police below raced down the sidewalk, trying to obtain a better firing angle at the new threat.

Daniels' limousine approached the intersection of East 42nd and Lexington Avenue.

The rocket launcher pivoted.

He needed to do something.

The rifle he straddled continued to fire, one shot after another, every five seconds. Bullets pinged off the opposite buildings and the street below. Stretching his body out farther on the aluminum superstructure, he wrapped an arm around the container and wrenched the assembly left. Gears inside strained, then stripped, as he forced the barrel parallel to the hotel's exterior.

Bullets now whirred through the air toward the rocket launcher.

He adjusted his aim, searching for the right trajectory.

One round found the mark, spanking off the aluminum.

The box he grasped felt thin, the aluminum pliable. He hoped the other was made of the same.

Two more high-powered rounds found the target.

A third bullet penetrated.

Blue sparks exploded.

Flames erupted as a rocket left the launcher.

Wyatt finished his salad as Cadillac One sped toward the intersection. He'd heard the second window shatter. men below raced down the sidewalk and were now firing upward. But the Secret Service's P229 Sig Sauers would do little good, and the submachine guns that usually followed the president in support vehicles had been left in Washington. As had the snipers.

Mistakes, mistakes.

He heard an explosion.

Rocket away.

He dabbed his mouth with a napkin and glanced down. Daniels' car cleared the intersection, heading toward the United Nations building and the East River. It would probably take Roosevelt Drive and find either a hospital or the airport. He recalled from days gone by when a special subway train was kept waiting on a dedicated track near the Waldorf Astoria hotel, ready to whisk the president out of Manhattan without delay.

Not anymore.

Useless.

The two suited agents rushed from the restaurant, heading for an adjacent stairway that wound down to the Hyatt's main entrance.

He laid his napkin down and stood.

All of the servers, the hostess, even the kitchen staff were crowded at the windows. He doubted anyone would bring a check. He recalled the price of the salad, compensated for the wine, added a 30 percent tip – he prided himself on being generous – and laid down a fifty-dollar bill. Probably too much, but he had no time for change.

The rocket never found the ground, and a second and third never fired. Obviously, the hero had completed his performance.

Now it was time to watch Cotton Malone's luck run out.

4

Clifford Knox severed the radio connection and shut down the laptop. The rocket launcher had fired only once, and the projectile had not found the presidential limousine. The closed-circuit television feeds – courtesy of cameras installed in both automated units – had delivered jerky images, shifting right and left. He'd repeatedly had trouble keeping the rifle aimed downward, the thing not responding to his commands. He'd ordered both the propellants and the explosives modified, ensuring that the three warheads could destroy a heavily armored vehicle.

Everything had been in working order this morning.

So what had happened?

The image from the television screen, blaring at him from across his hotel room, explained the failure.

Cellphones from the street had captured pictures and videos that had already been emailed to the networks. They showed a man balancing out of a shattered window in the Grand Hyatt, high above East 42nd Street. He straddled a metal structure and jerked the device one way, then another, finally directing its rifle fire toward the rocket launcher, destroying its electronics just as the weapon fired.

Knox had delivered the firing command. Three rockets should have discharged, one after the other. But only one emerged, and it flew off into the southern sky.

The room's phone rang.

He answered and a gravelly voice on the other end said, 'This is a disaster.'

His gaze stayed on the television screen. More images showed the two devices projecting outward from dark rectangles in the Grand Hyatt's glass facade. A scrolling banner at the bottom of the screen informed viewers that there was no word yet on the president's condition.

'Who was the man who interfered?' a new voice asked in his ear.

He imagined the scene on the other end of the line. Three men, each in their early fifties, dressed casually, sitting in an elegant salon, crowded around a speakerphone.

The Commonwealth.

Minus one.

'I have no idea,' he said into the phone. 'Obviously, I didn't expect any interference.'

Not much could be gleaned about the intruder, except that he was Caucasian, with sandy-colored hair, a dark jacket, and light-colored pants. His face had been impossible to see thanks to the cellphone cameras' low resolution and plenty of lens movement. The scrolling banner on the screen informed viewers that the man had appeared, been fired upon, diverted one weapon onto the other, then disappeared back inside.

'How would anyone have known about this?' came a question in his ear. 'Much less be in a position to stop it.'

'We obviously have a security leak.'

Silence on the other end of the phone confirmed that they agreed.

'Quartermaster,' one of the men said, using Knox's official title, 'you were in charge of this operation. Its failure is your responsibility.'

He realized that.

Like the ship's captain of long ago, a quartermaster was chosen by the crew, charged with safeguarding the company's interests. While a captain retained absolute authority during any conflict, a ship's everyday administration rested with the quartermaster. He allocated provisions, distributed spoils, adjudicated conflicts, and meted out discipline. A captain could undertake little without the quartermaster approving. That system remained today, except with the further complication that *four* captains commanded the Commonwealth. Knox reported to each of them, both individually and collectively. He also oversaw the crew, those who worked directly for the Commonwealth.

'We clearly have a spy among us,' he repeated.

'Do you realize what will happen from this? The repercussions will be enormous.'

Knox sucked in a breath. 'The worst of which is that Captain Hale was excluded from your decision.'

His comment would not be deemed insubordinate. A good quartermaster spoke his mind, unafraid, since his power came from the crew, not the captain. He'd cautioned them a week ago that this plan was ill advised. He'd kept to himself a further observation that he thought it bordered on desperation. But when three of the four in charge issued an order, it was his duty to obey.

'Both your counsel and objections have been noted,' one of the men said. 'We made the decision.'

But that might not be enough once Quentin Hale realized what the others had done. This particular course was one the Commonwealth had sailed before, but not in many decades. Knox's father had been the last quartermaster to attempt the feat, and he'd succeeded. But that had been a different time, with different rules.

'Perhaps Captain Hale should be told,' he advised.

'Like he doesn't already know,' one of the men said. 'We'll hear from him soon enough. In the meantime, what are you going to do?'

He'd been considering that move. No way existed for anyone to trace the mechanisms found in the two hotel rooms. They'd been manufactured in secret by crew members, every piece sanitized. No matter the outcome the machinery would have been discovered, so precautions had been taken. The two hotel rooms at the Grand Hyatt were registered to fictitious individuals – crew members who'd appeared at the front desk in disguise and paid with credit cards that relied on false identifications. Suitcases had held the various parts, and through the night he'd personally assembled the devices piece by piece. A DO NOT DISTURB sign on the door had ensured privacy all day. He'd controlled both weapons from here – blocks away – by radio, and the signals were now severed.

Everything had been carefully designed.

At times, in centuries past, quartermasters had been allowed to assume the helm, steering the ship's course. The Commonwealth had just handed him the wheel.

'I'll handle things.'

Malone wrestled with a decision. He'd spotted agents heading for the Grand Hyatt's main entrance. The Secret Service was thorough, which meant there were most likely agents already in the hotel, stationed where they could have observed the street below. They'd surely been contacted and ordered to head for both rooms. Should he leave? Or just wait for them?

Then he recalled the envelope in his pocket.

He tore it open to see a typewritten note.

I needed you to see these. Disable them before the president arrives. This could not be accomplished any sooner. I'll explain why later. You can't trust anyone, especially Secret Service. This conspiracy reaches far. Leave the hotel and I'll contact you before midnight by phone.

Stephanie

Decision made.

Time to go.

Apparently Stephanie was into something huge. He should at least follow her instructions.

For now.

He realized cellphones carried cameras and the sidewalks below had been crowded. His image would soon be splattered on every media outlet. He'd only been exposed for a couple of minutes, so he hoped that whatever pictures had been captured were not of the best quality.

He opened the door, not worrying about leaving evidence. His fingerprints were all over the device dangling out the window.

He calmly walked down the deserted hall toward the elevators. A lingering scent of nicotine reminded him that this was the smoking floor. No one appeared from any of the rooms that opened on either side.

He turned a corner.

Ten elevators serviced the hotel. Nothing indicated where those cars were currently located. He decided none of them was the smart play. His gaze searched left, then right, and he spotted the stairway exit.

He opened the metal door, listened, heard nothing, then slipped out.

He climbed two stories and hesitated at the 17th floor. All quiet. He stepped out into another elevator foyer nearly identical to the one two floors below. A similar side table with a flower arrangement and mirror adorned the wall.

He stared at himself.

What in the world was happening?

Somebody had just tried to kill the president of the United States and, at the moment, he was a prime person of interest.

He removed his jacket and exposed a pale blue button-down shirt underneath. They'd be searching for a man with light hair and a dark jacket. He spotted a trash bin, topped by more artificial flowers, between two of the elevator doors, and stuffed the jacket inside.

From his left, down the hall, a family approached. Mom, Dad, three kids. They seemed excited and were talking about Times Square and one of its neon signs. Dad pressed the UP button, summoning the elevator. Malone stood patiently with them and waited for the car to arrive. These people had somehow missed the whole thing. You'd think it would have been hard to ignore a rocket propelling out into the sky, leaving a trail of smoke in its wake. Tourists, though, had always baffled him. Højbro Plads, back in Copenhagen where his bookstore sat, was filled with them daily.

The elevator arrived and he allowed the family on first. Dad inserted a room card into a slot that granted access to the thirty-first floor. Apparently, that was reserved for special guests, probably the concierge level. Malone decided it might be a good place to think.

'Oh, you got it for me,' he said.

They rode in silence up another fourteen floors, then they all stepped off. Just as he suspected, the hotel's concierge lounge was there, available only to guests who'd paid for the privilege. He allowed Dad to go first and the guy inserted his key card into another slot and opened the glass-paneled door.

Malone followed the family inside.

The L-shaped lounge was crowded with people enjoying a cold buffet of meats, cheese, and fruit. He surveyed the room and immediately spotted two suits with ear fobs and lapel mikes glued to the windows that faced East 42nd Street.

Secret Service.

He grabbed an apple from a wooden bowl on a table, along with a copy of the day's *New York Times*. He retreated to the far side of the room, munched on his apple, and sat, one eye on the newspaper, the other on the agents.

And hoped he hadn't just made a third mistake.

5

Pamlico Sound, North Carolina

Hale sat in *Adventure's* main salon and noticed they'd veered west, leaving open ocean behind and entering the sound. What had been blue-gray water now turned coffee-colored, thanks to a steady flow of sediment brought east by the meandering Pamlico River. Log-hewn canoes, pole-propelled periaugers, and shoal-draft steamboats all once plied these waters. But so had sloops, corsairs, and frigates, manned by opportunists who'd called the densely wooded shores of the isolated Carolina colony home. The Pamlico comprised some of the most complex waterways on the planet. A vast array of oyster-rock islets, tidal marshes, hammocks, and sloughs. Its farthest coasts were stunted by dangerous capes whose names – Lookout and Fear – warned of tragedy, the open sea beyond so treacherous it had earned the title Graveyard of the Atlantic.

He'd been born and raised nearby, as had Hales back to the early part of the 18th century. He learned to sail as a boy and was taught how to avoid the ever-changing shoals and negotiate the dangerous currents. Ocracoke Inlet, which they'd just traversed, was where in November 1718 Black Beard himself had finally been cut down. Locals still spoke of both him and his lost treasure with reverence.

He stared down at the table where the two documents lay. He'd brought them with him, knowing that once the matter of his accountant had been resolved, he would need to turn his attention back to a mistake made by Abner Hale, his great-great-grandfather, who'd tried, on January 30, 1835, to assassinate President Andrew Jackson.

The first time in history that a sitting president's life had been directly threatened.

And Jackson's response to that attempt – a handwritten letter to Abner, now sheathed in plastic – had tortured Hales ever since.

So you have at last yielded to traitorous impulses. Your patience is no longer restrained. I am content with that. This shall be war, as great as when the martial hosts of this nation are summoned to tented fields. You have clamored for a fight and I shall not skulk in a corner now that the first shot has been fired. Because I would not yield to your advances, accede to your demands, or bow in your presence, my life is deemed unnecessary? You dare send an assassin? To retreat from such a gross offense would be shameful. My feelings are most alive and, I assure you, so am I. Your assassin spends his days muttering nonsense. You chose this servant well. He shall be adjudged insane and secreted away, not a single person ever believing a word he might utter. No evidence exists of your conspiracy, but we both are aware that you convinced the man named Richard Lawrence to aim those pistols. At this moment, when my feelings are thus so alive, I should do violence to them if I did not hasten your downfall. Yet I have been perplexed as to a response. And so, after seeking counsel and guidance from some who are wiser than I, a proper course has been chosen. My object in making this communication is to announce that what legal authority existed to shield your thievery is gone. I have stripped all reference to your letter of marque from the official congressional reports. When you approach another president and ask that your letter be respected, he will not be bound by the law as I have been. To increase your

torment, and thus to prolong the agony of your helpless situation,
I have not destroyed the authority. That would have been my
course, I confess, but others have convinced me that such
certainty might make your situation so helpless that it would
inspire further acts of desperation. Since you adore secrets and
plot your life along a path in the shadows, I offer you a challenge
that should suit you. The sheet attached to this letter is a code,
one formulated by the esteemed Thomas Jefferson. I am told he
thought it to be the perfect cipher. Succeed in learning its message
and you will know where I have hidden what you crave. Fail
and you remain the pathetic traitors that you are today. I must
admit, I like this course much better. I shall soon retire home to
Tennessee and the final years of my life, awaiting the day when I
will sleep beside my beloved Rachel. My sincerest hope is that the
unmanly course ascribed to you shall be your ruin and that I
shall live to enjoy that day.

Andrew Jackson

Hale stared at the second sheet, it also encased in plastic.

His family had tried to solve Jefferson's cipher for 175 years. Experts had been hired. Money had been spent.

But the key had eluded them.

He heard footsteps approaching from the ship's forward and his personal secretary entered the salon.

'Switch on the television.'

He saw the look of concern in the man's eyes.

'It's bad.'

He found the remote and activated the screen.

Malone finished his apple and kept the newspaper open before him. He noticed no story about any presidential trip to New York. Odd. Presidents usually appeared with much fanfare. He should leave the hotel, and quickly. Every second he lingered was making the effort that much more difficult.

He knew the Grand Hyatt lived up to its name, a massive, multistoried complex that thousands of people streamed into and out of twenty-four hours a day. Doubtful that the police or Secret Service could seal off every access, at least not this fast. Two televisions played in the room, and he saw how cell-phone cameras had indeed captured images – but thankfully, most were blurred messes. No word as yet on Daniels' condition. People chattered about the attack, remarking how it had occurred right below them. A few had heard the bangs and seen the rocket. The two suits with radios on the other side of the lounge kept their attention below, talking into their radios.

He stood to leave.

The agents abandoned the window and rushed straight for him. He braced himself to react, noting that the thick wooden table supporting the apples and newspapers could be used to break their advance.

Of course, they carried guns and he didn't, so a table would go only so far.

The two agents brushed past him and bolted out the door, straight for the elevators, one of which they entered when an open car arrived.

He heaved a silent sigh, then left, pressing the DOWN button, deciding to take the direct approach.

Straight out the main doors.

6

Wyatt waited in the Grand Hyatt's busy lobby, filled with tourists here for a weekend in the Big Apple, now made that much more exciting by someone trying to kill the president of the United States. He'd listened to snippets of conversations from a nearby lounging area and learned that no one knew if Daniels had been hit, just that he sped from the scene. Some recalled the Reagan assassination attempt from 1981, when only after the president was headed into surgery had an official statement been made.

At least a dozen New York City police and half that many Secret Service were now racing through the two-story lobby. Voices were raised and positions were assumed near escalators and exits. Hard to say where Malone would make his move, but the paths out of this hotel were limited to an entry down one floor, to his left, that led out onto East 42nd Street – as well as another set of adjacent glass doors that opened into a tunnel connecting with Grand Central Terminal – and a second set of glass doors one level up, which he could observe from his vantage point. If he knew his adversary as well as he thought he did, Malone would simply walk out the main doors. Why not? No one had seen his face, and the best place to hide was always in plain sight.

He realized the authorities would love to clear the hotel, but that could prove impossible. There were simply too many people on the twenty-plus floors. With the usual six months of prep time for a presidential visit, the Secret Service would have been able to handle this. As it was, they'd barely had eight weeks, their main tactic secrecy since no travel announcement had been made until this morning, when the White House simply said that Daniels would be in New York on a personal visit. The precedent for that came from a past president who'd made an unannounced trip with his wife to see a Broadway production. That jaunt had gone off without a hitch, but Danny Daniels was probably kicking himself right now, provided his organs weren't failing or he wasn't losing large quantities of blood.

Wyatt loved it when people screwed up.

It made things so much easier.

More than likely Malone had fled upward, at least initially. He'd yet to exit any of the elevators Wyatt could see. He certainly would not be using the stairs, as the police would have those sealed first thing. But the note he'd left in the room should drive Malone forward. He'd be the Lone Ranger, as always. Good and faithful to his beloved Stephanie Nelle.

He liked being back in the fray.

It had been a while since his last contract. Work had come less frequently the past few years, and he missed his job as a full-time agent. Eight years now since he'd been forced out. Still, he'd made a living peddling his services, which seemed the future of the intelligence business. Fewer agents on the payroll, more hired by the job – independent contractors who offered deniability and required no pension. But he was fifty years old and should have risen, by now, to deputy administrator, or maybe even head of an agency. He'd been called one of the best field agents ever.

Until—

'What are you going to do?' Cotton Malone asked him.

They were trapped. Two gunmen had them pinned from above, and another two were positioned in the dark recesses that stretched before them. He'd suspected a trap and now that fear had been confirmed. Thankfully, he and Malone had come prepared.

He reached for the radio.

Malone grabbed his arm. 'You can't do that.'

'Why not?'

'We know what's out there. They don't.'

They *were three agents told to watch the perimeter.*

'We have no idea how many guns are here,' Malone said. 'Four we know of, but there could be a lot more.'

His finger found the SEND *button. 'We have no choice.'*

Malone yanked the radio from his grasp. 'If I agreed with that, we'd both be wrong. We can handle this.'

More rounds came their way. They kept low, among the crates.

'Let's divide,' Malone said. 'I'll take the left, you the right, and we'll meet in the center. I'll keep the radio.'

He said nothing.

Malone stared out into the blackness, seemingly assessing the danger, readying himself to advance.

Wyatt decided on another course.

One swipe of his gun across the temple and Malone slumped to the concrete, out cold.

He retrieved the radio and ordered the three men to move in.

A loud voice snapped his mind back to reality.

Another wave of police had invaded the lobby. People were now being herded toward the exits, the hotel staff assisting. Apparently, somebody had finally made a decision.

His gaze raked the mayhem.

The main elevators opened on the ground floor and people streamed out. One of them was Cotton Malone.

Wyatt smiled.

Malone had ditched his jacket, just as Wyatt knew he would. That would be one of the things agents would be looking for. He watched as Malone melded into the crowd and hustled across the lobby to the escalator, riding it down toward the hotel's main entrance. Wyatt stayed back, using a tall curtain for cover. The agents and police were making their way toward where he stood, gesturing for everyone to leave.

Malone stepped off the escalator and, instead of leaving through the center doors, turned right and headed for the exit that led into Grand Central Terminal. Wyatt drifted toward one of the hotel meeting rooms, closed for the evening, and reached for the radio in his pocket, already set on the frequency being used by the Secret Service.

'Alert to all agents. Suspect is wearing pale blue button-down shirt, light trousers, no jacket at this time, presently exiting Grand Hyatt hotel from main lobby into tunnel that accesses Grand Central Terminal. I'm headed in that direction.'

He waited an instant, pocketed the radio, then turned toward the lobby.

Malone disappeared through the exit doors.

Secret Service agents elbowed their way through the crowd in pursuit.

7

Knox left the Plaza Hotel. He knew at least three members of the Commonwealth were bordering on panic. As they should be. What they'd authorized came fraught with risk. Too much in his opinion. Always before they'd worked with the encouragement and blessing of the government, their actions and authority sanctioned. Now they were renegades, sailing stormy, uncharted waters.

He crossed the street and entered Central Park. Sirens blared in the distance, as they would for hours to come. Still no word on the president's condition, but the whole thing had happened less than an hour ago.

He'd always liked Central Park. Eight hundred plush acres of trees, grass, lakes, and footpaths. A backyard for an entire city. Without it Manhattan would be one unbroken block of concrete and buildings.

He'd made a call from the Plaza and requested an immediate meeting. His contact had likewise wanted to talk – no surprise there – and was nearby, so they chose the same bench past the Sheep Meadow, near Bethesda Fountain, where they'd met before.

The man who waited for him was unremarkable in nearly every way, from his forgettable features to his plain manner of dress. Knox walked over and sat, immediately disliking the smug look on Scott Parrott's face.

'The man hanging out the window,' he asked Parrott. 'One of yours?'

'I wasn't told how it would be stopped, only that it would be.'

The answer raised more questions than it resolved, but he let it go. 'What now?'

'We want this to be a message to the captains,' Parrott said. 'We want them to know that we know everything about the Commonwealth. We know its employees—'

'Crew.'

'Excuse me?'

'The crew works the company.'

Parrot laughed. 'You're a bunch of friggin' pirates.'

'Privateers.'

'What the hell's the difference? You steal from anyone you can.'

'Only from the enemies of this country.'

'It doesn't matter what you are,' Parrot said. 'We're all supposed to be on the same team.'

'It doesn't look that way from our perspective.'

'And I sympathize with your bosses. I know they're being squeezed. I get it. But there are limits. You have to understand that. They have to know that we would never allow them to kill the president. I'm shocked that they'd think we would. Like I said, this is a message.'

Which the National Intelligence Agency apparently wanted him to personally deliver. Parrott was Knox's contact with the NIA. A year ago, when it became apparent that factions within the intelligence community had decided to destroy the Commonwealth, only the NIA had stood with them.

'The captains will wonder why you're sending them messages. Why you interfered.'

'Then tell them I have some good news. Good enough that they should thank us for what we did today.'

He doubted that, but he was listening.

'The solution to your Jefferson cipher should be loading on my laptop as we speak. Our guys solved it.'

Had he heard right? The key? Found? After 175 years? Parrott was right – the captains would be thrilled. But there was still the matter of the foolishness that had just occurred. He could only hope he'd covered their tracks with no mistakes. If not, no cipher key would matter.

'If there's anything that could help them climb out of the hole they dug for themselves today,' Parrott said, 'this is it.'

'Why not just tell us that?'

The agent chuckled. 'Not my call. I doubt you left a trail that will lead anywhere and we were there, ready to stop the attempt, so it doesn't matter.'

He kept calm and silently reaffirmed the decision he'd made on the walk over.

It had to be done.

'I thought maybe you'd buy me dinner,' Parrott said. 'Something that once had parents. You can afford it. Then we can go back to my hotel and you can find out what Andrew Jackson had to say.'

Could good fortune have actually come from this disaster? Even Quentin Hale, who should be furious, would be ecstatic to hear that the cipher had been solved.

Knox had served as quartermaster for nearly fifteen years, earning the job his father once held. He'd always smiled when he watched pirate movies with their caricatures of the all-powerful captain who mercilessly inflicted pain on his crew. Nothing could be further from the truth. Pirate communities had operated as loose democracies, members deciding for themselves who led them and for how long. The fact that both the captain and the quartermaster were elected ensured that the treatment of those below them would be fair and reasonable. As a further check and balance, crew votes could be taken for a new captain or quartermaster at any time. And many a captain who went too far found himself banished to the first speck of dry land the ship spotted, another man elevated to leadership. A quartermaster walked an even tighter line, serving both the crew and the captain.

A good one understood how to please both.

So he knew what had to be done.

'Okay,' he said, adding a smile. 'Steak's on me.' He reached over and patted Parrott twice on the shoulder. 'I get it. You guys are in charge. I'll take your message back.'

'I was hoping you'd see it that way.'

He withdrew his hand and tapped the exposed skin on Parrott's neck, penetrating the short needle. A tad more pressure, then a squeeze, and the contents of the bubble syringe injected.

'Hey.' Parrott's hand reached for the pain.

One. Two. Three.

Parrott's body went limp.

Knox kept him upright, then gently laid him on the bench. The concoction he'd used was derived from a Caribbean reef fish. *Karenia annulatus*. A fast-acting, lethal toxin. Centuries ago, during the glory days when sloops roamed that southern sea, more than one enemy had been dispatched with its nearly instant effect.

A shame this man had to die.

But there was no choice.

Absolutely none.

Carefully, he arranged Parrott's hands beneath his cheek, as if he'd dozed off. Nothing unusual for a Central Park bench. He patted Parrott's trousers and found a hotel room key for the Helmsley Park Lane. Not bad. He'd stayed there a few times himself.

Then he left.

8

Malone calmly walked down a low-ceilinged passage that connected the Hyatt with Grand Central Terminal. He knew that, once he was inside the busy concourse, he could take a train back to the St. Regis, where Cassiopeia was waiting. Together they could figure out what to do next.

Interesting that he thought that way.

Together.

For years he'd lived and worked alone. He'd met Cassiopeia two years back but only a few months ago, in China, had they both finally acknowledged how they felt. At first he'd thought their closer connection simply the emotional fallout from all that had happened.

But he'd been wrong.

They'd been combatants, competitors, then friends. Now they were lovers. Cassiopeia was confident, smart, and beautiful. They shared a pleasant, trusting intimacy, knowing that whatever one needed the other would provide. Like now, when a cadre of police, surely trigger-happy considering what had just happened, were on the hunt.

He could use a little help.

Actually, he could use a lot.

He exited the tunnel, passing through a set of glass doors that opened into a concourse lined with busy shops. A street exit loomed 150 feet to his right. He turned left and entered the most recognized terminus in the world, nearly a football field long and a third that wide. The famous ceiling – a gold-leaf zodiac of stars atop a cerulean blue sky – soared a hundred feet above. Atop a central information booth rose the famous four-faced, brass clock. It read 7:20 PM. Hallways and passageways branched off in all directions, leading to train platforms. Escalators moved up and down to more levels striped by tracks. Beneath him, he knew, was a massive dining concourse overflowing with cafés, bakeries, and fast-food outlets. Farther down were the subway lines. His destination.

His gaze searched the open restaurants that dominated two sides of the cavernous hall one floor up. He heard snippets of conversations from passing commuters. No word yet on Daniels' condition.

Two suits entered the terminal from the same passage he'd just negotiated.

Three more followed.

He told himself to stay cool. There was no way he'd been tagged. They had practically nothing to go on. They were simply reconnoitering. Searching. Hoping for a break.

Three New York City cops rushed in from one of the street exits. Several more appeared to his right, emerging off escalators that led up to 45th Street.

Wrong. They were zeroing in on a target. But what had Stephanie's note said? *You can't trust anyone.* He needed to head down two levels to the subway. Unfortunately, there was now no option but to head left and take the exit out onto 42nd Street.

Had that been their plan?

He crossed a wide pedestrian bridge that spanned a concrete walk. One of the police emerged from the far side of the information booth and rushed his way.

He kept walking.

No police or suits stood before him.

A marble balustrade, waist-high, protected the bridge's edges. He spotted a narrow ledge on the other side of the rail that led off the bridge and angled down to the walkway below.

The unexpected always was best, but he'd have to move fast. The cop behind him was surely only a few steps away.

He sidestepped, whirled, then brought a knee to the man's gut, shoving his attacker to the ground. He hoped a few precious seconds had been bought, enough that he could evade the others still in the main hall.

He leaped the marble railing and balanced himself on the ledge, cautious of the fact that the drop down was a good thirty feet. Too much for a jump. He hustled forward, arms out for balance, moving down, leaping off the ledge when the drop was less than ten feet.

Agents and police appeared above.

Guns were drawn.

Alarm spread through the people on the lower path as they saw the weapons and began to scatter. He used their confusion as cover and raced forward, beneath the overpass, out of the line of fire. It would take the cops above him a few seconds to dart to the other side of the bridge, which should be enough time for an escape. The Oyster Bar restaurant opened to his left, the main dining concourse to his right. He knew that a dozen or more exits led from the dining concourse to tracks, trains, stairs, elevators, and ramps. He could catch any one of the trains and buy a ticket once on board.

He hustled into the dining hall and started for one of the exits on the far side. A maze of eateries, tables, chairs, and people lay in between.

Plenty of cover.

Two men appeared. They'd been waiting on the far side of a central pillar. They leveled weapons and an old cliché came to mind.

You can't outrun the radio.

He raised both arms.

Shouts came, ordering him to the floor.

He dropped to his knees.

9

Cassiopeia Vitt stepped from the shower and reached for a terry-cloth robe. Before nestling her damp skin within its soft folds she did what she usually did after a bath, at least whenever possible – she weighed herself. She'd tested the digital scale yesterday, after rinsing away the transatlantic flight with another long hot soak. Of course, flying always added kilograms. Why? Something about dehydration and fluid retention. She wasn't obsessed with her weight. More curious. Middle age was approaching, and what she ate and what she did seemed to matter so much more than five years ago.

She studied the scale's LCD display.

56.7 KG.

Not bad.

She tied the robe and wrapped her wet hair in a towel. The CD player in the other room offered a classical medley. She loved the St. Regis, a legendary landmark smack in the heart of Manhattan, a stone's throw from Central Park. It had been where her parents had stayed when they'd visited New York, and where she always stayed. So when Cotton suggested a weekend across the Atlantic, she'd immediately offered to arrange the accommodations.

She chose the Governor's Suite not only for its views but also for its two bedrooms. Though they'd made great strides, she and Cotton were still exploring their fledgling relationship. Granted, one of the bedrooms had yet to be utilized, but it was there – just in case.

They'd spent a lot of time together since returning from China, both in Copenhagen and at her French château. So far the emotional plunge, new to them both, seemed okay. She felt safe with Cotton – comfortable, knowing they were equals. He said all the time that women were not his strong point, but he underestimated himself. This trip seemed a perfect example. Though its primary purpose had been for him to meet with Stephanie Nelle, she'd appreciated the simple fact that he'd wanted her along.

But she, too, had combined pleasure with some business.

One of her least favorite tasks was looking after the family concerns. She was the sole heir to her father's financial empire, which totaled in the billions and stretched across six continents. A central management team, headquartered in Barcelona, ran the everyday operations. She was provided weekly reports but occasionally her input, as the only shareholder, was required. So yesterday afternoon, and again today, she'd met with her American managers. She was good at business, but smart enough to trust her employees. Her father taught her always to invest those in charge with a stake in the outcome – a percentage of the profits, however small – and he was right. She'd been blessed with a team that treated her companies as their own, and they'd actually multiplied her net worth.

Cotton had left a couple of hours ago, having decided to walk to 42nd Street. That was the thing about New York – so much traffic, it was far easier to stroll the thirteen blocks. Tonight was dinner and a show. Her choice, he'd said. So she'd purchased the tickets a few days ago and made reservations for afterward at one of her favorite eateries. She'd also stopped at Bergdorf Goodman and bought a new dress.

Why not? Every once in a while a girl had to splurge.

She'd been lucky in the store. The Armani she chose fit perfectly, not a single alteration required. Black silk, backless, decadent.

Just what they both needed.

She liked thinking about pleasing someone else. Those thoughts had been foreign to her for the majority of her life. Was that love? Maybe a part of it. Or at least she hoped.

The doorbell rang.

She smiled, thinking back to yesterday when they'd arrived.

I learned something a long time ago, Cotton had said. *If you come to your hotel room and there's double doors, something pretty good is on the other side. If there's a doorbell, that's always a good sign, too. But if there's double doors and a doorbell, holy crap, look out.*

She'd ordered wine and hors d'oeuvres since it would be a while until dinner. Cotton didn't drink alcohol – never had, he said – so she'd substituted cranberry juice for him. He should be back soon. His meeting with Stephanie was at 6:15 and it was now pushing eight o'clock. They'd need to be leaving shortly.

The bell rang again.

She left the bathroom and walked through a spacious living room to the double doors. She turned the latch, but the door was suddenly forced toward her, the unexpected action reeling her back.

Two men rushed inside.

She reacted and spun, driving her leg into a stomach and thrusting with her right fist, aiming for the second man's throat. Her kick found flesh and the man doubled forward, but she missed the other. She spun again, the towel in her hair falling away, and saw the gun.

Aimed straight at her.

Three more armed men appeared.

She froze and realized her robe was askew, providing her visitors with a view. Her fists were raised, nerves ready. 'Who are you?'

'Secret Service,' one of them said. 'You're under arrest.'

What had Cotton done now? 'Why?'

'Assassination of the president of the United States.'

Rarely was she genuinely surprised. It happened, but not often. But assassination of the president of the United States?

That was a new one.

'You need to lower your arms and place them behind your back,' the agent calmly said. 'And maybe close that robe.'

She did as he suggested and composed herself. 'Am I allowed to dress before you take me away?'

'Not alone.'

She shrugged. 'I can handle it, if you can.'

IO

Malone realized they weren't headed to any police station. He'd been cuffed and quickly led from Grand Central. They'd confiscated his wallet and St. Regis room key, so he assumed Cassiopeia was going to have visitors. Too bad about dinner and the show. Would have been fun. He'd even bought some new clothes for the occasion.

They'd given him no time to speak. Instead he was stuffed into a waiting car, left alone for a few minutes, then driven away. Now they were crossing the East River and entering Queens, heading away from Manhattan. Police cars ahead cleared a path. If he didn't know better he'd swear they were headed for JFK airport. Were they transporting him to a place under their exclusive control?

You can't trust anyone.

Stephanie's caution.

Perhaps she was right.

He doubted anyone in the car was going to volunteer anything, but there was one thing he wanted to say. 'Fellows, you know my name, so you know my background. I didn't try to kill anybody.'

Neither of the agents in the front seat nor the one sitting next to him in the rear responded. So he tried a different tack.

'Is Daniels all right?' he asked.

No response again.

The guy beside him was young and eager. Probably his first time in a situation like this.

'I need to speak with someone at the Magellan Billet,' he said, changing his tone from friendly to irritated.

The agent in the front, sitting on the passenger side, turned toward him. 'You need to sit there and shut up.'

'How about you stick it up your ass.'

The man shook his head. 'Look, Malone, make this easy and just ride. Okay?'

This conspiracy reaches far.

More of Stephanie's warning.

Which they now had, the note taken from him when he was searched.

So they knew he knew.

Fantastic.

They rode in silence for ten more minutes, then motored into JFK, passing through a gate that led directly to where planes were busy coming and going. One, though, sat alone, away from the others, ringed by police. A 747, painted blue and white, an American flag on its tail, the words UNITED STATES OF AMERICA stenciled in gold on its fuselage.

Air Force One.

A navy-blue jacket was tossed from the front seat. 'Put it on,' came the command.

He noticed three gold letters stamped on the front and back.

FBI.

They wheeled to the stairs that led up into the plane. The cuffs on his wrists were removed and he stepped from the car, slipping on the jacket. A man appeared from the far side of the stairs. Tall, lanky, with thin gray hair and a tranquil face.

Edwin Davis.

'They're watching us,' Davis said. 'From the terminal.

Every network has a camera here with a telescopic lens. Careful with your words. They hire lip-readers.'

'I heard you got promoted.'

Last time they'd met in Venice, Davis was a deputy national security adviser. Now he served as White House chief of staff.

Davis motioned to the rolling stairs and muttered, 'Lucky me. Let's go up.'

'What about Daniels?'

'You'll see.'

Hale watched the television. ADVENTURE was nearing home, now under engine power as they cruised west on the murky Pamlico River. He'd turned the volume down, tired of the anchors speculating in hope of holding viewers' attention while the same grainy videos of two mechanical devices sprouting from the Grand Hyatt hotel played over and over. Twenty-four-hour news was good for the first thirty minutes of a crisis, but after that it was overkill.

He shook his head, thinking of his fellow captains.

The damn fools.

He knew it was their right to do as they pleased – majority ruled in the Commonwealth – but he'd been excluded from their vote, and that ran contrary to the Articles. Unfortunately, desperate situations bred desperate acts, and he understood their frustration. They were all facing prison and the forfeiture of everything their families had accumulated for the past three centuries. Their only hope rested with the single sheet of paper he now held, encased within its own plastic sheath.

The second page of Andrew Jackson's scathing letter.

Since you adore secrets and plot your life along a path in the shadows, I offer you a challenge that should suit you. The sheet attached to this letter is a code, one formulated by the esteemed Thomas Jefferson. I am told he thought it to be the perfect cipher.

Succeed in learning its message and you will know where I have hidden what you crave. Fail and you remain the pathetic traitors that you are today.

He stared at the page.
Nine rows of random letters and symbols.

XQXFEETH
APKLJHXREHNJF
TSYOL:
EJWIWM
PZKLRIELCPΔ
FESZR
OPPOBOUQDX
MLZKRGVKΦ
EPRISZXNOXEΘ

Gibberish.

My sincerest hope is that the unmanly course ascribed to you shall be your ruin and that I shall live to enjoy that day.

For 175 years the failure to solve Jefferson's cipher had been a source of concern. Four times that concern had risen to possible ruin, and four times the situations had been handled.

Now a fifth scenario had arisen.

But contrary to what his colleagues might think, he hadn't sat idle. He was working on a solution to their problem. Two separate paths, actually. Unfortunately, his compatriots may have now endangered both of those efforts.

On the television, something new appeared.

The image of Air Force One on the ground at John F. Kennedy International Airport. A scrolling banner at the bottom of the screen announced that a suspect had been apprehended trying to flee the Grand Hyatt, but had been released.

Mistaken identity.

NO WORD AS YET ON THE CONDITION OF THE PRESIDENT, WHOM WE ARE TOLD WAS TAKEN DIRECTLY TO AIR FORCE ONE.

He needed to speak with Clifford Knox.

Malone entered Air Force One. He knew the plane contained 4,000 square feet of carefully designed space on three levels, including a suite for the president, an office, staff accommodations, even an operating room. Usually when the president traveled, an entourage tagged along with him including a doctor, senior advisers, Secret Service, and the press.

But the deck was devoid of anyone.

He wondered if Daniels had been brought here for treatment and everyone cleared out.

He followed Davis, who led him through the empty mid-deck to a closed door. Davis turned the knob to reveal a plush conference room, its exterior windows shuttered closed. At the far end of a long table sat Danny Daniels. Unscathed.

'I hear you tried to kill me,' the president said.

'If I had, you'd be dead.'

The older man chuckled. 'On that you're probably right.' Davis closed the door.

'You okay?' he asked the president.

'No holes. But I got my skull popped when they threw me back into the car. Luckily, as many people have noted through the years, I have a hard head.'

He noticed the typewritten note from the hotel room lying on the table.

Daniels stood from the leather armchair. 'Thanks for what you did. Seems like I'm constantly owing you. But as soon as we learned who they had in custody, and I read that note you were carrying, supposedly from Stephanie, we knew the shit had really hit the fan.'

He didn't like the tone. This conversation was leading somewhere.

'Cotton,' Daniels said. 'We have a problem.'

'We?'

'Yep. You *and* me.'

11

Wyatt exited from the subway and stepped into Union Square. Not as bustling as Times or Herald, or as high-toned as Washington, to him Union possessed its own personality, attracting a more eclectic crowd.

He'd watched as Cotton Malone had been wrestled into custody inside Grand Central, then led from the terminal. But he wouldn't stay a captive long. Not once Danny Daniels learned that one of his fair-haired boys had been involved – and Malone was definitely a member of that exclusive club.

He crossed 14th Street and walked south, down Broadway, toward the Strand – four floors of overstock, used, rare, and out-of-print books. He'd chosen the location for the meeting in deference to his adversary, whom he knew loved books. Personally, he despised the things. Never read a novel in his life. Why waste time on lies? Occasionally he did consult a nonfiction volume or two, but he preferred the Internet or simply asking someone. What all the fascination was with words on paper he'd never understand. And why people would hoard the things by the ton, treasuring them as they would a precious metal, made no sense whatsoever.

He caught sight of his contact.

She stood on the sidewalk, perusing carts of dollar books that lined the Strand's Broadway storefront. Her reputation was one for being sharp-eyed, distant, and coy. A bit difficult to work with. Which was in stark contrast with her physical appearance, her curvy figure, black hair, dark eyes, and swar-thy complexion representative of a Cuban ancestry.

Andrea Carbonell had commanded the NIA for more than a decade. The agency was a holdover from the Reagan years, when it had been responsible for some of the country's best intelligence coups. CIA, NSA, and just about every other agency had hated them. But the NIA's glory days were over, and now it seemed just another annoying multimillion-dollar line item in the black-ops budget.

Danny Daniels had always preferred the Magellan Billet, headed by another one of his fair-haired favorites, Stephanie Nelle. Her twelve agents had accomplished many of the country's recent successes – ferreting out the treason of Daniels' first vice president, stopping the Central Asian Federation, eliminating the Paris Club, even effecting a peaceful transition of power in China. And all without ever contracting for any services from Wyatt. The Magellan Billet worked internally with no outside help.

Except for Cotton Malone, of course.

Nelle hadn't seemed to mind recruiting her glamour boy when necessary. He knew that Malone had been involved with nearly all of the Billet's notable efforts. And, according to his sources, had worked for free.

The idiot.

Wyatt had received his call from Andrea Carbonell three weeks ago.

'Do you want the job?' she asked him.

'What you're asking may not be possible,' he told her.

'For you? No way. Everything is possible for the Sphinx.'

He hated the nickname, which referred to his tendency toward silence. He'd long ago acquired the skill of being in a conversation, saying nothing, yet appearing fully part of it. The tactic unnerved most listeners, nudging them to talk more than they ever would ordinarily.

'Is my price acceptable?' he asked.

'Perfectly.'

He kept walking, passing the dollar carts, knowing that Carbonell would follow. He turned the corner and headed east on 12th Street for half a block, ducking inside the doorway of a closed business.

'Daniels is fine,' Carbonell said as she drew close.

He was glad to hear that. Mission accomplished.

'How close were you going to cut that?' she asked.

'Where is Daniels?'

He saw she did not appreciate the inquiry, but then again he didn't appreciate her tone.

'At JFK. Inside Air Force One. I heard before I got here he's about to make a statement. Let the world see he's okay.'

He decided to answer her question now. 'I did my job.'

'And that meant involving Cotton Malone? The Secret Service grabbed him in Grand Central Station. They were led there by a radio alert. You wouldn't know who provided that information, would you?'

'Why do you ask questions you already know the answer to?'

'What if Malone had failed?'

'He didn't.'

She'd hired him to stop the assassination attempt, telling him she could not trust the assignment to anyone in-house. She'd also told him that her agency was on the budgetary chopping block, the official word being that it would be eliminated in the next fiscal year. He had little sympathy for her. He'd been eliminated eight fiscal years ago.

'I did what you asked,' he said.

'Not exactly. But close enough.'

'Time for me to go home.'

'Don't want to stick around and see what happens? You realize, Jonathan, that if NIA is hacked from the budget you'll lose money, too. I think I'm the only one who still employs you on a regular basis.'

No matter. He'd survive. He always had.

She motioned at his wristwatch. A Rolex Submariner. 'You like it?'

What was not to like? Gilt-faced. Gold lettering. Accurate to a tenth of a second on a battery that lasted practically forever. A gift to himself a few years ago after a particularly lucrative assignment.

He stared hard into her dark eyes.

'Do you know how the Swiss rose to be such superb watch-makers?' she asked.

He said nothing.

'In 1541 Geneva outlawed jewelry on religious grounds, so the jewelers were forced to learn a new trade – watchmaking. Over time they became good at it. During World War I, when foreign competition had factories either seized or destroyed, the Swiss thrived. Today they produce half of the world's watches. The Geneva seal is the gold standard by which all others are judged.'

So what?

'Jonathan, you and I are not the gold standard of anything any longer.'

Her gaze bore into his eyes.

'But just like those Swiss jewelers, I have an exit strategy.'

'I wish you well with it. I'm done.'

'Don't want to play with Malone anymore?'

He shrugged. 'Since no one shot him, that will have to wait for another day.'

'You really are nothing but trouble,' she said. 'That's what the other agencies say about you.'

'Yet they seem to come my way when they get their asses stuck in deep cracks.'

'Maybe you're right. Go back to Florida, Jonathan. Enjoy

yourself. Play golf. Walk on the beach. Leave this business to the grown-ups.'

He ignored her insults. He had her money and he'd done his job. Winning a war of words meant nothing to him. What *did* interest him was that they were being observed. He'd spotted the man on the subway and confirmed his presence when the same face reappeared at street level in Union Square. He was currently positioned on the other side of Broadway, a hundred yards away.

And not being all that subtle.

'Good luck, Andrea. Perhaps you'll fare better than I did.'

He left her standing in the doorway and did not glance back.

Twenty yards away a car wheeled around the corner and headed straight for him.

It stopped and two men emerged.

'Do you think you could be a good boy and come quietly?' one of the men asked.

Wyatt was unarmed. Carrying a weapon around the city would have proved problematic, especially in the charged atmosphere he knew would be present after the assassination attempt.

'Some people want to talk to you,' the man said.

He turned back.

Carbonell was gone.

'We're not with her,' one of the men said. 'In fact, the chat is about her.'

12

Malone waited with Edwin Davis inside Air Force One and watched the spectacle below. The press had been allowed onto the asphalt and were now crowded ten-deep behind a hastily erected rope barricade, cameras pointed toward a crop of microphones that sprouted before Danny Daniels. The president stood tall, his baritone voice booming to the world.

'What did he mean that *we* have a problem?' Malone asked Davis.

'The past few months have actually been a little boring. The last year or so of a president's second term is like the last few months of a pope's life. Everybody's waiting for the old guy to exit so the new guys can take over.' Davis pointed at the press. 'Now there's something to report.'

They crowded close to one of the plane's windows, out of sight. A television to their right displayed what was being broadcast by CNN, the volume just high enough for Malone to hear Daniels reassure everyone that he was unhurt.

'You're not answering the question.'

Davis pointed out the window. 'He asked me to hold any explanations until he was finished.'

'You always do as he says?'

'Hardly. As you well know.'

Malone turned toward the monitor and heard Daniels proclaim, 'Let me say emphatically that I think the Secret Service and the law enforcement agents of New York City did a superb job, and I want to thank them for everything they did during this unfortunate incident. This was to be a personal trip to honor an old friend. This incident, under no circumstances, will prevent me from traveling throughout America and the world. It is regrettable that individuals still think murder or assassination is a way to effect change.'

'Mr. President,' one of the reporters shouted, 'can you give us an idea what you saw or felt at the time?'

'I'm not sure that I ought to describe what I saw beyond the fact that the window shattered and a metal device appeared. I then saw the quick and effective actions taken by the Secret Service.'

'Your own thoughts, sir?'

'I was thankful to the Secret Service for doing a superb job.'

'You used the word *individuals* a moment ago when referring to the assassination attempt. Who do you mean by that in the plural?'

'Do any of you believe that one person manufactured all that hardware?'

'Do you have specific individuals in mind?'

'That will be the focus of an intense investigation, which is starting as we speak.'

Davis pointed at the flat screen. 'He has to be careful. Just enough to send a message.'

'What the hell is going on?' Malone asked.

Davis did not answer. This punctilious man, with a knife-edge press to his trousers, simply stared at the television screen as Daniels retreated from the microphones and his press secretary fielded more questions. The president climbed the stairs back into the plane, camera lens following. In a few moments he would reenter through the door a few feet away.

'It's Stephanie,' Davis whispered. 'She's the one who needs our help.'

Cassiopeia sat in the rear seat of an SUV, one agent beside her, two more up front. They'd allowed her to dress, then to pack both her and Cotton's belongings, bringing everything with them.

Apparently, they were going somewhere.

They'd left the St. Regis quietly and driven unescorted out of Manhattan, across the East River into Queens. No one had said a word, and she hadn't asked anything.

No need.

The car radio told the story.

Someone had tried to assassinate Danny Daniels, and the president had just appeared before the press to assure everyone that he'd escaped unharmed. Cotton was somehow involved, and she wondered if this was what Stephanie Nelle had wanted to see him about.

Stephanie and Cotton were close – friends for fifteen years. He'd worked for her a dozen of those years at the Magellan Billet, a covert intelligence unit within the U.S. Justice Department. Cotton had been a navy commander, trained as both a pilot and a lawyer, personally recruited by Stephanie. While there, he'd handled some of her most sensitive assignments until retiring early three years ago. That's when he'd moved to Copenhagen and opened an old-book shop.

She hoped Cotton was okay.

They'd both thought the email from Stephanie strange but ignored the warning signs. A weekend in New York had simply sounded like fun. Unfortunately, she wasn't wearing her black Armani in a crowded theater. Instead she was in federal custody being driven who knew where.

Her long dark hair was still damp, curling as it dried. She wore no makeup, but rarely did anyway. She'd chosen a smart ensemble of brown leather trousers, a camel-colored cash-mere shirt, and a double-breasted camel-hair blazer. Vanity had never been a weakness, but that didn't mean she wasn't conscious of her appearance.

'Sorry about the kick,' she said to the agent sitting beside her. He'd been the one to first rush into the apartment.

He acknowledged the apology with a nod but kept his thoughts to himself. She realized prisoners rarely had luggage brought with them to jail. Apparently, after her identity had been discovered, new instructions had been provided.

Up ahead she spotted the grand expanse of John F. Kennedy International Airport. They motored through an open gate and she caught sight of Air Force One parked on the tarmac. A swarm of people were being led away from the plane.

'We'll wait until the press clears,' the agent in the front seat said.

'Then what?' she asked.

'You're going on board.'

13

Hale continued to watch the television coverage. *Adventure* was less than thirty minutes from home. They'd slowed to a crawl respecting the fact that the Pamlico, for all its vastness, was little more than twenty feet deep at best. He recalled what his grandfather had told him about the channel markers – once merely cedar saplings, they were routinely moved by the local pilots to encourage visiting boat captains to hire them. Thank God the days of tacking inland from the sand banks, dodging shoals that had not existed the day before, were over. Engines made quite the difference. He'd muted the TV and was listening to the *slap-slap* of the river's flow against the ship's smooth hull.

Waiting.

He'd placed a call twenty minutes ago and left a voice message.

Danny Daniels had been impressive before the press. Hale had caught the president's unspoken message. The investigations were already starting. He wondered how good the quartermaster had been. Thankfully, Knox was thorough, that he'd give him. Knox's father had been the same, serving Hale's father. But this situation was unusual, to say the least.

His phone chimed.

When he answered, Knox said, 'I told them not to do it, but they were insistent.'

'You should have told me.'

'It's no different from what I did for you, and they have no idea of that. I've never violated your confidence, so you can't expect me to violate theirs.'

True, only a few days ago Knox had indeed performed a clandestine mission for Hale. One of great importance.

And never had he violated any of their confidences.

Of the four families, the Hales were by far the most prosperous, with a net worth equal to the remaining three combined. That superiority had often bred resentment, evidenced from time to time by bursts of independence, the others' way of asserting themselves, so he should not be surprised by the day's events.

'What happened?' he asked.

He listened as the quartermaster reported, including the NIA's interference and the elimination of their agent.

'Why did they interfere?' he asked. 'They are the only ones who have stood by us.'

'Apparently, we went a bit too far. Beyond that, their agent offered no explanation. He seemed intent on sending us a message. I thought it important for them to know that we received the message, and don't appreciate what they did.'

He could not argue with that conclusion.

A sense of mission had always bound a pirate company, the team more important than any one individual. His father had taught him that missions required goals and rewards, the participants bound into a single purpose. That had been the way of his ancestors, and even today every good ship captain knew that a clearly defined mission transformed the hunted into hunters.

So he decided not to chastise Knox and simply said, 'From this point on, I want to be kept informed.'

The quartermaster did not object. 'I'm going to retrieve Parrott's laptop.'

His heart quickened. The prospect that Jefferson's cipher may have been solved excited him. Could it be? Still—

'I'd be careful.'

'I plan to.'

'Notify me the moment you have it. And, Clifford. No more moves like the ones today.'

'I assume you'll be dealing with the other three?'

'As fast as I can get to shore.'

He ended the call.

At least something might have gone right today.

He glanced over at the two pages sheathed in plastic.

In 1835, when his great-great-grandfather had tried to assassinate Andrew Jackson, there'd been hell to pay. And just like now, divisions existed within the Commonwealth. Only then a Hale had ordered the quartermaster to kill the president of the United States.

Richard Lawrence, an unemployed house painter, had been covertly recruited. Prior to the assassination attempt Lawrence had tried to shoot his sister and openly threatened two others, eventually believing that Jackson had murdered his father. He also thought himself the king of England and fervently pronounced that Jackson was interfering with his royal inheritance. He held the president responsible for his unemployment and for an overall shortage of money in the country.

Not a difficult matter to encourage him to act.

The problem came from Jackson, who'd sequestered himself within the White House during the bitter winter of 1834. A funeral at the Capitol finally brought the president out, so Lawrence was nudged to Washington and provided two pistols. He'd secreted himself within the crowd on a cold, rainy day and confronted his adversary.

But fate intervened and saved Old Hickory.

Thanks to wet powder, both guns misfired.

Immediately Jackson had blamed Senator George Poindexter of Mississippi, alleging a conspiracy. The Senate launched an official inquiry, but Poindexter was exonerated. Privately, though, Jackson targeted his real vengeance.

Hale's grandfather had told him the story.

The six presidents before Jackson had been easy to work with. Washington knew what the Commonwealth had done for the country during the Revolution. So did Adams. Even Jefferson tolerated them, and their help with America's war on the Barbary pirates removed any bad taste that may have lingered. Madison, Monroe, and the second Adams never presented a problem.

But that damn fool from Tennessee was determined to change everything.

Jackson fought with Congress, the Supreme Court, the press – anybody and everybody. He was the first president nominated by a political party, not political bosses, the first who campaigned directly to the people and won thanks solely to them. He hated the political elite and, once in office, made sure their influence waned. Jackson had even dealt with pirates before, as a general during the War of 1812 when he made a deal with Jean Lafitte to save New Orleans from the British. He actually liked Lafitte, but years later, as president, when a dispute arose with the Commonwealth, one that should have been an easy matter to resolve, Jackson refused to capitulate. The other captains at the time had wanted to maintain the peace so they voted to let it go.

Only the Hales said no.

And they'd sent Richard Lawrence.

But just like today, that assassination attempt failed. Thankfully, Lawrence was declared insane and locked away. He died in 1861, never uttering an intelligible word.

Could a similar good fortune emerge from today's fiasco?

Outside the salon's windows Hale spotted the Bayview car

ferry making another of its daily runs across the Pamlico, south to Aurora.

Home was not far away.

His mind continued to churn.

The path his great-great-grandfather had chosen remained bumpy. Andrew Jackson had left a scar on the Commonwealth that, on four previous occasions, had festered into an open wound.

My hope is that the unmanly course ascribed to you shall be your ruin.

Maybe not, you sorry SOB.

His secretary entered the salon. Hale had tasked him with finding the three other captains.

'They are in the compound at Cogburn's house.'

'Tell them that I want to see them in the main house within the hour.'

His secretary left.

He stared back at the choppy river and caught sight of a shark fin just beyond the boat's wake. An interesting sight fifty miles inland from the open sea. Of late he'd noticed more and more predators plying these waters. Just a few days ago one had snatched the bait from his fishing line, nearly yanking him into the river.

He smiled.

They were tough, aggressive, and relentless.

Like him.

14

Malone was becoming impatient. The comment about Stephanie Nelle being in trouble concerned him. And he hadn't missed what the president had first said.

I read that note supposedly *from Stephanie.*

Stephanie was not only his former boss, she was his close friend. Twelve years they'd worked together. When he'd retired out early, she'd tried to talk him out of it. Ultimately, she'd understood and wished him well. But over the past three years they'd come to each other's aid more than once. He could count on her, and she on him.

Which was the sole reason why he'd responded to her email.

The president reentered the plane and marched toward where he and Davis stood. They followed Daniels into the conference room. The cabin remained empty. Three LCD screens displayed images from Fox, CNN, and a local New York station of the 747's exterior as the press was being herded away. Daniels removed his suit jacket and yanked loose his tie, unbuttoning the collar.

'Have a seat, Cotton.'

'I'd rather you tell me what's going on.'

Daniels sighed. 'That could be a tall order.'

Davis sat in one of the chairs.

Malone decided to sit and listen to what they had to say.

'The planet should now be at ease knowing that the leader of the free world is still alive,' Daniels said, the sarcasm clear.

'It had to be done,' Davis made clear.

Daniels dropped himself into a chair. He was in the final sixteen months of his presidency, and Malone wondered what this man would do when he no longer occupied the head of the table. Being an ex-president had to be tough. One day the weight of the world rested on your shoulders. Then, at noon on the 20th day of January, nobody gave a rat's ass if you were even alive.

Daniels rubbed his eyes and cheeks. 'The other day I was thinking about a story somebody once told me. Two bulls were sitting atop a hill, staring down at a mess of pretty cows. The young one said, "I'm going to run down there and have me one of those beauties." The old bull didn't take the bait. He just stood there. The young bull egged him on, questioning his ability to perform, saying again, "Let's run on down there and have us one of 'em." Finally the old bull cocked his head and told his young friend, "How about we just walk down there and have 'em all?"'

Malone smiled. He could empathize with that young cow.

On the television screens a fuzzy, distant image of the plane and two cars approaching the stairway leading up inside could be seen. Three agents stepped out of the cars wearing FBI jackets like the one he still had on, along with caps.

One of them climbed the stairs.

He'd sensed they were waiting for something but, thinking about the story and its metaphor, he wanted to know, 'Who are you planning on sticking it to?'

The president pointed a finger at him and Davis. 'You two get reacquainted?'

'Like family,' Malone said. 'I feel the love. Do you, Edwin?'

Davis shook his head. 'Believe us, Cotton. We wish this wasn't happening.'

The conference room door opened and Cassiopeia stepped inside. She removed a navy jacket and cap, exposing damp, dark hair.

She looked great, as always.

'It's not exactly dinner and a show,' he said. 'But it is Air Force One.'

She smiled. 'Never a dull moment.'

'Now that the gang's all here,' Daniels said. 'We can get down to business.'

'And what might that be?' Cassiopeia asked.

'It's so good to see you again, too,' the president said to her.

Malone knew Cassiopeia had worked with Daniels before – on something she and Stephanie had teamed up on. The two women were close friends. Their connection stretched as far back as Stephanie's late husband, Lars. So she, too, would be concerned that Stephanie was in trouble.

Cassiopeia shrugged. 'I don't know how good it is. I'm accused of trying to kill you. Since you're obviously not dead, why are we here?'

Daniels' face turned hard. 'It's not good. Not good at all.'

15

Bath, North Carolina

Hale stepped from Adventure and marched down the dock. The crew was busy securing the sloop to the end of the two-hundred-foot expanse. The late-summer sun faded to the west, the air acquiring a familiar chill. All the land along the river, nearly twenty square miles, belonged to the Commonwealth – the tracts allocated centuries ago among the four families, the riverbank divided equally. Bath lay a couple of miles east, now a sleepy village of 267 residents – mostly weekend homes and river cottages – none of its former glory remaining. The Hales' quarter of the estate had always been meticulously maintained. Four houses dotted the surrounding woods, one for each of the Hale children and one for himself. He lived here most of the time, occupying apartments in New York, London, Paris, and Hong Kong only when necessary. The other clans were the same. It had been that way since 1793, when the Commonwealth formed.

An electric cart awaited him and he drove through groves of oak, pine, and cypress to his home, a mansion erected in 1883 in Queen Anne style, flush with irregular forms and dramatic rooflines. Balconies and porches wrapped each of its three levels, opening off twenty-two rooms. Warmth and character sprang from olive walls, shingles mixed in pale red and gray slate, glittering diamond-paned windows, and mahogany-stained doors. Its elaborate woodwork had been crafted in Philadelphia, then shipped south and hauled from the river by oxcart.

His ancestors had certainly known how to live. They'd built an empire, then passed it down to their children. Which made his current predicament even more compelling.

He was not going to be the last in a long line.

He stopped the cart and surveyed the grounds.

The grove beyond was quiet as a church, dotted with shadows, the dwindling open patches whitened by the setting sun. Crew kept the estate in superb working order. What was once a hip-roofed dairy had been remodeled into a workshop. The old smokehouse contained a communications and security center. The privies were long gone, but the saddle-notched log barns remained, each housing farming equipment. He was particularly proud of the grape arbors, his scuppernongs some of the state's sweetest. He wondered if any of his children were back on the property. They were all grown and married, but none, as yet, with children of their own. They worked in the legitimate family enterprises, aware of their heritage but ignorant of his responsibilities. That had always been kept between father and the singular chosen offspring. To this day his sister and brother knew nothing of the Commonwealth. The time was coming when he'd have to choose his successor and start the grooming process, just as his father had done with him.

He imagined what was happening a mile away as the other three captains, heads of their respective families, responded to his summons. He told himself to control his temper. In 1835 Hales had acted unilaterally to the detriment of the others. Now it was the other way around.

He depressed the accelerator and drove on.

The gravel road paralleled one of his most productive soybean fields, the thick woods on the opposite side loaded with deer. The deep alto of a blackbird, singing the last strophes of a ballad, could be heard in the distance. His life had always been about the outdoors. Hales first came to America from England in 1700, on a voyage across the Atlantic that took so long the pet rabbits had bred three times.

He'd always liked how that first Hale had been described.

A vigorous, intelligent man of wit and charm and diverse abilities.

John Hale arrived at Charles Town, in South Carolina, on Christmas Day. Three days later he plunged northward along trails known only to Natives. Two weeks after that he found the Pamlico River and a blue, tree-ringed bay where he built a house. He then founded a port, sheltered from attack by water, but navigable on an easterly course to the sea. He named it Bath Town, and five years later its incorporation was formally approved.

Always ambitious, John Hale built ships and made his fortune in the slave trade. As his wealth and reputation grew, so did Bath, the town becoming a center of nautical activity and a hotbed for piracy. So it was only natural that Hale became a pirate, preying off British, French, and Spanish shipping. In 1717, when King George announced his Act of Grace, granting absolution for men who swore they would not resume buccaneering, Hale pledged his oath and, openly, became a respected planter and Bath councilman. Secretly, his ships continued to wreak havoc, but he targeted only the Spanish, which the British would care little about. The colonies became an ideal market for the buying and selling of illegal goods. Under British law American exports could be shipped only on English ships with English sailors – a nightmare relative to cost and supply. Colonial merchants and governors greeted pirates with open arms since they could supply what was needed at the right price. Many American ports became pirate dens, Bath the most notable and productive. Eventually the Revolutionary War changed allegiances and led to the formation of the Commonwealth.

Ever since, the four families had been bound.

To pledge our Unity and assert our Cause, every Man has a Vote in Affairs of Moment; has equal Title to the fresh provisions, or strong Liquors, at any Time seized, and may use them at Pleasure. No man is better than Another and each Shall rise to the Defense of the Other.

Words from the Articles, which he took to heart.

He stopped the cart before another of the estate's buildings, this one with a hipped roof, gables, dormers, and a tower at one end. It rose two stories with a cantilevered stairway. The delightful nature of its exterior concealed the fact that it acted as a prison.

He punched in a code for the heavy oak door and released the latch. Once the walls had been fashioned of only brick and timber. Now they were soundproofed with the latest technology. Inside were eight cells. Not a horrible prison, but a prison nonetheless. One that came in handy.

Like a few days ago, when Knox moved on the target.

He climbed to the second floor and approached the iron bars. The prisoner on the other side rose from a wooden bench and faced him.

'Comfortable?' he asked. The cell was ten feet square, roomy actually considering what his ancestors had been forced to endure. 'Anything you need?'

'The key to the door.'

He smiled. 'Even if you had that, there would be no place to go.'

'They were right about you. You're no patriot, you're a thieving pirate.'

'That's the second time today I've been called that.'

The prisoner stepped close to the bars. Hale stood just on the other side, a foot or so away. He noted the dingy clothes, the tired face. He'd been told that his captive had eaten little over the past three days.

'Nobody gives a damn that you have me,' he was told.

'I'm not so sure about that. They don't, as yet, realize the danger you're in.'

'I'm expendable.'

'Caesar was once captured by Sicilian pirates,' he said. 'They demanded a ransom of 25 gold talents. He thought himself worth more and demanded they raise the ransom to 50, which was paid. After he was freed, he hunted his captors down and slaughtered them to a man.' He paused. 'How much do you think you are worth?'

Spit flew through the bars and splattered on his face.

He closed his eyes as he slowly reached into his pocket for a handkerchief and wiped it away.

'Stick it up your ass,' his captive said to him.

He reached into his other pocket and found his lighter, plated with German silver and engraved with his name, a gift from his children two Christmases ago. He ignited the handkerchief and tossed the flaming cloth through the bars, straight at his prisoner.

Stephanie Nelle reeled back and allowed the burning bundle to drop to the floor where she extinguished it with her shoe, never taking her gaze off him.

He'd snatched her as a favor for someone else, but over the past couple of days, he'd been thinking how to make use of her for his own purposes. She might even become expendable if Knox's news from New York – that the cipher may be solved – proved true.

Considering what just happened he hoped that was the case.

'I assure you,' he said to her. 'You will regret what you just did.'

PART TWO

16

Malone held tight in his chair as Air Force One rose from the runway and vectored south back to Washington, DC. Everyone still occupied the conference room.

'Tough day at the office, dear?' Cassiopeia asked him.

He caught the playful look in her eyes. Any other woman would be highly irritated at the moment, but Cassiopeia handled the unexpected better than any person he'd ever known. Cool, calculated, focused. He still recalled the first time they'd encountered each other – in France, at Rennes-le-Château, one dark night when she'd taken a shot at him then sped away on a motorcycle.

'Just the usual,' he said. 'Wrong place, right time.'

She smiled. 'You missed out on a great dress.'

She'd told him before he left the hotel about the stop at Bergdorf Goodman. He'd been looking forward to seeing her purchase.

'Sorry about our date,' he told her again.

She shrugged. 'Look where we ended up.'

'It's good to finally meet you,' Edwin Davis said to Cassiopeia. 'We missed each other in Europe.'

'This trip to New York was a lark,' Danny Daniels said. 'Or as much of a lark as a president is allowed to have.'

Malone listened as Daniels explained how a close friend and lifetime supporter was having a retirement gathering. Daniels had been invited but had not decided to attend until a couple of months ago. No one outside the White House was told of the journey until yesterday, and the press was informed only that the president would be visiting New York. No location, time, or extent of the visit had been provided. Once inside Cipriani, attendees would have passed through a metal detector. By not forewarning anyone, and keeping even the press in the dark until the last minute, the Secret Service thought they had the trip reasonably secure.

'It's always the same,' Daniels said. 'Every assassination, or attempted one, happened because of screwups. Lincoln, McKinley, and Garfield had no guards. Just walk right up and shoot 'em. Kennedy's protection was waved off for political reasons. They wanted him as close to the people as possible. So they announced that he'd be parading down a crowded street in an open car. "Come on out and see the president."' Daniels shook his head. 'Reagan took a bullet solely because his layers of protection broke down. Always some screwup. This time it was mine.'

Malone was surprised to hear the admission.

'I insisted on the trip. Told everyone it would be fine. They took some precautions, and wanted to take more. But I said no.'

The plane leveled off from its climb. Malone popped his ears to the altitude.

'When you decided to go,' Cassiopeia said. 'Who knew?'

'Not enough people,' Daniels said.

Malone thought the response curious.

'How did you get into that hotel room?' the president asked him.

He explained about Stephanie's email, the key card waiting for him at the St. Regis, and what he found. Cassiopeia was handed the note from the envelope, which she read.

Daniels motioned to Davis, who produced a pocket tape recorder and slid it across the table.

'This is a recording of secured radio traffic, after the

shooting, while you were trying to get out of the Hyatt,' Davis said.

Daniels activated the unit.

Alert to all agents. Suspect is wearing pale blue buttondown shirt, light trousers, no jacket at this time, presently exiting Grand Hyatt hotel from main lobby into tunnel that accesses Grand Central Terminal. I'm headed in that direction.

The president stopped the machine.

'There's no way anyone could have known that,' Malone said.

'None of our agents posted that alert,' Davis said. 'And as you know, those frequencies are not available to the general public.'

'You recognize the voice?' Daniels asked.

'Hard to say. The static and the radio mask a lot. But there is something familiar about it.'

'Seems you have an admirer,' Cassiopeia said.

'And you were set up,' Daniels made clear. 'Just like we were.'

Wyatt was driven past Columbus Circle to Manhattan's Upper West Side, an area less commercial, less congested, and loaded with quaint shops and brick-faced apartments. He was escorted to the second floor of one of the many brick buildings and into a spacious dwelling, sparsely decorated, wooden blinds covering the windows. He assumed it was some sort of safe house.

Two men waited for him.

Both deputy directors – one for the CIA, the other NSA. The National Security Agency face he knew, the other he simply recognized. Neither man seemed glad to see him. He was left alone with them, as the two who brought him waited outside in the elevator foyer.

'You want to tell us what you were doing today?' CIA asked. 'How you happened to be at the Grand Hyatt?'

He hated anything and everything related to CIA. He'd only worked for them, on occasion, because they paid well.

'Who says I was there?'

CIA was antsy, pacing the room. 'Don't screw with us, Wyatt. You were there. Why?'

Interesting that these two clearly knew at least some of his business.

'You responsible for Malone showing up?' NSA asked.

'Why would you think that?'

CIA produced a pocket tape recorder and flicked it on. He heard his voice, over the radio, informing the Secret Service about Malone heading for Grand Central Station.

'I'll ask you again. Was Malone your idea?'

'Seems it was fortunate he was there.'

'And what if he'd failed to stop things?' NSA asked.

He gave them the same response he'd provided Carbonell. 'He didn't.' And he wasn't about to explain anything more to these idiots. But he was curious. 'Why didn't you stop things? You were obviously there.'

'We didn't know spit,' CIA hollered back. 'We've been playing catch-up all day.'

He shrugged. 'Seems you caught up.'

'You cocksure SOB,' CIA said, his voice still loud. 'You and Carbonell are interfering in our business. You're both trying to save that stinking Commonwealth.'

'You're confusing me with someone else.'

He'd decided to take Carbonell's advice and play golf tomorrow. He'd actually come to enjoy the game, and the course inside his gated community was spectacular.

'We know all about you and Malone,' NSA spit out.

This man was a degree calmer than CIA, but still anxious. Wyatt knew NSA represented billions in the annual intelligence budget. They were into everything, including the covert monitoring of nearly every overseas phone call made to and from the United States.

'Malone was the chief witness against you at your admin hearing,' NSA said. 'You coldcocked him so you could order three men into a shoot-out. Two of whom died. Malone brought charges against you. What was the finding? *Unnecessary risks taken in disregard of life.* You were sectioned out. A twenty-year career gone. No pension. Nothing. I'd say you owe Cotton Malone.'

CIA pointed a finger at him. 'What did Carbonell do, hire you to help out with the Commonwealth? To try and save their hides?'

He knew little about the Commonwealth besides the meager information contained in the dossier she'd provided, all of which related to the assassination attempt, little in the way of broad background. He'd been briefed about Clifford Knox, the organization's quartermaster, who would be directing the threat on Daniels' life. He'd watched as Knox moved about the Grand Hyatt the past few days, preparing the guns, waiting for him to leave so that he could inspect their handiwork and leave Malone the note.

'Are those pirates the ones who tried to kill Daniels?' NSA asked. 'You know who planted those guns, don't you?'

Since he doubted the trail of those automatic weapons led anywhere past the Grand Hyatt, he was not about to become their chief accuser. His immediate problem, though, was even more substantial. Obviously, he'd managed to insert himself into some sort of spy civil war. CIA and NSA apparently were at odds with NIA, and the Commonwealth was at the center of the dispute. Nothing new. Intelligence agencies rarely cooperated with one another.

Still, this feud felt different.

More personal.

And that concerned him.

17

Bath, North Carolina

Hale entered his house, still seething from Stephanie Nelle's insult. Just the latest example of America's continued ingratitude. All that the Commonwealth had done for the country, during and since the American Revolution, and he got spit on.

He stopped in the foyer at the base of the main staircase and gathered his thoughts. Outside, his secretary had told him the other three captains were there. He had to handle them carefully. He stared up at one of the canvases that dotted the oak-paneled walls – his great-great-grandfather, who'd lived on this same land and attacked a president, too.

Abner Hale.

But surviving had been a lot easier in the mid-19th century, as the world was a much larger place. You could actually disappear. He'd often imagined what it would have been like to sail the oceans back then, going about, as one chronicler had written, *like roaring lions seeking whom you might devour.* An unpredictable life on a rolling sea, no home, no bounds, few rules save for those all aboard had agreed upon in the articles.

He sucked a few deep breaths, straightened his clothes, then walked down the corridor, entering his library, a spacious rectangle with a vaulted ceiling and a wall of windows framing a view of the orchards. He'd remodeled the room a decade ago, removing most of his father's influences and purposefully evoking the mood of an English country estate.

He closed the library doors and faced three men seated in tufted, burgundy velvet chairs.

Charles Cogburn, Edward Bolton, and John Surcouf.

Each was lean, two wore mustaches, all bore sun-squinted eyes. They were men of the sea, like him, signers of the Commonwealth's current Articles, heads of their respective families, bonded to one another by a sacred oath. He imagined that their stomachs were tossing similar to Abner Hale's in 1835 when he, too, had acted like a fool.

He decided to start with a question he already knew the answer to. 'Where is the quartermaster?'

'In New York,' Cogburn said. 'Doing damage control.'

Good. At least they planned to be reasonably honest with him. Two months ago he'd been the one to inform them of Daniels' unannounced New York trip, wondering if perhaps an opportunity might present itself. They'd debated the proposed course at length, then voted. 'I don't have to say the obvious. We decided not to do this.'

'*We* changed our minds,' Bolton said.

'Which I'm sure you championed.'

Boltons had always displayed irrational aggression. Their ancestors had helped found Jamestown in 1607, then made a fortune supplying the new colony. On one of those voyages they imported a new strain of tobacco, which proved the colony's saving grace, thriving in the sandy soil, becoming Virginia's most valuable export commodity. Bolton descendants eventually settled in the Carolinas, at Bath, branching out into piracy, then privateering.

'I thought the move would solve the problem,' Bolton said. 'The vice president would have left us alone.'

He had to say, 'You have no idea what would have happened, *if* you'd been successful.'

'All I know, Quentin,' John Surcouf said, 'is that I'm at risk of going to prison and losing everything my family has. I'm not going to sit by and allow that to happen. Even if we failed, we sent a message today.'

'To whom? Do you plan on taking responsibility for the act? Does someone in the White House know that you three sanctioned the assassination? If so, how long do you think it will be before you're arrested?'

None of them spoke.

'It was foolish thinking,' he said. 'This is not 1865, or even 1963. It's a new world, with new rules.'

He reminded himself that Surcouf family history differed from the others. They'd started as shipbuilders, immigrating to the Carolinas just after John Hale founded Bath. Surcoufs eventually financed much of the town's expansion, reinvesting their profits in the community and helping the town grow. Several became colonial governors. Others took to the sea, manning sloops. The early part of the 18th century had been piracy's Golden Age, and Surcoufs reaped their share of those spoils. Eventually, like others, they legitimized themselves with privateering. One interesting story came at the dawn of the 19th century when Surcouf money helped finance Napoleon's wars. Enjoying friendly relations, the Surcouf then living in Paris asked the emperor if he might build a terrace at one of his estates tiled of French coins. Napoleon refused, not wanting people traipsing across his image. Undaunted, Surcouf built the terrace anyway but with the coins stacked upright, edges to the surface, which solved the problem. Unfortunately, later Surcouf descendants had been equally foolish with their money.

'Look,' Hale said, softening his voice, 'I understand your anxiety. I have my share as well. But we are in this together.'

'They have every record,' Cogburn muttered. 'All my Swiss banks caved.'

'Mine, too,' Bolton added.

Combined, several billion dollars of their deposits lay overseas, on which not a dime of income tax had ever been paid. Each of them had received a letter from the U.S. attorney notifying him that he was the target of a federal criminal investigation. Hale assumed that four separate prosecutions – as opposed to one – had been chosen to divide their resources, pit one against the other.

But those prosecutors underestimated the power of the Articles.

The Commonwealth's roots lay squarely within pirate society, a raucous, reckless, rapacious bunch for sure, but one with laws. Pirate communities had been orderly, geared to profit and mutual gain, always advancing the enterprise. They'd smartly adhered to what Adam Smith had observed. *If there is any society among robbers and murderers, they must at least abstain from robbing and murdering one another.*

Which pirates did.

What became known as the custom of the coast called for articles to be drawn before every voyage specifying the rules of behavior, all punishments, and dividing the booty among officers and crew. Each swore on a Bible to obey the articles. While swallowing a swig of rum mixed with gunpowder they would sign along the borders, never beneath the last line, which demonstrated that no one, not even the captain, was greater than the whole. Unanimous consent was required for the articles' approval, and any who disagreed were free to search elsewhere for more satisfactory terms. When multiple ships joined together additional articles were drawn for the partnership, which was how the Commonwealth had been formed. Four families united to further a singular goal.

To betray the Crew, or each other, desert, or abandon a battle is punished as the Quartermaster, and or the Majority, shall think fit.

None would turn on the other.

Or at least, none would live to enjoy the benefit.

'My accountants are under siege,' Bolton said.

'Deal with them,' Hale said. 'Instead of killing a president, you should have been killing them.'

'It's not that easy for me,' Cogburn said.

He stared at his partner. 'Killing never is, Charles. But occasionally it has to be done. The skill is in choosing the right time and how.'

Cogburn did not reply. He and the others had clearly chosen the wrong time.

'I'm sure the quartermaster has done his job,' Surcouf said, attempting to break the tension. 'Nothing will lead back to us. But we still have a problem.'

Hale stepped over to an English bamboo console table flanking one of the pine-paneled walls. None of this should be happening. But perhaps that had been the whole idea. Toss out the threat of prosecution, then wait and see what happened when fear set in. Maybe it was thought they would self-destruct and save everyone the trouble of trials and jail. But surely no one had assumed that the president of the United States would be attacked.

He'd tried his own form of diplomacy, which had failed. The humiliation of his White House trip remained fresh in his mind. Similar to a visit made in 1834 by Abner Hale, which also failed. But he intended to learn from his ancestor's mistakes, not repeat them.

'What are we going to do?' Cogburn asked. 'We're about at the end of the plank.'

He smiled at the reference to the stereotype of a blind-folded man being forced to walk into the sea at the end of a plank. In reality that punishment had been used only by squeamish captains, those who avoided bloodshed or wanted to convince themselves that they were not responsible for another's death. The bold and daring adventurers, the ones who forged legends that continued to be told in countless books and movies, were not afraid to stare their adversaries down, even in the face of death.

'We shall raise the flag,' he said.

18

Air Force One

Cassiopeia listened as Danny Daniels explained how the voice on the recorder had alerted everyone where to look.

'He had to be there,' Malone said. 'In the lobby of the Grand Hyatt. It's the only way he would have known where I went. They were clearing the place out as I left.'

'Our mystery man also knew what to say and how,' Davis noted.

She caught the implications. One of their own, or at least someone who knew all about their own, was involved. She spotted a look in Daniels' eye, one she'd seen before – at Camp David, with Stephanie – one conveying that this man knew more.

Daniels nodded at his chief of staff. 'Tell 'em.'

'About six months ago, I received a visit at the White House.'

Davis stared at the man sitting across from his desk. He knew him to be fifty-six years old, a fourth-generation American, with family ties that dated to before the American Revolution. He was tall, with luminous green eyes and a shadowy chin that appeared as tough as armor. His smooth head was bounded by a crescent of long, thick silver-black hair, swept back like the mane of an aging lion. His teeth shone like pearls, marred only by a noticeable gap in the front two. He wore an expensive suit that fit as comfortably as his voice projected.

Quentin Hale commanded a massive corporate empire that involved manufacturing, banking, and retail. He was one of the largest landowners in the country, mainly shopping malls and office buildings located in nearly every major city. His net worth lay in the billions and he consistently made the Forbes wealthiest list. He was also a supporter of the president, having contributed several hundred thousand dollars to both campaigns, a fact that had earned him the right to personally meet with the White House chief of staff.

But what Davis just heard took him aback. 'Are you saying that you're a pirate?'

'A privateer.'

He knew the difference. One was a criminal, the other worked within the law on an official grant from the government to attack its enemies.

'During the American Revolution,' Hale said, 'there were but 64 warships in the Continental navy. Those vessels captured 196 enemy ships. At the same time, there were 792 privateers, sanctioned by the Continental Congress, which captured or destroyed 600 British ships. During the War of 1812 it was even more dramatic. Only 23 navy ships, 254 enemy vessels captured. At the same time, 517 congressionally authorized privateers captured 1,300 ships. You can see the service we performed for this country.'

He could, but wondered about the point.

'It wasn't the Continental army who won the Revolutionary War,' Hale said. 'It was the devastation on English commerce that turned the tide. Privateers brought the war across the Atlantic to the shores of England and threw the British coasts into continual alarm. We endangered shipping within their harbors and nearly halted trade. That sent merchants into an uproar. Insurance rates for shipping rose to the point that the Brits started using French ships to transport their goods, something unheard of until that time.'

He caught a tinge of genteel dignity in the recounting.

'Those merchants ultimately pressured King George to abandon the fight in America. That's why the war ended. History makes clear

*that there would have been no victory in the American Revolution
without privateers. George Washington himself publicly acknowledged that on more than one occasion.'*

'How does this relate to you?' he asked.

*'My ancestor was one of those privateers. Together with three other
families, we floated many ships during the Revolution and organized
the rest into a cohesive fighting force. Somebody had to coordinate the
attack. We did it.'*

*Davis delved through his brain and tried to remember what he
could. What Hale had said was true. A privateer bore a letter of
marque, authorizing him to prey on a nation's enemies, free from
prosecution. So he asked, 'Your family possessed a letter?'*

Hale nodded. 'We did, and still do. I brought it.'

*His guest reached into his suit jacket and removed a folded sheet
of paper. Davis opened it to see a photocopy of a two-hundred-plus-
year-old document. Most of it printed, some of it handwritten:*

George Washington, President of the United States
of America

To all who shall see these presents, greeting:

Know Ye, that in pursuance of an Act of Congress of the
United States, on this case provided and passed on the
Ninth day of February, One Thousand Seven Hundred and
Ninety-Three, I have commissioned and by these presents
do commission Archibald Hale, licensing and authorizing
the said individual, his lieutenants, officers and crews, to
subdue, seize, and take all property and wealth of any and
all enemies of the United States of America. All items seized,
including apparel, guns, appurtenance, goods, property,
effects, and valuables shall belong to the recipient of this
grant, after paying an amount equal to twenty percent of the
value seized to the government of the United States of
America. To further encourage a robust and continuous

attack on our said enemies, in a manner that we have all enjoyed during the recent conflict, the said Archibald Hale shall be exempt from all regulatory and pecuniary laws of the United States, and any State thereto, that may affect or discourage any and all aggressive actions, except that of willful murder. This compilation is to continue in force from the date of this grant in perpetuity and shall inure to the benefit of any and all heirs of the said Archibald Hale.

Given under My Hand and the Seal of the United States of America, at Philadelphia, the Ninth day of February, in the year of our Lord, One Thousand Seven Hundred and Ninety-Three **and of the Independence of the said States,** the Twenty-Seventh.

George Washington

Davis glanced up from the page. 'Your family essentially has a grant from the United States to wreak havoc on our enemies? Exempt from the law?'

Hale nodded. 'Given in thanks by a grateful nation for all that we did. The other three families likewise have letters of marque from President Washington.'

'And what have you done with this grant?'

'We were there in the War of 1812 and helped end that conflict. We were involved in the Civil War, the Spanish-American War, and both world wars. When the national intelligence community was created after World War II, we were recruited to assist them. Of late, for the past twenty years, we have plagued the Middle East, disrupting financial activities, stealing assets, denying funds and profits. Whatever is needed. Obviously we have no sloops or corsairs today. So instead of sailing off in ships armed with men and cannons, we travel digitally, or work through established financial systems. But as you can see, the letter of marque is not explicit to ships.'

No, it was not.

'Nor to time.'

Davis rose and reached for a small pamphlet he kept handy on a shelf titled The Constitution of the United States.

Hale saw the title and said, 'Article One, Section 8.'

The man had read his mind. He was looking for legal authority and found it exactly where Hale had said.

The Congress shall have the power to declare War, grant Letters of Marque and Reprisal, and make Rules concerning Captures on Land and Water.

'*Letters of marque have existed since the 1200s,*' *Hale said.* '*Their first recorded use was by Edward III in 1354. It was considered an honorable calling, combining patriotism with profit. Contrary to pirates, who are but thieves.*'

That rationalization was interesting.

'*For 500 years privateering flourished,*' *Hale said.* '*Francis Drake was one of the most famous, devastating Spanish shipping for Elizabeth I. European governments routinely issued letters of marque not only in war, but in peacetime. It was so common a practice that the Founding Fathers specifically granted Congress the power to issue such letters, and the people approved when the Constitution was ratified. That document has been amended twenty-seven times since our founding, and never has that power been modified or removed.*'

Hale seemed not to attack his listeners so much as to persuade them. Instead of thundering out his point, he dropped his voice, exhibiting a focused attention.

Davis raised a half-open hand to say something, then changed his mind as the pragmatist within him reasserted itself. '*What do you want?*'

'*A letter of marque grants the holder legal protection. Ours is quite specific on that. We simply want our government to honor its word.*'

'He's a damn pirate,' Daniels blurted out. 'So are the other three.'

Malone nodded. 'Privateers were the nursery of pirates. That's not my observation, but Captain Charles Johnson's. He wrote a book in the 18th century, *A General History of the*

Robberies and Murders of the Most Notorious Pyrates. A big seller for its time, still in print today. An original edition is worth a fortune. It's one of the best records of pirate life that exists.'

Cassiopeia shook her head. 'I didn't realize you had such an interest.'

'Who doesn't love pirates? They declared war against the world. For a century they attacked and looted at will, then they vanished, leaving almost no record of their existence. Hale's right about one thing. It's doubtful America would be here except for privateers.'

'I admit,' Daniels said, 'that I never knew just how much these opportunists did for us. A lot of brave and honest men took to privateering. They gave their lives, and obviously Washington felt an obligation toward them. But our merry band today isn't quite that noble. They can call themselves what they want, but they're pirates, pure and simple. Incredibly, though, the 1793 Congress sanctioned their existence. I bet there aren't too many Americans who know that the Constitution allowed that to happen.'

They sat in silence for a moment while the president seemed lost in thought.

'Tell them the rest,' he finally said to Davis.

'After the Revolution ended, Archibald Hale and his three compatriots formed a Commonwealth. Using their letters of marque, together they fattened their pockets. They also added to the Treasury, paying out the specified twenty percent they owed to the new national government. That's something else I'm sure most Americans have no idea about. We made money off those thieves. With the current bunch, their income tax returns bear little relation to their lifestyles. And yes, for the past couple of decades their talents have been used by our intelligence community. They managed to do some damage in the Middle East, pillaging financial accounts, stealing assets, devaluing companies whose profits were being funneled to extremists. They're good. Too good, actually. They don't know when to stop.'

'Let me guess,' Malone said. 'They started stealing from folks that we'd prefer they leave alone.'

'Something like that,' Daniels said. 'They're not real good on taking direction, if you know what I mean.'

'A dispute broke out between the Commonwealth and the CIA,' Davis said. 'The last straw came with all the trouble in Dubai and its financial meltdown. The CIA determined that the Commonwealth had been engineering most of that chaos. As the Dubai national debt skyrocketed, the Commonwealth cherry-picked the best assets, buying them for pennies on the dollar. They also thwarted certain debt restructures that nations in the region were offering to solve the crisis. In general, they were a giant pain in the ass. But we couldn't let Dubai go under. They're one of the few moderates in that region. Somewhat of an ally. The Commonwealth was told to stop, they said they would, but then they kept right on. So the CIA pointed the IRS at them. They then squeezed the Swiss, who caved and provided financial records on all four members of the current Commonwealth. It's been determined that those four owe hundreds of millions in back taxes. If done right, we can seize all their assets, which total in the billions.'

'That's enough to make a bunch of pirates real nervous,' Cotton said.

Davis nodded. 'Hale came to me and wanted protection under his letter of marque. And he has a point. The language specifically immunizes them from all laws, save for murder. White House counsel tells us the letter is legally binding. The Constitution of the United States directly authorizes it, and the letter itself mentions an act of Congress that approved it.'

'So why isn't it being honored?' Cassiopeia asked.

'Because,' the president said, 'Andrew Jackson made that impossible.'

19

New York City

Wyatt had not appreciated the reminder about his firing. True, charges had been brought against him by Malone, a hearing was held, and three mid- to high-level paper pushers, none of them a field operative, had determined that his actions were unwarranted.

Was I simply to shoot it out with Malone? he had asked the tribunal. *He and I, guns blazing, hoping we make it, while three agents wait outside?*

He'd thought the question fair – it was the most he'd said at the entire hearing – but the tribunal decided to accept Malone's assessment that the men had been used as targets, not as protection. Incredible. He knew of half a dozen agents who'd sacrificed themselves for less reason. No wonder intelligence gathering was rife with problems. Everyone seemed more concerned about being right than being successful.

With little choice, he'd accepted his termination and moved on.

But that did not mean he'd forgotten about his accuser. Yes, these men were right. He owed Malone.

And he'd tried to repay that debt today.

'Do you realize that Carbonell is all but gone?' NSA said. 'NIA is useless. Nobody needs it or her anymore.'

'The Commonwealth is going away, too,' CIA made clear. 'Our modern-day pirates will live out their lives in a federal prison, where they belong. And you never answered our question. Were the pirates responsible for what happened today?'

The dossier Carbonell had provided about the Commonwealth had contained a brief overview of its four captains, noting that they were the last remnants of 18th-century adventurers, direct descendants of pirates and privateers. An excerpt from a psychological evaluation had explained how a navy man went to sea knowing that if he fought the good fight and won, rewards would come his way in the form of praise and advancement. Even if he failed, history would record his exploits. But it required a person of unusual bravery to face danger when he knew that no one would learn of his deeds. Especially when, if he failed, most would cackle at his misfortune.

Privateers had labored under both conditions.

If successful, their reward was a division of the spoils. Vary from their letter of marque in any way and they became pirates and were hung. A privateer could capture one of the king of England's most formidable cruisers and the act would scarcely have been known. If along the way life or limb were sacrificed, too bad.

They were on their own.

Easy to see, the report had concluded, why they might play loose with the rules.

NSA stepped close. 'You set Malone up, then led him straight into a trap. You knew what was going to happen there today. You wanted someone to shoot him, didn't you? What's the matter, Wyatt, lost your taste for killing?'

He stayed calm and asked, 'Are we through?'

'Yep. You're through,' CIA said. 'Here. But since you're not going to tell us anything, we have people who can be more successful in acquiring answers.'

He watched as they shifted on their feet, waiting for him to acknowledge their superiority. Perhaps that threat of a more intense questioning was designed to scare him. He wondered what possessed them to think that such a tactic would work. Luckily, he'd socked away enough tax-free money in foreign banks to live comfortably forever. He really needed nothing from any of these people. That was one advantage of being paid from a black-ops budget – no W-2s or 1099s.

So he debated his options.

He assumed the two men who'd brought him were just outside the door. Beyond the window, on the opposite side of the room, past the blinds, was surely a fire escape. All these older buildings possessed one.

Should he be quiet and take two down or make some noise and drop all four?

'You're coming with us,' NSA said. 'Carbonell has a lot of explaining to do and you're going to be witness number one for the prosecution. The man who can contradict her lies.'

'And you think I would actually do that?'

'You'll do whatever you have to do to save your hide.'

Interesting how little they knew about him.

A mechanism from deep within seized control, and he allowed it.

One swing of his body and his right fist found CIA's throat. Then he doubled NSA over with a kick to the chest, careful for the legs not to lose their balance. While the one man fought to breathe, he pounded NSA's neck with a short chop, breaking the man's collapse with his arms, then gently laying the stunned man on the floor.

He then stepped behind CIA and wrapped an arm around his neck.

'I could choke you to death,' he whispered in the man's ear.

He gritted his teeth and increased the pressure on the windpipe.

'I'd actually enjoy watching you suck your last breath.'

Tighter.

'Listen to me,' he said. 'Stay. The hell. Out of my way.'

CIA reached for his arm.

He increased the hold. 'Do you hear me?'

Finally, the man nodded, then a lack of oxygen sucked all resistance from the muscles.

He released his grip.

The body folded to the floor, hardly making a sound.

He checked for pulses. Faint, but there. Breathing was shallow, but constant.

He stepped to the window, opened it, and left.

Malone was waiting for both Daniels and Davis to explain what was happening with Stephanie. But he also realized the president had much to say. So, since they were 30,000 feet in the air with nowhere to go, he decided to sit back and listen as Daniels explained what happened in the spring of 1835.

'Jackson was furious over the assassination attempt,' the president said. 'He openly blamed Senator Poindexter from Mississippi, called the whole thing a Nullifiers' conspiracy. He hated John Calhoun. Called him a traitor to the Union. That one I can understand.'

Calhoun had been Jackson's vice president and, initially, a big supporter. But in the face of a rising southern sympathy, Calhoun had turned on his benefactor and started the Nullifier Party, advocating states' rights – especially southern states' rights. Daniels, too, had seen his share of vice-presidential traitors.

'Jackson had dealt with pirates before,' Daniels said. 'Jean Lafitte in New Orleans he liked. Together they saved that city during the War of 1812.'

'Why do you call these people pirates?' Cassiopeia asked. 'Were they not privateers? Specifically authorized by America to attack its enemies?'

'That they were and, if they'd stopped there, it might have

been okay. Instead, once they received that letter of marque in perpetuity, they were hell on water.'

He listened as Daniels explained how during the Civil War the Commonwealth worked both sides of the conflict.

'I've seen classified documents from that time,' Daniels said. 'Lincoln hated the Commonwealth. He planned on prosecuting them all. By then privateering was illegal, thanks to the Declaration of Paris in 1856. But here's the rub. Only fifty-two nations signed that treaty. The United States and Spain refused.'

'So the Commonwealth kept going?' Cassiopeia said. 'Using that failure to their advantage?'

Daniels nodded. 'The Constitution allows for letters of marque. Since the United States never renounced privateering by signing the treaty, it was essentially legal here. And even though we didn't sign the treaty, during the Spanish-American War both we and Spain agreed to observe the treaty's principles. The Commonwealth, though, ignored that agreement and attacked Spanish shipping, which so angered William McKinley that he finally had Congress pass an act in 1899 making it unlawful to capture shipping or distribute any proceeds taken as a prize.'

'Which meant nothing to the Commonwealth,' Malone said. 'Their letters of marque would give them immunity to that law.'

Daniels pointed a finger at him. 'Now you're beginning to see the problem.'

'Some presidents,' Davis said, 'used the Commonwealth to their advantage, some fought them, most ignored them. No one, though, ever wanted the public to know that George Washington and the U.S. government had sanctioned their actions. Or that the U.S. Treasury profited from their actions. Most simply let them do as they please.'

'Which brings us back to Andrew Jackson,' Daniels said. 'He's the only one who stuck it up their ass.'

Davis reached beneath the table and found a leather satchel. He withdrew a sheet of paper and slid it over.

'That's a letter,' the president said, 'Jackson wrote to Abner Hale, who, in 1835, was one of the four in the Commonwealth. Jackson kept a copy in a cache of presidential papers that have remained sealed in the National Archives. Papers only a few can access. Edwin found it.'

'I didn't know there was such a repository,' Malone said.

'Neither did we, until we went looking,' Daniels said. 'And I'm not the first to read that. They keep a log at the archives. A lot of presidents took a look at that letter. But none in a long while. Kennedy was the last. He sent his brother Bobby for a gander.' The president pointed to the page. 'As you can see, Abner Hale sent the assassin after Jackson, or at least that's what Jackson thought.'

Malone read the page, then passed it to Cassiopeia and asked, 'Abner is related to Quentin Hale?'

'Great-great-granddaddy,' Daniels said. 'Quite a family tree they've got there.'

Malone smiled.

'Andrew Jackson,' the president said, 'was so mad at the Commonwealth, he ripped the two pages from the House and Senate journals where the letters of marque had been congressionally authorized for the four families. I saw both journals myself. A jagged tear in each volume.'

'Is that why you can't simply revoke the letters?' Cassiopeia asked.

Malone knew the answer. 'No congressional record of their passage means no legal authority stating that they have to be honored. Presidents can't sign letters of marque unless Congress okays them, and there's no record of Congress ever approving these.'

'Presidents can't do it on their own?' Cassiopeia asked.

Daniels shook his head. 'Not according to the Constitution.'

'And,' Malone said, 'if you went proactive and actually revoked these letters of marque, you'd be implying that they were valid in the first place. Also, any revocation would not affect past acts. They'd still be immune to those, which is exactly what the Commonwealth wants.'

Daniels nodded. 'That's exactly the problem. A classic damned if we do, damned if we don't. It would have been better if Jackson had just destroyed those two journal pages. But the crazy SOB hid them away. Like he said, he wanted to torment them. Give them something to worry about besides killing a president. But all he did was pass the problem down to us.'

'If you had the two pages,' Cassiopeia asked, 'what would you do?'

'That's part of what I had Stephanie looking into. Those possibilities. I don't pass problems down to my successors.'

'So what happened?' Malone asked.

Daniels sighed. 'It got complicated. After Hale came to see Edwin, we became curious, so we started asking questions. We discovered that the head of the NIA, Andrea Carbonell, is linked to the Commonwealth.'

He knew about Carbonell from his days with the Magellan Billet. Cuban American. Tough. Wary. No nonsense. He also knew what the president meant. 'A bit too close?'

'We're not sure,' Davis said. 'It was an unexpected discovery. One that caused us concern. Enough that we needed to know more.'

'So Stephanie offered to look into it,' Daniels said. 'On her own.'

'Why her?' Malone asked.

'Because she wanted to. Because I trust her. NIA is at odds with the rest of the intelligence community on the Commonwealth. They want the pirates in jail, but Carbonell doesn't. Involving another agency would have compounded that conflict. Stephanie and I spoke about this last week. She agreed that her doing it herself was the best way. So she went DNC to meet with some former NIA agents who could shed light on Carbonell and the Commonwealth. She was to call in to Edwin four days ago. That didn't happen and, unfortunately, we have no idea why. We can only assume she's been taken.'

Or worse, Malone thought. 'Squeeze Carbonell. Go after the Commonwealth.'

Davis shook his head. 'We don't know they have her. We also have zero proof on Carbonell. She would simply deny everything and go to ground. All four members of the Commonwealth are respected businessmen with no criminal records. We accuse them of being pirates, they go public, and we have a PR nightmare.'

'Who cares?' Malone asked.

'We do,' Daniels said. 'We have to.'

He heard the frustration.

But something else ate at him.

Four days gone.

If that were the case, 'Then who sent me an email two days ago and who left that note in the Grand Hyatt?'

20

Bath, North Carolina

Hale watched as the other three considered his proposal about raising the flag. He knew they understood its significance. During the glory days pirates and privateers survived on their reputations. Though violence was certainly a way of life, the preferred method of taking a prize was *without* a fight. Attacking cost in many ways. Injuries, deaths, damage to the ship or, worse, to the booty. Battles unnecessarily escalated operating costs and, inevitably, reduced revenue. Plus, the vast majority of crewmen could not even swim.

So a better way to fight developed.

Raise the flag.

Display your identity and your intentions.

If the target surrendered, then lives would be spared. If the target resisted, the crew, to a man, would be slaughtered.

And it worked.

Pirate reputations became infamous. The cruelties of George Lowther, Bartholomew Roberts, and Edward Low were legendary. Eventually, simply the sight of a Jolly Roger became enough. Merchantmen who spotted the distinctive flag knew their choices.

Surrender or die.

'Our former friends in the intelligence community,' he said, 'need to understand that we are not to be taken lightly.'

'They know it was us who took the shot at Daniels,'

Cogburn said. 'The quartermaster has already reported in. NIA stopped us.'

'Which raises a list of new troubling questions,' Hale said. 'Most important of which is – What has changed? Why has our last ally turned on us?'

'This is nothing but trouble,' Bolton said.

'What is wrong, Edward? Another bad decision gone worse?'

He couldn't resist the jab. Hales and Boltons had never really cared for one another.

'You think yourself so damn invulnerable,' Bolton said. 'You and all your money and influence. Yet it can't save you or us now, can it?'

'I've been a bad host,' he said, ignoring the insult. 'Would anyone care for a drink?'

'We don't want drinks,' Bolton said. 'We want results.'

'And killing the president of the United States would have achieved those?'

'What would you have done?' Bolton asked. 'Go back to the White House and beg some more?'

Never again. He'd hated sitting across from the chief of staff, after being denied a face-to-face with Daniels. And the call that came a week after his meeting with Davis had been even more insulting.

'*The U.S. government cannot sanction your breaking the law,*' Davis said to him.

'*That's what privateers do. We pillage the enemy with the blessing of the government.*'

'*Two hundred years ago, perhaps.*'

'*Little has changed. Threats still remain. Perhaps more so today than ever. We have done nothing but support this nation. Every effort of the Commonwealth has been directed toward thwarting our enemies. Now we are to be prosecuted?*'

'*I'm aware of your problem,*' Davis said.

'Then you know our dilemma.'

'I know that the intelligence people are fed up with you. What you did in Dubai almost brought the entire region crashing down.'

'What we did was frustrate our enemies, attacking them when and where they were most vulnerable.'

'They are not our enemies.'

'That's a matter of debate.'

'Mr. Hale. If you'd kept on there and bankrupted Dubai, which was a real possibility, the repercussions would have disrupted this nation's entire Middle East policy. The loss of such a key ally in that region would have been devastating. We have so few friends over there. It would have taken decades to cultivate another relationship like that one. What you were doing was counterproductive to anything reasonable and logical.'

'They are not our friends, and you know it.'

'Maybe so. But Dubai needs us, and we need them. So we put aside our differences and work together.'

'Why not do the same relative to us?'

'Frankly, Mr. Hale, your situation is not something the White House cares about one way or the other.'

'You should. The first president and the second Congress of this country legally granted us the authority to act, so long as it was directed toward our enemies.'

'With one problem,' Davis said. 'The legal authority for your letter of marque does not exist. Even if we wanted to honor it, that could prove impossible. There is no written reference in the congressional journals for that session addressing them. Two pages are missing, which I believe you are well aware of. Their location is guarded by Jefferson's cipher. I read Andrew Jackson's letter to your great-great-grandfather.'

'Am I to assume that if we solve the cipher and find those missing pages, the president will honor the letter?'

'You can assume that your legal position will be much stronger since, as of now, you don't have one.'

'Gentlemen,' he said to the other three. 'I am reminded of a story my grandfather once told me. A British merchant ship spotted a vessel on the horizon, its identity and intentions unknown. They watched for the better part of an hour as it bore down upon them. As it approached the captain asked his crew if they would stand and defend the ship. "If they be Spaniards," the crew said, "we will fight. But if they be pirates we will not." Once they learned that it was Black Beard himself, they all quit the ship, believing they would be murdered.'

The other three stared at him.

'It is time to raise our flag. To let our enemy know that we are bearing down upon them.'

'Why are you so smug?' Cogburn asked. 'What have you done?'

Hale smiled.

Charles knew him well.

'Perhaps enough to save us all.'

21

Knox entered the Helmsley Park Lane, the upscale hotel located at the south end of Central Park. Though he possessed a key, he did not know which room it opened. That was the thing about plastic cards. No information. He stepped across the lobby to the front desk. There a bright-eyed woman in her early twenties asked if she could be of help.

'Scott Parrott, checking out,' he said to her, adding a smile and handing her the key.

He was hoping Parrott had not made himself noticeable. If by chance the woman knew Parrott, he was ready with a cover story. *I'm the one paying the bill. Scott works for me.* But not a word was uttered as she pounded computer keys and printed out a bill.

'Leaving a day early?' she said.

He nodded. 'Necessary.'

She plucked a page from the printer and handed it to him. He pretended to peruse the statement, focusing only on the room number.

'Oh, no,' he said. 'I just realized I left something upstairs. I'll be right back. Hold this for me.'

He thanked her and headed for the elevators, riding an empty car to the fifth floor. There he inserted the key card and opened the door. Inside was a spacious suite with an unmade king-sized bed. Picture windows consumed the south wall and offered an impressive view of Central Park's colorful treetops, hinting at their autumn glory to come, along with the buildings of the Upper West Side.

His gaze raked the décor until he found the laptop on the desk. He stepped over and yanked the power cord from the wall socket.

'And who are you?' a female voice said.

He turned.

A woman stood inside the bathroom doorway. She was short, petite, with straight brown hair, wearing jeans and a sweater.

Her right hand held a revolver.

'Scott sent me to get the computer.'

'That all you got? Or the best you could do on short notice?'

He shrugged, gesturing with the laptop in his grasp. 'Best I could do.'

'Where's Scott?'

'Now, is that all *you* have?'

'I don't know, Knox. I seem to be the one with the gun, so answer the question.'

Just what he needed – another problem. Hadn't he had enough of those for one day. But his suspicions were now confirmed.

This was a trap.

Still, he'd been forced to take the chance.

She advanced farther into the room, keeping her gun trained on him. She reached into her back pocket and found a cellphone. One push of a button and she said, 'Our pirate has arrived.'

This just kept getting better.

She stood too far away, maybe ten feet, for him to do anything that would not get him shot. He noticed that her weapon was sound-suppressed. Obviously, the NIA wanted minimum attention drawn to this effort, which might work to his advantage. He had to do something, and fast, since he did not know how far away that assistance was located.

She tossed the phone aside.

'The laptop,' she said. 'Toss it on the bed.'

He nodded his assent and started to lob it onto the mattress. At the last second he propelled the device straight at her, spinning it across the room.

She dodged and he lunged, kicking the gun from her grasp. She spun, raised her arms, and attacked. He slammed his right fist into her face, driving her onto the bed. Dazed from the blow, she reached for her bloody nose.

He found the gun on the carpet.

Finger on the trigger, he grabbed a pillow from the bed, pressed the gun into one side, the other onto her head, and fired once.

She stopped moving.

The pillow had muffled the sound-suppressed report to almost nothing.

Dammit. Killing was not something he enjoyed doing. But he hadn't set this foolish trap.

He tossed the pillow aside.

Think.

He'd touched only the laptop, its power cord, and the door handle.

He retrieved the computer from the floor. It had landed on one of the upholstered chairs and seemed okay. He would keep the gun. He found a washcloth in the bathroom and opened the exit door with it, then wiped the knob on both sides. He stuffed the cloth in his pocket and headed for the elevators.

He turned the corner just as a sound announced the arrival of a car.

Two men stepped off, both young and clean-cut. Surely

the radioed assistance. He casually brushed past, never giving them a second glance. It would take them less than a minute to discover the body and begin their pursuit. He wasn't necessarily worried about these two, but the ones they could radio would be a problem.

He pressed the button with his sleeved elbow and waited.

'Hey,' a voice said.

He turned.

Both men were rushing back his way.

Crap.

His right hand rested in his pocket, fingers on the gun.

He withdrew the weapon.

22

Wyatt hopped down from the last rung of the fire escape to the pavement and grabbed his bearings, deciding to walk the few blocks east toward Central Park and find a cab. The quiet side street was tree-lined, light on traffic, but heavy with parked cars. Several displayed violation tickets on their windshields. Night had arrived with a chill that matched his mood. He did not like being used or manipulated.

But Andrea Carbonell had done both.

That woman was a problem.

She was a career intelligence operative who'd risen from low-level analyst to agency head, managing to keep NIA useful even in difficult times. His previous dealings with her had been varied – occasional jobs for which she paid well – and there'd never been any problems out of the ordinary.

So why was this time so different?

None of this really concerned him. Yet he was curious. More of that operative inside him seeping back to the surface.

He approached an intersection and was about to cross when he noticed a black sedan parked fifty feet away. The face that stared at him from an open rear window was familiar.

'Forty-two minutes,' Carbonell called out to him. 'I gave you forty-five. You hurt them?'

'They're going to need a doctor.'

She smiled. 'Get in. I'll give you a lift.'

'You fired me, then you allowed those idiots to take me. I'm going home.'

'I was hasty on both counts.'

That curiosity inside him swelled. He knew he shouldn't but he decided to accept her offer. He stepped across the street, and the sedan left the curb as soon as he settled into the rear seat.

'We found Scott Parrott,' she said. 'Dead in Central Park. The pirates are predictable, I'll say that for them.'

He'd worked with Parrott for the past month. He was NIA's conduit to the Commonwealth, the source of all of his intel. Of course, he hadn't told NSA or CIA any of that. None of their damn business.

'I knew Clifford Knox would do something,' she said. 'He'd have to.'

'Why?'

'It's all part of the pirate thing. We insulted them by interfering so they have to retaliate. It's their culture.'

'So you sacrificed Parrott?'

'That's a harsh way of putting it. What did you say at your admin hearing? Part of the mission. People get killed sometimes.'

Yes, he had said that. But he didn't catch the connection between his comment, referring to agents under fire who required help, and sending a man to meet with someone you knew was going to kill him.

'Parrott was careless,' she said. 'Too trusting. He could have protected himself.'

'And you could have provided him a warning or backup.'

She handed him a file. 'That's not how it works. It's time you learn more about the Commonwealth.'

He handed the packet back. 'I'm done.'

'You realize there'll be repercussions over what happened back there.'

He shrugged. 'I didn't kill anybody.'

'They won't see it that way. What did they want? For you to turn on me? Give up the Commonwealth on the assassination attempt?'

'Something like that.'

'You're a smart guy, Jonathan. The only one for this job.' She smiled. 'I know they're after me. I've known that for a while. They think I'm on the take to the Commonwealth.'

'Are you?'

'Not in the least. I have no use for their ill-gotten gains.'

'But apparently, you have use for them.'

'I'm a survivor, Jonathan. I'm sure you don't have to worry about a paycheck. You have millions stashed away, no danger of anybody ever getting their hands on it. I'm not that fortunate. I have to work.'

No, that wasn't right. She *loved* the work.

'Even in a changing job market,' she said, 'courtesy of a presidential downsizing, opportunities still exist. I simply want one of those for myself. That's all. No payoffs. No bribes. Just a job.'

Since clearly no one at NSA or CIA would touch her, and she wouldn't settle for anything less than a deputy administrator or a director's post, her choices were limited. She'd also want to go somewhere safe. Nothing on the chopping block. Why jump from one fire into another?

He caught her gaze.

She seemed to read his mind.

'That's right. I want the Magellan Billet.'

Knox whirled, the sight of the sound-suppressed gun stopping the two men's advance.

'Hands to the side,' he said. 'Step back.'

They obliged and slowly retreated down the hall.

Another elevator arrived, and the doors opened.

Two more threats stood inside, similar to the first pair. The sight of his gun momentarily caught them off guard, as neither of them held a weapon. He fired twice into the elevator, angling the shots up, trying not to hit anybody, just rattle them into a frenzy.

The doors closed as the two men dove to the floor, arms shielding their heads, trying to avoid the rounds. But the few seconds used to discourage the new threat encouraged the old one, and a body slammed into him broadside.

He hit the carpet and lost his grip on the laptop.

Using his legs, he pivoted upward and flipped himself, propelling the man off him. He rolled right and fired at the second agent rushing down the hall, dropping the body to the carpet.

The other man recovered and swung a fist.

Which connected.

Wyatt considered what Carbonell had told him.

The Magellan Billet.

'Seems like a good place to be,' she said. 'Daniels loves it. Odds are his party will retain the White House after next year. It's the perfect spot for a career woman like me.'

'Except that Stephanie Nelle heads it now.'

He noticed their route, toward Times Square, in the direction of his hotel, the location of which he'd never mentioned to Andrea Carbonell.

'I'm afraid Stephanie has come on some hard times,' she said. 'The Commonwealth took her prisoner a few days ago.'

Which explained how his email to Malone in Copenhagen had worked so easily. He'd opened a Gmail account in Stephanie Nelle's name. Nothing unusual would have flagged on Malone's end. Field agents regularly used common email providers since they drew no attention, revealed nothing about the sender, and blended perfectly with the billions of others. If Malone hadn't taken the bait, or had communicated with Nelle outside the email, he would have waited for another time to repay his debt. Luckily, that had not occurred.

He was curious, though. 'The Commonwealth is helping you acquire a new job?'

'They're about to.'

'And what is it you have that *they* want?'

She laid the folder in his lap. 'It's all explained in here.'

He listened as she told him about privateers, letters of marque from George Washington, an attempt on Andrew Jackson's life, and a cipher Thomas Jefferson considered unbreakable.

'A friend of Jefferson's,' she said, 'Robert Patterson, a professor of mathematics, conceived what he called the perfect cipher. Jefferson was fascinated with codes. He loved Patterson's so much that, as president, he passed it to his ambassador in France for official use. Unfortunately, there is no record of its solution. Patterson's son, also named Robert, was appointed by Andrew Jackson as director of the U.S. Mint. That's probably how Jackson learned of the cipher and its solution. It's logical to assume that the son knew. Old Hickory was a big fan of Thomas Jefferson.'

She showed him a copy of a handwritten page that contained nine rows of letters in seemingly random sequence.

'Most people don't know,' she said, 'that prior to 1834 there were few records of Congress. What existed was contained within the separate journals for the House and Senate. In 1836 Jackson commissioned the *Debates and Proceedings in the Congress of the United States,* which took twenty years to finish. To create that official record, they used journals, newspaper accounts, eyewitnesses, whatever or whoever they could find. It was mainly secondhand information, but it became the *Annals of Congress* and is now the official congressional record.'

She explained that nowhere in the *Annals* was there any mention of four letters of marque granted to any Hale, Bolton, Cogburn, or Surcouf. In fact, two pages were missing from the official House and Senate journals for the congressional sessions of 1793.

'Jackson tore those pages out and hid them away,' she said, 'concealed behind Jefferson's cipher. It has done its job well, protecting that hiding place—' She paused. 'Until a few hours ago.'

He spotted his hotel down Broadway.

'We hired an expert a few months ago,' she said. 'A particularly smart individual who thought he could solve it. The Commonwealth has tried, but none of their hired guns were successful. Our man is in southern Maryland. He's privy to some computer programs we use for Middle East decoding that apparently worked. I need you to go see him and retrieve the solution.'

'It can't be emailed or couriered?'

She shook her head. 'Too many security risks associated with that. Besides, there's a complication.'

He caught the implications. 'Others know about this?'

'Unfortunately. Two of whom you just sent to the hospital, but the White House knows as well.'

'And how do you know that?'

'I told them.'

23

M alone waited for an answer to his questions – who *contacted me two days ago and who left the note?* – but none came. Instead Edwin Davis handed him another sheet of paper, this one with nine lines of random letters, written in the same script featured on Andrew Jackson's letter to Abner Hale.

'That's the Jefferson cipher,' Davis said. 'The Commonwealth has tried since 1835 to crack it. Experts tell me it's not a simple substitution, where you replace one letter of the alphabet with another. It's a transposition, where letters are placed in a defined order. To know the sequence, you have to know the key. There are something like 100,000 possibilities.'

He studied the letters and symbols.

> XQXFEETH
> APKLJHXREHNJF
> TSYOL:
> EJWIWM
> PZKLRIELCPΔ
> FESZR
> OPPOBOUQDX
> MLZKRGVKΦ
> EPRISZXNOXEΘ

'Someone obviously deciphered it,' Malone said. 'How else did Jackson compose the message?'

'He had the good fortune,' Daniels said, 'to appoint the son of the cipher's creator as head of the U.S. Mint. We're assuming Daddy told his boy, who told Jackson. But Jackson died in 1845 and the son in 1854. Both took the solution to their graves.'

'Do you think the Commonwealth tried to kill you?' Cassiopeia asked Daniels.

'I don't know.'

But Malone was more concerned about Stephanie. 'We can't just sit here and do nothing.'

'I don't plan to,' Daniels said.

'You have thousands of agents at your disposal. Use them.'

'As the president told you,' Davis said, 'it's not that simple. CIA and several other intelligence agencies want the Commonwealth prosecuted. NIA wants to save them. We're also about to eliminate NIA and about fifty more redundant intelligence agencies in the next fiscal year.'

'Does Carbonell know that?' he asked.

'Oh, yes,' Daniels said.

'And drawing attention to the Commonwealth would only escalate the problem,' Davis made clear. 'They'd love a public spectacle. In fact, they may be baiting us into one.'

Daniels shook his head. 'This has to be handled quietly, Cotton. Trust me on this. Our intelligence people are like a bunch of roosters I once saw on a farm. All they do is fight one another to see who's going to be the cock of the walk. In the end, it takes the life out of 'em all, and none amounts to much of anything.'

Malone had personal experience with those turf wars, which was another reason he'd opted to retire out early.

'The big boys have decided to take the Commonwealth down,' Daniels said. 'Which is fine with me. I don't care. But if we start publicly interfering with that effort, then it becomes *our* fight. We're then going to have more problems, which will include my least favorite kind. Legal problems.' The president shook his head. '*We* have to handle this quietly.'

He didn't agree with that at all. 'To hell with the CIA and NIA. Let me go after the Commonwealth.'

'To do what?' Cassiopeia asked.

'You have a better idea? Stephanie needs our help. We can't do nothing.'

'We don't even know the Commonwealth has her,' Cassiopeia said. 'Seems this Carbonell is the better lead.'

His friend was in trouble. He was frustrated and angry, as in Paris, last Christmas, when another friend had been in peril. He'd been two minutes too late that time, which he still regretted.

Not this time. No way.

Daniels pointed to the sheet. 'We have a trump card. That cipher was solved a few hours ago.'

The revelation grabbed both his and Cassiopeia's attention.

'An expert the NIA hired deciphered it, using some secret computers and a few lucky guesses.'

'How do you know that?' he asked.

'Carbonell told me.'

More dots connected. 'She's feeding you info. Playing both sides. Trying to make herself useful.'

'What irks me,' Daniels said, 'is she thinks I'm too stupid to see through her.'

'Does she know Stephanie was looking into her?' Cassiopeia asked.

'I don't know,' Daniels said, his voice trailing off. 'I hope not. That could mean big trouble.'

As in death, Malone thought. The intelligence business was hard-pitch fastball. The stakes were high and death common.

So finding Stephanie was *the* priority.

'Those presidential papers I told you about in the National Archives?' Daniels said. 'Like I said, only a few people can get into them. An intelligence agency head is one of those.'

'Carbonell was on the log sheet?' he asked.

Davis nodded. 'And she's the one who contracted for the cipher to be solved.'

'She reminds me,' Daniels said, 'of one of those roosters. A little scrawny thing who watches all the fights from the side, hoping to become the top bird simply by being the last one standing.' The president hesitated. 'I'm the one who sent Stephanie out there. It's my fault she's missing. I can't use anyone else on this one, Cotton. I need you.'

Malone noticed that Cassiopeia was watching the muted TV screens, the three stations replaying the video of the assassination attempt over and over.

'If we have the cipher solution,' Davis said, 'then we have something both the Commonwealth *and* Carbonell want. It gives us a bargaining position.'

Then he realized. 'Carbonell provided you the information so you'd obtain the solution. She wants you to have it.'

Daniels nodded. 'Absolutely. I assume it's to keep it away from her colleagues, who would like nothing better than to destroy it. Fortifying those letters of marque could become problematic to their prosecutions. If I hold the key, then it's safe. Our problem, Cotton, is that right now we don't even have a pair of twos to bluff with, so I'm willing to take anything.'

'And don't forget,' Cassiopeia said to him, 'you were invited. With a special engraved invitation. Your presence has been requested.'

He stared at her.

'Somebody specifically wants *you* here.'

'And they wanted you to leave the Grand Hyatt,' Daniels

said, lifting the typewritten note from the table. 'Stephanie didn't write this. It was designed to flush you out. Ever thought that whoever sent it might have wanted some cop or a Secret Service agent to shoot you dead?'

The thought had occurred to him.

'Go to the Garver Institute in Maryland and get that cipher solution,' Daniels said. 'Carbonell tells me the people there are expecting you. She's provided us a password that will gain you access.'

He wasn't stupid. 'Sounds like a trap.'

Daniels nodded. 'Probably is. The people who want to prosecute the Commonwealth do not want that cipher solved.'

'Aren't you the president? Don't they all work for you?'

'I'm a president with not much more than a year left in office. They don't really care what I think or do anymore. They're more interested in the next person who'll be sitting in this chair.'

'We could be wasting time,' he said. 'Whoever has Stephanie could just kill her and be done with it. We'd never know.'

'Killing her would be counterproductive,' Davis pointed out.

'And killing the president was productive?' Cassiopeia asked.

'Good point,' Daniels said. 'But we play the odds. We have to. And the odds, at least to me, say she's alive.'

He did not like the passive approach, but recognized that what Daniels said made sense. Besides, it was getting late and the Garver Institute seemed the best use of his time until morning. Owning that cipher solution would indeed provide bargaining power.

'Why am I here?' Cassiopeia asked the president.

'I assume to grace us with your beauty wouldn't work?'

'Any other time, maybe.'

Daniels sat back in his chair, which groaned under his tall frame. 'Those contraptions that fired on me took time to make. The whole thing required a crap load of planning.'

That was obvious.

'There were half a dozen people in the White House,' Davis said, 'who were aware of the New York trip for the full two months after we decided to go. All high-level aides or Secret Service. They'll be interviewed and investigated, but I'd stake my life on each one of them. A few more were told two days ago, but Secret Service tells us that those rooms were reserved at the Hyatt five days ago, using phony credit cards.'

Malone spotted an unusual concern on Daniels' face.

'We have to investigate every avenue,' Davis said. 'And there's one possible problem that Cassiopeia must handle. We don't want the Secret Service or FBI involved there.'

'A possible leak?' Malone asked.

'Yep,' Daniels said. 'And it's a doozy.'

He waited.

'My wife. The First Lady.'

24

Knox still held the gun but it was of little use since the man on top of him kept a vise grip on his arm. He had to get out of here. The two men from the elevator had surely exited a floor below or above and were making their way back.

He rolled and reversed positions, but the man below him kept a lock on his arm. He pivoted and rammed his knee into the gut. Repeating the blow drew the breath from his opponent and he used that instant to wrench his right arm free, swinging the gun around and firing point-blank into the man's chest.

An agonized cry rang out.

He pushed away.

The body bucked and squirmed, then went still.

He retrieved the laptop and sprang to his feet.

One of the room doors opened. He planted a shot into the jamb, and the door slammed shut. The last thing he needed was for one of the hotel occupants to become involved.

His mind assessed his situation.

Certainly no one was going to come back up the elevator. Far too risky. So he pushed the button and quickly dragged the wounded agent out of the car's line of view. The other agent farther down the hall lay still. The stairway was ten feet away, around a corner.

But people with guns could be there.

The elevator arrived.

He stuffed the weapon in his pocket but kept hold of the trigger.

Three people were inside the car. Two women and a man, dressed as if they'd been out for the evening. One of them held shopping bags. He composed himself and stepped on board. The car was headed down and stopped on the second floor, where the three exited.

As did he.

Clearly, Parrott had intended on rocking him to sleep with dinner, then luring him into a trap. He'd avoided that, but this was foolishness, brought on by more nonsense from his bosses. He'd just killed two people for sure, and maybe two more. Never had an operation gyrated so out of control.

He walked the hallway and turned a corner, spotting a maid's cart parked outside an open door. He spotted a trash bag at one end, a shopping tote from Saks Fifth Avenue protruding from the top. He grabbed the tote and kept walking, dropping the laptop inside.

This was a tight spot.

How many agents could be here? And how much attention were they willing to bring on themselves? With four of their people down, probably a hell of a lot.

He decided there was no choice.

He'd walk out the front door.

And fast.

Wyatt entered his hotel room and immediately packed his bag. He'd brought little in the way of clothes, learning a long time ago the value of traveling light. He switched on the television and watched more of the assassination attempt coverage. The station reported that Danny Daniels was on his way back to Washington, aboard Air Force One.

With a passenger, no doubt.

Cotton Malone.

Which meant that if the White House knew about the cracking of the Jefferson cipher, as Carbonell had made clear, Malone knew, too.

'Two men are dead because of you,' Malone said to him.

The administrative hearing was over, a verdict rendered, and for the first time in a long while he was unemployed.

'And how many owe their graves to you?' he asked.

Malone seemed unfazed. 'None because I wanted to save my own ass.'

Wyatt slammed his adversary into the wall, one hand finding the throat. Strangely, there was no defensive reaction. Instead Malone simply stared back, fear or concern nowhere in his eyes. Wyatt's fingers tightened into a ball. He wanted to jab a fist into Malone's face. Instead he said, 'I was a good agent.'

'That's the worst part. You were good.'

He squeezed the throat harder but still Malone did not react. This man understood how to handle fear. How to quell, conquer, and never show it.

He'd remember that.

'It's over,' Malone said. 'You're done.'

No, I'm not, he thought.

Carbonell had reveled in telling him about the Garver Institute, providing him its location and a password to gain entrance. She said a man there was expecting him, and once he had the cipher key he should contact her.

'What are you going to do with that solution?' he asked her.

'I plan to save Stephanie Nelle.'

He doubted that. Not from a woman who'd just sacrificed one of her own agents.

'In return for performing this errand for me,' she said. 'I'll double your fee.'

That was a lot of money for something she could send one of her own to do or, better yet, do herself. Then he understood. 'Who else will be there?'

She shrugged. 'Hard to say, but they all know. CIA, NSA, and several others who don't want that cipher solved or those pages found.'

He was still undecided.

Her eyes softened. She was damn attractive and knew it.

'I'll fly you to Maryland myself,' she said. 'I have a helicopter standing by. On the way, I'll deposit your doubled fee into whatever offshore account you like. Do you want the job?'

She knew his weakness. Why not? Money was money.

'There's a fringe benefit to this, too,' she noted. 'Cotton Malone is aboard Air Force One. Since I gave the White House this information, my guess is he'll be there, too.' She smiled. 'Maybe someone will finish what you started today.'

Maybe so, he thought.

Knox stepped off the elevator into the Helmsley Park Lane's lobby. Thankfully, though it was approaching nine-thirty PM, the place bustled with activity. His gaze scoured the faces, searching for problems, but he sensed nothing. He calmly walked toward the front door, one hand holding the shopping bag, the other stuffed into his jacket pocket where the gun lay. If necessary, he'd shoot his way out.

He exited onto Central Park South.

The sidewalk was crowded with more excited people and he followed the flow toward Fifth Avenue and the Plaza Hotel. He needed to collect his things and leave New York. Any remaining agents in the Helmsley Park were certainly occupied, discovering by now the extent of the carnage and cleaning up the mess. NIA would want the situation contained. No local police or press involved. Hopefully, that would consume them long enough for him to leave the city.

This had to end, but the nightmare seemed far from over. The captains were safe on their North Carolina estates. He was the point man, taking incoming rounds, trying to stay alive.

Had it all been a ruse? Was there any cipher solution?

He had to know.

He rode the Plaza's elevator to his floor, and immediately upon entering the room powered up the laptop. Only a moment was needed for him to realize that the machine held nothing. Just a few standard programs that came with any computer.

He clicked on the email program and saw no accounts.

This thing had just been purchased.

As bait.

For him.

Which meant a bad day had just become worse.

25

Cassiopeia sat in the car. They'd traveled in a motorcade straight from Andrews Air Force Base – she, Edwin Davis, and Danny Daniels. Cotton had been provided transportation and directions to the Garver Institute, which lay about forty-five minutes south into Maryland. She hadn't liked the idea of him going alone, especially with the prospect of trouble, but agreed that it seemed the only course. Stephanie Nelle was her friend, too, and she was worried. They all had to play their part.

'I need you to handle this situation carefully,' Daniels said to her as they motored onto the White House grounds.

She wanted to know, 'Why me?'

''Cause you're here, you're good, and you're an outsider.'

'And a woman?'

The president nodded. 'It could help. Pauline has her moods.'

She tried to recall what she could about the First Lady, but knew next to nothing. American politics was not her specialty, since her business concerns lay largely outside of North America. Her first foray into the Daniels administration had been with Stephanie a couple of years ago – the first time she'd visited the White House – which had been an eye opener in more ways than one.

'What makes you suspect your wife of leaking information?'

'Did I say I suspect her?'

'You might as well have.'

'She's the only one,' Davis said, 'besides myself, the president, and a few staffers, who knew from the start.'

'That's a big leap, accusing her.'

'It ain't as far a jump as you think,' Daniels muttered.

They were both holding back, which irritated her.

The motorcade came to a stop beneath a portico. She spotted a cadre of people waiting at the lighted entrance. Daniels emerged to a round of applause and cheers.

'At least someone loves me,' she heard him mutter.

Daniels acknowledged the well-wishers with handshakes and smiles.

'He's actually a joy to work for,' Davis said as they watched from the car. 'When I took over as chief of staff I quickly learned this is a happy White House.'

She had to admit, the welcoming committee seemed genuine.

'It's not every day someone tries to kill a president,' Davis said.

She stared across at the chief of staff. Davis was cold and calculating, with a mind that never seemed to stop working. The perfect person, she concluded, to watch your back.

'Notice anything?' he quietly asked her.

Yes, she had.

Of the forty or so who'd waited in the dark to greet Danny Daniels, no where was the First Lady to be seen.

Hale paced in his study. The other three captains had left an hour ago. Hopefully, by morning the Jefferson cipher would be solved and they could regain their constitutional immunity. Then those federal prosecutors, with their tax evasion charges, could go to hell.

He stared out at the blackened Pamlico River. Solitude was one of the things he cherished most about his family's refuge. He checked his watch. Nearly 10:30 PM. Knox should have reported in by now.

He resented being called a pirate. By his accountant. By Stephanie Nelle. By anyone and everyone who did not understand his heritage. True, the Commonwealth drew heavily from pirate society, implementing policies and practices pioneered during the 17th and early 18th centuries. But those men had not been fools, and they taught one lasting lesson Hale never forgot.

Embrace the money.

Politics, morality, ethics – none of that mattered. Everything was about profit. What had his father taught him? *It is not from the benevolence of the butcher, the brewer, or the baker that we expect our dinner, but from a regard to their own interest.* Greed was what compelled every business to serve its customers. It's what guaranteed the best product at the best price.

The same was true with privateering. Take away the lure of riches and you removed all motivation. Everyone wanted to get ahead.

What was wrong with that?

Apparently, everything.

The crazy part was that none of this was revolutionary. Letters of marque had existed for 700 years. The word *marque* had been chosen from the French, meaning 'seizure of goods.' Privateers had first come from well-educated merchant families, some even noblemen. They were described with respect as 'gentlemen sailors.' Their credo? *Never come back empty-handed.* Their spoils increased royal treasuries, which allowed kings to lower taxes at home. They provided protection from national enemies and aided governments during times of war. As an institution piracy itself ended in the 1720s, though privateering continued for another hundred and fifty years. Now it seemed the United States had decided to erase its last vestiges.

Was he a pirate?

Maybe.

His father and grandfather had not minded the label. They'd actually taken pride in their buccaneer ways. Why not him?

The house phone rang.

'I have some bad news,' Knox said when he answered. 'They set me up.'

As he listened to what had happened in New York, his anxiety returned. Salvation seemed fleeting once again. 'I want you back here. Now.'

'I'm on the way. That's what delayed my call. I wanted to get out of New York first.'

'Come straight to the house on your return. And no reports to the others. Not yet.'

He ended the call.

And immediately dialed another number.

26

Wyatt surveyed the forested campus of the Garver Institute. The cluster of five brick buildings, each three stories high, sat in a wooded glen a quarter mile off a state highway. Clouds rolled across the black sky, veiling a half-moon. A splatter of rain had followed him from the small airport a few miles away where Andrea Carbonell had left him. Thunder clapped in the distance.

He'd purposefully not driven into one of the lit parking lots, the hundred or so spaces vacant. In fact, he'd left the car Carbonell had provided him on the highway and walked in. Ready for whatever might be waiting.

He'd watched as Carbonell left, flying south, toward the Potomac and Virginia. Washington lay north. Where was she going now?

He used a progression of pine trees lining the lane for cover and kept easing toward the one building where lights still burned on the second floor. Carbonell had said that the office he sought was located there, a Dr. Gary Voccio, supposedly some mathematician supreme. The good doctor was told to wait until an agent appeared with the appropriate password, then to provide all data and information on the Jefferson cipher only to him.

His gaze raked the darkness, his alert level rising from

yellow to orange. A chill coursed through his body. He wasn't alone. Though he couldn't see them, he sensed them. Carbonell had warned they'd be here. Why hadn't they moved on the institute already? The answer was clear.

They were waiting for him.

Or someone else.

Prudence advised caution, but he decided to not disappoint them.

So he stepped from his cover and walked straight for the lit building.

Hale listened as the phone rang in his ear.

Once. Twice. Three times.

'What is it, Quentin?' Andrea Carbonell finally said in his ear. 'Don't you sleep?'

'As if you weren't waiting for my call.'

'Knox made a mess at the Helmsley Park Lane. One dead agent, two wounded, another dead in Central Park. I can't let that go unanswered.'

Noise on the line, like the rotor of a helicopter, signaled that she was on the move.

'What do you plan to do? Arrest us? Good luck, considering how deep you're into this. I'd love to explain on television what a lying bitch you truly are.'

'A little touchy tonight.'

'You have no idea.'

'I have as much faith in the justice system as you do,' she made clear. 'And like you, I prefer my own forms of retribution, administered my way.'

'I thought we were allies.'

'We were, until you decided to do something stupid in New York.'

'I didn't do that.'

'Nobody would ever believe you.'

'Have you solved the Jefferson cipher? Or was that another lie?'

'Before I answer, I want to know something.'

He wasn't thrilled at the prospect of discussing much with this woman, but what choice did he have? 'Go ahead.'

'How long did you think you could do as you pleased?'

This he could discuss. 'We have a constitutional grant of authority from the Congress and the first president of United States to attack, at will, this nation's enemies in perpetuity.'

'You're an anachronism, Quentin. A relic from the past that no longer has any place.'

'Our Commonwealth has managed to do things that could never have been accomplished through conventional avenues. You wanted economic chaos in certain Middle East nations. We provided that. You wanted assets stripped from certain persons of interest. We stripped them. Politicos who weren't cooperating started to cooperate after we finished with them.' He knew she would not want this information broadcast to the world, so if anyone was listening they were enjoying an earful.

'And while you did all that,' she said. 'You stole for yourself, keeping far more than the eighty percent allowed.'

'Can you prove that? We make considerable payments to several intelligence agencies on a yearly basis, yours included – payments in the millions. I wonder, Andrea, does all of that end up in the U.S. Treasury?'

She laughed. 'Like we're getting our full share. All you pirates and privateers perform your own special form of accounting. Centuries ago it happened on the high seas, the spoils divvied up per your precious Articles before anyone could see how much had been plundered. What did they call it? The ledger? I'm sure two sets of ledgers were kept. One to show the government to make them happy and another to make sure that everyone privy to the Articles didn't complain.'

'We are at an impasse,' he said. 'We're accomplishing nothing.'

'But it explains why we're speaking at this godforsaken hour.'

He tried again. 'Have you solved the cipher?'

'We have the key.'

He didn't know whether to believe her or not. 'I want it.'

'I'm sure you do. But I'm not currently in a position to give it to you. I'll admit that I was planning on taking Knox hostage, using him as a bargaining chip. Maybe even just killing him and be done with it. But your quartermaster moved fast and we took casualties. That's the price my people pay for their failure.'

Had any corsair or buccaneer regarded his crew with the same callous disrespect, he would have been marooned on the first island encountered.

And she called *him* a pirate.

'Don't forget,' he said, 'I have what you really want.'

He'd moved on Stephanie Nelle only because Carbonell had specifically asked him to. If she was to be believed, Nelle had been asking questions about Carbonell, investigating her relationship with the Commonwealth or, more specifically, her relationship with Hale. None of the other three captains knew of her existence, or at least that's what he'd been led to believe. Carbonell had become aware of a meeting Nelle had arranged with a terminated NIA agent, one who harbored no loyalty to his former boss. She'd provided him the Delaware location and Knox had snatched Nelle at the scene, under cover of darkness, no witnesses, quick and clean. She'd wanted him to hold her discreetly for a few days. He could not have cared less. Just a favor done. But with all that had happened over the past few hours, the circumstances had altered.

NIA was no longer a friend.

'How is your guest?' she asked.

'Comfortable.'

'Too bad.'

'What is it you want with her?'

'She has something I want and will not voluntarily relinquish it.'

'So you thought I'd trade Nelle for Knox?'

'Worth a try.'

'I want the cipher key,' he made clear. 'If you're not interested, I could make some arrangements with Stephanie Nelle. I'm sure she'd love to know why I have her. She looks the bargaining type.'

The silence on the other end of the line confirmed that his suspicions had proven correct. That was something she feared.

'Okay, Quentin. Things have obviously changed. Let's see what you and I can now agree to.'

Malone turned off the highway and entered the Garver Institute. Edwin Davis had told him that the facility was a well-financed think tank that specialized in cryptology, the harder the better, and was privy to some sophisticated encryption programs.

It had taken a little longer than he thought to drive the forty miles south from DC into rural Maryland. A storm was shifting north from Virginia. Wind whipped the foliage into a torrid fury. No security of any kind guarded the entrance and none was visible in the lighted parking lots. A depth of trees provided a margin of privacy from the highway. Davis had explained that the lack of any overt security kept the place anonymous. Of the five bland corporate rectangles, four were black stains on the night, one was lit. Daniels had said that a Dr. Gary Voccio was waiting. A password had been provided by the NIA that would gain him access to the solution.

He wheeled into the parking lot and stopped the car,

then stepped out into the night, silent save for some distant thunder.

Back in the fray. Seemed he could not escape.

A car suddenly screeched from the far side of one of the buildings. No headlights, its engine revving. The vehicle veered right, hopping a curbed median and careening across the empty lot.

Heading straight for him.

An arm extended from the front passenger-side window.

Holding a gun.

27

Cassiopeia was led by Edwin Davis upstairs to the second-floor residence that contained the First Family's private living space. *A safe retreat,* Davis had said, guarded by the Secret Service. *Perhaps the only place in the world where they can actually be themselves.* She was still trying to gauge Davis. She'd watched him as the staff greeted Daniels. How he'd kept out of the way. Off to the side. There, but not overtly so.

They came to the top of the stairs and stopped in a lighted hallway that extended from one end of the building to the other. Doorways lined either side. One was guarded by a woman who stood straight against the ornate wall. Davis motioned to a room across the hall. They stepped inside and he closed the door. Pale walls and simple draperies were warmed by the golden glow of lamps. A magnificent Victorian desk sat atop a colorful rug.

'The Treaty Room,' Davis said. 'Most presidents have used this as a private study. When James Garfield was shot, they turned this into an icehouse with some crude air-conditioning machines, trying to make him comfortable as he lay dying.'

She saw he was anxious.

Odd.

'The Spanish-American War ended here when President McKinley signed the treaty on that table.'

She faced Davis. 'What is it you have to say?'

He nodded. 'I was told you were direct.'

'You're a little on edge and I'm not here for a tour.'

'There's something you need to know.'

Danny Daniels woke from a sound sleep and smelled smoke.

The darkened bedroom was thick with an acrid fog, enough that he choked on his next breath, coughing away a mouthful of carbon. He shook Pauline, waking her, then tossed the covers away. His mind came fully awake and he realized the worst.

The house was on fire.

He heard the flames, the old wood structure crackling as it disintegrated. Their bedroom was on the second floor, as was their daughter's.

'Oh, my God,' Pauline said. 'Mary.'

'Mary,' he called out through the open doorway. 'Mary.'

The second floor was a mass of flames, the stairway leading down engulfed by fire. It seemed the whole house had succumbed save for their bedroom.

'Mary,' he yelled. 'Answer me. Mary.'

Pauline was now beside him, screaming for their nine-year-old daughter.

'I'm going after her,' she said.

He grabbed her arm. 'There's no way. You won't make it. The floor is gone.'

'I'm not going to stand here while she's in there.'

Neither was he, but he had to use his brain.

'Mary,' Pauline shrieked. 'Answer me.'

His wife was bordering on hysterical. Smoke continued to build. He bolted to the window and opened it. The bedside clock read 3:15 AM. He heard no sirens. His farm sat three miles outside of town, on family land, the nearest neighbor half a mile away.

He grabbed a lungful of fresh air.

'Dammit, Danny,' Pauline blurted out. 'Do something.'

He made a decision.

He stepped back inside, grabbed his wife, and yanked her toward the window. The drop down was about fifteen feet into a line of shrubs. There was no way they could escape out the bedroom door. This was their only avenue out and he knew she would not go voluntarily.

'Get some air,' he said.

She was coughing bad and saw the wisdom in his advice. She leaned out the window to clear her throat. He grabbed her legs and shoved her body through the open frame, twisting her once so she'd land sideways in the branches. She might break a bone, but she wasn't going to die in the fire. She was no help to him here. He had to do this on his own.

He saw that shrubbery broke her fall and she came to her feet.

'Get away from the house,' he called out.

Then he rushed back to the bedroom door.

'Daddy. Help me.'

Mary's voice.

'Honey. I'm here,' he called out to the fire. 'Are you in your room?'

'Daddy. What's happening? Everything's burning. I can't breathe.'

He had to get to her, but there was no way. The second-floor hall was gone, fifty feet of air loomed between the doorway and his daughter's room. In a few more minutes the bedroom where he stood would be gone. The smoke and heat was becoming unbearable, stinging his eyes, choking his lungs.

'Mary. You still there?' He waited. 'Mary.'

He had to get to her.

He rushed to the window and stared below. Pauline was nowhere to be seen. Maybe he could help Mary from the outside. There was a ladder in the barn.

He climbed out through the window and stretched his tall frame downward, gripping the sill. He released his grip and fell the additional nine feet, penetrating the shrubbery, landing on his feet. He pushed through the branches and ran around to the other side of the house. His worst fears were immediately confirmed. The entire second floor was engulfed, including his daughter's room. Flames roared out the exterior walls and obliterated the roof.

Pauline stood, staring upward, holding one arm with the other.

'She's gone,' his wife wailed, tears in her voice. 'My baby is gone.'

'That night has haunted him for thirty years,' Davis said, his voice a whisper. 'The Daniels' only child died, and Pauline could not have any more.'

She did not know what to say.

'The cause of the fire was a cigar left in an ashtray. At that time Daniels was a city councilman and liked a good smoke. Pauline had begged him to quit, but he'd refused. Back then, smoke detectors were not commonplace. The official report noted that the fire was preventable.'

She comprehended the full extent of that conclusion.

'How did their marriage survive that?' she asked.

'It didn't.'

Wyatt entered the second-floor office of Dr. Gary Voccio, who'd answered the intercom and released an electronic lock only after being provided the appropriate password. The doctor greeted him from behind a desk cluttered with paper and three active LCD monitors. Voccio was in his late thirties with a Spartan vigor and reddish hair cut in a boyish fringe. He appeared disheveled, shirtsleeves rolled up, eyes tired.

Not the outdoor type, Wyatt concluded.

'I'm not a night person,' Voccio said as they shook hands. 'But the NIA's paying the bill, and we aim to please. So I waited.'

'I need everything you have.'

'That cipher was a tough one. It took nearly two months for our computers to crack the thing. And even then, it was a little luck that did the trick.'

He wasn't interested in details. Instead he stepped across the cluttered office to the plate-glass windows, which offered a view of the front parking lot, wet asphalt glistening beneath the sodium vapor lights.

'Something wrong?' Voccio asked.

That remained to be seen. He kept his eyes out the window.

Headlights appeared.

A car turned from the entrance lane, wheeled into the vacant lot, and parked.

A man emerged.

Cotton Malone.

Carbonell had been right.

Another car materialized from his left. No headlights. Speeding straight for Malone.

Shots were fired.

Hale listened to Andrea Carbonell. Her tone was not that of someone cornered, more the frivolity of somebody genuinely bemused.

'You realize,' he said, 'that I can easily turn Stephanie Nelle loose after I make some arrangements with her. She is, after all, the head of a respected intelligence agency.'

'You'll find her difficult to work with.'

'More than you?'

'Quentin, only I control the key to the cipher.'

'I have no idea if that is true. You've already lied to us once.'

'The mishap with Knox? I was simply hedging the bet. Okay. You won that round. How about this. I'll provide the key to you. And once you find those missing two pages, then we'll both be in a better position to negotiate.'

'I assume that, in return, you would want what I have stored eliminated?'

'As if that's a problem for you.'

'I'm not immune to that particular charge, even if I find

the missing pages.' He knew she was aware that the letter of marque did not protect against willful murder.

'That hasn't seemed to bother you in the past, and there's a man at the bottom of the Atlantic Ocean who would agree with me.'

Her comment caught him off guard, then he realized. 'Your informant?'

'Spies do come in handy.'

But she'd tossed him a bone. He now knew where to look. And she knew what he'd do.

'Cleaning up loose ends?' he asked.

She laughed. 'Let's just say I can be quite generous when I want to be. Call it a demonstration of my good faith.'

The hell with Stephanie Nelle. Maybe she was more valuable dead. 'Give me the key. Once I have those two pages in hand, your problem will go away.'

28

Cassiopeia entered a casual space adjacent to the presidential master bedroom, the room decorated as a cozy den.

Perched on a settee, upholstered in a bright chintz print, sat Pauline Daniels.

The female Secret Service agent outside had closed the door behind her.

They were alone.

The First Lady's dull blond hair fell in wisps over dainty ears and a short brow. Her features cast a more youthful appearance than the early to midsixties she had to be. Octagonal glasses without rims fronted attractive blue eyes. She sat in an unnatural pose, back straight, veined hands folded in her lap, wearing a conservative wool suit and flat-soled Chanel ballet slippers.

'I understand you want to question me,' Mrs. Daniels said.

'I'd prefer we just talk.'

'And who are you?'

She caught the defensive edge in the question. 'Someone who doesn't want to be here.'

'That makes two of us.'

The First Lady motioned and Cassiopeia sat in a chair facing the sofa, two meters separating them, like some sort of demilitarized zone. This was uncomfortable on a multitude of levels, not the least of which was what Edwin Davis had just told her about Mary Daniels.

She introduced herself, then asked, 'Where were you when the attempt on the president's life happened?'

The older woman stared down at the rug on the wood floor. 'You make it sound so impersonal. He's my husband.'

'I have to ask the question, and you know that.'

'Here. Danny went to New York without me. He said he'd only be a few hours. Home by midnight. I didn't think a thing about it.'

The voice remained distant, far off.

'What was your reaction when you heard?'

The First Lady glanced up, her blue eyes focused. 'What you're really asking is, was I glad?'

She wondered about the bluntness, searching her memory, recalling nothing in the press about any animosity, whether perceived or real, between the first couple. Their marriage had always been regarded as strong. But if this was the direction the woman wanted to go, then, '*Were* you glad?'

'I didn't know what to think, especially during those first few minutes after it happened, before we were told he was okay. My thoughts were . . . confused.'

An uneasy silence passed between them.

'You know, don't you?' the older woman asked her. 'About Mary.'

She nodded.

The face remained frozen, a mask of indifference. 'I never forgave him.'

'Why did you stay?'

'He's my husband. I swore for better or worse. My mother taught me those words meant something.' The First Lady sucked in a deep breath, as if steeling herself. 'What you really want to know is, did I tell anyone about the trip to New York.'

She waited.

'Yes. I did.'

Malone dove behind his parked car and reached for the semi-automatic the Secret Service had provided. He'd expected something, but not necessarily this fast. The car speeding toward him slowed as the gun projecting from the open window fired three rounds. The weapon was sound-suppressed, the shots popping more like those of a cap pistol than the bangs of a high-caliber weapon.

The car wheeled to a stop fifty yards away.

Two men emerged, one from the driver's side, the other from the rear passenger door. Both armed. He decided not to give anyone time to think and shot the man closest to him in the thigh. The body dropped to the ground, his victim crying out in pain. The other man reacted, assuming a defensive position behind the vehicle.

The rain quickened, drops stinging his face.

He glanced around to see if there were any more threats and spotted none.

So instead of aiming for the man with the gun, he pointed his weapon at the open driver's-side door and fired into the car.

Hale hung up the phone. Of course, he did not believe a word Andrea Carbonell had said. She was buying time.

But so was he.

He was bothered by the fact that she knew about the earlier murder at sea. There was indeed a spy among them.

Which had to be dealt with.

He mentally assessed *Adventure*'s crew. Many of them performed other tasks around the estate, some in the metallurgy workshop where Knox had surely fashioned his remote-controlled weapons. Each man derived a designated share of the Commonwealth's annual spoils, and it pained him to think that one of them had betrayed the company.

Justice must be done.

The Articles provided an accused a trial before his peers with the quartermaster presiding and crewmen, captains included, serving as jury. A simple majority vote would determine his fate, and if he was found guilty, the punishment was not in doubt.

Death.

Slow and painful.

He recalled what his father had told him about a convicted traitor from decades ago. They'd resorted to the old ways. About a hundred of the crew assembled to deliver one blow each from a cat-o'-nine-tails. But only half were able to inflict the punishment before the man died.

He decided not to wait for the quartermaster.

Though it was approaching midnight, he knew his secretary was down the hall. Never would he retire before Hale.

He called out and a few moments later the door opened.

'I want the crew of the sloop assembled at once.'

Cassiopeia stayed calm. Apparently, Danny Daniels' instincts had proven correct.

'Are you married?' the First Lady asked her.

She shook her head.

'Someone special in your life?'

She nodded, though it felt strange to actually admit the fact.

'Do you love him?'

'I told him I did.'

'Did you mean it?'

'I wouldn't have said it otherwise.'

A sly grin came to the older woman's thin lips. 'I wish it were that simple. Does he love you?'

She nodded.

'I met Danny when I was seventeen. We married a year later. I told him I loved him on our second date. He told me on the third. He always was a little slow. I've watched him rise up the political ladder. He started as a city councilman and ended up president of the United States. If he hadn't killed our little girl, I do believe I would worship him.'

'He didn't kill her.'

'But he did. I begged him not to smoke in the house and to be careful with his ashes. Back then nobody knew anything about secondhand smoke, all I knew was that I didn't want him smoking.' The words had come fast, as if they needed to be said. 'I relive that night every day. Earlier, when they told me somebody had tried to kill Danny, I thought about it again. I hated him for tossing me out the window. Hated him for being stubborn. Hated him for not saving Mary.' She caught herself. 'But I also love him.'

Cassiopeia sat silent.

'I bet you think I'm a crazy person,' the First Lady said. 'But when I was told someone would be coming to interrogate me, someone from outside the White House, I knew that I had to be honest. You do believe that I'm being honest?'

That was the one thing she was sure of.

'Who did you tell about the New York trip?' she asked, trying to get back on point.

Pauline Daniels' face cast an expression of profound sympathy. Her blue eyes seemed on the verge of tears, and Cassiopeia wondered at the thoughts swirling through this troubled woman's mind. From everything she knew the First Lady was a poised, well-respected figure, never a cruel word uttered about her. At all times she conducted herself in a proper manner, but apparently this woman kept her emotions bottled inside, the relative safety of these walls, home to her for the past seven years, the only place where they might be exposed.

'A friend of mine. A close friend. That's who I told.'

The eyes conveyed more.

'A friend I don't want my husband to talk to.'

29

Wyatt watched as Cotton Malone fended off the attackers, firing at the car stopped a hundred and fifty feet away.

Carbonell had been right about the others coming, too.

'What's happening out there?' Voccio said, stepping toward the window.

Wyatt turned to face him. 'We have to go.'

More shots rang out from below. Concern filled the other man's face, the anxious eyes like those of a cornered animal.

'We need to call the police,' Voccio said.

'Do you have all the data?'

The man nodded and produced a flash drive. 'On here.'

'Give it to me.'

The academician handed over the device. 'Why are you even here to get it?'

A strange question.

'I emailed it to the NIA director several hours ago.'

Really? A point Carbonell had failed to mention. But he should not be surprised. 'Do you have a car downstairs?'

'In the rear parking lot.'

He gestured for the door. 'Bring the keys and let's go.'

The room suddenly went dark.

Every light extinguished with a loud bang, except for the three computer monitors. Even the rumble of the ventilation system stopped. Wyatt's alert level moved from orange to red.

Seemed they might be the subject of this attack, too.

'The computers are on a battery backup,' Voccio said, the uneven light from the screens washing over them. 'What in the world is going on?'

He couldn't say that men were probably coming to kill them both.

So he kept it simple.

'We need to leave.'

Malone aimed not to hit anyone, but to spur the driver to move the car, and bullets close enough to feel should do the trick.

And they did.

The engine revved, the wheels spun, and the vehicle sped away.

The gunman on the other side suddenly realized that his only cover had vanished. Now he stood in the center of an empty parking lot, awash in light from the overhead lamps, nowhere to go. So he laid down a spread from his automatic weapon, indiscriminate rounds tearing through Malone's car, shattering glass.

Malone huddled close, listening to the thumping report of lead ripping through metal, and waited for his moment. When the firing stopped, he rose, aimed, and brought the gunman to a wavering halt with a bullet to the shoulder.

He rushed over and kicked the rifle away.

The man writhed in pain on the wet pavement, and blood poured from the wound.

The storm freshened as gusts of wind molested the trees. His eyes swept the darkness, and he noticed something.

All the lights in the building that had been illuminated were now out.

Knox stepped off the plane at the Greenville, North Carolina, airport. He'd flown to NewYork aboard the Commonwealth's jet, piloting the twelve-seater himself. He'd learned to fly while in the air force. His father had encouraged him to join, and the six years he'd spent on active duty had been good for him. His sons had followed suit, one of them just finishing a Middle Eastern tour, another planned to enlist. He was proud that his children wanted to serve. They were good Americans, as was he.

The small, regional airport lay forty minutes west of Bath, and he quickly made his way to a Lincoln Navigator parked beside the Commonwealth's private hangar. Ostensibly, both the plane and the building belonged to one of the Hale business concerns, used by executives for corporate travel. Three pilots stayed on the payroll, but Knox never used them. His trips were private, the fewer witnesses the better. He was still concerned about New York and all that had gone wrong. But at least he'd managed to escape in one piece.

He unlocked the rear door and tossed his travel bag inside. The place was quiet and still for late on a Saturday night. Movement out of the corner of his eye diverted his attention. A form emerged from the darkness and said, 'I've been waiting.'

He stared at the faceless shadow, an inkblot on the night, and said, 'I should kill you.'

The woman chuckled. 'Funny, I was thinking the same thing about you.'

'Our deal is over.'

Andrea Carbonell stepped forward. 'Hardly. We are far from through with each other.'

Malone retrieved the weapons from the two downed men then ran toward the building's entrance. He saw that its glass doors had been shattered, the electronic latch destroyed. He entered the lobby, immediately finding cover behind a sofa grouping with chairs. A reception counter fronted one wall, two elevators another. Three sets of glass doors led into what he assumed were other offices, but they were dark. Another set of glass doors at the far end opened out to the rear of the building. His gaze found the stairway, an EXIT sign burning a dull crimson from battery power.

He crept close and eased the door open.

He heard movement.

Footsteps.

Above him.

Wyatt led Voccio out of the office and down the hall, passing both open and closed doorways. Emergency lighting indicated where the stairs waited and, in the soft glow from the illuminated panel, he caught sight of the exit door.

Which was being eased open.

He grabbed Voccio by the arm, signaling for quiet, then diverted them both into the first open space. Some sort of conference room, the opposite wall lined with windows, the plate glass smeared with rain and lit from the outside by lamps below. He motioned for the doctor to wait in one of the corners, then peered out into the hall, his eyes struggling to define shapes.

Two forms disturbed the darkness, both moving ahead toting automatic rifles. He thought he caught the silhouette of night goggles around their heads. It would make sense that these men would have come equipped.

Thank goodness he'd also thought ahead.

Knox was in no mood for Carbonell's theatrics. He'd sold his soul to her, doing something that ran counter to every fiber in his being.

But she'd made a convincing case.

The Commonwealth was finished.

All four captains would spend a decade or more in federal prison. Every penny they'd made and every tangible asset they owned would be seized by the government. No more crews. No more letters of marque. No more quartermasters.

Knox could either survive the calamity or become part of it.

God help him, he chose survival.

The NIA knew about the assassination attempt because he'd told them. That had been his bargaining chip, the one piece of information that neither NIA nor anyone else had known.

His ticket out.

Carbonell had listened to him intently.

'They're going to kill Danny Daniels?' she asked.

'Three captains think that's the solution.'

'And what do you think?'

'They're crazy and desperate. That's why I'm talking to you.'

'What do you want?'

'To see my children graduate from college. To enjoy my grandchildren. I don't want to spend the rest of my life in prison.'

'I can make that happen.'

Yes, she could, he thought.

'Keep their plan moving forward. Do nothing out of the ordinary. But keep me informed.'

He hated himself for selling out. He hated the captains for forcing him into the position.

'One thing,' she said to him. 'If you hold out or give me one shred of bad information, the deal is off. But you won't go down with them.'

He knew what she'd do.

'I'll tell them that you sold out, and let them handle you for me.'

Of which he was sure.

So he'd fabricated the weapons, delivered them to New York, then provided Carbonell with card keys to both rooms, per her request. She'd then told him to carry out the attempt, as planned, with no stops.

He'd wondered about that.

'You cut that close,' he said to her. 'I wasn't sure you were going to end it or not. The guy dangling out the window. Yours?'

'An unplanned complication, but it worked out. Good work on Scott Parrott.'

He'd killed Parrott only because that's what the captains would have expected from their quartermaster. Duplicity could never be tolerated. Anything less than direct force would have been suspect.

'You gave him up easily,' he said to her.

'Would you have preferred one more live witness around who could sell you out?'

No. He wouldn't. Which was another reason why he'd acted. 'Were you going to kill me in New York?'

She laughed. 'Far from it. That was a favor from me to you. In the event that, for some reason, you didn't move on Parrott.'

He didn't understand.

She said, 'How better to shield the fact that you're a traitor to all those you once held dear than to place your life in dire jeopardy, from which you manage to escape?'

'That whole thing was an act?'

'Not from the agents' perspectives. They knew nothing, except to stop you. But I knew you could handle yourself.'

'So you sacrificed them, too? Do you care anything for the people who work for you?'

She shrugged. 'They had a better-than-fair shot at besting you. Five against one. It's not my fault they failed.'

Damn her. None of that had been necessary.

Or had it?

Both incidents would indeed provide him with excellent cover.

'Captain Hale,' she said, 'and the rest of the Commonwealth are surely in a panic. But it seems the captains work together about as efficiently as the intelligence community.'

He could not argue with that conclusion. They were all becoming more combative, more irrational. He knew about what Hale had done earlier, killing his long-term accountant. Who was next?

'Hale wants the cipher solution,' she said. 'But I don't particularly want to give it to him.'

'So don't.'

'I wish it were that easy.'

'Like I said, we're through. I've done my part.'

'I taped our conversations. I'm taping you right now. Your captains might find our talks enlightening.'

'And I could kill you right now.'

'I'm not alone.'

He glanced around at the darkness and realized that if the captains learned of his treachery, there would be nowhere on the planet for him to hide. Though they called themselves privateers, there was a pirate within every one of them. Treason had never been tolerated – and the higher on the pole you were the more grotesque the punishment.

'Not to worry, Clifford,' Carbonell finally said, 'I did you one other favor.'

He was listening.

'I cultivated a second informant. One who provided information to me independent of you.'

More news.

'And I just sold that source out to Hale.'

He'd wondered how he was going to satisfy the captains' demand that the spy be found.

'All you have to do in gratitude,' she said, 'is one little thing.'

He realized that any gesture from her came with a price.

'Kill Stephanie Nelle.'

30

Cassiopeia gunned the motorcycle and sped onto Interstate 95, heading south toward Virginia. Edwin Davis had offered her a choice of transportation, and she'd selected one of the Secret Service's two-wheelers. She'd also changed, donning jeans, leather boots, and a black sweater.

Her talk with the First Lady still disturbed her.

Pauline Daniels was one conflicted woman.

'I don't hate my husband,' the First Lady told her.

'You just resent him, and you've kept that bottled up for thirty years.'

'Politics is a powerful drug,' the older woman said. *'If you're successful at it, the effects are like a sedative. Adoration. Respect. Need. These can make you forget. And sometimes those of us who receive too much of this drug begin to believe that everyone loves us, that the world would be worse off if we weren't around to help run it. We even begin to feel entitled. And I'm not talking about being president of the United States. Political worlds can be as big or small as we create for ourselves.'*

She roared on, quickening her pace down the blackened highway. Not much traffic out at this hour beyond a procession of eighteen-wheelers taking advantage of uncrowded asphalt.

'When Mary died,' Pauline said, 'Danny was a city councilman. He became mayor the next year, a state senator after that, then governor. It seemed that the depths of our tragedy gave birth to his success. He suppressed his grief through politics. He succumbed to the sedative. I wasn't so lucky.'

'Have you two discussed this? Dealt with it?'

She shook her head. 'It's not his way. He never spoke of Mary again after the funeral. It is as if she never existed.'

'But that's not what happened for you.'

'Oh, no. I didn't say that. I'm afraid I wasn't immune to politics, either. As Danny rose, so did I.' The voice drifted farther away and she wondered, Who was she really talking to? 'God forgive me, but I tried to forget my daughter.' Tears welled in the older woman's tired eyes. 'I tried. I just couldn't.'

'Why are you telling me this?'

'When Edwin told me you were coming, he also told me you're a good person. I trust him. He's a good person. Maybe it's time I rid myself of this burden. All I know is that I'm tired of carrying the grief.'

'What are you saying?'

A few moments of strained silence passed.

'I've come to expect Danny to be around,' the First Lady said, her voice still a monotone. 'He's always been there.'

But she heard what had not been spoken. Yet you still blame him for Mary's death. Every day.

'But when they told me that someone had tried to kill him—'

She waited for the sentence to be finished.

'I found myself glad.'

She roared passed a car and crossed into Virginia, headed for Fredericksburg, which lay about forty kilometers away.

'Living with Danny isn't easy,' Pauline said. 'He compartmentalizes everything. Moves from one thing to the next without a problem. I suppose that's what makes him a good leader. And he does it all without emotion.'

Not necessarily, she thought. *The same had been said about her – even Cotton had chastised her once on her lack of feeling. But just because they weren't shown didn't mean emotions did not exist.*

'He's never gone to her grave,' the First Lady said. 'Not once since the funeral. We lost everything we owned in that fire. Mary's room, and the rest of the house, was nothing but ash. Not a photo of her survived. I think he was almost glad. He wanted no reminders.'

'And you wanted too many.'

Eyes brimming with pain stared back at her.

'Perhaps I did.'

She noticed that the black sky overhead was shrouded in clouds. Not a star visible. The asphalt was damp. Rain had come and gone. She was headed to a place that she preferred not to go. But Pauline Daniels had confided in her, telling her something only two other people knew – neither one of which was Danny Daniels. Before leaving, the president had questioned her on her destination, but she'd refused to tell him.

'You wanted me to handle it,' she'd said. 'Let me handle it.'

Wyatt reached into his pocket and found the flash bomb. His own invention, developed years ago. He'd taken Carbonell's warning to heart and anticipated that there might be visitors waiting here, people not all that friendly, and it was reasonable to assume that they might come equipped with night-vision goggles.

'Close your eyes,' he whispered to Voccio.

He freed the igniter pin and tossed the paper-wrapped wad out into the hall.

A blinding flash of light lit up inside his closed lids, lingered a couple of seconds, then faded.

Cries rang out.

He knew what was happening.

The two assailants, caught unawares, were momentarily

blinded, their pupils, dilated by the goggles, violently closing to the unexpected brightness.

Pain would be next, then confusion.

He found his gun, swung around the doorway, and fired.

Malone heard two shots. He was in the stairway, waiting at a metal door that led into the second floor. Cracks around the frame illuminated with a bright flash, which immediately diminished. Something pinged off the other side, then the door flung open and two forms bolted into the stairwell, both reaching for their heads, cursing, ripping night goggles from their faces. He used their confusion to slip up the stairs, toward the next floor, and hide on the landing.

'Son of a bitch,' one of the men breathed.

A moment of quiet passed as the two reclaimed their emotions and readied their weapons.

'Leave the eyes off,' one of them said.

He heard the door ease open.

'They have to be headed toward the far side.'

'Hopefully for the other stairway down.'

'Three, this is Two,' he heard a man say in a low voice. A pause. 'Subjects are headed your way.' Another pause. 'Out.'

'Let's finish this,' one of the men said.

A gentle click signaled the metal door had closed.

He risked a look down through the darkness.

Both men were gone.

'Why would I kill Stephanie Nelle?' Knox asked Carbonell.

'Because you have no choice. If the captains learn of your betrayal, how long do you think you'd last? It's a simple task, killing one person. Shouldn't be a problem for you.'

'Is that what you think I do? Kill people all the time?'

'You certainly have in the past few hours. I have two dead agents as proof, and two more in the hospital.'

'All thanks to you.' And he was curious as to her reversal. 'You realize that Hale went to a lot of trouble to capture her for you. Your instructions were that she not be harmed in any way.'

She shrugged. 'He was accumulating a favor from me. I get that. But things have changed. Nelle is more of a problem now.'

'I assume you won't explain why.'

'Clifford, you wanted out. I offered you a way out. Now I'm telling you the price.'

Her tone bore no trace of anger, contempt, or amusement.

'Once the Commonwealth ceases to exist,' she said, 'which is going to happen, you'll be free to do as you please. You can live your life. Enjoy your spoils. And no one will know a thing. If you like, I'll even hire you.'

He wanted to know, 'Did you actually solve the Jefferson cipher?'

'Does it matter?'

'I want to know.'

Carbonell hesitated a moment before saying, 'Yes. We did.'

'So why didn't you just kill Nelle yourself? Why involve us in the first place with her?'

'First off, I didn't have the cipher key when I asked Hale to move on Nelle. I do now. Second, contrary to the movies, it's not that easy eliminating targets in my line of work. People who do those types of jobs want too much in return for their silence.'

'And I don't?'

She shrugged. 'Not anything I can't provide.'

'You didn't answer my question. What if Hale doesn't want Nelle dead?'

'I'm quite sure that he doesn't, not at the moment anyway. But I do. So find a way to make it happen. Quickly.'

He was exasperated. This was way too much. 'You said

you sold out another source. Hale knows the identity?'

'He knows where to start looking, which I'm sure he's doing right now. He'll surely turn that matter over to you soon enough. His faithful servant, returned from doing battle in New York. See what I've done for your image?. You're a hero. What more could you want? And to demonstrate my good faith, to make clear that we're all one-for-all-and-all-for-one, I'm going to tell you the name of my source and exactly how to prove he's a traitor.'

That was exactly what he wanted to know. The captains would demand that the man be tried, convicted, and punished immediately. If he personally managed to accomplish that task, his value would rise immeasurably.

Most of all, it would divert even more attention from himself.

Damn her.

'Give me the name and I'll make sure Stephanie Nelle goes away.'

31

Fredericksburg, Virginia

Cassiopeia said hello to the woman who answered the door. The house was a large, airy Georgian filled with plants, three cats, and exquisite antiques. The exterior had been awash with yellow light and an iron gate blocking a brick-paved drive had hung open. Her host wore a loose-fitting Nike jogging suit with Coach tennis shoes. She was clearly a contemporary of the First Lady, their ages and appearances not far off except that Shirley Kaiser's wavy hair hung long and was tinted a faint golden-red.

Their attitudes were also different.

Where Pauline Daniels' face had stayed pale and drawn, Kaiser's brimmed with civility, her animated features high-lighted by firm cheekbones and bright brown eyes. They stepped into a room lit by crystal wall sconces and Tiffany lamps. She was offered and refused a drink, though a glass of water would have been welcomed.

'I understand you have some questions for me. Pauline told me that you were a person I could trust. I wonder. Can we?'

She caught the use of third-person plural and decided to approach this woman with greater care than she'd used with Pauline. 'How long have you and the First Lady known each other?'

A crease of amusement marked Kaiser's face. 'You're a clever one, aren't you? Get me talking about me first.'

'I'm not new to this.'

The amusement increased. 'I bet you aren't. What are you, Secret Service? FBI?'

'Neither.'

'No, you don't look like either one.'

She wondered what that look entailed, but only said, 'Let's just say I'm a friend of the family.'

Kaiser smiled. 'That one I like. Okay, friend, Pauline and I have known each other twenty years.'

'Which makes that about a decade after her daughter died.'

'Something like that.'

She'd already surmised that Kaiser was a night person. Eyes that should be misty brimmed with life. Unfortunately, this woman had been given two hours to prepare herself. The First Lady would not allow an unannounced visit. Cellphones had been used to send a brief text message.

'Have you known the president for twenty years?' she tried.

'Unfortunately.'

'I assume then that you didn't vote for him.'

'Hardly. I wouldn't have married him, either.'

Where Pauline had wanted to purge, this woman sought to vent. But Cassiopeia had no time for anger. 'How about you quit with the games and explain what's on your mind.'

'I'd love to. Pauline is dead inside. Couldn't you see that?'

Yes, she had.

'Danny has known that from the day they buried Mary. But does he care? Does he give a damn? Has anyone asked themselves, if he treats his wife with such callousness, imagine how he treats his enemies. Is it any wonder somebody took a shot at him?'

'How do you know what he feels?'

'I've been there for twenty years. I've never once heard him mention Mary's name. Never has he even acknowledged that there was a daughter. It is as if she never lived.'

'Maybe that's how he handles his grief,' she had to say.

'That's just it. He has no grief.'

Wyatt used the moments the flash bomb bought him to advance himself and Voccio toward another stairway that the doctor had told him existed on the far side of the second floor, used by employees as a quick route down to the cafeteria. His charge was in a panic, clearly never having been in a fight like this before.

Luckily, this was not his first.

Somebody had come to *sweep and clean*, as they said in the trade. He'd been a party to a few himself. He wondered if it was CIA, NSA, some other combination, or whether Carbonell herself sent them.

That actually made the most sense.

He rushed down the hall and opened the exit door, listened, then motioned for Voccio to follow. He led the way down the black stairway, using the metal railing as his guide, keeping Voccio close behind him.

He halted just before they found the ground.

'How far to your car?' he whispered.

Wyatt heard deep, ragged breaths, but Voccio did not answer him.

'Doctor, to get us out of here I need your help.'

'Not far . . . just outside the rear exit door. To the right . . . when we get to the bottom and the lobby.'

He eased down the remaining few risers. His hand found the exit door and he eased it open.

The lobby loomed still.

He motioned for them to crouch low and head right.

They cleared the doorway.

And shooting started.

Malone had watched from the stairway door as the two gunmen negotiated the doglegged hallway and turned about fifty feet away. He noticed an ambient glow from one of the office doorways. Odd, considering the power was gone.

He hustled ahead and glanced inside.

Three computer screens glowed. A nameplate on the door read VOCCIO. The man he'd come to see.

He started to search the office, but a cacophony of gunfire erupted below.

Cassiopeia felt the need to defend Danny Daniels. Why, she wasn't sure, but this woman seemed unapologetic in her harsh judgments.

'What Danny has,' Kaiser said, 'is guilt, not grief. Once, about a year before Mary died, his smoking caused a small fire at the house. That one only destroyed a chair. Pauline begged him to stop, or smoke outside, or something – anything but what he was doing. For a while, he did. Then he did what Danny always does. Whatever he wants. That fire should have never happened, and he knows that.'

She decided to come to the point of her visit. 'When did you and the First Lady first speak of the New York trip?'

'You don't want to hear my opinions anymore?'

'I want you to answer my question.'

'To see if my answer and Pauline's match?'

'Something like that. But since you two have already communicated, that shouldn't be a problem.'

Kaiser shook her head. 'Look, missy, Pauline and I talk every day, sometimes more than once. We discuss everything. She told me about Danny's New York visit about two months ago. She was home alone in the White House. People haven't really noticed, but she's doing less and less in the way of appearances. I was here.'

Which was exactly what she already knew. The First Lady had also made clear that she never used a mobile or cordless phone when talking to Kaiser. Always a landline. So she asked, and was told the same was true on this end.

'The text earlier was a first for us,' Kaiser said. 'Did I pass the test?'

She stood. 'I have to check for listening devices.'

'That's why I'm up at this hour. Do what you have to do.'

She removed from her pocket an EM detector provided by the Secret Service. She doubted the house itself was wired. That would require every square inch being within range of a listening device. So she decided to start with the phones themselves.

'Where are the outside electrical, cable, and phone boxes?'

Kaiser stayed seated. 'On the side of the garage. Behind the hedge. The floodlights are already on for you. I'm here to please.'

She left the house and followed the brick-paved drive around to the side. They hadn't even approached the most uncomfortable questions, but they would have to be asked either by her, or by people whom neither one of these two women wanted to talk to. She told herself to be patient. There was a lot of history here, most of it bad.

She located the junction boxes where utility service tied to the house. She eased her way down the side of the building, between damp chest-high hedges, and activated the EM detector. Not a one hundred percent accurate device, but good enough to sniff out any electromagnetic emissions that might warrant closer inspection.

She pointed the unit at the metal boxes.

Nothing.

Wires ran from the telephone connector up through the soffit, into the house, feeding each of the inside jacks. She'd need to check them individually, since what she was looking for could well be concealed within the phones themselves.

'Find anything?' a voice asked.

Startled, she lost her grip on the detector and it dropped to the ground.

She turned.

Kaiser watched from the corner of the building, beyond where the hedge ended. 'Didn't mean to frighten you.'

She didn't believe a word of that.

The detector began to pulsate, its green indicator light shifting to red, blinking at an ever-increasing rate. If she hadn't muted its audio, a beep would now be disturbing the night. She bent down and pointed the unit in several directions, finally determining that down was correct. She dug through the wet soil, her fingers scraping something hard. Clearing away the mud she discovered a small plastic box, about eight centimeters square, the underground telephone wire running through it from one end to the other.

The detector continued to alert.

A bad situation had just became worse.

Kaiser's phones had been tapped.

32

Wyatt dove to the tiled floor and made sure Voccio was low alongside of him.

Bullets banged off the walls.

He couldn't tell how many shooters they faced. The lobby remained in darkness, only a peripheral glow from the parking lot offering any assistance. Two wide chairs blocked them from the source of the gunfire, about fifty feet away.

He pulled Voccio closer to him.

'Stay down,' he whispered.

The glass doors he sought, the ones Voccio had said led to the rear parking lot, were twenty feet away at the end of a short alcove. He was determined to get them both out of here. His heart pounded with a familiar alarm, the silence around him broken only by Voccio's nervous breathing. He laid a reassuring hand on the other man's arm and shook his head, signaling for him to remain calm. If he could hear each breath, so could their attackers.

He was curious about Malone. How had his adversary fared? He hadn't seen the end of the parking lot standoff and wondered if Captain America was hurt, dead, or across the room firing.

Outside, the rain had slackened.

'I can't take this anymore,' Voccio said.

He was in no mood for defeatism.

'Stay with me. I know what I'm doing.'

* * *

Malone descended the stairs, retracing his route to the ground floor, coming ever closer to the loud retorts. He found the exit door, eased it open, and caught sight of shadows advancing across the lobby. Not much light, but enough to see two men with automatic rifles concerned with a target on the far side of the room. These could not be the same two from before. They'd disappeared down the second-floor corridor, headed to the other side of the building and another staircase.

These must be the ones on the other end of the radio.

Whoever these people were after, their quarry was now caught in a pincer, men ahead and behind. He could not reveal himself, as anonymity seemed his best defense, but he also could not just wait to see what happened.

So he aimed and fired.

Wyatt heard shots and saw muzzle flashes beyond where he'd spotted the shadows advancing.

Somebody was behind his two problems.

Malone?

Had to be.

Malone fired again, catching one of the shadows in the shoulder, hurling the form forward into the wall with a dull thump. The other shadow reacted, whirling around and unleashing a burst of rounds. He jerked himself back inside the stairway and allowed the metal door to close.

Bullets dinged off the other side.

Apparently, his presence had not been expected.

Wyatt heard the stairway door – behind where he and Voccio lay – open and he turned as movement disturbed the darkness.

Men were also behind him.

The shooter whom he assumed was Malone had taken down one of the men in the lobby, and the other was now firing at a second illuminated exit. He rotated on the floor, spine down, and fired at the door less than ten feet away.

They had to get out of here.

Voccio was apparently thinking the same thing. The doctor belly-crawled toward the outside exit.

Not smart.

Little cover existed between here and there, though the main threats across the lobby seemed occupied.

He watched as Voccio found the glass doors, slammed a hand into a quick-release latch, and slipped outside. The other gunman, the one firing at Malone, heard the escape, turned, and aimed toward the doors. Before he could fire a shot, Wyatt sent three bullets the man's way. The form spun, flailed backward, then shrank to the floor.

Two attackers down.

Voccio raced outside.

An instant later both downed forms came to their feet, rifles in hand.

Then he realized.

They wore body armor.

Neither he nor Malone had stopped a thing.

Malone abandoned the stairwell door, climbing back to the first floor, negotiating another hall nearly identical to the one a floor above and finding the second stairway on the far side. He was going to make an end run on the two men he'd seen earlier, but just as he turned the corner for the exit, the stairway door opened.

He darted into the first office he saw and carefully peered around the jamb. A man with a rifle took measure of the hall, then, satisfied that all appeared quiet, emerged. Malone laid his gun down on the carpet and prepared himself, keeping his back to the wall, waiting for the target to pass. As that happened, he lunged, wrapping an arm around the man's neck from behind, the other hand going for the rifle.

He wrenched the weapon free, spinning the man around and driving a knee into his groin. He'd already felt the body armor and knew that blows above the waist would be futile.

His opponent buckled forward and cried out in pain.

Another knee into the man's jaw and the body recoiled backward. He readied a third blow, this time a fist to the face, when the man suddenly planted a foot into Malone's left kidney.

A mist of pain engulfed him.

His adversary ignored the rifle on the carpet and beat a retreat toward the stairway door.

Malone shook off the blow and started his pursuit.

The fleeing shadow turned, pistol in hand.

A backup weapon.

The gun fired.

Wyatt crouched low and headed for the exit doors. As he came close to the glass he turned back, ready to fire, but no one was there.

He took advantage of the quiet and released the doors, fleeing out into the night. Immediately he assumed a position adjacent to the exit, using the exterior brick wall as cover, glancing with caution through the doors back into the lobby.

Three men rushed from the building, out the main entrance.

At first he thought they were circling, readying an attack from the outside, but then he saw the glow of headlights from the front parking lot, the three bolting toward a waiting vehicle.

No way these guys were such bad shots.

They'd been waiting for him and Malone, prepared and equipped, but they'd accomplished nothing except making a lot of noise and shooting up the lobby.

Another shot disturbed the silence.

From inside, an upper floor.

Where was Voccio?

He scanned the blackness and caught sight of the doctor, fifty yards away, hustling toward a parked car. He tore out the gun's magazine and slammed home a fresh one from his pocket. He glanced back inside and spotted another form emerging from the stairway across the lobby and leaving through the front doors.

Apparently the party was over.

Something was wrong.

He stared back toward where Voccio was entering the car. He should leave, too, with the doctor.

Then it hit him.

That's exactly what they wanted him to do. His mind performed a rapid calculation and the result struck him like iron.

A growl signaled a cold engine starting.

He opened his mouth to yell.

Voccio's car exploded.

33

Cassiopeia examined the device revealed by her digging. Somebody had gone to a lot of trouble to listen in on Kaiser's telephone. Somebody who knew exactly where and what to listen for.

'Who knows you talk to the First Lady?' she asked Kaiser. 'And it has to be someone who knows those conversations are numerous and intimate.'

'It's Danny Daniels. Who the hell else?'

She stood from the wet ground and walked closer, exiting the shrubbery that encased the garage.

'It's not the president,' she said in a whisper.

'He knows Pauline and I are close.'

'Are you married?'

The question seemed to take Kaiser aback. Edwin Davis had told her about the house, the neighborhood, and that Kaiser was a player in both the Virginia and the capital social scenes. Her extensive charity work included serving on the board of directors for the Library of Virginia and on several state advisory councils. But he hadn't mentioned much about her personal life.

'I'm a widow.'

'Mrs. Kaiser, somebody tried to kill the president of the United States today. Somebody who knew exactly when and where he would be in New York. Your phones are being monitored. I need you to answer my question. Who would know to do this? Either talk to me or I'm calling the Secret Service and you can talk to them.'

'Pauline is on the verge of a nervous breakdown,' Kaiser said. 'I've heard it in her voice for weeks now. She's been through hell far too long. What happened today with Danny could send her over. If you keep this pressure on her, she's going to snap.'

'Then she needs professional help.'

'That's not so easy when you're the First Lady.'

'It's not so easy for a woman who wants to blame her husband for the tragic death of their daughter. A woman who did not have the courage to leave the man, but instead stays, keeps everything welled inside her, and makes life all his fault.'

'You're one of Danny's groupies, aren't you?'

'Yep. I love men with power. It's a turn-on.'

Kaiser caught the sarcasm. 'That's not what I meant. He has an effect on women. They did a poll a few years ago and nearly eighty percent of women favored him. Since they're a majority of the voters, it's easy to see why he's never lost an election.'

'Why do you hate him?'

'I don't. I just adore Pauline, and I know he could not care less about her.'

'You still haven't answered my question,' she said.

'Nor you mine.'

She appreciated strong women. She was one herself. She assumed Kaiser's talent was simply being herself – easy, natural – giving and accepting without question, never thinking much beyond the moment. She'd hoped there would be nothing to find here. A dead end. Unfortunately, that was not the case.

'Pauline has always needed someone to talk to,' Kaiser

said. 'A person she could trust. Long ago, I became that for her. Since she moved into the White House, that's become even more important.'

'Except that you can't be trusted.'

She saw that Kaiser realized the implications of what lay in the ground a meter or two away.

'Who else knew about that New York trip?' she asked her again.

'I can't say.'

'Okay. We can do this another way.'

She found her cellphone and hit the speed dial button for the White House. Two rings and a male voice answered.

'Do it,' she told him, then ended the call.

'There's a Secret Service agent in contact with your telephone provider, both landline and mobile. You have two accounts. The company has already been served a subpoena and has the information prepared. Under the circumstances, we weren't going to invade your privacy unless necessary.'

Her phone rang. She answered, listened, then clicked off.

Defeat filled Shirley Kaiser's face.

As it should.

'Tell me about the one hundred and thirty-five calls between you and Quentin Hale.'

Hale entered what had once been an outdoor kitchen and smokehouse. Now the building, with its pine walls, sash windows, and glazed cupola, served as a meeting hall that all four families utilized. The sixteen members of *Adventure*'s crew had been roused from their beds, including the yacht's captain. Most lived within half an hour of the estate on land bought by their families generations ago. He could not fathom that any one of them would betray their heritage.

But apparently someone had.

All sixteen men standing before him had signed the current

Articles, pledging their loyalty and obedience in return for a specified portion of the Commonwealth's plunder. Granted, their respective percentages were small, but combined with health insurance, workers' compensation, and disability pay, theirs was a comfortable living.

He caught the uncertain looks on their faces. Though it wasn't unusual for things to happen in the middle of the night, it was definitely unusual for events to involve the entire complement on land.

'We have a problem,' he told them.

He watched the faces, assessing them, recalling the four who'd lifted the gibbet and tossed his screaming accountant into the ocean.

'One of you is a traitor.'

He knew those words would grab their attention.

'Today we all were involved on a mission, one that was of great concern to the entire company. A traitor died, and one of you breached the silence we all pledged to maintain.'

None of the sixteen said a word. They knew better. The captain spoke until he said he was ready to listen.

'It saddens me to think that one of you betrayed us.'

And that was how he viewed his world. *Us.* A grand society, built on loyalty and success. Long ago pirate ships learned to strike with speed, skill, and urgency, the crews functioning as tight, cohesive units. Laziness, incompetence, disloyalty, and cowardice were never tolerated since those endangered everyone. His father had taught him that the best plans were simple, easy to understand, and flexible enough to deal with any contingency.

And he was right.

He paced the floor.

Captains must always be bold and daring tacticians. Crews intentionally elected them in defiance of a naval tradition that bestowed leadership regardless of competency.

But captains today were not elected.

Heredity accounted for their ascendency. He often imagined himself at the helm of one of those long-ago ships, stalking prey, following at a safe distance for days, all the while determining strengths and weaknesses. If the target proved a powerful man-of-war, he could veer away and seek weaker prey. If she seemed vulnerable they could take her either by surprise or by frontal attack.

Choices.

All born through patience.

Which he intended to exercise here tonight.

'None of you will leave this room until I find the traitor. When morning breaks your bank accounts will be examined, your houses searched, your phone records obtained. You will sign whatever releases are needed, or grant whatever permissions required—'

'That won't be necessary.'

He was taken aback by the interruption until he realized the voice belonged to Clifford Knox, who'd entered the room.

Quartermasters were not bound by the same rules of silence.

'I know who the traitor is.'

34

Malone dove into the office six feet away. The bullet fired his way thudded into drywall. More slugs cracked and hummed through the air. He readied his gun and scampered for the desk. But all he heard was the click of a door closing from out in the hall.

The man had left.

An explosion rattled the windows, followed by a flickering glow that signaled something was burning outside.

He approached the glass, keeping low, alternating his attention between the doorway behind him and a flaming car below. Across the hall, in another office, he caught a spray of light across more windows. He quickly made his way there and spotted a man leaping into a car in the front parking lot, then speeding away. He should leave, too, and fast. Though this facility was in the countryside, somebody may have heard the gunfire or the explosion and called the police.

But first . . .

He hustled back into Voccio's office and noticed that the three computer screens still burned. He squinted at the glare off the first machine and caught a break.

The displayed file explained the solution to the Jefferson cipher.

Voccio had apparently left in a hurry.

He closed the file, found the machine's email program,

attached the document to a message, and forwarded it to himself. He then deleted the message and file from the machine.

No great security measure, but enough to buy him time.

He stared past the black square of night framed by the window.

The car still burned.

Needles of rain clawed the glass. To his right, a hundred yards away from the flaming chaos, he spotted a dark figure.

Running.

Away.

Wyatt decided that a propitious retreat seemed the best option. Voccio was dead. He'd told the frightened idiot to stick with him, and if he'd done that the man would still be alive.

So he shouldn't feel bad. Yet he did.

He kept running.

Carbonell had lured him here with a double fee, wanting him not to escape. Those men were hers.

They needed to chat.

On his terms.

And he knew exactly how to do that.

Knox entered the hall and stared at *Adventure*'s crew. Quentin Hale stood silent, clearly waiting to see what his quartermaster had to say.

'Captain Hale, when we spoke earlier I could not say all that I knew since we were on an open phone line.'

He was practicing, to the max, one of the strategies his father had taught him. *Always have a plan.* Contrary to popular myth, buccaneers never attacked anything blind. Whether their target be on land or sea, to ensure success an advance party would first reconnoiter. The preferred time for any assault was dawn, or a Sunday, or a holy festival, or, as here, late at night, the element of surprise used to prevent escapes and to overwhelm resistance.

'Periodically, I run checks,' he said. 'Looking for anything out of the ordinary. Big purchases. Unusual lifestyle. Trouble at home. It's strange, but a woman can drive a man to do crazy things.'

He allowed the last sentence to linger and watched the yacht's crew. He was careful to keep his gaze roving, from one man to the next, never settling in one place.

Not yet, anyway.

He was playing to an audience of one. Quentin Hale. So long as Hale was convinced, that was all that mattered.

He focused.

Make your case.

Then figure out how to kill Stephanie Nelle.

Malone fled the building and made a quick inspection of the destroyed car. Indeed, somebody had been behind the wheel, the body now burning with a fury. The license plate was charred but readable and he committed the numbers to his eidetic memory.

He rounded the building and found his government-issued sedan. The rear windshield and most of the windows were gone, the sidewalls riddled with holes. No gas had leaked, though, and the tires were intact, so at least two things had gone right. Soon this place would be awash with the corona of blue and red revolving lights, police everywhere.

The wind moaned through the trees, as if telling him to leave. He glanced up at the sky, clearing of clouds and rain, revealing half-lit stars.

The wind was right.

Time to go.

35

Cassiopeia sat in Shirley Kaiser's living room. Her parents had owned a similar parlor in their Barcelona home. Though billionaires, they'd been simple, private souls, staying to themselves, devoting their lives to her, to each other, and to the family business. Never once had she heard a hint of scandal associated with either. They seemed to live exemplary lives, both dying in their seventies within months of each other. She'd always hoped to find someone to whom she could equally devote herself.

Perhaps she had in Cotton Malone.

At the moment, though, she was concerned with the woman sitting across from her who, unlike her parents, harbored a great many secrets.

Starting with 135 telephone calls.

'Quentin Hale and I are lovers,' Kaiser said.

'How long?'

'Off and on for the past year.'

She listened as Kaiser explained. Hale was married with three grown children. He'd been separated from his wife going on a decade – she lived in England, he in North Carolina. They met at a social occasion and immediately liked each other.

'He insisted that we keep things discreet,' Kaiser said. 'I thought he was concerned about my reputation. Now I see it may have been something else altogether.'

Cassiopeia agreed.

'I'm a fool,' Kaiser said. 'I've gotten myself into a deep mess.'

No argument there.

'I never had children. My husband . . . he couldn't. The fact never really bothered me. No motherly instincts overtook me.' A squint of regret appeared on Kaiser's face. 'But as I get older, I find myself rethinking my attitude toward children. It's lonely sometimes.'

She could relate to that. Though a good twenty years younger than Kaiser, she, too, had felt those motherly pangs.

'Are you going to tell me how my relationship with Quentin connects to what's in the ground outside?' Kaiser asked. 'I'd like to know.'

Answering that inquiry could prove difficult. But since she'd already determined that they were going to require this woman's cooperation, she decided to be honest. 'Hale may have been involved with trying to kill the president.'

Kaiser did not react. Instead, she sat contemplative.

'We often spoke of politics,' Kaiser finally said. 'But he seemed to care nothing about it. He was a supporter of Danny's, contributing a lot of money to both presidential campaigns. He never had anything bad to say. Contrary to myself.' The words were expressionless, as if Kaiser was talking to herself, arranging her thoughts in order, readying her mind for what she was about to be asked. 'But why would he say anything bad? He was gaining my trust.'

'Who exactly did you tell about the trip to New York?'

'Only Quentin.' Kaiser stared at her with a look of undisguised fear. 'We talked about Pauline often. You have to understand, Pauline and Quentin are my two closest friends.'

She heard the unspoken comment.

And one betrayed me.

'We discussed it a couple of months ago, right after Pauline mentioned the New York trip. I didn't think anything of it. Pauline never said the trip was a secret. I had no idea it wasn't being publicly announced. She simply said Danny was headed to New York for a retirement dinner.'

Which meant Hale had grasped the significance of the White House withholding the information and decided to act.

'I need to know more about you and Hale,' Cassiopeia said. 'The Secret Service is going to want every detail.'

'It's not complicated. Quentin is well known in social circles. He's an avid yachtsman. He participated twice in the America's Cup. He's rich, handsome, charming.'

'Does Pauline know about him?'

Kaiser shook her head. 'I kept that relationship to myself. There was no need to tell her.'

The cocky attitude had been shed, the voice growing more penitent as the realization of what had happened pounded its way home.

'He used you.'

She could only imagine the emotions churning inside the older woman.

'Ms. Kaiser—'

'Don't you think we can be Shirley and Cassiopeia? I have a feeling you and I will be seeing more of each other.'

So did she. 'I'm going to have to report everything, but it will stay contained. That's why I'm here and the Secret Service isn't. I do have a proposition for you. Would you like an opportunity to repay the favor to Hale?'

She'd already been thinking on how to do just that since they now possessed a way to draw Hale from the shadows. What better route than a source he thought his own?

'I'd like that,' Kaiser said. 'Truly, I would.'

But something was still bothering her. What Pauline Daniels had said. *A friend I don't want my husband talking to.*

Pauline was afraid of what Kaiser knew about her. Something that might not remain secret if questions were asked.

And she suddenly realized what that was.

'The First Lady is having an affair. Isn't she?'

The question did not catch Kaiser off guard. It was as if she'd been expecting it.

'Not exactly. But close enough.'

Malone stepped from the car, now stopped under the covered entrance of The Jefferson, Richmond, Virginia's most impressive hotel. The Beaux-Arts-style building, built at the end of the 19th century, sat downtown a few blocks from the state capitol. Its grand lobby was reminiscent of the Gilded Age, highlighted by a white marble statue of Jefferson himself. Malone had stayed there several times. He liked the place. He also liked the strange look the bellman tossed him when he handed over a five-dollar bill and the keys to the bullet-ridden car.

'Soon-to-be-ex-wife found me.'

The guy seemed to understand.

Though it was pushing three AM the front desk was manned and ready. A room was available but, before he headed up, a twenty-dollar tip bought him entrance to the locked business center. Inside, with the door closed, he rubbed his temples, closed his eyes, and tried to empty his mind. His body was drained with fatigue but, even though he understood the risk he was about to take, he had to do it.

He tapped the keyboard and found the email he'd sent to himself.

Hale stared at the accused traitor. One of *Adventure*'s crew, a man who'd been with the company for only eight years. Not one of the generationals, but a trusted associate nonetheless. A trial had been immediately convened – presided over, as specified in the Articles, by the quartermaster. Hale, along with the rest of *Adventure*'s crew, served as jury.

'My contact in the NIA bragged they had a spy among us,' Knox said. 'He knew all about today's execution aboard *Adventure*.'

'Exactly what do they know?' Hale asked.

'That your accountant is at the bottom of the Atlantic. The names of the crewmen who tossed him, and all the others on board. All of them, yourself included, being guilty of willful murder.'

He saw how those words sent a shiver through the jury, each one of them now implicated. This was justice at its purest. Men who lived, fought, died, and sat in judgment together.

'What say you?' Knox asked the accused. 'Do you deny this?'

The man said nothing. But this was not a court of law. No Fifth Amendment privileges existed. Silence could, and would, be used against him.

Knox explained how the prisoner's marriage was in trouble and he'd turned to another woman who'd become pregnant. He'd offered her money for an abortion, which she refused, telling him she intended on having the baby. She also threatened to inform the wife if he did not support her.

'The NIA offered cash for information,' Knox said. 'And this man took it.'

'How do you know that?' one of the crewmen asked.

Questions were encouraged and could be offered at will.

'Because I killed the man who made the deal.' Knox faced the accused. 'Scott Parrott. A NIA agent. He's dead.'

The accused stood stoic.

'I spoke to Parrott at length,' Knox said. 'He was gloating about how he knew exactly what we were doing. That's how he was ready today to stop the attempt on President Daniels' life. He knew exactly where and when. He was planning on killing me as well, which is why he was so free with information. Fortunately, he failed.'

Hale stared straight at the accused and wanted to know, 'Did you sell us out?'

The man bolted for the door.

Two men cut off his escape and tackled him to the floor, where he struggled to get free.

Knox faced the jurors. 'Have you seen and heard enough?'

They each nodded.

'The judgment is guilty,' one of them shouted.

Knox asked, 'Does anyone object?'

None did.

The prisoner kept struggling, screaming, 'No way. This is wrong.'

Hale knew what the Articles provided. *To betray the crew, desert, or abandon a battle is punished as the Quartermaster or Majority shall think fit.*

'Bring him,' Hale ordered.

The man was yanked to his feet.

This sorry no-good had placed him in an untenable position with Andrea Carbonell. No wonder she'd been so damn smug. She knew it all. Everything he'd anticipated might now be compromised. This man's death would be excruciating. An example to everyone.

Knox produced a gun.

'What are you doing?' he asked the quartermaster.

'Meting out punishment.'

A panic came over the accused's face as he realized his fate. He renewed his struggle against the two men restraining him.

'It's as the quartermaster, *or majority*, shall think fit,' Hale said, quoting the Articles. 'What say the majority?'

He watched as *Adventure*'s crew took their cue from him

and, to a man, echoed, 'Whatever you want, Captain,' each grateful that it wasn't him about to die. Normally, a captain never questioned the quartermaster in front of the crew or vice versa. But this was wartime, when the captain's word went unquestioned.

'He'll die at seven AM, with the entire company present.'

36

Cassiopeia drove away from Shirley Kaiser's neighborhood, found an empty shopping mall parking lot, and called the White House.

'You're not going to like this,' she said to Edwin Davis.

And she told him everything, holding back only the last thing she and Kaiser had discussed.

'This has potential, though,' she said. 'We could draw Hale out, if played right.'

'I see that.'

There was a lot more to say, but she was tired, and it could wait. 'I'm going to get some sleep. We can talk in the morning.'

A moment of silence passed before Davis said, 'I'll be here.'

She ended the call.

Before she could restart the motorcycle and find a motel the phone dinged again. She checked the display. Cotton. About time.

'What happened?' she asked.

'Just another fun night. I need the Secret Service to run a license plate. But I think I already know who the car belongs to.'

He gave her information for a Maryland tag.

'But there's a bright spot,' he said.

She could use one of those.

'The cipher's been broken. I now know the message Andrew Jackson left for the Commonwealth.'

'Where are you?' she asked.

'Richmond. At a lovely hotel called The Jefferson.'

'I'm in Fredericksburg. Is that nearby?'

'About an hour away.'

'I'll join you.'

During my preliminary research in the National Archives, I found correspondence that Robert Patterson, a mathematics professor at the University of Pennsylvania, wrote to Thomas Jefferson in December 1801. By then, Jefferson was president of the United States. Both Patterson and Jefferson were officials at the American Philosophical Society, a group that promoted scholarly research in the sciences and humanities. Both were also enthusiasts of ciphers and codes, regularly exchanging them. Patterson wrote, 'The art of secret writing has engaged the attention both of the statesman and philosopher for many ages.' But Patterson noted that most ciphers fall 'far short of perfection.' For Patterson the perfect code came with four properties: (1) It should be adaptable to all languages; (2) be simple to learn and memorize; (3) easy to read and write; and (4) most of all, 'be absolutely inscrutable to all unacquainted with the particular key or secret for deciphering.'

Patterson included with his letter an example of a cipher so difficult to decode that it 'would defy the united ingenuity of the whole human race.' Bold words from a man of the 19th century, but that was before the existence of high-speed computer algorithms.

Patterson made the task especially difficult, explaining in his letter that, first, he wrote a message text vertically, in column grids, from left to right, using lowercase letters or spaces, with rows of 5 letters. He then added random letters to each line. To solve the cipher meant knowing the number of lines, the order in which those lines were transcribed, and the number of random letters added to each line.

Here are the letters from Andrew Jackson's message:

XQXFEETH
APKLJHXREHNJF
TSYOL:
EJWIWM
PZKLRIELCPΔ
FESZR
OPPOBOUQDX
MLZKRGVKΦ
EPRISZXNOXEΘ

    The key to deciphering this code is a series of two-digit number pairs. Patterson explained in his letter that the first digit of each pair indicated the line number within a section, the second digit the number of letters added to the beginning of that row. Of course, Patterson never revealed the number keys, which has kept his cipher unsolved for 175 years. To discover this numeric key, I analyzed the probability of diagraphs. Certain pairs of letters simply do not exist in English, such as dx, *while some almost always appear together, such as* qu. *To ascertain a sense of language patterns for Patterson and Jefferson's time I studied the 80,000 letter characters contained in Jefferson's State of the Union addresses and counted the frequency of diagraph occurrences. I then made a series of educated guesses such as the number of rows per section, which two rows belong next to one another, and the number of random letters inserted into a line. To vet these guesses I turned to a computer algorithm and what's called dynamic programming, which solves massive problems by breaking the puzzle down into component pieces and linking the solutions together. The overall calculations to analyze were fewer than 100,000, which is not all that tedious. It's important to note that the programs available to me are not available to the general public, which might explain why the cipher has remained unbroken. After a week of working the code, the computer discovered the numerical key.*

    33, 28, 71, 12, 56, 40, 85, 64, 97.

To utilize the key, let's return to the cipher rows themselves and lay them one after the other, per Patterson's instructions:

XQXFEETHAPKLJHXREHNJFTSYOL:
EJWIWMPZKLRIELCPΔFESZROPPOB
OUQDXMLZKRGVKΦEPRISZXNOXEΘ

If we apply the first numerical key, 33, to the letters we would count 3 over on the first row then identify the next 5 letters, FEETH. The next number, 3, indicates the original position of this letter row. Using 28, you would count 2 more letters over and identify 5 letters that would be placed in the row 8 position. By applying the remaining keys to the letters, the grid reappears in its original order:

JWIWM
EHNJF
FEETH
FESZR
ELCPΔ
RGVKΦ
SYOL:
OUQDX
NOXEΘ

The message can be read vertically down the 5 columns from left to right:

JEFFERSONWHEEL
GYUOINESCVOQXWJTZPKLDEMFHR
ΔΦ:XΘ

Malone read again Voccio's report and Andrew Jackson's coded message.

Jefferson Wheel.

Followed by twenty-six random letters and five symbols.

He'd already surfed the Internet and determined what the words *Jefferson Wheel* meant. Twenty-six wooden disks, upon which were carved the letters of the alphabet in random sequence. Each disk was numbered 1 through 26 and, depending on the order in which the disks were threaded onto an iron spindle, and the manner in which they were aligned, coded messages could be passed. The only requirement was that the sender and receiver had to possess the same collection of disks and arrange them in the same order. Jefferson conceived the idea himself from cipher locks he'd read about in French journals.

The problem?

Only one wheel still existed.

Jefferson's own.

Which had been lost for decades but now was on display at Monticello, Jefferson's Virginia estate. Malone assumed the twenty-six random letters in Jackson's message would align the disks.

But what order should the disks be in?

Since none was specified, he would assume numerically. So when the disks were threaded in the correct sequence, then properly arranged, twenty-five lines would contain nonsense.

One would reveal a cohesive message.

He hadn't told Cassiopeia what he'd found.

Not on the phone.

Monticello was less than an hour to the west.

They'd go there tomorrow.

Wyatt found a hotel just outside Washington, a boutique establishment that came with a computer in the room. He figured in the not-too-distant future that accessory would be as standard as a hair dryer and a television.

He inserted the flash drive and read what Voccio had deciphered.

Smart guy.

A shame he was dead, but it was his own fault. Those men had come to herd them both to that waiting car. Just fire some shots, allow him to do his thing and think he succeeded, then wait and watch as the bomb took care of two problems at once.

Carbonell was covering her tracks. The NSA and CIA moving on him may have spooked her. One less witness against you was never a bad thing.

He was mad with himself, though. He knew better. But he'd wanted the money, and thought he could stay a step ahead.

Thank goodness for a little luck.

On a website for Monticello, he read about the Jefferson Wheel, noting that it was on display inside the mansion. The estate was located not far away. He'd go there tomorrow and do what he had to do to obtain the wheel.

He checked his watch.

4:10 AM.

A few clicks on the keyboard and he learned that Monticello opened at nine AM.

That gave him five hours to deal with Andrea Carbonell.

PART THREE

37

Wyatt admired the condominium. Roomy, stylish, pricey. He'd easily gained entry, the door secured by a simple lock. No alarm, no dog, no lights. It was located outside the Beltway in an upscale area replete with trendy stores and upscale eateries, the attractive complex iron-gated. He assumed a remote-controlled entry made for a good selling point to potential tenants who liked the status of having their guests wait for the bars to open. His own condominium in Florida came with gate and guard, which cost him and several thousand others a few hundred dollars a month in assessments.

But it was worth it. Kept the riffraff out.

He studied the décor, an odd mixture of minimalist style and Caribbean influences from onyx, wrought iron, and terra-cotta. Dim light leaking past the windows revealed a vibrant mixture of color and tone. He found a CD stack and noted a theme – mostly mambo, salsa, and Latin jazz. None of it his taste, but he could see how it would suit the condo's owner.

Andrea Carbonell.

He'd called on longtime sources and learned where she lived. Unlike most of her colleagues, she resided beyond the DC limits and was ferried to and from work each day in a government car with driver. That same source had also told him that Carbonell was aboard an NIA helicopter that would land at Dulles in thirty minutes. She'd already informed her office that she would not be at her desk until eight AM. He hoped that meant she planned to come home for a quick stop. She'd been out all night, traveling somewhere south after she'd dropped him in Maryland. For someone so careful about her thoughts and plans, he wondered about her carelessness when it came to her schedule. He also wondered about the attack in Maryland. Did Carbonell already know that Dr. Gary Voccio was dead? No doubt.

All yesterday she'd stayed a step ahead of him.

Today was his turn.

He noticed nothing personal or intimate on display anywhere. No photographs, keepsakes, nothing. She apparently had no husband, boyfriend, children, girlfriend, pet.

But who was he to talk?

He possessed none of those, either. He lived alone, always had. There hadn't been a woman in years. Several prospects – divorced, widowed, or still married – had expressed an interest, but he'd never reciprocated. Simply the thought of sharing himself, in return for the other person offering up their vulnerabilities, turned his stomach. He preferred solitude, and the quiet that now enveloped him.

But a sound intruded.

His gaze shot toward the front door.

A scraping.

Not of a key entering the lock, but of someone working the mechanism.

As he'd just done.

He found his gun and retreated into one of the bedrooms, positioning himself so that he could spy around the jamb.

The front door slowly opened and a dark formed stepped inside.

Male. About Wyatt's height and build, wearing black clothing, moving in silent steps.

Apparently, he was not the only one interested in Carbonell.

Knox detoured to his house for a shower and change of clothes. His wife greeted him with her usual cheerfulness, not asking a thing about where he'd been or what he'd done. That was made clear long ago. His work for the Commonwealth was confidential. Of course, she believed the reasons for that involved legitimate corporate concerns and trade secrets. Not presidential assassinations, kidnappings, murder, and a variety of other lesser felonies he committed on an almost daily basis. She knew only that her husband loved her, their children were provided for, and they were happy. The secrecy of his life had afforded him countless opportunities to do as he pleased. He'd learned from his father, who'd also been a quartermaster, that with risk came reward.

Is it unfair to your mother, his father had said, *that I have other women? Damn right it is. But I'm the one out there, not her. I'll go to prison, if caught. Not her. Always, in the end, I come home to her. I provide for her. I'll grow old with her. But while I can, I'm entitled to live as I please.*

He hadn't understood that selfish attitude until his turn came and he witnessed the demands of the job firsthand. Two hundred fourteen men made up the current company, spread among the four families. He served at their pleasure and they counted on him. But the four captains also demanded that he safeguard their interests. And though the captains could not fire him, they could make his life an utter hell.

Fail either and the penalty was severe.

A good quartermaster came to understand that balance. And yes, an occasional roll in the sack here and there with women he encountered might relieve the stress. But he'd never succumbed. He loved his wife and his family. Cheating on either was not an option. His father had not been right about everything. Not on married life – nor the

Commonwealth. Things had changed since his father's time, and he often wondered what that man would have done if faced with the current challenges. The captains fought among themselves with a rising intensity, one that was threatening the company's existence. The long-standing ties that bound them together seemed ready to snap. Even so, he'd made a horrible mistake becoming entangled with Andrea Carbonell. Thank God the traitor she'd pointed him toward had implicated himself beyond question. In a strange way, he could sympathize with that doomed soul.

Trapped. Nowhere to go.

At the mercy of others.

'You look tired,' his wife said to him from the bathroom door.

He was about to shower and shave. 'Long night.'

'We can go to the beach next weekend and rest.'

They had a cottage near Cape Hatteras, which he'd inherited from his father.

'That sounds great,' he said. 'You and me. Next weekend.'

She smiled and hugged him from behind.

He studied her face in the mirror.

They'd been together twenty-five years, marrying young and raising three children. She was his best friend. Unfortunately, a huge part of his life remained a mystery to her. Where his father had kept secrets and cheated, he only kept secrets. He wondered what she'd do if she knew what he really did.

That he killed people.

'The weather should be great,' she said. 'Nice and cool.'

He turned and kissed her, then said, 'I love you.'

She smiled. 'That's always nice to hear. I love you, too.'

'I wish I didn't have to go back to the estate.' He saw she registered what he meant.

'How about tonight?'

He smiled at the prospect. 'You've got a date.'

She kissed him again, then left him alone.

His thoughts returned to the problem.

He needed the matter of the traitor ended. The captains' fears must be eased. Nothing could point his way. He now knew why Carbonell had allowed him to kill Scott Parrott. Why not? Sure, it helped him with the captains, doing what they expected, but Parrott's death also eliminated the only other person at NIA he'd ever dealt with.

Making him totally dependent on her.

Not good.

He steadied himself.

Two more hours and he should be in the clear.

Wyatt watched the newcomer. The burglar had made no search, apparently aware that the condo would be empty. He'd toted in a dark bundle, laying the bag on the floor and quickly emptying its contents. A chair from the dining area was brought close to the front door. What looked like a gun was attached with clamps to its back, the legs braced with the couch that was slid into position. He then installed screw eyes in the ceiling, the jamb, and the door itself, threading string from the gun's trigger, through each one, to the knob.

He realized what was being created.

A spring gun.

Once used to protect property in remote locations. Rigged to a door or window so anyone who broke inside would be shot. They'd been illegal for decades. A bit old-fashioned and out of date.

But effective.

The man finished his work, testing the string's tautness, then he carefully opened the door and slipped out.

He wondered.

Who else's patience had run out?

38

Bath, North Carolina

Hale could not sleep. He'd hoped to after the trial, return-ing home and retiring to his bedroom. But too many troubling thoughts swirled through his head. At least the matter of the traitor seemed resolved. Knox had handled the situation exactly as a quartermaster should. Shortly, the captains would demonstrate to the entire company what happened to those who violated the Articles. Reminders of that fact were never a bad thing. What truly concerned him, though, was the cipher's solution.

Could Carbonell provide it?

Parrot had lied to Knox.

Was she lying to him?

Would he finally succeed where his father, grandfather, great-grandfather, and great-great-grandfather failed?

'It is indecipherable,' his father told him. 'Just letters on a page. No order or reason.'

'Why do we need it?' he asked with the innocence of someone not yet twenty. 'We're not threatened. Our letter of marque is being respected.'

'That's true. This president has been mindful, and most have been. Wilson, during World War I, was grateful for all our efforts. Roosevelt, too, during the Second World War. But four times our government chose not to honor its agreement, resting on the fact that there was no express congressional approval for our letter. They laughed at us, as

Andrew Jackson did, knowing that, legally, our letter of marque was not enforceable. Those four men became problems.'

His father had never spoken of this before.

'Which four?'

'The ones who died from a gun.'

Had he heard right?

'Quentin, your brother and sisters know nothing of what I do, only that we own and control many business entities. They, of course, are aware of our sea heritage, as you are, and they are proud of the role we played in forming this country. But they are ignorant of what we have done afterward.'

And so was he, but his father was teaching him by the day.

'During the Civil War, the Union called on us to stop the Confederacy from being supplied by sea. We were encouraged to attack French and English cargo vessels. While the Union navy blockaded key southern ports, we ravaged ships at sea. But we could not forget that we were of the South. So we allowed some to sneak through. Enough that the Confederacy lingered longer than it should have.'

He'd never heard this before.

'Lincoln was furious. During the war, he needed us. He knew what Jackson had done — that our letters of marque were foundationless — but he ignored that weakness and encouraged our strengths. When the war was won, he changed course. Arrest warrants were issued, and the Commonwealth was to be tried for piracy.' His father paused, the dark eyes focused intently on his son. 'I remember when Papa told me what I am about to tell you.'

His father was nearing seventy and in poor health. Hale was the youngest of the brood, not coming along until his father was nearly fifty. His older brother and sisters were far more accomplished and successful than him, yet he'd been chosen.

'Lincoln knew that with two missing pages from the congressional journals our letters of marque were flawed. Foolishly, we'd trusted him. If tried, we had no defense. The captains would have gone to prison, or perhaps been shot as traitors.'

'But no Hale has ever gone to jail.'

His father nodded. 'Because he made sure that Abraham Lincoln died.'

He still recalled the amazement when his father told him what the Commonwealth had done, completing the connection between Andrew Jackson and Abraham Lincoln.

'Abner Hale tried to assassinate Andrew Jackson. He recruited and encouraged Richard Lawrence to kill the president. Jackson realized this immediately. That's why he retaliated, gutting the letters of marque. The reason Abner acted was because Jackson refused to pardon two pirates convicted of robbing an American ship. It was a popular case in its time, one with all the things we've come to expect: celebrated lawyers, interesting personalities, allegations of official misconduct. The guilty verdicts were so controversial that they inspired death threats on Jackson. One came from a flamboyant Shakespearean actor. He wrote a scathing note and threatened to cut the president's throat while he was sleeping, or to have him burned at the stake in Washington, DC, if a pardon was not issued. The man who wrote those words was Junius Brutus Booth.' His father paused. *'The father of John Wilkes who, twenty-six years later, was used by the Commonwealth to assassinate Abraham Lincoln.'*

Now he knew how the captains in 1865 escaped prosecution.

'We ended the threat,' his father said, *'by recruiting the younger Booth, which wasn't all that difficult. People with causes in their hearts are common. Most are unstable and easily manipulated. Lincoln's assassination threw the government into chaos. All talk of arrests ended. Even better, Booth died while trying to escape. Four other conspirators were quickly arrested, tried, and hung. Five more were imprisoned. Those nine knew nothing of us. So we survived.'*

And the Commonwealth would this time, too.

But everything rested on Andrea Carbonell, and how desperately she wanted Stephanie Nelle dead.

He had to play that card carefully.

A knock on his bedroom door caught his attention.

His secretary stepped inside. 'I saw the light and decided to alert you.'

He was listening.

'The prisoner has asked to see you.'

'Which one?'

'The traitor.'

'For what reason?'

'He did not say. Only that he wishes to speak with you. Alone.'

Malone awoke and checked the bedside clock.

6:50 AM.

Cassiopeia lay beside him, still sleeping. They'd been out for a little over two hours. He wore his undershirt and boxers. She was naked, her preferred bedclothes, which he liked. He studied her contoured curves. Not a blemish disturbed the swarthy patina. She was a beautiful woman.

If only they had more time.

He swung his legs to the floor.

'What are you doing?' she asked.

He'd learned she was a light sleeper.

'We have to get going.'

'What happened last night?'

He'd promised her an explanation when they awoke. So he told her, then said, 'I deleted the cipher solution off the Garver server but that's only going to stop the people who went there for a few hours. They probably already know I emailed a copy to myself.'

He waited for it to hit her.

'Which means they know you're here,' she said.

'I used another name to register and paid in cash. It cost me a hundred-dollar tip, but the clerk didn't ask for any identification. I told him I didn't want my wife to know where I was.' He reached for his clothes. 'I knew when I accessed that email last night, they'd trace it here. But I want to know who *they* are. It's possible they could lead us to Stephanie.'

'You think they'll make a play?'

'Oh, yeah. My guess is they're downstairs waiting. The question is, how much attention do they want to draw? We do have one advantage. An unknown factor to them.'

And he saw she understood.

'That's right. You.'

39

W yatt stared out the window as an SUV cruised into the parking lot. No further visitors had entered Carbonell's condominium, and the spring gun sat waiting. He'd inspected the gadget and wondered if the Commonwealth had planted it. It was certainly a device that fit their operating mode. But that could have been exactly why someone else chose the method. Clearly, Carbonell had double-crossed more than one participant in this dispute, and neither the Commonwealth nor the intelligence community could be happy with her. But he could not help thinking that perhaps, like last night, she'd ordered it herself.

What was she thinking?'

He watched as Carbonell stepped from the vehicle, the interior cabin light revealing her wearing the same clothes from yesterday. She said something to the driver, then marched toward the building entrance. Her apartment was on the second floor, past an unlocked ground-floor door. The SUV waited in its parking spot, lights off.

He stepped over to the gun.

The ingenious array of screw eyes had been geometrically arranged so that the door, as opened, gradually tightened the twine, working the trigger. The gun was an automatic rifle. He'd already checked. Fully loaded with more than enough rounds to obliterate any and all the flesh and bone standing less than two feet away.

He tested the nylon one more time.

Taut as a guitar string.

Would it matter if she died?

Cassiopeia strolled off the elevator and into The Jefferson's lobby. She'd already called down and asked that her motorcycle be brought to the front entrance. She'd valet-parked it on arrival.

Four policeman waited to her left, near the marble statue of Thomas Jefferson that dominated the lobby's center.

Apparently, this was not to be a subtle encounter.

She casually drifted their way, the click of her boots announcing her presence. Outside, past the glass doors, she spotted three Richmond city police cars. Whoever had attacked Cotton last night had apparently decided to stay in the shadows today and allow the locals to take the heat. She caught a few concerned looks on the faces of guests who milled back and forth, carrying their morning paper, or a briefcase, or navigating a roller bag.

But she ignored them all and assessed the geography.

The lobby was L-shaped and huge. To her left a grand staircase swept down into an atrium lined with what appeared to be marble columns – which she discovered, on closer inspection, were faux-painted. The ceiling reached twenty-plus meters to a stained-glass skylight. Tapestries and Victorian-era furniture added to an Old World feel. At the far side of the two-story atrium she spotted another set of glass exit doors, adjacent to a restaurant.

Her mind worked out a plan.

Could she do it?

Sure.

Plenty of room to maneuver.

* * *

Hale entered the prison that had once acted as a stable for the estate's horses. Stephanie Nelle was confined on the second floor, the traitor on the ground. He'd specifically ordered that they not see each other, much less have an opportunity to speak. He'd initially resisted the urge to come, but he wanted to hear what this man had to say.

The accused sat on a cot and remained seated when Hale appeared. He opted to stand outside the cell and speak through the bars. He'd ordered that the upstairs door be closed and a radio played on the next floor so nothing of their conversation could leak upward.

'What do you want?' he quietly asked.

'There are things you need to know.'

No hint of fear laced the words. This man seemed to be facing his fate with courage. He liked that. His crew was tough. He always laughed at the image of a sailor being conscripted by a pirate ship, forced, kicking and screaming, into unwilling service. In reality, when a captain dropped the word that his ship was 'going on the account,' every tavern, brothel, and alleyway buzzed with anticipation. If that captain had been successful on previous voyages, former shipmates were usually first to sign on. Others wanting to join in success came next. Pirating paid well, and men of that time were interested in the most return for their risky investment. None of them wanted to die. All wanted to return to port and enjoy their share of the spoils. Still, a captain had to be cautious in his choices – once the articles were agreed upon and the ship sailed, he could be removed by that crew. Of course, that was no longer the case. Heredity now determined a captain. But there remained risks, and this man was a perfect example.

'I'm here. Talk.'

'I told the NIA about the murder on *Adventure*. I admit that. They offered me money, so I took it.'

Hale already knew that, but wanted to know, 'Are you proud of what you did?'

'I realize this whole company thing is important to you. All for one, one for all, and all that. But let's face it, you get the cake and we get the crumbs.'

'Those crumbs are far more than anyone else was giving you.'

'They are. But I never really bought into all this.'

Recruitment had always been accomplished by the quartermaster, usually from proven families who'd worked for the Commonwealth. Just as in former times, modern crews were generally ill educated and came from poor to modest backgrounds. But still—

'Is your word not good for anything?' he asked. 'You signed the Articles and swore an oath. That means nothing?'

The man shrugged. 'I did it for the money. Also, Knox got me out of some bad trouble. I appreciated that. I'm good with metal. So when he offered me a job, I took it.'

'You apparently did not appreciate things enough to keep your word and be loyal.'

'You're the one who killed that guy on the boat. He was a threat to you. Not me, or any of the others. I betrayed you, not them.'

'Is this what you wanted to say to me?'

He caught the hard look of disgust on the man's face. 'I wanted you to know that I didn't know a damn thing about any assassination attempt. The first I heard about it was on television, after it happened. Yeah, I worked on the gun in the metal shop and recognized it when I saw it on the news. But we weren't told a thing about when, or where, it was going to be used. I had no clue, and I didn't say a word about it to the NIA.'

'You're a liar and a traitor. Not to be believed.'

The man shrugged. 'Suit yourself. But just know that there

are two traitors in your precious company, and one of them is still out there.'

'Why are you telling me this?'

'Two reasons. One, like I said, I never betrayed my friends and they need to know that there's a spy among them. And two, since there's no way I'm going to get of here, when it comes time for me to die, I hope you'll at least be merciful.'

40

Malone entered the elevator. Cassiopeia had reconnoitered The Jefferson's ground floor, noting that three Richmond city police cars guarded the main entrance, but the second exit that opened onto West Main Street at the south end of the lobby was unguarded. She'd reported by cellphone that this seemed a local operation, which meant he would learn nothing by hanging around. He'd hoped some of the principals would reveal themselves. Knowing the solution to Jefferson's cipher gave him bargaining power, and he'd wanted an opportunity to use it. Since that was not going to be the case, what waited at Monticello now seemed more promising.

Unfortunately, there was the matter of the police.

Cassiopeia had descended three long flights of carpeted stairs into a faux-marble hall, then walked a hundred feet to glass doors at the south end of the lobby. They were locked and the hostess in a nearby restaurant explained that the doors were not opened until nine each day. Apparently the police had decided the locked doors were enough protection, and controlling the upper lobby, the stairwells, and the main exit would be their play. Since he hadn't registered using his real name, searching every room was impractical. Easier to simply wait for him to walk off the elevator and into their arms.

But they'd never met Cassiopeia Vitt.

She'd told him her escape plan over the phone. He'd shook his head, then said, *Okay. Why not?*

The elevator door opened.

He stepped off, turned left, and walked toward the main desk,

intending on making another left and descending the stairs to the lower level. He realized he'd never get that far and, just as predicted, three uniformed officers appeared from his right and yelled for him to stop.

He did.

'Cotton Malone,' the lead officer said, who appeared to be a captain. 'We have a warrant for your arrest.'

'I know I have a lot of unpaid parking tickets. I tear 'em up. I shouldn't, but –'

'Put your hands behind your back,' a second officer ordered.

Cassiopeia watched as the attendant roared up on the motorcycle. The Honda NT700V came with a liquid-cooled, 680cc, V-twin, eight-valve engine that packed a kick, and the young man seemed to enjoy the jaunt from the parking lot. He climbed off, leaving the engine running, holding the two-hundred-plus-kilogram machine steady while she climbed on.

She handed him a fifty-dollar bill.

He nodded in appreciation.

Two police cars were parked beyond the porte cochere, ahead of her, another positioned behind her, all with drivers inside. She'd caught the officer at her flank giving her ass the once-over, her tight jeans doing their duty.

'I need you to do something for me,' she said to the attendant.

'Name it.'

She pointed to one of the entrances that led into the lobby. 'Could you hold that glass door open for me?'

*   *   *

Malone turned and complied with the officer's command. The important thing was to keep the guns in holsters and, so far, none of them had drawn a weapon.

'What's this about?' he asked.

'You're a person of interest,' the first cop said as he gripped Malone's wrists. 'The feds want to talk to you.'

'Why aren't they here?' he asked.

The grip on his wrists tightened.

'Cotton,' one of the other cops said. 'Where'd you get a name like that?'

The growl of a motorcycle grew louder as a glass door opened fifty feet to his left.

'Long story,' he said, spotting Cassiopeia, outside, astride the motorcycle.

He smiled.

You had to love her.

Cassiopeia revved the sixty-five-horsepower engine and noticed in her rearview mirror that the policeman behind remained more concerned with her ass than where she might be going. Clearly he hadn't paid the attendant, standing ten meters away holding the door open, any attention.

She yanked the handlebars to the right, popped the clutch into first, and strained the engine. Tires spinning, she swung right, straightened out, and sped through the open doorway into the lobby.

Knox stood before the company, which had assembled in the yard before the jail at precisely seven AM. Two hundred and four of the 214 were present, the absentees excused only because they were out of town. One rule was clear. A call to assemble could not be ignored.

Since none of the three Hale children was on the estate, the gathering could be held in private. The front gates were locked, video-monitored by staff in the security building who were witnessing punishment electronically. This was sacred ground. Where the company had gathered since the Commonwealth's formation. For 250 years, thousands of men had stood and listened to pronouncements, buried captains, elected quarter-masters, or, as today, bore witness to punishment.

He'd personally supervised the prisoner's preparation, making sure the hands were bound and the mouth gagged. He did not want any outbursts or speeches. This matter had to end here and now.

But he'd been troubled by what the jailer had reported. The prisoner had requested to speak privately with Hale and the captain had obliged, spending a few minutes alone with the man.

Disturbing. No question.

His gaze focused on the four captains, clustered at the far end of the yard. The prisoner was tied to a pine stake in the center, the company assembled at the other end.

He stepped forward.

'This man has been tried and convicted of treason. Punishment was proclaimed to be death.'

He allowed those words to take hold. The whole idea of discipline was for it to be memorable.

He faced the captains. 'What say you as to the method?'

In centuries past there were options. Shackled and chained, then locked away with no food or water? That took days. Dangled from a mast until exposure and starvation proved fatal? Faster. Flogging with a cat-o'-nine-tails? Even quicker since the knotted leather strips killed in a matter of minutes.

Today, options existed, too.

Hanging. Shooting. Drowning.

'Woodling,' Hale called out.

41

Wyatt waited beside the spring gun as a key was inserted into the lock on the other side of the door.

He watched the knob turn.

Andrea Carbonell was about to enter her residence. Was she oblivious to the fact that the simple act of coming home would end her life?

The door opened.

Nylon whined as it tightened through the screw eyes.

Hinges pivoted thirty degrees, forty, forty-five.

He'd already determined that at least a sixty-degree arc would be needed for the trigger to engage.

His foot stopped the door's advance and he snipped the line with scissors.

He withdrew his shoe and the door fully opened.

Carbonell stared at him, then the gun, the nylon swinging in the dim light. Not a hint of surprise flooded her face.

'Was it a tough choice?' she asked.

He still held the scissors. 'More than I thought it would be.'

'Obviously not your doing. Who?'

He shrugged. 'A man came, did his thing, and left.'

'Whom you did not stop.'

He shrugged. 'Not my business.'

'I suppose I should be grateful you're here.'

'How about grateful that I snipped the string.'

She stepped inside and closed the door. 'Why'd you do it? You have to be angry about what happened last night.'

'I am. You wanted me dead.'

'Come now, Jonathan. I have a much greater respect for your skills.'

He lunged at her, his right hand clamping tight on her neck, slamming her thin frame into the wall. Framed pictures nearby rattled on their hangers.

'You wanted my skills to kill me. You wanted me to get Voccio out of there. Flush us both to the car, then blow us up.'

'Did you come to kill me?' she breathed out, his grip still tight. Not a hint of concern seeped from her.

He'd made his point. He released his grip.

She stood and stared at him, composing herself. Then she caressed the spring gun, admiring its workmanship. 'High caliber, automatic fire. How many rounds? Thirty? Forty? There would have been little left of me.'

He could not care less. 'You have the cipher solution.'

'Voccio emailed it to me a few hours before you arrived. But I suppose you already know that. Hence, your anger.'

'I have more than that to be angry about.'

She apprised him with a long gaze. 'I suppose you do.'

'That solution will not remain a secret for long.'

'Jonathan, *you* have such little faith in *my* abilities. I had it emailed from outside the institute. Only Voccio knew from where. Now he's dead.'

'Isn't that convenient?'

She caught his drift. 'You believe those men there last night came from me.' She pointed to the spring gun. 'You probably believe that I planted this here, too.'

'Both are entirely possible.'

'It would do no good for me to deny either. You wouldn't believe me. So I won't.' She relieved him of the scissors, which he still held. 'From my desk?'

He said nothing.

'I like you, Jonathan. I always have.'

'I didn't know you liked cigars.' He'd caught the lingering scent in the air and found three antique humidors, each filled with smokes.

'My father once made them. My family lived at Ybor City, in Tampa. Many of the 1960s Cuban immigrants settled there. Florida was like home. It was once quite a place. Ever been?'

He shook his head.

'Spaniards, Cubans, Italians, Germans, Jews, Chinese. We all coexisted, thriving off one another. What an exciting place. So alive. Then it all ended, and they built an interstate highway straight down its middle.'

He kept silent and let her talk. She was buying time. Okay. Buy it.

'My father opened a cigar factory and did well. There were many in Ybor back in the 1920s, before the Great Depression, but gradually they all disappeared. He was determined to bring them back. No machines for him. All of his smokes were hand rolled, one at a time. I acquired a taste for them early in life.'

He knew that her parents had fled Castro in the 1960s and that she'd been born and raised here. Beyond that, she was a mystery.

'Have you always been a man of few words?'

'I say what I need to say.'

She stepped around the gun and came closer. 'My parents were quite wealthy when they lived in Cuba. They were capitalists, and Castro hated capitalists. They left everything they owned and came here, starting over, intent on proving themselves a second time. They loved America, and at first this country gave them another chance. Then bad economies and bad choices took it all away. They lost everything.' She paused and stared at him through the dark. 'They died broke.'

He wondered why she was telling him this.

'The opportunists who fled Cuba in the 1980s? The Mariel boat people? They tried to buy into Castro, and when it didn't work out they decided to come here. All they did was make it hard for the others, my parents included. They should be sent back to live with what they embraced.' She paused. 'I worked my way up. Every step. No one gave me anything. When my father died I swore to him that I would not make the mistakes he made. That I'd be careful. But unfortunately, I made an error today.' Her eyes locked on him. 'Yet you gave me a reprieve. Why? So you could kill me yourself?'

'I'm going after the Jefferson Wheel,' he told her. 'If you interfere, I'll kill anyone you send, then I *will* kill you.'

'Why do you care? This really doesn't concern you anymore.'

'A man died last night for no reason other than he did his job.'

She laughed. 'And that affects you?'

'It *affects* you.'

He saw she understood. He could cause her problems. Change all of her plans. Screw up her life.

'Malone has the cipher key, too,' she said. 'He emailed it to himself last night from Voccio's computer, then deleted it from the institute's server. There is no other record of the solution. Only you, he, and I have it.'

'He'll go straight to Monticello.'

He stepped around her toward the door.

She grabbed his arm, her face only inches away. 'You can't do this alone and you know it.'

That he did. Too many unknowns. Too much risk. And he was not properly prepared.

'You don't fool me, Jonathan. This isn't about me and what happened last night. It's Malone. You don't want him to succeed. I can see it in your eyes.'

'Maybe I just want you to fail.'

'Go to Monticello. Get what we both want. What you do with Malone is your business. What you and I do is between us. I'm betting you can keep those two separate. You need me. That's why I'm still alive.'

She was right.

The only reason.

'Get that wheel,' she said.

'Why don't you get it yourself?'

'As I told you in New York, I prefer to owe only you.'

That meant she was hearing the end of whatever she'd planned. Involving any of her agents would only require more cleanup.

'You actually wanted Scott Parrott dead, didn't you?'

'If he'd done his job, he wouldn't be dead.'

'He never had a chance.'

'Unlike those three agents you ordered in after banging Malone in the head with a gun? They *had* a chance, right?'

The fingers in his right hand tensed into a fist, but he caught himself. That was exactly the reaction she wanted.

'Get the wheel, Jonathan. Then we'll talk.'

Malone spun and kicked one of the Richmond city cops in the shin. He then planted a right cross to another and kneed the third in the gut.

All three went down.

The sound of a motorcycle roaring into the lobby had provided the few moments of distraction he'd needed to act.

Cassiopeia raced toward him across the marble floor. She slowed enough for him to hop onto the saddle, then gunned the engine, turning left, heading for the staircase fifty feet away. He wrapped one arm around her midsection while the other hand found his gun. He turned back to see the cops coming to their feet and unholstering weapons.

The cycle slowed as the staircase approached.

Risers descended in three long, straight flights, maybe a hundred feet from top to bottom, two wide landings in between.

This was the part he hadn't been looking forward to.

'Here we go,' she said.

He aimed and fired a shot over the cops' heads.

They plunged to the floor, scrambling to use Jefferson's statue as cover.

Cassiopeia had never actually driven a motorcycle down a staircase. A carpet runner lining the stone risers should help with traction, but it was going to be a bumpy ride.

She downshifted to second and plunged forward.

The suspension bucked as she and Malone fought for balance. She worked the handlebars, keeping them stable. She knew this machine. A low center of gravity made it easy to handle. European police had successfully utilized them for years. An earlier model was parked in her French château's garage. Familiarity was exactly why she'd chosen it for the trip to Fredericksburg, as opposed to one of the Secret Service cars.

Cotton was holding her tight, her grip on the handlebars equally firm.

They found the first landing.

She added a quick burst of speed, then a nudge of the disk brakes, before dropping down more stairs. At the second landing the front end twisted hard left. She immediately yanked the handlebars right, the front wheel slamming into the final set of risers as gravity kept sending them toward the floor below.

'Company,' she heard him say.

Then a shot.

From Cotton.

A few more bumpy meters and they found a smooth surface.

She revved the engine and they sped ahead, threading a path across rugs through chairs and sofas, across the faux-marble hall, beneath the stained-glass ceiling.

People who'd been sitting rushed out of the way.

The exit doors waited thirty meters away.

Malone was surprised they'd made it this far. He'd given the whole thing about a 30 percent chance of success. They'd caught the police off guard, and he was glad to see that the way ahead was clear. Behind was their problem. He caught sight of the cops, bounding down the stairway, finding the first landing and readying themselves to shoot. He fired three times at the second set of risers, bullets ricocheting off the marble and scattering the would-be attackers.

He hoped none of the rounds hit anybody.

'Cotton,' he heard Cassiopeia say.

He turned back and stared ahead.

Glass doors, locked as she'd told him until nine AM, blocked their path ahead. Beyond, a bright morning sun signaled freedom.

Forty feet.

'Anytime now,' she said, as they kept racing ahead.

He aimed the gun over her shoulder and fired three times, obliterating a set of glass doors.

Cassiopeia aimed the cycle for the center of the exposed opening.

They roared out onto the sidewalk and she braked.

Both of their feet found pavement.

A busy street ran perpendicular to the hotel.

He checked traffic, spotted a break for a merger, then said, 'Get us out of here.'

42

Bath, North Carolina

Hale was satisfied with all of the preparations. The choice of woodling had certainly surprised Knox, who'd openly hesitated an instant before nodding his consent, then requesting a few extra minutes so the necessary items could be readied. He noticed that the other three captains were anxious. The choice of punishment had been on his motion, but they'd all voted in favor.

'Killing your accountant was foolish,' Surcouf said to him.

'Like this crewman, he disappointed me.'

'You take too many chances,' Cogburn noted. 'Far too many.'

'I do what I have to do in order to survive.'

One captain was not required to explain himself to the others so long as what he did remained personal to him, and the death of his family accountant certainly fell into that category. No different from when captains controlled their own ships, and another captain's opinion was relevant only when companies grouped together.

Knox caught his attention and signaled that all was ready.

He stepped forward and called out to those assembled in the morning sun, 'We each pledged loyalty to the Articles. You have a good life, a good living. Our company works because we work together.' He pointed at the man bound to the pole. 'He spit in the face of all that we hold dear, and jeopardized each and every one of you.'

The men stirred.

'Traitors deserve what they get,' he called out.

A clamor arose signifying that they all agreed. A chill crept down his spine. What a feeling, to be in charge. Only the tang of salt air and the sway of a deck was missing.

'Bear witness to punishment,' he yelled.

Knox stood near the bound and gagged man and Hale watched as the quartermaster directed two other crewmen. The chosen punishment was especially harsh, though simple in design. Two boards were connected at each end by leather straps, about three feet long. The prisoner's head was positioned between the two straps, the men standing on either side, gripping the boards with both hands.

He hoped Stephanie Nelle was watching. He'd had her moved from a windowless cell to one where she could see the yard. He wanted her to know what he was capable of doing. He still had not heard from Andrea Carbonell about any cipher solution, so Nelle's fate remained undecided.

The two crewmen began rotating the boards, twisting the straps until they embraced the man's skull. The prisoner wiggled his head, trying to thwart their effort, but the gesture proved useless.

Knox threw Hale a final look.

He glanced at the other three captains, who nodded.

He stared back at Knox and added his own nod.

The command to continue was given and the boards were rotated more. For a few turns, as the straps tightened, the skull endured. By the sixth, pressure was building. The prisoner's body wiggled against the restraints. If he hadn't been gagged, the man would surely be screaming in agony.

The boards continued to turn.

Pupils went wide, the eyeballs bulging unnaturally. Hale knew what was happening. Pressure from inside the compressed skull was literally forcing them outward.

The other three captains noticed, too.

He knew these men were not accustomed to witnessing violence. They could order it done with no remorse. Watching it, though, seemed another matter.

More turns.

The man's face turned crimson from the pressure.

An eyeball burst from its socket.

Blood poured from the gaping hole.

The tightening continued, slower now as the straps had little give left in them.

His father had told him about woodling. How the last few seconds were the worst. Once the eyes gave way all that remained was for the skull to crack. Unfortunately for the victim, the skull was tough. That was the one thing about this particular form of punishment – many times it did not kill the victim.

The other eyeball escaped and more blood soaked the face.

Hale walked toward the yard's center.

The prisoner had stopped all movement, his body limp, the head held aloft only by the straps.

Knox ordered the twisting to stop.

'Just know that there are two traitors in your precious company.'

'Why are you telling me this?'

'When it comes time for me to die, I hope you'll at least be merciful.'

He'd thought about little else since the man uttered those words less than an hour ago.

Two traitors in your precious company.

Though the prisoner had said he'd never bought into the company mentality, he was wrong. *I betrayed you, not my friends.* He cared about his fellow crewmen.

And that made him believe the man.

He stared at the bloodied face. Then he reached beneath his jacket, brought out a pistol, and fired one shot to the head.

'Punishment has been administered,' he called out. 'Dismissed.'

The crewmen began to drift from the yard.

He turned to Knox. 'Have the body dumped at sea. Then come to my house. We need to talk.'

Cassiopeia shifted the Honda into fifth and kept the cycle moving down U.S. 250. They'd purposefully avoided Interstate 64 west, opting for a secondary highway, hoping they could avoid any alerts to adjoining counties. But she agreed with Cotton's assessment. After having failed with the easy catch, whoever had ordered his arrest might not be so willing to involve others again. Next time they'd do it them-selves, their way.

Cotton tapped her on the belly and said in her ear, 'Pull over up there.'

She veered into an abandoned restaurant, the building collapsing, an asphalt parking lot infested with weeds and grass. She wheeled to the rear and brought the cycle to a stop.

'No sign of anybody on our tail,' he told her as he climbed off. 'We need to talk to Edwin Davis again.'

She found her phone and dialed the number. Davis answered on the second ring. She pressed SPEAKER. They'd talked with him earlier, just before Cassiopeia descended to the lobby on her reconnoiter mission.

'Glad to hear you made it out,' Davis said. 'Not too much damage to the hotel, I hope.'

'It's insured,' Cotton told him.

'The dead man in the car at the Garver Institute was Dr. Gary Voccio,' Davis said. 'We have an ID on the body, and it was his car.'

They listened as Davis explained how the FBI and CIA had descended on the institute. Power and phones had been deliberately cut, one building's lobby obliterated, bullet holes spread across two floors.

'The big man isn't happy,' Davis said. 'More casualties.'

'We're headed to Monticello,' Cotton said.

'When you deleted the cipher key off the institute's server,' Davis said, 'you eliminated it. Voccio had not saved anything. It's gone. That file contained all of his notes and results.'

'At least we have it,' she said.

'But we have to wonder who else managed to get it, too.'

'We're going to need access to the wheel,' Cotton said. 'The estate's website says it's displayed in Jefferson's cabinet, near his library and bedroom.'

'I'm headed to Monticello,' Davis said. 'I'll be at the visitor center, waiting for you to arrive.'

Cotton smiled. 'Aren't we Johnny-on-the-spot today.'

'This has to be handled, along with the other situation Cassiopeia has uncovered with the phones.'

He was right about that, Cassiopeia thought, in more ways than one. 'We'll be there in about forty-five minutes.'

She ended the call.

'What's the problem?' Cotton asked her.

'Who said there was one?'

'Call it boyfriend intuition. I saw it on your face. What happened with the First Lady? You only gave me the short version.'

True. She'd abbreviated the events, leaving off the last part of her conversation with Shirley Kaiser.

The First Lady is having an affair. Isn't she?

Not exactly. But close enough.

'I'm thinking how we can use that phone tap to our advantage,' she said. 'It's our fastest ticket to flush out Hale.'

He gently grabbed her arm. 'There's something else. You're holding back. That's okay. I do it, too. But whatever it is, if you need my help, ask.'

She liked that he didn't try to be the fixer. Instead, he was her partner, watching her back.

And she just might take him up on his offer.

But for now that *something else* was her problem.

43

Knox was troubled. Quentin Hale had met privately with the traitor before the execution and now he'd been ordered to the main house with no explanation. The corpse was on its way to sea, where it would be weighed down and tossed into the Gulf Stream. Perhaps the traitor had told Hale that he'd compromised the murder but not the assassination. But why would Hale have believed him? And even if Hale harbored doubts, nothing pointed Knox's way, except that he was one of four men who knew every detail, from the beginning, the other three all being captains. True, at least a dozen had worked on the weapons in the metal shop, but they were not told of any planned use. Were they suspects? Of course, but weak ones.

He entered the Hale house and walked straight for the study. All four captains were there, waiting, which immediately raised his anxiety level.

'Good,' Hale said, as Knox closed the door. 'I was just about to play something for the others.'

A digital recorder lay on the tabletop.

Hale activated it.

'My marriage has been a problem for a long time, Shirley. You know that.'

'You're the First Lady of this country. Divorce is not an option.'

'But it is once we leave, and that's only a year and a half away.'

'Pauline, do you realize what you're saying? Have you thought this through?'

'I think about little else. Danny's held office nearly our entire marriage. It's been a distraction for us both, neither one of us wanting to face reality. In twenty months his career is over. Then it will only be him and me. No distractions. I don't think I can stand that.'

'It's the other thing. Isn't it?'

'You talk like it's dirty.'

'It's clouding your judgment.'

'No, it's not. He actually clears my head. For the first time in many years I can see. Think. Feel.'

'Does he know that we talk about this?'

'I told him.'

Hale clicked off the recorder. 'Seems the First Lady of the United States has a boyfriend.'

'How did you record that?' Surcouf asked.

'About a year ago I cultivated a relationship, one I hoped might provide us with some valuable information.' Hale paused. 'And I was right.'

Knox had researched Shirley Kaiser and learned of her long-standing friendship with Pauline Daniels. Luckily, Kaiser was outgoing, attractive, and available. A supposed accidental introduction was arranged and a relationship blossomed. But neither he nor Hale had realized the deep chasm that existed in the Daniels' marriage. That had been an unexpected bonus.

'Why didn't you tell us what you were doing?' Cogburn asked.

'That's easy, Charles,' Bolton said. 'He wanted to be our savior so we'd be in his debt.'

Which wasn't too far off the mark, Knox thought.

'You berate us,' Bolton said, 'for acting alone. But you've done the same thing, and for a long time.'

'With the difference being that my actions were calculated and private. Yours were stupid and public.'

Bolton rushed across the room, heading straight for Hale, arm cocked back, fist balled. Hale's right hand reached beneath his jacket and the same gun used to ease the prisoner's misery appeared.

Bolton stopped.

The men glared at each other.

Cogburn and Surcouf stood silent.

Knox was delighted. They were fighting among themselves – again – the perfect distraction from him. But it only went to prove what he'd already concluded before dealing with NIA. These men would not survive the waves that were about to wash across their decks. Too much conflict, too many egos, too little cooperation.

'One day, Quentin,' Bolton said.

'What will you do? Assassinate me?'

'I'd love to.'

'You'll find killing me far harder than any president.'

Wyatt arrived at Monticello. He'd driven the 120 miles from Washington in less than two hours and parked in a treed lot, adjacent to an attractive complex of low-slung buildings identified as the Thomas Jefferson Visitor Center and Smith Education Center. Its rooflines followed the contour of the adjacent hillside, the wooden walls blending naturally into the surrounding forest and encompassing a café, gift shop, theater, classrooms, and exhibit hall.

Carbonell had been right. He could not allow Malone to succeed. He'd involved his adversary in New York to place him in danger, perhaps even eliminate him, not provide another opportunity for him to save the day.

Carbonell had also been right about one other thing.

He needed her. At least for the short haul.

She'd provided some useful information on Monticello, including its geography, security system, and maps for roads leading in and out. He walked from his car up a stairway into a courtyard dotted with locust trees. He found the ticket center and bought a spot on the first tour of the day, leaving in less than twenty minutes, when the mansion opened at 9 AM.

He wandered around and read the placards, learning that Jefferson had labored forty years on the estate – naming it Monticello, Italian for 'little mountain' – creating what he eventually called his 'essay in architecture.'

It had been a working estate. Livestock, hogs, and sheep had all been bred there. A sawmill produced lumber. Two other mills provided corn and wheat. A barrel shop fashioned casks for flour. Firewood was harvested and sold from the surrounding forests. Jefferson had raised tobacco for sale to the Scots, then switched to rye, clover, potatoes, and peas. At one point he could ride ten miles in any direction and never leave his land.

He envied that independence.

But inside the exhibit hall he learned that Jefferson had died broke, owing thousands of dollars, and that his heirs sold everything, including his slaves, to satisfy his creditors. The house survived through a succession of owners until being repurchased in 1923 by a foundation, which had labored to restore its original glory.

He drifted among the various exhibits and learned more. The house's main floor consisted of eleven rooms, each part of the official tour. The careful use of space and natural light, one room easing into another, once divided by glass doors, was meant to convey a sense of a free and open life – nothing hidden, no secrets. The second and third floors were not accessible to visitors, but the cellars were open to the public.

He studied a diagram.

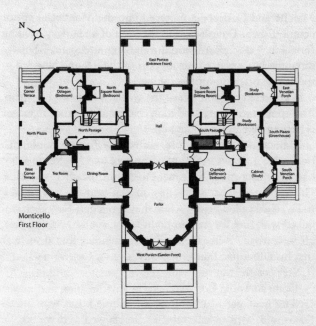

Monticello
First Floor

Satisfied, he stepped back outside into a beautiful late-summer morning and decided that quick and fast was the only way to get this job done.

He made his way toward where a shuttle bus would ferry him and the first group nearly nine hundred feet up the mountainside. The fifty or so people consisted of many teenagers. A life-sized bronze of Thomas Jefferson waited with them near the curb. A tall man, he noticed, over six feet. He studied the likeness with a few of the youngsters.

'This ought to be neat,' one of them said.

He agreed.

A little fun.

Like the old days.

Malone and Cassiopeia motored into the Monticello visitor center. Edwin Davis stood at the base of a stairway, waiting for them. Cassiopeia ignored a parking attendant, who was directing her toward a vacant part of the lot, and wheeled to the curb, switching off the engine.

'I arranged for you to see the wheel,' Davis said to them. 'I've spoken with the foundation chair, and the estate manager is here to take us up to the house.'

Malone had never before visited any former president's home. He'd always meant to come here and Mt. Vernon, but had just never made the time. One of those father–son trips. He wondered what Gary, his sixteen-year-old, was doing today. He'd called Friday when they arrived in New York and talked with him for half an hour. Gary was growing up fast. He seemed a levelheaded kid, particularly pleased to hear that his father had finally made a move on Cassiopeia.

She's hot, the boy had said.

That she was.

'The manager is waiting by the shuttle buses with a car,' Davis said. 'Only estate vehicles are allowed to drive up. We can slip in with the first tour and see the wheel. It's displayed on the ground floor, then we can take it upstairs where there's privacy.'

'Cotton can go,' Cassiopeia said. 'You and I need to talk.'

Malone caught the look in her eye – that something was troubling her – and one other thing.

Her suggestion was not open for debate.

'Okay,' Davis said. 'You and I will stay here.'

44

Hale waited for Bolton to cow to him and, finally, the weak soul, as expected, retreated to the other side of the room. Tensions eased but did not dissipate.

'President Daniels will not want his private life exposed,' he said. 'There has never been a hint of scandal regarding him or his wife. America believes them to be the perfect couple. Can you imagine what the twenty-four-hour news channels and the Internet would do with this? Daniels would forever be known as the cuckold president. He'll never allow that to happen. Gentlemen, we can use this.'

He saw that the other three did not necessarily agree.

'When were you going to tell us?' Cogburn asked again. 'Edward is justified in being angry. We're all angry, Quentin.'

'There was no sense speaking of it until I was sure that it could be used. Now, I am sure.'

Surcouf stepped to the bar and filled a glass with bourbon. Hale could use one himself, but decided a clear head would be better.

'We can quietly apply pressure and stop these prosecutions,' he said. 'As I told all three of you a month ago, there's no need to kill a president. The talking heads on television and bloggers of the Internet will do it for you. This president has shown us no courtesy. We owe him nothing, unless he wants to accommodate us now.'

'Who is the woman you're holding in the prison?' Cogburn asked.

He'd wondered when they'd finally ask. 'The head of an intelligence unit within the Justice Department called Magellan Billet. Stephanie Nelle.'

'Why do we have her?'

He could not tell them the truth. 'She was becoming a problem for us. Investigating.'

'Isn't she a little late?' Bolton asked. 'We've been investigated to death.'

'I saw her watching the execution from a cell window,' Cogburn said.

Finally. One of them had paid attention. 'My hope was that it would send her a message.'

'Quentin,' Surcouf said, 'do you have any idea what you're doing? It seems like you're headed in three different directions. Taking a hostage could bring even more heat on us.'

'More so than trying to kill a president? And I truly hate to keep harping on that, but not a soul knows my prisoner is here, besides us. Right now, as far as they are concerned, she is simply missing.'

Of course, he did not include Andrea Carbonell in that disclaimer. Which brought to mind the second traitor. If that person existed, he or she could well know of Stephanie Nelle's presence. But if that was the case, why hadn't anyone acted to save her?

The answer to that inquiry reassured him.

Surcouf pointed at the recorder. 'You could be right, Quentin. Daniels may not want this made public.'

'And the price for our silence is quite reasonable,' he said. 'We simply want the American government to keep its word.'

'There's a chance Daniels won't give a damn,' Bolton said. 'He may tell you to stick it up your ass, like they did the first time you went begging.'

He resented the comment, but there was something else that required mentioning. 'Did you notice an omission during that taped conversation?'

'I did,' Cogburn said. 'No name. Who's the man the First Lady is messing around with?'

He smiled. 'Now, that's what makes this so intriguing.'

Wyatt stepped inside Monticello with the first tour group of the day. He'd learned that visitors came in bunches of thirty, escorted by a guide who explained each room and answered questions. He noticed the guides were mainly older, volunteers most likely, and groups stayed clustered, spaced about five minutes apart.

He stood in what the guide called the entrance foyer, just inside the east portico. The spacious two-story room cast the appearance of a museum – which had been Jefferson's intention, the guide explained – displaying maps, antlers, sculptures, paintings, and artifacts. The second floor was visible through a semi-octagonal balcony. Thin, closely spaced balusters topped by a mahogany rail protected the outer edge. Everyone's attention was directed to Jefferson's dual-faced clock, displaying time and day of the week, its cannonball-like weights traveling through holes in the floor to the cellar. He feigned interest in two Old Master paintings and the busts of Voltaire, Turgot, and Alexander Hamilton while absorbing the layout.

They drifted into a sitting room adjacent to the hall.

Jefferson's daughter, Martha, and her family had used the cramped space as their private living quarters. He retreated to one corner so the rest of the group could enter the next room on the tour before him. He noticed that the guide would wait and close the door of the preceding room before addressing the group in the next. He assumed that was so the tour behind them could enjoy their visit uninterrupted.

'This is Jefferson's *sanctum sanctorum*. His most private place,' the guide told the group in the new space.

Wyatt studied the library.

Many of the walls remained lined with shelving. In Jefferson's time, the guide explained, they would have been fronted by pine boxes, stacked one atop the other – folios at the bottom, followed by quartos, octavos, duodecimos, with petit-formats on top. Nearly 6700 volumes at its peak, all of them eventually sold to the United States to form the Library of Congress after the British burned the capitol in 1814, destroying the nation's first collection of books. Tall windows that opened like doors led out to a louvered porch and greenhouse.

But what drew Wyatt's attention lay at the far end.

A semi-octagon lined with windows.

What the guide called the cabinet.

He spied a writing desk, a revolving leather chair, an astronomical clock, and Jefferson's famous polygraph that duplicated letters as they were drafted. An architect's table fronted one of the windows. Among a profusion of scientific instruments on a side table lay the cipher wheel. Maybe eighteen inches long. Its carved wooden disks were about six inches in diameter, resting beneath a glass lid. The guide was droning on about how Jefferson spent much of his morning and late afternoons reading and answering correspondence in the cabinet, surrounded by his books and scientific instruments. Few were allowed here, save those close to the former president. Wyatt recalled what he'd read at the visitor center about glass doors, openness, and no secrets, realizing that it had all been an illusion. In reality, there were a great many private spaces in this house, especially here in the south wing.

Which were about to come in handy.

The tour continued into Jefferson's bedroom, which rose double-height, at least eighteen feet to a skylight, joined with the cabinet by an alcove bed. The next room beyond that was the large parlor, located in the ground-floor center, with windows and doors facing the rear yard and west portico. The guide dutifully closed the bedroom door after the last visitor entered the parlor. Oil portraits dominated the cream-colored walls. Crimson draperies crowned its tall windows. English, French, and American furniture sat intermingled.

He reached into his pocket and found a flash bomb. Discreetly, he freed the igniter and, while the guide explained about the works of art on the walls and Jefferson's admiration of John Locke, Isaac Newton, and Francis Bacon, he bent down and rolled the explosive across the wood floor.

One. Two. Three.

He closed his eyes as a burst of light and smoke flooded the room.

He already held a second surprise, so he yanked its igniter and dropped it on the floor, reaching for the knob that opened back into the bedroom just as another *swoosh* of thick air terrorized the parlor.

Malone rode with the estate manager on the two-lane road that wound up the mountainside. Traffic moved only one way, rounding the house at the summit, then working its way back down, past Jefferson's grave, to the visitor center.

'We were lucky to get the wheel back,' the manager said. 'Nearly everything Jefferson owned was sold after his death to pay his creditors. Robert Patterson, the son of the man who was Jefferson's longtime friend, bought the wheel then from the estate. His father had helped Jefferson make it, so there was a sentimental attachment. The elder Patterson and Jefferson shared a love of codes.'

Malone made the connection with what Daniels had told him. The son Robert Patterson had worked for the government and provided Andrew Jackson with his father's cipher. Apparently, he'd also suggested incorporating the wheel into the decoding process. Since there was only one in the world, which Patterson himself owned, Old Hickory probably rested easy knowing that the Commonwealth would never decipher a thing.

'Jefferson stopped using the wheel in 1802,' the manager said. 'It was resurrected in 1890 by a French government official and used for a while. Then again, during World War I, the Americans brought it back, and it was utilized for coding until the start of the Second World War.'

They rounded a bend and approached a small paved lot, devoid of cars. One of the shuttle buses was just easing away after depositing more visitors. The house's main entrance stood about a hundred feet away.

'Nice to be with the man in charge,' he said. 'Gets you real close.'

'It's not every day the White House chief of staff and the head of the Secret Service conference call with you.'

The manager switched off the engine.

Malone stepped out into the bright morning, the late-summer air dry and warm. He stared up at the mansion and its distinctive dome, the first ever, he knew, constructed above an American house.

A flash momentarily illuminated some of the house windows.

Screams came from inside.

Another flash.

Someone bolted out the front door.

'There's a bomb inside. Run.'

45

Cassiopeia and Edwin Davis stood alone, at the far end of a parking lot, beyond which more visitors were arriving by the carload.

'I want to know about you and the First Lady,' she said to him.

Defeat clouded Davis' face. 'Now you see why it had to be you working on this?'

She'd already understood that fact.

'When the Secret Service told us who they had in custody, I convinced the president to involve you both. It wasn't a hard sell. He has great trust in both you and Cotton. He hasn't forgotten what you did for him last time. I knew Pauline would instantly become a suspect, since only a handful of us knew of the trip that far in advance, so any investigation of her had to be controlled.'

'You knew she was the leak from the start?'

'The idea of her saying something to someone made sense.'

'When did your relationship with the First Lady start?'

A wave of uneasiness passed between them. She knew this was tough. But he'd involved her and she had to do her job.

'I came to the White House three years ago as a deputy national security adviser. I met Pauline . . . the First Lady . . . then.'

'Don't worry about correctness,' she said. 'This is just you and me. Tell me what happened.'

'I do worry about it.' A wave of anger flashed across his face.

'I'm mad at myself. Never have I behaved in such a manner. I'm sixty years old and have never placed myself in such an awkward situation. I'm not sure what's come over me.'

'Welcome to the club. Have you ever been married?'

He shook his head. 'I've had precious few relationships in my life. Work was always the most important thing. I was the person other people turned to in time of trouble. A steady hand. Now—'

She reached out and lightly grasped his arm. 'Just tell me what happened.'

His defensiveness seemed to abate. 'She's a terribly unhappy woman and has been for a long time. Which is such a shame, because she's a good person. What happened with her daughter profoundly affected her. She just never dealt with it.'

And neither had Danny Daniels, she thought.

'She rarely travels with the president anymore,' Davis said. 'Differing schedules, which isn't unusual. So there were times when he was gone that she and I would visit with each other. Nothing improper, mind you. Nothing at all. Just a lunch or a dinner where I'd keep her company and we'd talk. She likes to read, mainly romance novels. That's something few know. The steamier the better. Shirley would sneak them to her.' He smiled. 'They bring her joy, and not because of the sex. That isn't the allure. It's the happy endings. They all end on a high note, and that she likes.'

He was relaxing, opening up, as if he'd been living on his raw nerves far too long.

'We talked about books, the world, the White House. There was no reason to pretend with me. I was the closest person to the president. There was nothing I didn't know. Eventually, we explored Mary, her husband, and her marriage.'

'She made it clear to me that she blames the president for everything.'

'That's not true,' he quickly said. 'Not in the way you think.

Maybe in the beginning she did blame him. But I think she came to realize that was foolish. Sadly, a part of her died that night with Mary. A part that could never be reclaimed, and it's taken her decades to understand that loss.'

'Were you a factor in that understanding?'

He seemed to feel the hint of criticism in her words.

'I tried hard not to be. But when I was promoted to chief of staff, we spent more time together. Our discussions progressed to ever-deeper topics. She trusted me.' He hesitated. 'I'm a good listener.'

'But you were doing more than listening,' she said. 'You were empathizing. Relating. Drawing something equally beneficial, for yourself, from her.'

He nodded. 'Our conversations were a two-way street. And she came to know that.'

She, too, had wrestled with those same emotions. Sharing yourself with someone was tough business.

'Pauline is a year older than me,' he said, as if that mattered in some way. 'She jokes that I'm her younger man. I have to confess, I like it when she says that.'

'Does Daniels have any idea?'

'Heavens, no. But like I said, absolutely nothing improper has occurred.'

'Except the two of you have fallen in love.'

Resignation filled his face. 'I suppose you're right. That's exactly what happened. She and the president have not been man and wife for a long time, and they both seem to have accepted that. There's no intimacy in their relationship. And I don't mean in the physical sense. There's no sharing of each other. No vulnerabilities exposed. It's as if they're roommates. Colleagues. With a physical wall between them. No marriage can survive that.'

She knew what he meant. Never before had she been intimate with anyone on the level she was with Cotton. There'd been men, and she'd shared some of herself, but never all. To reveal your hopes and fears, trusting that another person will not abuse them, involved a huge leap of faith.

And not only for her, but for Cotton, too.

Yet Davis was right.

Intimacy seemed the mortar that bound love together.

'Did you know about Quentin Hale's connection to Shirley Kaiser?' she asked.

'Absolutely not. I've only met Shirley once, when she came to the White House. But I know Pauline talks to her every day. Without her, she would have folded long ago. If Pauline would tell anyone about the New York trip, it would have been Shirley. I also know that Shirley knows about me. That's why I needed you on this one. I figured things could rapidly get out of hand.'

Which had happened.

'Now Quentin Hale knows,' she said. 'But, interestingly, he hasn't done a thing with the information.'

'When he met with me that day in the White House, he surely knew. That get-together was probably a way for him to see if he had to play the trump card.'

She agreed. That made sense. As did something else. 'I'm convinced that Hale has Stephanie. Though she was looking into Carbonell, it involved the Commonwealth, too. There's no doubt about it now.'

'But if we act imprudently, we risk not only exposure and embarrassment for all concerned, but Stephanie's life.'

'That's true but—'

An alarm sounded from the visitor center.

'What now?' she said.

They raced back toward the cluster of buildings and into the estate manager's office.

Concern filled the manager's assistant's face. 'Some sort of bomb went off in the main house.'

46

Wyatt's toys had done the trick. Panic now reigned inside the mansion. People screaming, shoving, trying to escape. He'd used a modified mixture that added smoke, which only amplified the effects. Thank goodness he'd shipped a supply to New York, since he'd been unsure just what would happen once Cotton Malone entered the picture.

He'd retreated into Jefferson's bedroom and jammed a chair under the doorknob. He knew another tour would be making their way from the sitting room into the library, then the cabinet. He stepped lightly across the room's plank floor toward the bed. He recalled the guide earlier babbling about how Jefferson would rise as soon as he could see the hands of an obelisk clock that sat across from the bed. A crimson silk counterpane – sewn to Jefferson's specifications, the guide had pointed out – covered the mattress, which filled an alcove between the bedroom and the cabinet. He crawled onto the bed and carefully peered around the edge, past arches, to see people in the library, about twenty feet away. The guide seemed to be assessing the unusual situation and, upon hearing the screams from the other end of the house, asked for everyone to stay calm.

Wyatt tossed a light bomb their way, jerking his head back just as the flash and smoke appeared.

Shouts came as fear set in.

'This way,' he heard a voice say over the commotion.

He glanced back and saw the guide leading the group through the smoke, out the louvered doors, into the adjacent greenhouse and fresh air.

He turned his attention to the cipher wheel.

Which rested two feet away.

Malone stood inside Monticello's two-story entrance hall. Smoke billowed from open glass doors at the opposite end, followed by screams and yells that signaled something had just happened to his left.

The estate manager stood beside him.

A wave of people had fled the house a moment ago through the main doors behind him, their voices excited, their eyes alight with fear.

'What's that way?' he asked, motioning to the left where the commotion now seemed centered.

'Jefferson's private rooms. The library, cabinet, bedroom.'

'Is that where the wheel is displayed?'

The man nodded.

He found his gun. 'Out. And don't let anybody in.'

He realized there was no bomb. Just flash and pan. A diversion. The same swishing sound from last night and the attack on the men with the night-vision goggles.

Who the hell was here?

Wyatt slipped the nylon carryall he'd brought with him from his pant pocket. The wheel was larger than he'd expected, but the thin bag could handle it. He'd have to be careful since the wooden disks seemed brittle. Understandable, considering they were over two hundred years old.

He climbed off the bed into the cabinet, removed the glass cover, and lifted out the spindled disks. Carefully, he worked the device into the nylon bag. He then grabbed two loose disks that had been displayed separately and laid them in the bag. He would have to cradle the bundle in his arms, holding it close to his chest to ensure no damage.

He tested the weight.

About five pounds.

No problem.

Malone passed through a room with pale green walls and a fireplace. A placard identified it as the South Square Room. Above a white mantel hung a woman's portrait. Another door led into what he recalled from some reading as Jefferson's *sanctum sanctorum*, which consumed the entire south end of the building.

Gun in hand, he opened the door and was met by a wall of smoke.

He stared through the fog and caught glimpses of people outside, through the room's windows, which stretched floor-to-ceiling, opening like doors into a sunlit porch bright with potted plants. He grabbed a breath and plunged into the smoke, keeping close to the wall, seeking cover behind a wooden cabinet. Ahead, to his left, rose narrow bookshelves lined with old leather-bound volumes. Archways supported the ceiling and led to the far end where, in a semi-octagonal alcove, he spotted a man, bagging up the wheel.

He focused on the face.

One he knew.

And everything made sense.

Wyatt caught movement through the fog. Somebody had entered the library at the far end.

He finished his task, cradled the wheel in one arm, and found his gun.

He saw a man staring at him.

Cotton Malone.

And fired a shot.

★ ★ ★

Malone dropped behind the wooden cabinet as Wyatt sent a bullet his way. What had it been? Eight years. At least. He'd never known what had happened to Wyatt after he was forced out, though he'd heard something about freelancing.

The person who'd set the trap using Stephanie Nelle as bait, luring him to that hotel room. The author of the note left for him to find. The voice on the radio from the Grand Hyatt that fingered him. The manipulation of the police and the Secret Service.

All Wyatt.

Something flew through the fog and landed on the floor.

Small, round, rolling his way.

He knew what was coming and whirled his head to the right, shutting his eyes.

Wyatt abandoned the cabinet, then the bedroom, and made his way back into the parlor, away from Malone. As much as he'd like to stay and play, he couldn't.

Not now.

He had the wheel and that was all that mattered. He could use it to discover what lay next in the search for the two missing congressional pages. Or maybe he'd just destroy the thing and be done with it.

That way, nobody would win.

At the moment, he was unsure.

Malone decided not to follow Wyatt. He knew the ground-floor rooms wound their way back to the center, so he opened a door to his right, revealing a short corridor that emptied twenty feet ahead into the entrance hall.

Smoke drifted his way.

Visibility wasn't good, and Wyatt certainly wasn't going to walk out the front door. To his immediate right, a set of narrow, wedge-shaped steps rose in a vertical spiral to the second floor. A chain with a sign indicated no admittance. He recalled the entrance hall and the open second-floor railing and decided the high ground might be better, so he stepped over the chain and headed up.

Wyatt intended on leaving, but not from the ground floor. His plan was to make his way to the cellar, then out through the lower, north exit into the woods beyond the service road. That had always seemed the safest route, considering the excitement would be centered on the house's east side. But Malone was just a few feet away, probably trying to make his way back toward the entrance hall.

He stopped in the parlor and listened.

Smoke remained thick. No one was around. Malone probably had the house sealed. Then a thought occurred to him and his gaze drifted to the ceiling.

Of course.

That's exactly what he would have done.

47

Bath, North Carolina

Knox watched the three other captains as Quentin Hale reveled in his moment. He, too, had been impressed when he first listened to the taped conversations. The fact was startling. The First Lady of the United States romantically involved with the White House chief of staff?

'How long has this been going on?' Cogburn asked Hale.

'Long enough that neither of them can deny it. The conversations are, at a minimum, hugely embarrassing. Never before has American politics been subjected to something like this. The sheer novelty will drive the press and the public insane. Daniels would be impotent for the remainder of his term.'

Even Edward Bolton, who as a matter of course denied all things that emanated from a Hale as either self-serving, impractical, or stupid, sat silent, certainly realizing the possibilities.

'Let's use it,' Surcouf said. 'Now. Why wait?'

'Its use must be timed with precision,' Hale said. 'As you three like to remind me, when I went *begging* to the White House, I knew about this information. But I went there to see if we would have to use it. I asked that our letters be respected and was rebuked. So now we have little choice. Still, going straight to the president with this would be counterproductive. Instead we must pressure the two individuals involved, allow them to consider the ramifications of their actions, then wait as they do our persuading for us.'

Knox agreed, the First Lady and the chief of staff would have the most influence over President Daniels. But would they do the Commonwealth's bidding? Hardly. This was more irrational thinking. The kind that had convinced him that making a deal with the NIA was preferable to riding out the storm on this leaky ship.

'They can choose for themselves what to tell Daniels,' Hale said. 'We don't care. We just want the U.S. government to honor the letters of marque.'

'How did you acquire these tapes?' Bolton asked. 'Is there anything that leads this way? How do you know that you're not being played? This whole thing is a bit fantastic. Too damn good to be true. We could be walking into a trap.'

'That's a good point,' Cogburn said. 'It is awfully convenient.'

Hale shook his head. 'Gentlemen, why are you so suspicious? I have been involved with this woman for over a year. She shares with me things she really should not.'

'Then why tape her phone calls?' Bolton asked Hale.

'Because, Edward, do you think she tells me everything? And for this to work, we need the First Lady herself to speak about it. So I took the chance and monitored her phone line. Thank goodness I did, or we would not have such damning evidence.'

'I'm still concerned,' Cogburn said. 'It could be a trap.'

'If this is a ruse, then it is one on an elaborate scale.' Hale shook his head. 'This is real. I'd stake my life on it.'

'But the question is,' Bolton said, 'will *we* stake *our* lives on it?'

Malone crept down a corridor that stretched north-to-south, from one end of the second floor to the other. Though he'd never been inside Monticello, he knew enough about Thomas Jefferson to know that there would be another staircase at the far end. Jefferson had been an admirer of all things French. Double-height rooms, domes, bed alcoves, skylights, indoor privies, narrow staircases – all common elements in Franco architecture. As was symmetry. Which meant there should be a second stairway at the north end that would lead down. But between here and there was the balcony that opened out into the entrance hall, smoke filling the path ahead confirming that fact.

He came to the end of the corridor and gazed down into the entrance hall. Beyond the railing he spotted no movement. Smoke hung thick, dissipating as it drifted upward. He kept away from the rail, hugging the wall, and crossed the balcony to the other side. Ahead, a few feet down another hall, he spotted the second staircase, winding a steep path down and up to the third floor.

Something flew up from that stairway and bounced on the hall's wood floor. Rolling his way. He dove back to the balcony just as the flash bomb exploded with light and smoke.

He raised his head and glanced down, beyond the railing.

Wyatt stood, aiming a gun upward.

Hale glared at Edward Bolton and said, 'I'd say you have little choice but to trust this will produce the desired results.' He paused. 'For us all. Unless you have a better idea.'

'I don't trust anything you do,' Bolton said.

Charles Cogburn stepped forward. 'I have to agree with him, Quentin. This could be as foolish as what we tried.'

'Assassination wasn't foolish,' Bolton was quick to say. 'It's worked in the past. Look at what happened to McKinley. He was determined to prosecute us, too.'

Hale's father had told him about William McKinley, who like Lincoln had at first made use of the Commonwealth. By the time of the Spanish-American War, thanks to the 1856 Treaty of Paris, more than fifty nations had outlawed privateering. And though neither Spain nor America signed that treaty, they agreed not to engage in privateering during their war at the turn of the 20th century. Not bound by any international agreement, the Commonwealth preyed on Spanish shipping. Unfortunately, the war lasted only four months. Once peace was declared the Spanish demanded retribution, calling into question America's veracity since it had violated its prewar agreement. McKinley finally relented to pressure and authorized prosecutions, resting on the fact that the Commonwealth's letters of marque were legally unenforceable. So a deranged would-be anarchist was covertly recruited and encouraged to kill McKinley, which he did on September 6, 1901. The assassin was apprehended at the scene. Seventeen days later he was tried and convicted. Five weeks after that he was electrocuted. The new president, Theodore Roosevelt, had no qualms with the Commonwealth's attacks and cared nothing about appeasing the Spanish.

All prosecutions ended.

Of course, neither Roosevelt, nor anyone else, knew of the conspiracy to kill McKinley.

'That is the difference between you and me,' Hale said to Bolton. 'I merely cherish our past. You insist on repeating it. As I said, bullets and violence are not the way to take down a president any longer. Shame and humiliation work in the same manner with the advantage that others willingly take up the fight for us. We have to do nothing more than light the fire.'

'It's your damn family that created this mess,' Bolton said. 'Hales were nothing but trouble in 1835, too. We were fine. No one bothered us. We'd provided a great service to the country and the government left us alone. But instead of accepting Jackson's decision not to pardon those pirates, your great-great-granddaddy decided to kill the president of the United States.' Bolton pointed his finger at Hale. 'About as stupid a move as the one we tried. The only difference is, we didn't get caught.'

Hale could not resist. 'Not yet, anyway.'

'What's that supposed to mean?'

He shrugged. 'Just that the investigations have barely begun. Don't be so sure that there is no trail to follow.'

Bolton lunged forward, apparently taking the words as a threat, then stopped, realizing that the gun, though lowered, was still in Hale's hand.

'You'd sell us out,' Bolton said. 'Just to save your own hide.'

'Never,' Hale said. 'I take my oath to the Articles seriously. It is *you* that I take lightly.'

Bolton faced Surcouf and Cogburn. 'Are you going to stand there and let him talk to us that way? Does either of you have anything to say?'

Cassiopeia rode with Edwin Davis up the inclined road toward Monticello's main house. Buses up and down had been halted, the local sheriff called. They wheeled into a parking lot in front on the mansion. The estate manager waited at the end of a paved walk that led to a columned portico. Twenty meters away, people were being herded onto another bus.

'Where's Cotton?' she asked.

'Inside. He told me to seal the house and let no one in.'

'What's happened?' Davis asked.

A *swoosh* could be heard from inside, followed by a bright flash of light that illuminated some of the windows.

'What was that?' she asked.

'There've been others like that,' the manager said.

She ran down the walk toward the house.

'He said for no one to enter,' the manager called out to her.

She found her weapon. 'That doesn't apply to me.'

A loud retort echoed from inside.

That sound she knew.

Gunfire.

48

Malone dropped to the floor just as Wyatt fired, the bullet shattering one of the wooden spindles. He beat a hasty retreat on all fours toward the back wall, away from the railing, using the angle below for protection. Another shot and a bullet came up through the floorboards a few feet away, the two-hundred-year-old timbers offering little resistance.

A third shot.

Closer.

Wyatt was searching for him.

Something arced through the air and bounced on the balcony floor. He'd seen this movie before and quickly shielded his head as the light bomb did its thing, adding a fresh wave of smoke to the confusion.

He sprang to his feet and found the hall that led back to the stairs he'd taken earlier. Spying movement below, he stared up toward the third floor and decided to reverse the roles.

Time for Wyatt to play rabbit and for him to be the fox.

Wyatt crept up the stairs, gun leading the way, searching through the smoke for Malone.

Two things happened at once.

He heard the house's main doors open and a woman yell, 'Cotton.'

Then, up above, he caught sight of Malone.

Climbing to the third floor.

* * *

Knox waited for Captains Surcouf and Cogburn to answer Bolton's question.

'I don't know, Edward,' Surcouf finally said. 'I'm not sure what to think. We're in a mess. Frankly, I don't like what either one of you proposes. But I have to wonder, Quentin. There's no way you're depending totally on Daniels caving simply from embarrassment.'

'If it were me,' Cogburn said, 'I'd call the wife a lying whore and hang her out to dry. Nobody would have any sympathy for her.'

Typical, Knox thought. Cogburns had long viewed the world in black and white. He wished life were that simple. If it were, none of them would be in the mess they were in. But he, too, doubted that the tactic alone would pressure the White House into doing anything productive.

'I still have Stephanie Nelle,' Hale said.

'And what are you going to do with her?'

Knox wanted to hear the answer to that question, too.

'I haven't decided. But she could prove valuable.'

'Talk about a thing from the past,' Bolton said. 'Do you hear yourself? A hostage? In the 21st century? Like you told us about the assassination attempt. Are you going to call up the White House and say you have her? Let's make a deal? You can't do diddly-squat with that woman. She's useless.'

Unless her corpse could be shown to Andrea Carbonell, Knox thought. Then, she was worth a great deal.

At least to him.

'Why don't you let me worry about her value,' Hale said.

Cogburn pointed an accusing finger. 'You're plotting something else. What is it, Quentin? Tell us or, by God, I'll join with Edward and make your life a living hell.'

Cassiopeia could distinguish little through the smoke. The two-story entrance hall was enveloped in a gray fog. She sought cover close to the wall, behind a pine table, beneath a wall dotted with antlers.

She realized what she had to do.

Not the smartest move, but necessary.

'Cotton,' she called out.

Malone came to the top of the stairway on the third floor. He'd made no attempt to disguise his path. Surely Wyatt had seen or heard him and was headed this way.

Or at least he hoped.

He heard his name called out.

Cassiopeia.

Wyatt had no idea as to the woman's identity, but she obviously was connected to Malone. He should simply descend to the cellar and leave, but he recalled that the staircase before him led down, not into a public area, but into a private room the staff utilized. He wondered if any of them was still there, or if they'd been told to evacuate. The one thing he did not want to do was shoot anyone. That would bring immeasurable grief his way. Better to be a simple thief, inflicting nothing more than a little property damage.

He stared up.

The third floor contained the room beneath the dome. Only the north and south staircases led there. Malone was clearly drawing him that way into a confined space.

Not today, Cotton.

He crept away from the stairs to the end of the corridor and peered out into the entrance hall. The woman had taken cover on his side of the room, behind a table, near the front windows and door. He aimed the gun above her head and obliterated a set of

eighteen-paned windows directly behind her.

★ ★ ★

Hale debated what to say in response to Cogburn's threat. For the first time, he saw a semblance of backbone in one of these men.

So he opted for the truth.

'I am solving the cipher,' he told them.

'How?' Cogburn asked, clearly not impressed.

'I made a deal with the head of NIA.'

Malone stood just inside an octagon-shaped room with bright yellow walls, crowned by a dome and a glass oculus. Circular paned windows in six of the walls allowed bright morning sun inside. Little smoke had, as yet, drifted to this floor.

He debated how best to confront Wyatt.

Gunfire erupted below.

Knox kept his composure, but what he'd just heard sent a chill down his spine.

Carbonell was playing every angle. Squeezing him. Dealing with his boss. Had he been compromised? Was that why he was here? He readied himself to react, but Hale still held a gun and he was unarmed.

'What kind of deal have you made?' Bolton asked Hale.

'The NIA has solved the cipher.'

'Then what's the problem?' Surcouf asked.

'There is a price.'

The other three waited for him to tell them.

'Stephanie Nelle has to die for us to obtain the solution.'

'Then kill her,' Cogburn said. 'You're always chastising us on being blood-shy. What are you waiting for?'

'The NIA director is not to be trusted. And we can, of course, only kill Ms. Nelle once. So that death has to produce the desired results.'

Bolton shook his head. 'You're telling us you can end

this simply by killing that woman in the prison? We'll all be safe? Our letters of marque fortified? And you're playing games?'

'What I am doing, Edward, is assuring that, if that happens, we will indeed be safe.'

'No, Quentin,' Bolton said. 'What you're ensuring is that *you* will be safe.'

Cassiopeia crouched low, using the table as cover.

Two retorts.

Close by.

And the windows behind her shattered from bullets.

She recovered and sent a round in reply, aiming for the spot in the fog where she'd spotted muzzle flashes.

By eliminating the set of windows behind the woman, Wyatt had provided her an easy escape route. They stretched six feet from the floor, like doors, an easy matter to step through.

But she wasn't leaving.

He aimed his next shot at the table she was using for cover.

On the fourth round, he might not be so generous.

Malone had to return to ground level and see about Cassiopeia. She and Wyatt were engaged in a gun battle. But the south stairway, to his right, the one he'd used to ascend, was not the way. He decided to head to the north side of the building and the second set of risers.

He quickly found them and descended.

Cassiopeia decided that retreat was the smart move. Too many bullets, too much smoke.

How many assailants were there?

And why had Cotton not answered?

She fired another round, then darted out the open frame behind her, leaping from the portico.

Wyatt saw the woman flee and decided to do the same.

Malone was surely on his way back down.

Enough of this.

Malone found the first floor. A short hall to his left led back to the entrance hall, but he avoided that and stepped into what appeared to be a dining room.

A large parlor opened through another doorway, the interior walls dotted with paintings, the exterior lined with draped windows and a set of doors, the air inside consumed by swirling smoke.

He entered and peered through another set of glass doors, back out into the entrance hall.

Cassiopeia rolled onto the portico, staying low, advancing to the shattered window.

She had to get back inside.

She came to her feet and pressed her body close to the outer bricks, then slipped into the smoke-filled hall.

Her gaze raked the murky scene.

On the opposite side, beyond a set of glass doors, in another smoke-filled room dotted with windows and portraits, she caught movement.

She aimed and fired.

49

Bath, North Carolina

Hale's patience ended. These three imbeciles had no conception of what was required to win this war. It had been that way from the start. Hales had always dominated the Commonwealth. They were the ones who'd approached George Washington and the Continental Congress with the idea of coordinating the privateers' offensive efforts. Before that, vessels had operated independently, doing what they pleased when they pleased. Sure, they'd been effective, but not like what happened after they unified under a single command. Of course, for their trouble Hales derived a specified cut from every seizure, partnering with privateers from Massachusetts to Georgia, ensuring that attacks on British shipping continued unabated. Surcoufs, Cogburns, and especially Boltons had been there, but had not done nearly as much as what the Hales did. His father had cautioned him to cooperate with his fellow captains, but also always to keep a distance and maintain his own connections.

You can't rely on them, son.

He agreed. 'I'm about sick to death of being accused and threatened.'

'We're sick to death of being kept in the dark,' Bolton said. 'You're making deals with the same people who are trying to put us in prison.'

'The NIA is our ally.'

'Some ally,' Cogburn said. 'They've done nothing to stop any of this. They then cultivated a spy within the company and interfered with our move on Daniels.'

'They solved the cipher.'

'And have not, as yet, provided it to us,' Bolton said. 'Some friend.'

'What effect has that traitor had on your dealings with NIA?' Surcouf wanted to know. 'Why would they need a spy among us?'

That was the first good question he'd heard. And the answer remained unclear, except that 'The NIA director wants Stephanie Nelle dead—'

'Why?' Cogburn asked.

'There's something personal there. She did not explain, only that Nelle was investigating both her and us. It was to our advantage to stop that. She asked me to do it, so I obliged. That is what friends do for each other.'

'Why the need for the spy if she had you?' Surcouf asked.

'Because he's a liar, a thief, and a murderer,' Bolton spat out. 'A stinking, crooked pirate who can't be trusted. His great-great-granddaddy would be proud.'

His spine stiffened. 'I have had enough of your insults, Edward. I challenge you. Here and now.'

Which was his right.

Whenever ships in the past joined for a common purpose, the possibility of conflict had been great. By their nature captains were independent – mindful of their own crew, uncaring about anyone else's. But civil wars were deemed counterproductive. The idea was to loot merchant shipping, not fight among themselves. And never were disputes settled at sea, as crews rarely chanced their own lives or damage to the ship over a silly quarrel.

So another way evolved.

The challenge.

A drama in which the captains could show their courage while at the same time not endangering anyone or anything, besides themselves.

A simple test of guts.

Bolton stood silent and stared.

'Typical,' Hale said. 'You have no stomach for a fight.'

'I accept your challenge.'

Hale turned to Knox.

'Prepare it.'

Malone heard the shot and dove to the floor, scrambling beneath a table surrounded by chairs.

Glass doors six feet away shattered.

More shots came his way, keeping him close to the floor.

Cassiopeia decided to attack. She fired once, twice, then a third time, taking no chances, advancing toward the source of movement.

Malone kept his head down and waited for the shooting to stop. He was going to take Wyatt out, but he needed to make his one move count. He lay flat on the floor beneath the table and gripped the gun, readying himself.

Through the smoke, a shadow came his way.

From the entrance hall, toward the parlor.

He waited for the target to grow larger.

Then he'd take Wyatt down with some well-placed shots.

Wyatt found the cellar, pleased to see that no staff occupied the small office at the base of the stairway. A series of brick-lined rooms formed both the house's foundation and subterranean storage. They lined a long passage that stretched the building's length, lit by incandescent fixtures springing from the rough stone walls. He recalled from the exhibits at the visitor center that the rooms served as food, beer, and wine cellars. He stared at the end of the north passage, maybe seventy-five feet away, which opened out into the morning sun.

All clear.

He rushed ahead.

He knew that behind him were what Jefferson had called the dependencies. The south set held the kitchen, smokehouse, dairy, and some slave quarters. Here, on the north side, were the carriage house, stables, and ice cellar. He came to the passage end and hesitated near a door identified as the north privy.

Good placement, he thought. Ground level, outside the walls, private.

He found his cellphone and hit SEND for the message he'd prepared earlier.

READY FOR PICKUP. NORTH SIDE.

That had been the plan.

If anything had changed, so would have the message.

He'd known from the start that getting into Monticello would be easy. Getting out? An entirely different matter. That was why he'd accepted help from Andrea Carbonell.

He fled the north dependency and crossed the asphalt road. His location, on the far side from the main entrance, among trees and shrubs, provided ample cover. A check on Google Maps earlier had revealed an open field about a hundred yards northeast of the house.

A perfect landing spot.

He heard three shots from inside the house and smiled.

With any luck, the woman would shoot Malone for him.

Cassiopeia knew someone was in the next room. She'd caught movement before her barrage, but had not seen any other disturbances through the fog. She was still concerned about Cotton.

Where was he?

Who had shot at her?

A hallway opened to her right where less smoke had collected. She spotted the base of a stairway.

Whoever was in the next room knew she was here.

But they were lying low. Waiting.

For her.

Malone aimed at the black smudge drifting across the smoke.

Just a few more feet and he'd have a clean shot. He didn't want to miss. He'd tried to draw Wyatt in upstairs. That effort failed.

Now he had him.

He held his breath, finger tightened on the trigger.

One.

Two.

Cassiopeia had advanced too far.

She was exposed, and knew it.

She darted right, used the hallway for protection, then called out, 'Cotton, where are you?'

Malone exhaled.

He lowered his gun.

'In here,' he said.

'Better for you to come out here,' she called out.

He came to his feet and stepped from the parlor. Cassiopeia appeared from the smoke to his left.

'That was close,' he said.

He saw in her eyes that she agreed.

'What happened in here?'

'I found the source of all our trouble.'

A new sound invaded the silence. A low rhythmic thump of deep bass tones beating air. Approaching.

Helicopter.

Wyatt cradled the wheel in his arms, careful not to damage it. A couple of glances back and he saw no one following him. He disappeared into the trees and eased down an incline toward the field.

A chopper swooped in from the west, clearing the trees lining the field, and settled on the grass.

He jumped in the open cabin door.

Malone and Cassiopeia stepped outside onto the east portico and saw a helicopter landing about a quarter mile away.

Way too far to do anything about it.

After only a minute below the trees, the rotors' thump increased and the chopper climbed back into the morning sky, heading west.

Malone realized that without the wheel there was no way to know what Andrew Jackson had done. And since only one existed, the cipher's solution had just flown away.

'We can track that thing, can't we?' Cassiopeia asked.

'Not quick enough. He'll set down somewhere not far away and drop his passenger off.'

'The person who shot at me?'

He nodded.

The estate manager rushed up to where they stood, along with Edwin Davis. Malone stepped back inside and headed straight for Jefferson's cabinet.

The others followed.

He found the table where an empty glass cover sat.

'Those windows outside,' the manager said, 'were 19th-century glass. The frames were original to Jefferson's time. Irreplaceable.'

'This isn't a World Heritage Site, is it?' he asked, trying lighten the tension.

'Actually, it has been since 1987.'

He smiled. Stephanie would love that one. How many of those had he damaged? Four? Five?

He heard windows being opened throughout the house and saw the smoke dissipating. A new face appeared. A middle-aged woman with dark red hair and freckled skin. She was introduced as the senior curator, in charge of the estate's artifacts. She was visibly upset at the site of the missing wheel.

'It's the only one in the world,' she said.

'Who was here?' Edwin Davis asked him.

'An old friend, who apparently holds a grudge.'

He motioned for Davis and Cassiopeia to walk with him toward the library while the curator and the estate manager talked in the cabinet. He told them about Jonathan Wyatt, then said, 'Last I saw him was eight years ago, at the admin hearing when he was fired.'

Davis immediately withdrew his phone, placed a call, listened a few moments, then hung up.

'He's a contract agent now,' Davis said. 'Works for hire. Lives in Florida.'

Malone thought back to the coded message from the sheet Jackson had written. Twenty-six letters, five symbols.

GYUOINESCVOQXWJTZPKLDEMFHR
$$\Delta \, \Phi : X \, \Theta$$

'Without that wheel, the final message is indecipherable,' he said. 'We're done. We need to focus on Stephanie now.'

'Mr. Malone,' a female voice said.

He turned at the call of his name.

The curator.

'I understand it was the cipher wheel that interested you.' She walked toward him beneath the room's arches.

He nodded. 'It's what we came for. We needed it but, like you said, that's the only one in the world.'

'The only original in the world,' she said. 'Not the only wheel.'

He was listening.

'At the learning center, down in the visitor center, we wanted the kids to experience Thomas Jefferson hands-on. So we re-created many of his inventions and devices. We made them so they could touch and feel them. There's a wheel there. I had it made myself. It's plastic, and looks somewhat like the original. There are twenty-six disks, each one with twenty-six letters carved on the edge. I had nothing else to go on, so I told the company who made it to copy the disks exactly as Jefferson made them.'

50

Bath, North Carolina

Hale watched as Knox made the necessary preparations. Six glasses were brought from the bar and laid out in a row on one of the tables. Into each was poured a swallow of whiskey. Knox produced a glass vial that held a yellow-tinted liquid. The captains stared at the contents. Bolton nodded his consent to proceed. At any time, a captain challenged could withdraw, conceding defeat.

But not today.

Into one of the glasses Knox trickled a few drops of the yellowish liquid. The poison came from a Caribbean fish. Odorless, tasteless, fatal in seconds. A Commonwealth staple for centuries.

'All is ready,' Knox said.

Hale stepped to the table, his gaze on the third glass from the left where the poison rested within the amber-colored whiskey.

Bolton approached.

'Do you still accept my challenge?' Hale asked.

'I'm not afraid to die, Quentin. Are you?'

That wasn't the issue. Teaching these three a lesson was the point – one they would never forget. He kept his gaze locked on Bolton and said to Knox, 'Shuffle the glasses.'

He heard the bottoms slide across the tabletop as Knox rearranged the glasses, making it impossible to know which one contained the poison. Tradition required that the two participants lock eyes. Centuries ago, the crew would study the shuffle, then wager among themselves when a captain would make the wrong choice.

'It's done,' Knox said.

The six glasses waited in a row, their swirling contents settling. Since Hale had extended the challenge, he was required to pick first.

One in six the odds.

The best they would be.

He reached for the fourth glass, lifted it to his lips, and downed the contents with one swallow.

The liquor burned his throat.

He bore his gaze into Bolton's eyes and waited.

Nothing.

He smiled. 'Your turn.'

Wyatt settled into the helicopter's passenger compartment. He'd made his escape exactly as planned, leaving Malone empty-handed. Now no way existed to learn the next part of Andrew Jackson's message.

Mission accomplished.

He laid his gun on the seat beside him and arranged the nylon bag in his lap. Carefully, he extracted the device and balanced its metal frame across his knees. The chopper had risen from the field and was now flying west, away from Monticello, the sunny morning air clear and smooth.

He found the two loose disks and studied how to add them. A metal rod ran through the center of the other twenty-four disks, attached to the frame and held in place by a retaining pin. He noticed that the disks, about a quarter inch wide, fit tightly, no spare room except at the end where there was space for two more.

He examined the two loose ones. Each, like the others,

contained the letters of the alphabet, carved into their edge, broken by crooked lines above and below. He'd read enough about the wheel to know that the disks had to be arranged on the rod in a certain order. But Jackson had not included any instructions as to that, only adding the five curious symbols at the end. He decided to try the obvious and rotated the first visible disk on the rod and saw a carved 3 on its inside face. The two loose disks showed a 1 and 2 in the same spot.

Perhaps the order was simply numerical.

He freed the center post from the frame, held it firm so the remaining disks would not shake loose, and slipped the two disks onto the rod in the correct order.

He reattached the rod and found Andrew Jackson's message, which he'd jotted down earlier.

Hale could feel the tension in the room, thick after only one selection.

Now it was Bolton's turn.

His adversary glared at the remaining five glasses. Surcouf and Cogburn watched in apparent disbelief. Good. Those two should understand that he was not a man to challenge.

Bolton focused on the glasses.

Interesting that the usually hapless fool showed no fear. Was it anger that protected him? Or recklessness?

Bolton chose, lifting the glass and swallowing its contents. One second. Two. Three. Four.

Nothing.

Bolton smiled. 'Back to you, Quentin.'

Wyatt studied the sequence of twenty-six letters that Andrew Jackson had hidden behind the Jefferson cipher.

GYUOINESCVOQXWJTZPKLDEMFHR

Starting at the left, and the disk he knew was labeled 1, he rotated until he found a G. He continued with the next disk, locating a Y. He kept finding the relevant letters in the sequence.

The chopper brushed the outskirts of Charlottesville, flying over the University of Virginia. Carbonell was waiting for him a few miles ahead. They'd agreed to no calls or radio contact during the flight to lessen the chance of anyone listening in or following. The pilot was payroll NIA, loyal to his boss. He began to realize why the disks were so tightly packed on the spindle. Friction kept them from moving once the desired letter was found.

A forest of foliage spread out below as they flew westward toward more trees.

He had little time left.

So he kept finding letters.

Hale gulped his second glass of whiskey, wasting no time in his selection. He waited five seconds, knowing that the poison worked incredibly fast.

His father had told him about another challenge, one that happened long ago with Abner Hale. After the failed attempt on Andrew Jackson's life, and the gutting of the Commonwealth's letters of marque, tension among the four captains reached a climax when a Surcouf challenged a Hale. Kentucky bourbon had been the beverage of choice then. On the second selection, the one he'd just swallowed, Abner's eyes had rolled to the top of his head and he'd dropped dead. That had happened not in the room they now occupied, but somewhere within the current house's footprint in a parlor not all that dissimilar to this one. Abner Hale's death had relieved the pressure within the Commonwealth. His successor, Hale's great-grandfather, was more moderate and did not suffer the stigma of what his father had done.

That was another thing about pirate society.

Each man proved himself.

The whiskey settled in his stomach.

No poison.

The odds had just worsened for Bolton.

One in three.

Wyatt spotted their destination about a mile away. An under-developed industrial park with a paved lot that spanned out before a couple of dilapidated metal buildings. Two SUVs waited. A single person stood on the asphalt, looking his way.

Andrea Carbonell.

He found the twenty-sixth letter.

An R.

He pressed the tips of his fingers on the far left and far right disks and rotated all twenty-six in unison. He knew that somewhere in the circle, among the twenty-six different arrangements of letters there should be a coherent message that spanned the disks' length.

A quarter turn later he saw it.

Five words.

He committed them to memory, then rescrambled the disks.

Knox saw Edward Bolton labor over his second choice and, for the first time, spotted hesitation as the captain debated the remaining three glasses.

Just watching rattled his nerves.

He never dreamed that he would actually witness a challenge. His father had told him about them, none of which had ever gone this far. But that was the whole point of something so unpredictable, its message clear. Don't fight. Work it out. Still, no captain had ever wanted to show cowardice, so Edward Bolton held firm, knowing that one of the three remaining glasses would prove fatal.

Hale's dark eyes, oily and alive, stared unblinking.

Bolton brought a glass to his lips.

Mouth open, he threw the contents to the back of his throat and swallowed.

Five seconds passed.

Nothing.

Surcouf and Cogburn exhaled together.

Bolton grinned, an undisguised hint of relief at the corners of his mouth.

Not bad, Knox thought.

Not bad at all.

51

Hale studied both remaining glasses. Six inches of polished wood separated them.

One contained death.

'Enough of this,' Cogburn said. 'You've both proven your point. Okay. You're men, you can take it. Stop this now.'

Bolton shook his head. 'No way. It's his turn.'

'And if I choose wrong, you're rid of me,' Hale said.

'You challenged me. We're not stopping. Choose a damn glass.'

Hale stared down. The amber liquid lay still as a pond in each. He lifted one glass and swirled its contents.

Then, the other.

Bolton watched him with an intense glare.

He reached for a glass. 'This one.'

He lifted it to his lips.

All three captains and Knox stared at him. He kept his eyes locked on their faces. He wanted them to know that he possessed true courage. He poured the contents into his mouth, swished the liquor between his gums, and swallowed.

His eyes went wide, his breathing shallow.

He choked, as the muscles in his face contorted.

He reached for his chest.

Then he dropped to the floor.

* * *

Wyatt waited as the helicopter settled on the landing area, the wheel back in the nylon bag. He'd worked intelligence since graduating from college, recruited while in the military. He was neither liberal nor conservative, neither Republican nor Democrat. He was simply an American who'd served his country until deemed too reckless to be kept on the payroll. He'd made his contribution to intelligence gathering in some of the hottest spots on the planet. He'd been instrumental in uncovering two sleeper agents within the CIA, both tried and convicted as spies. He'd also taken down a double agent, carrying out a clandestine order to kill the man, despite the fact that, officially, America assassinated no one.

Never once had he violated orders.

Not even that day with Malone, when two men died. But he was no longer bound by any rules or ethics.

He could do as he pleased.

Which was another reason why he'd stayed in this fight.

He stepped from the chopper, which immediately lifted from the ground and departed. Most likely it would soon be in a hangar, safe from any prying eyes.

Carbonell waited for him alone. No driver in the SUV.

'I see you were successful,' she said.

She'd changed, and was now dressed in a short navy-blue skirt and white jacket that clung to her curvy frame. Sandals with medium heels adorned her feet. He stood a few feet away, holding the bagged wheel. His gun rested at the base of his spine, tucked behind his belt.

'What now?' he asked her.

She motioned at one of the vehicles. 'The keys are in it. Take it wherever you want.'

He feigned interest in the SUV. 'Can I keep it?'

She chuckled. 'If it'll make you happy. I don't really give a damn.'

He faced her.

'You worked the wheel and know the location, don't you?' she asked.

'I do.'

'Can you get those two missing pages?'

'I'm the only person on the planet who can.'

He realized the unique position he presently found himself in. Standing here, holding the one thing in the world that this woman needed more than anything else. With it she could find the missing two congressional pages and complete whatever scheme she'd devised. Without it, she was no better off than anyone else.

He slammed the nylon bag to the pavement and heard two-hundred-year-old wooden disks shatter.

'You can glue them back together. Should take a week or so. Good luck.'

And he walked toward the SUV.

Knox locked his eyes on the body of Quentin Hale, lying on the floor. Neither Surcouf nor Cogburn had moved.

Bolton stared with visible relief, before saying, 'Good riddance.'

One glass remained on the table.

The victor reached for it. 'Hales are the reason we're in this mess, and they never would have gotten us out. I say we use that woman in the prison to our advantage and make a bargain.'

'Like that's going to work,' Cogburn said.

'You got a better idea, Charles?' Bolton asked. 'Do you, John? How about you, Quartermaster?'

But Knox could not have cared less about them. He wanted only to save himself, and now more than ever. These men were not simply reckless, they were idiotic. None of them paid attention to anything.

Bolton lifted the final glass in a toast. 'To our fallen captain. May he enjoy hell.'

Knox lunged forward and slapped the whiskey from Bolton's fingers. The glass rattled across the wood floor, its contents scattering.

Bolton stared at him in shock. 'What the hell—'

'Dammit, Clifford,' Hale said, rising from the floor.

Shock invaded the three captains' faces.

'I had him right where I wanted him,' Hale said. 'He would have drunk himself straight to death.'

Bolton was visibly shaken.

'That's right, Edward,' Hale said. 'Another second and you would have been dead.'

'You cheating bastard,' Bolton spat out.

'Me? Cheating? Tell me. If I had not faked dying, would you have drunk the last glass, knowing it contained the poison?'

Which would have been expected by the others to complete the challenge. Of course, if the final glass was the one with the poison, the captain faced with the choice of drinking could always withdraw, thereby declaring the other the winner.

'I need to know, Edward. Would you?'

Silence.

Hale chuckled. 'Just what I thought. I wasn't cheating. I was merely helping you along a path you never would have taken.'

Knox had immediately realized Hale was not dead. The way he'd reacted to the poison was atypical. He'd used the substance enough to know precisely how it affected the human body, Scott Parrott being the latest example just a few hours ago.

Hale glared at his three compatriots. 'I do not want to hear another word out of any of you. Do not screw with me anymore.'

None of them spoke.

Knox was pleased on two counts.

First, Edward Bolton knew that he'd just saved his life. Second, so did the other two captains.

Both should definitely count for something.

52

Monticello

Malone entered the Griffin Discovery Room, located on the ground floor of the visitor center. The curator had explained that the facility was designed as a hands-on activity center for children, intended to teach them about the estate, Jefferson, and life in the late 18th and early 19th centuries. Scattered about the organized space was a reproduction of the estate, a facsimile of Jefferson's alcove bed, a nail-making shop, a slave dwelling, a weaver's studio, an exhibit that allowed the wielding of a blacksmith's hammer, and a duplicate of Jefferson's polygraph machine. Several children, their parents watching, enjoyed the self-directed activities.

'This place is popular,' the curator told him.

Cassiopeia, Edwin Davis, and the estate manager had come, too.

He spotted the replicated wheel. Three kids were spinning its tan-colored disks.

'It's made of resin,' the curator said. 'The original is far more fragile. Those disks are carved wood, over two hundred years old, about a quarter inch thick, and crack easily.'

He caught the concern in her voice. 'I'm sure the thief is going to be careful.'

At least until he deciphers the message, he silently added.

The kids fled the wheel exhibit heading for something new. Malone walked over and examined the twenty-six disks threaded onto a metal rod. On the edge of each were black letters, separated by black lines.

'Do you have the sequence written down?' the curator asked.

'He doesn't need it,' Cassiopeia said, adding a smile.

No, he didn't.

His eidetic brain rattled them off.

GYUOINESCVOQXWJTZPKLDEMFHR

He spun the disks, assembling them in the correct order.

Wyatt kept walking toward the car.

'I knew you'd read the message,' she called out.

He stopped and turned.

She stood in the sun, her face a mask. The nylon bag remained on the asphalt. He realized that her calculating brain had rattled through the options and quickly determined that there was no play left, except to deal with him. Destroying the disks had ensured his safety, since now only he knew the location.

She walked toward him and kept coming, stopping only when she was inches away. 'Triple your fee. One-half deposited within the next two hours in the bank of your choice. The remaining part when you deliver the two documents to me intact.'

There was the obvious. 'You realize the Commonwealth would pay far more for them.'

'Of course. But, like this morning, you apparently need something only I can provide. That's why you're talking with me right now instead a driving away in your new SUV.'

She was right. In order to do as Andrew Jackson directed he required a few items and had no time to procure them himself. 'I need a clean passport.'

'And where would you be going?'

Since he doubted he could shield his movements from her anyway, he told her about Paw Island, Nova Scotia, then made clear, 'Only you and I know this location. So only you and I can tell someone else.'

'Your way of keeping me honest?'

'If anyone else appears there, whatever I find goes up in flames. And you and the Commonwealth can go to hell.'

'This your way of showing that you're better than me?'

He shook his head. 'It's just my way.'

She tossed him an understanding grin. 'That's what I like about you, Jonathan. You know exactly what you want. Okay. We'll do this your way.'

Cassiopeia glanced over Cotton's shoulder as he arranged the disks. She and Edwin Davis had never finished their conversation, and there was much still to be said, but it would have to wait. And to think that she'd flown to New York simply to have a romantic weekend. Now she was embroiled in a true sticky wicket. She smiled at the phrase, one her father liked to use. He'd loved cricket, sponsoring several Spanish national teams. Sports had been important to him. Unfortunately, she hadn't inherited his passion. But this was one sticky wicket, and just as hard crust atop wet soil caused a cricket ball to bounce in any direction, the same was true here. Lots of secrets, egos, and personalities. Not to mention the fact that two of the players were among the best-known people on the planet.

Cotton finished his task and said, 'Those five symbols at the end of Jackson's message are not on these disks. So they must be part of something else.'

He held all twenty-six disks in place and rotated them as a unit.

'There it is,' he said.

She focused on the black letters. One row, all the way across, formed words connected without spaces.

PAWISLANDMAHONEBAYDOMINION

'We need a computer,' Cotton said.

The curator led them to an office off the exhibit room where a desktop waited. Cassiopeia decided to do the honors and typed PAW ISLAND, MAHONE BAY.

The screen filled with sites. She selected one.

Mahone Bay was located at 44°30 N, 64°15 W, just off the coast of Nova Scotia, a respectable body of water that opened to the Atlantic Ocean. Named after the French *mahonne*, which was a type of boat once used by the locals. Dotted with nearly 400 islands, the most famous of which was Oak Island, where for more than two hundred years treasure hunters had excavated a deep pit into the bedrock, searching to no avail for gold. Paw Island was south of Oak, upon which lay a British fort, long abandoned, once called Dominion.

'Jackson chose his site with care,' Cotton said. 'That's about as out of the way as you can get. But it's appropriate. That area has long been associated with piracy. It was a haven for pirates in the 18th century.' He faced Davis. 'I'm going.'

'I agree. It's the best thing for Stephanie. We need those pages.'

She already knew what Cotton wanted her to do. 'I'll slow them down through the phone tap. We can feed Hale whatever we like.'

He nodded. 'Do it. Wyatt has the wheel and he'll be headed north, too.'

'I'll find Stephanie,' she told him.

He turned to the curator. 'You said you created that duplicate wheel. Is the fact that it's an exact duplicate of the original advertised anywhere?'

The woman shook her head. 'The manufacturer and I are the only ones who know. I didn't even tell the estate manager until a little while ago up in the house. It really wasn't that important.'

But Cassiopeia realized exactly why that fact was critical. 'Wyatt thinks he's the only one who knows.'

Cotton nodded.

'Yep. Which means, for the first time, we're ahead of the game.'

PART FOUR

53

Knox paced the grass beneath a canopy of oaks and pines. He'd been excused from the captain's meeting just after Hale's resurrection and told to wait outside. Not unusual for the four captains to discuss things without him, but he remained concerned about Hale's private talk with the traitor.

Was that what the captains were discussing?

Adventure had, by now, made its way through the Ocracoke Inlet into the open Atlantic, heading out to dispose of the body.

What was he to do next?

The front door opened.

Bolton, Surcouf, and Cogburn emerged into the midday sun. They descended the veranda and headed for an electric cart. Bolton spotted him and walked over as the other two kept pace toward the vehicle.

'I wanted to thank you,' Bolton said.

'My job is to look after all of the captains.'

'What Hale is doing is wrong. It's not going to work. I know, what we tried to do was desperate, or even worse than that. But he's no better.'

Knox shrugged. 'I'm not sure any of us knows what to do anymore.'

Defeat clouded the other man's face. Bolton extended his hand, which Knox shook.

'Thanks again.'

Good to know that his move may have paid off. He might need Edward Bolton before this was done.

'Mr. Knox.'

He turned.

Hale's private secretary waited on the porch.

'The captain will see you now.'

Hale poured himself a drink as Knox reentered the study. It held some of the same whiskey that had been used for the challenge. He tipped the glass to his quartermaster and said, 'At least this one won't kill me.'

The tumbler Knox had slapped from Bolton's hand still lay on the hardwood floor, its liquid death soaked into the nearby planks.

'No one should touch that stain,' Knox made clear. 'It will need to evaporate.'

'I'm keeping it there as a reminder of my triumph over idiocy. You should have let him die.'

'You know that I couldn't.'

'Ah, yes. That duty of yours. The loyal quartermaster who walks the line between captain and crew. Elected by one group, yet dominated by the other. How *do* you do it?'

He made no attempt to mask his sarcasm.

'Did you make your point to them?' Knox calmly asked.

'What you really want to know is what we just discussed without you.'

'You'll tell me when necessary.'

He threw the whiskey toward the back of his throat and swallowed.

He then banged the glass down on the table, reached for his gun, and pointed the weapon straight at Knox.

★ ★ ★

Malone settled into the seat of an executive Gulfstream and fired up the LCD screen beside the white leather seat. He was alone in the spacious cabin, taxiing down the runway at Reagan National Airport, readying himself for what lay 800 miles to the north, across the Canadian border.

He needed the Internet and, thankfully, did not have to wait until 10,000 feet before using any approved electronic devices. He zeroed in on a few websites and learned what he could about Nova Scotia, a narrow Canadian peninsula barely connected to New Brunswick, surrounded by the Atlantic Ocean. Three hundred miles long, 50 miles wide, 4800 miles of coastline. A mix of old and new with craggy coves, sandy beaches, and fertile valleys. The south shore, from Halifax to Shelburne, contained countless inlets, the largest of which was Mahone. Though the French had discovered the bay in 1534, the British took control in 1713.

Something he hadn't known came up on one site.

During the American Revolution colonial forces had occupied the region, attempting to make Canada the fourteenth colony. The idea had been to woo the many angry French still living there into becoming allies against the English, but the move failed. Canada remained British and, after the Revolution, became even more so, as Loyalists emigrated northward, fleeing the newly formed United States.

And he'd been right.

Mahone Bay became a haven for pirates.

Shipbuilding developed into an industry. Thick fogs and sinister tidal marshes provided ideal cover for several hundred islands. The locale was not all that dissimilar to Port Royal, Jamaica, or Bath, North Carolina, both of which had also once been notorious pirate dens.

Oak Island, which lay in Mahone Bay, appeared on many of the websites, so he read what he could. Its history began on a summer day in 1795 when Daniel McGinnis, a young man in his early twenties, discovered a clearing where oak trees had been felled, leaving only stumps. At the center of the clearing lay a circular indentation, maybe twelve feet wide. A large branch protruded over the depression. One version said that a ship's pulley had been attached to the branch. Another stated there were strange markings on the tree. A third account noted that the clearing had been blanketed with red clover, which wasn't native to the island. No matter which version was accepted as true, what happened next was beyond dispute.

People started digging.

First McGinnis and his friends, then others, then organized treasure consortiums. They bore down nearly two hundred feet and found layers of charcoal, timber, coconut fibers, flagstones, and clay. If their accounts could be believed, they unearthed a strange stone with curious markings. Two ingenious flood tunnels tied into the shaft, designed to ensure that anyone who dug deep enough would encounter nothing but water.

And that was exactly what they found.

Flooding had thwarted every attempt to solve the mystery.

Countless theories abounded.

Some said it was a pirate cache, dug by Captain William Kidd himself. Others gave ownership to the privateer Sir Francis Drake or the Spanish, as an out-of-the-way place to stash their wealth. More pragmatic people suggested military involvement – pay chests concealed by the French or English in their seesawing struggle to control Nova Scotia.

Then there were the far-outers.

Antediluvian Atlanteans, interplanetary travelers, Masons, Templars, Egyptians, Greeks, Celts.

Several men lost their lives, many their fortunes, but no treasure had ever been found.

Oak Island wasn't even an island any longer. A narrow

causeway, built to allow heavy digging equipment to easily pass back and forth, now connected it to the mainland. One recent Canadian news article mentioned that the provincial government was considering buying the land and turning the place into a tourist attraction.

Now that would yield a treasure, he thought.

He located a few mentions of Paw Island, a few miles southeast of Oak. About a mile long, and half that wide, shaped liked its name. Two coves indented its center facing north, while smaller ones cracked the remaining shoreline. Its rounded west side was covered with trees, while rocky cliffs dominated the east and south shores. The French had explored it in the 17th century looking for furs, but the English had built a fort, which they dubbed Wildwood, that faced the Atlantic and guarded the bay. He read how Nova Scotia was generally devoid of ruins. Nothing was ever wasted. Houses were dismantled timber by timber, the hinges, door handles, nails, bricks, mortar, and cement all reused. *Twenty-first-century boards, driven by 18th-century nails, over 19th-century joists,* was how one site described it.

But the limestone fort on Paw Island stood as an anomaly.

And history was the explanation.

In 1775 when the American Continental army invaded, seizing control of the British forts, Wildwood was taken early and renamed Dominion. But the Americans were soon defeated at the Battle of Quebec and withdrew from Canada in 1776. Before leaving Paw Island, though, they torched the fort. Nothing was ever rebuilt, the site abandoned to the elements, the fire-blackened walls left standing as a reminder of the insult.

Now only birds occupied them.

'Mr. Malone,' a voice said over the intercom. 'We have a weather delay. They're asking us to hold on the runway.'

'I didn't think those rules applied to the Secret Service.'

'Unfortunately, there's a nasty storm between here and Maine and even the Secret Service has to bow to that.'

'Keep in mind, we're in a hurry.'

'It could be a little bit. They didn't sound encouraging.'

He tapped the keyboard and found a map of Mahone Bay, deciding how best to arrive on Paw Island. They would be landing at a small airstrip to the south, specifically avoiding Halifax and its international hub, since Wyatt could be traveling through there. The Secret Service had run a check of all flights to Nova Scotia, but no seats had been booked in Wyatt's name. No surprise. He was surely flying under an alias with a clean ID, or he may have chartered something.

It didn't matter.

He wanted his adversary to have a clear run to the island.

There, they would get reacquainted.

54

Cassiopeia followed Edwin Davis into a room not much larger than a closet. Inside was a small table that supported a console with an LCD monitor. The screen displayed a room dotted with oil portraits dominated by a conference table, whose seats were rapidly filling with men and women. She'd returned with Davis to Washington. Later, she'd head back south to Fredericksburg to make use of Kaiser's phone tap.

'He had me order them here,' Davis said, pointing to the screen. 'Heads of the eighteen largest intelligence agencies. CIA, NSA, NIA, Defense Intelligence, National Counter-Terrorism, Homeland Security, Foreign Terrorist Asset Tracking, National Geospatial, Underground Facility Analysis – you name it, we have somebody spending money on it.'

'Bet they're wondering what's going on.'

Davis smiled. 'These people don't like surprises, or one another for that matter.'

She watched on the screen as the president of the United States burst into the room and moved out of view to the head of the table. The camera had apparently been installed behind where he sat so only the participants would be recorded.

Everyone sat.

'It's good to see you're okay,' one of the participants said to Daniels.

'It's good to be okay.'

'Mr. President, we had little notice of this meeting so nothing has been prepared. We weren't even told of the subject matter.'

'Head of Central Intelligence,' Davis told her. 'The president owes me five dollars. I bet he'd be the first to probe. He said NSA.'

'You people love to tell me how good you are,' Daniels said. 'That this country would be in dire jeopardy if we didn't spend billions of dollars every year on what you do. You also like to hide behind that secrecy you so righteously demand. I don't have the luxury of working in secret. I have to do what I do with a cadre of reporters camped out less than a hundred feet away from where I work. Hell, I don't even know where half of your offices are located, much less what you do.'

'Do they know we're watching?' she asked.

Davis shook his head. 'Pinhole camera. The Secret Service installed it a few years ago. Nobody knows but senior staff.'

'This monstrosity of government called homeland security,' the president said, 'is absurd. I have yet to find anyone who knows how much it costs, how many are employed, how many programs there are and, most important, how much duplication there is. Best I can tell there are nearly 1300 separate organizations working homeland security or foreign intelligence. That's on top of nearly 2000 private contractors. Nearly 900,000 hold a top secret clearance. How could anything possibly be kept secret with that many eyes and ears?'

No one said a word.

'Everyone said they were going to streamline things after 9/11. You folks swore you were finally going to start working together. What you did was create 300 new intelligence organizations. You produce over 50,000 intelligence reports each year. Who reads them all?'

No answer.

'That's right. No one does. So what good are they?'

'He's going right for their throats,' she said to Davis.

'It's all they understand.'

'I want to know who hired Jonathan Wyatt and had him in New York yesterday,' the president asked, breaking the room's silence.

'*I did.*'

'Is that her?' Cassiopeia asked.

Davis nodded. 'Andrea Carbonell. Head of NIA.'

She'd noticed the woman's entrance, her swarthy complexion, dark hair, and Latino influences similar to her own. 'What's her story?'

'Daughter of Cuban immigrants. Born here. She worked her way up through the ranks until finally snagging the head of NIA. Her service record is actually exemplary, except for her ties to the Commonwealth.'

Carbonell sat straight, hands folded on the table, eyes intent on the president. Her features remained expressionless, even in the face of an angry commander in chief.

'*Why did you have Wyatt in New York?*' Daniels asked her.

'*I required outside assistance to counter pressure I was receiving from CIA and NSA.*'

'*Explain yourself.*'

'*A few hours ago someone tried to kill me.*'

The room fell into a hush.

Carbonell cleared her throat. 'I wasn't planning on bringing it up in this meeting, but an automated weapon was waiting for me in my residence.'

Daniels hesitated only a moment. 'And the importance of that? Besides the fact that you could be dead.'

'*Wyatt was in New York to help me decipher the recent actions of some of my colleagues. We were meeting to discuss the situation. But a CIA deputy director and another deputy from NSA interrupted that meeting and took Wyatt. I would like to know the purpose of that action.*'

She was good, Cassiopeia thought. Carbonell had yet to answer a question, but she'd managed to shift attention away from herself. Her inquiry clearly interested some of the others around the table, who stared at CIA, and another man whom Davis identified as the NSA director.

'Mr. President,' CIA said. 'This woman has been conspiring with the Commonwealth. She may well have been involved in the attempt on your life.'

'Do you have proof of that?' Carbonell calmly asked.

'I don't need proof,' Daniels said to her. 'I just need to be convinced. So tell me, did you have any involvement with the attempt on my life?'

'I did not.'

'Then how did Wyatt get himself right smack in the middle of things? He was there, in the Grand Hyatt. We know that. He directed agents straight to Cotton Malone. He involved Malone in the whole thing.'

'He has a personal vendetta against Malone,' Carbonell said. 'He set Malone up, involving him in the attempt on your life, unbeknownst to me. I fired him just before CIA and NSA took him away.'

'Wyatt just shot up Monticello,' Daniels said. 'He stole a rare artifact. A cipher wheel. Did you arrange for that to happen?'

'The shooting or the stealing?'

'You choose. And, by the way, I've never liked a smart-ass.'

'As I said, Mr. President, I fired Wyatt yesterday. He no longer works for me. I think the CIA or NSA is in a better position to answer the question of what happened after I terminated him.'

'So, do any of you have any knowledge of the plot to kill me?' the president asked.

The table stirred at the pointed question.

'We were unaware there was a plot,' one of them said.

'You're damn right there was,' Daniels said. 'I asked a question. Ms. Carbonell, how about you answer first.'

'I knew nothing of any assassination plot.'

'Liar,' CIA said.

Carbonell kept her composure. 'I only know that Wyatt lured Cotton Malone to the Grand Hyatt, hoping Malone would stop the attempt. Then Wyatt directed agents toward Malone. He apparently was hoping one of them would shoot him. He reported this to me after *it happened. I realized immediately that things were way out of control. So I severed all connection with him.'*

'*You should have arrested him,*' one of the others around the table said.

'*As I've already said, he was in the custody of CIA and NSA after I did what I did. Seems they are the ones who need to explain why he was not arrested.'*

'She's good,' Cassiopeia said.

'And she's holding back,' Davis said.

Cassiopeia's eyes seemed to communicate exactly what she was thinking.

'I know,' Davis said. 'I'm doing the same thing. But can we keep things close a little while longer.'

'To what end?'

'Hell if I know.'

'*Where's Wyatt now?*' Daniels asked the room.

'*He attacked the two men we sent to interrogate him,*' CIA said. '*And escaped.*'

'*Were you planning on reporting any of this?*' the president asked. No reply.

'*Who sent the police after Cotton Malone in Richmond, Virginia?*'

'*We did,*' CIA said. '*We ascertained that Malone emailed to himself a classified document. He then accessed it from a hotel in Richmond. We asked the locals to pick him up for questioning.'*

'*Don't bother him again,*' Daniels ordered. '*Ms. Carbonell, are you in communication with the Commonwealth?*'

She shook her head. '*My contact to them was found dead last evening in Central Park, as was another of my agents in a nearby hotel. Two more were seriously injured. They were apparently shot by a Commonwealth operative they were attempting to apprehend.'*

'*You have four people down?*' CIA asked her.

'*I agree. It's tragic. We contained the situation quickly and kept a lid on it. We're searching for that Commonwealth operative now. He will be found.'*

'Why did CIA and NSA want to speak to Wyatt?' Daniels asked.

'We, too,' CIA said, 'were curious as to Wyatt's involvement with what happened in New York.'

'Why?'

The president's curt inquiry triggered more silence.

'It's simply a question,' Daniels said. 'How did you know Wyatt was even in New York?'

More silence.

Then, from NSA, 'We've been watching NIA and Ms. Carbonell.'

'Why?'

'He's screwing with them,' Davis said. 'He does that to me all the time. Just one why after another, forcing you down a path that he's already walked. He's just waiting for you to catch up.'

'She's interfering with our prosecution of the Commonwealth,' NSA said. 'That group is well known to us all and is a danger to our national security. The decision was made to eliminate it. NIA and Ms. Carbonell disagree with that decision. We wondered why. Too much loyalty there under the circumstances. We knew she'd employed Wyatt, we just didn't know all that was about to happen. If we had, we would taken preventive measures.'

'That's comforting to know,' Daniels said, his sarcasm clear.

'When we learned Malone was the man in the video,' CIA said, 'we realized something strange was up.'

'Okay, let me see if I have this straight,' Daniels said. 'Somebody, identity unknown, tries to blow me up. A contract player, Jonathan Wyatt, is involved. At least three intelligence agencies knew that Wyatt was in New York doing something. Two of you were already investigating NIA and its director. What Wyatt was doing in New York, none of you is willing to admit. But two of you are curious enough to take Wyatt into custody, yet he escapes. And most important, four agents are down.'

No one said a word.

'You folks are about as useful as tits on a boar hog. How about *this, which one of you sent men into the Garver Institute last night and murdered one of its employees?'*

No reply.

'No one going to claim that one? I wouldn't think so.'

'Carbonell probably did it herself,' Cassiopeia said.

Davis nodded. 'Makes the most sense.'

'I want each of you to know that we're investigating this, independent of you. If Wyatt lured Malone to New York, that meant he knew what was about to happen. If he knew, others knew. Hence, a plot.'

'We need to find Wyatt,' one of the men said.

'FBI director,' Davis noted. 'The only one around that table we can actually trust. A straight shooter.'

'I'd say that should be tops on your list,' Daniels said. 'What about those two automated weapons from the hotel rooms? What have you learned?'

'Sophisticated engineering,' the FBI director said. 'Well made. Malone disabled the one with shots from the other that shorted out its electronics. They were both radio-controlled. No way, though, to ascertain from where, though a radius of about three miles was the receiver's range.'

'That's a lot of real estate in New York City,' Daniels said. 'What, about 30,000 hotel rooms to choose from?'

'Something like that.'

'Since Wyatt seems the only one at the moment who knew anything in advance,' Daniels said, 'he's the best lead. At least he sent Malone in there. That's better than the rest of you can claim.'

'Is Cotton Malone conducting your inquiry?' NSA asked.

'Does it matter?'

'No, sir. I was simply curious.'

'Like I said. None of you bother Malone. That's a direct order. He's working for me. The people who murdered Dr. Gary Voccio last night also tried to kill Malone and, interestingly, Wyatt, too. That means Wyatt may not be my enemy. I intend to find out who ordered that strike.'

No one spoke.

'Also, Stephanie Nelle has been missing for several days.'

'Missing where?' CIA asked.

'I don't know. She's just gone.'

'Do you plan to release any of this to the public?' someone asked.

'I'm not going to do anything.' Daniels stood. 'Not until you folks do what you're supposed to do and provide me with some meaningful information.'

Daniels came back into the camera's view as he marched toward the door.

The people around the table rose for his exit.

'Mr. President.'

NSA director.

Daniels stopped at the door.

'Your assessment of our effectiveness is wrong,' NSA said. 'For my agency, we intercept nearly two billion emails, phone calls, and other international communications each day. Someone must listen to those. It's how threats directed toward us are communicated. It's how we became suspicious of Ms. Carbonell and her ties to the Commonwealth. We provide a vital service.'

'And who sorts though those two billion communications you intercept each day?' Daniels asked.

NSA started to speak, but Daniels held up a hand. 'Don't bother. I know the answer. No one. You sort a mere fraction. And every once in a while you luck onto something, like with NIA, then spout off about your importance. Interesting how, despite all of your money, people, and equipment a group of goat-herding terrorists from the wilds of Afghanistan managed to plow two planes into the World Trade Center and another into the Pentagon. If not for the bravery of some ordinary Americans another plane would have destroyed the White House. You didn't know a damn thing about any of that coming.'

'With all due respect, sir, I resent your insults.'

'With all due respect, I resent tossing $75 billion dollars a year – that we know of – away on your foolishness. I resent the fact that

those planes made it as far as they did. I resent your arrogance. We deserve an intelligence community that works together as a team in every sense of the word. Hell, if World War II had been run this way we would have lost. I wasn't planning on doing this but, before I leave office, I'm going to shake this rotting tree down to its roots. So get ready, people. Anybody else having something to say?'

No one spoke.

'Find Stephanie Nelle,' Daniels said.

'Before the assassins?' one of them asked.

'Find one and I believe you'll find the other.'

The president left.

The others lingered a few seconds, then they, too, began to leave.

'Okay,' Davis said. 'Our turn.'

55

Knox readied himself to be shot. The weapon was of modest caliber, and the bullet would surely pass straight through him.

But it was still going to hurt.

Apparently, the traitor had sold him out.

Hale lowered the gun. 'Don't you give me any more trouble, either. You should not have interfered in that challenge.'

He exhaled. 'Killing Captain Bolton was not the answer to the problem.'

Hale laid the gun on the table and grabbed his empty glass, refilling it with whiskey. 'The answer to our problem came a little while ago. The director of NIA called me.'

He told himself to listen carefully. Carbonell was maneuvering again. But so was Hale.

'NIA has solved the cipher. They know where that no-good scoundrel Andrew Jackson hid the two missing pages. She told me the location.'

'And you believe her?'

'Why not?'

'They stopped our assassination attempt and cultivated a spy within this company.'

Hale nodded. 'I know. But at the moment, the NIA director wants something from me. Something only I can provide.'

'Our guest in the lodge.'

Hale sipped his drink and nodded. 'Providing this information is NIA's way of demonstrating good faith. They hired a contract person who is going after the missing pages. But the man has no intention of turning over what he finds. The director made that clear. She wants him killed. It's a remote location, which offers a good opportunity to do that. Of course, in return, she says we can have whatever there is to find.'

He listened as Hale explained about Nova Scotia and a man named Jonathan Wyatt. 'Carbonell provided me everything she has on Paw Island and Fort Dominion.'

'What's to stop us from simply going after the two pages and ignoring Wyatt?'

'Nothing, provided Wyatt doesn't get in your way. From what she said, you'll have to kill him in order to get him out of the way. He's not the type to simply step aside.'

Everything about this sounded bad.

Hale pointed toward his desk. 'There's a photo and dossier on Wyatt. He was also the man who stopped the assassination attempt. I'd say you owe him.'

Perhaps he did, but he wasn't quite sure what.

'Take the file. Use the jet. NIA tells me Wyatt is flying commercially out of Boston, but weather is delaying him. Get there before he does and be ready.'

Apparently things had changed one more time and Carbonell had decided to provide the Commonwealth what it wanted.

Or had she?

'This could be a trap.'

'I am willing to take the chance.'

No, he was willing for *someone else* to take the chance. But Knox had no choice. He had to go to Canada. If he could be ready before this Wyatt arrived, it should be an easy kill. One more demonstration of his loyalty to the captains, which should buy him more time.

At least the traitor had not compromised him.

'Look, Clifford,' Hale said, conciliation in his voice. 'Why provide us this information if she's lying?'

'Apparently, so we can do her dirty work. The man she sent can't be trusted, so she wants us to eliminate him.'

Just like with Scott Parrott.

'If that makes her happy, so what? If she's lying, we still have Stephanie Nelle to do with as we please.'

He caught the message. *What do we have to lose?* So he knew the right response. 'I'll head north immediately.'

'Before you leave, there is another matter. Bolton was right about one thing. The equipment that we have secreted at Shirley Kaiser's residence. It's time to remove it before someone notices. It's not needed any longer. Do you have men who can accomplish that?'

He nodded. 'Two I've been training. They assist me often. They can handle it.'

'I spoke with Kaiser a day or so ago and she told me she would be out this evening at a fund-raiser in Richmond. That should give you an opportunity.'

Hale sipped more whiskey.

'Clifford, the others know nothing of my association with NIA, beyond the little bit I told them earlier. And I don't want to share any more until we have success. I'm asking you to keep this between us, for now. Contrary to what they think, I will not abandon them, though God knows I should. They are an ungrateful, stupid lot. But I take my oath to the Articles seriously. If we succeed, we succeed for all.'

He could not care less, but feigned interest. 'I'm curious about one thing. How did you know which glass to pick?'

'What makes you think I knew?'

'You're a bold man, but not a foolish one. For you to issue that challenge you must have known you could win.'

'My father taught me a trick,' Hale said. 'If you jiggle the glass ever so slightly, the poison comes out of suspension and blurs the alcohol. It's just for an instant but, if you pay close attention, you can see it. I swirled each glass before I drank. Granted, it's not foolproof, but it's better than blind luck.'

'That took guts,' he said.

Hale smiled at himself. 'Indeed. It certainly did.'

Wyatt stepped onto an Air Canada flight in Boston's Logan International Airport. He'd flown from Richmond, Virginia, and had now been laid over for nearly two hours. A bad storm was delaying every flight, and he wondered if this one would make it out anytime soon. Flight time to Halifax, Nova Scotia, was another two hours, which should place him on the ground by midafternoon – provided there were no more delays. With any luck he'd be on Paw Island by five PM. He'd checked the weather, and the temperature should be around seventy degrees. The area had lately been experiencing a September heat wave combined with a dry spell. If necessary, he'd sleep on the island and finish his business tomorrow. One way or the other he would leave there with those missing pages.

He'd come to New York fully prepared with flash bombs, guns, and ammunition, but his passport would be of little use. Airline manifests could be checked by law enforcement with nothing more than a click of a mouse.

Another identity was required.

So he'd been forced to deal with Carbonell.

The half of his triple fee had been deposited in his Liechtenstein account, as promised. A lot of cash, tax-free. But a lot of risk, too. The greatest of which was dealing with Carbonell. She'd rubbed him wrong. Riled-up feelings within him he'd thought long suppressed. He was an American intelligence operative. Always had been, always would be.

That meant something to him.

Contrary to what Carbonell seemed to think.

He resented her callous, selfish attitude. She had no business heading any intelligence agency. Operatives in the field had to know that their superiors were watching their backs. Things were dangerous enough without having to worry whether your boss was unnecessarily placing your life in jeopardy.

She had to be stopped.

And that was why he'd stayed in this fight.

Malone? The trail for Captain America ended at Monticello. He wasn't a factor any longer. That would have to wait for another time.

This would be his victory, and his alone.

He'd opted to fly commercial to draw less attention. He'd rent a car once on the ground and drive the fifty miles south to Mahone Bay. He'd bought appropriate outdoor clothing. Anything else needed he could buy once on the ground. The Nova Scotia peninsula was a mecca for outdoor enthusiasts, catering to cyclists, golfers, hikers, kayakers, boaters, and bird-watchers. It being Sunday might offer a few challenges with store hours, but he'd make do. Unfortunately, he was unarmed. No way to import a weapon. He'd read the intel Carbonell had provided, especially the information explaining the last word in the cipher's message – *Dominion* – which referred to Fort Dominion, located on the south side of Paw Island.

A ruin not only today, but in Andrew Jackson's time.

The site possessed a checkered history.

During the American Revolution, after the fort was seized by the Continental army, seventy-four British prisoners died there while in colonial hands. They'd been temporarily incarcerated beneath the fort, in a dungeon-like complex carved into its rocky foundation, and drowned when the level flooded. Three colonial officers were court-martialed over the incident, the charge being that they were told by others that the chamber would flood yet ignored the warning. They were acquitted, as the testimony regarding their knowledge of the danger was conflicted, at best.

He sympathized with those officers.

They'd simply been doing their duty, in a time of war, a long way from any command authority. Of course they hadn't had the luxury of instant communication. Instead, they had to make local decisions. Then, months later, someone came along and second-guessed them. Unlike him, those men escaped punishment, but he imagined that any military career those officers might have envisioned ended with their trial.

Just like his.

What happened at Fort Dominion remained a sore spot for American and British relations up to the War of 1812, when the two nations finally resolved their differences. He wondered if there was any connection between that tragic incident and what Andrew Jackson had done sixty years later.

Dominion had been specifically chosen by Jackson.

Why?

He'd also reviewed again Jackson's letter to the Commonwealth and his message hidden behind Jefferson's cipher. The five symbols remained unexplained.

$$\Delta \ \Phi : X \ \Theta$$

Carbonell had found nothing on them. Her advice? Deal with them once he was on the ground in Canada.

She'd assured him again that this mission was between the two of them. But a lie for her was far better than the truth, even when lying wasn't necessary.

This was the end of the line, though.

If she lied to him here, even in the slightest—

He'd kill her.

56

Cassiopeia sat in the Oval Office, Edwin Davis beside her on an upholstered settee. She'd been here once before and not much had changed. A couple of Norman Rockwells still adorned one wall. The same portrait of George Washington hung above the fireplace. Potted Swedish ivy dangled from the mantel – a tradition, Davis explained, dating back to the Kennedy administration. Two high-backed chairs framed the hearth, a scene she recognized from photo ops when the president sat to the left and a visiting head of state on the right. That had started, Davis explained, with Franklin Roosevelt so his guest would be seated, like him, downplaying his handicap.

The door opened and Daniels entered.

The president sat in one of the chairs before the fireplace.

'The press corps will be here shortly. I have some pictures to take with the new ambassador from Finland. They're not supposed to ask questions when they come here for the pictures, but they will. Hell, their minds are fixated on only one thing, and they do have to keep the public interested.'

She caught his exasperation.

'This assassination attempt will be *the* story for a while,' the president said. 'Of course, if we told them the real story, nobody would believe us. What did you two think of our little gathering?'

'That should rattle their cages,' Davis said.

'Those sons of bitches irk my ass,' Daniels said. 'You hear that arrogant NSA bastard as I left?'

'Carbonell is good,' Davis said. 'She held her own.'

'Smug as hell, too. With balls. She's our target. No question. In *The Godfather,* I love that book and movie, Don Corleone teaches Michael that "the one who comes to you with an offer of help will be your traitor." I know, I know. It's fiction. But that screenwriter was right.'

'Why did you tell them about Stephanie?' Cassiopeia asked.

'It couldn't hurt. At least they know finding her will please me and, right now, I imagine most of them want to do that. Maybe one of 'em will surprise me and actually do something. Is Cotton on his way?'

Davis told his boss that the Secret Service flight had been delayed because of weather, then said, 'We have no idea how, or when, Wyatt will get there.'

'But he'll be there,' Daniels said. 'Did you learn about the locale?'

Davis nodded. 'A letter exists in the National Archives, from a group in Cumberland, Nova Scotia, sent to George Washington. The locals expressed sympathy for the American revolutionary cause against the British and actually invited Washington and the Continental army to invade Nova Scotia. They wanted Halifax burned and the British gutted. We didn't take them up on that offer entirely, but we did capture a few strategic sites. Fort Dominion was one of those. It helped guard our flank, keeping British ships out of Mahone Bay while our forces moved on Montreal and Quebec. When the British defeated us at Quebec, we abandoned Dominion and burned it. Jackson, as a military man, definitely would have known of Fort Dominion, and he would not have used the British name, Wildwood, for the site.'

Cassiopeia listened as Davis explained about 74 British

soldiers who died at the fort under questionable circumstances during the American occupation. The colonial officers involved had been court-martialed, but were all acquitted. After the Revolution, Canada ceased being a military target, becoming more a haven for ambitious pirates and privateers. Nova Scotia ultimately attracted 30,000 British Loyalists from the newly formed United States, one-tenth of whom were fleeing slaves.

'But during the War of 1812 we tried to take Canada again,' Davis said. 'We lost that one, too.'

'And what were we going to do with it?' Daniels asked, shaking his head. 'Crazy thinking. Just like our roosters back there in the conference room. Accomplishing nothing but their own survival. What did you find out about the five symbols in the message?'

Davis reached for a file in his lap. 'I had the national security staff do the research, people I can trust here, in-house. Nothing flagged anywhere. But one of the staffers is a big conspiratorialist. Into a lot of the New Age stuff, and she recognized the symbols.'

Davis handed both Cassiopeia and the president a sheet of paper.

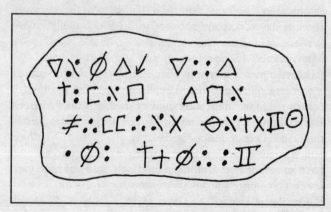

'That stone was supposedly found about ninety feet down in the Oak Island treasure pit. When they hit that slab they thought something valuable would be either with it or below it. Unfortunately, that was not the case.'

'What does it mean?' the president asked.

'It's a simple transposition code.'

Davis handed them another sheet.

'It supposedly says, Forty Feet Below Two Million Pounds Are Buried.' Davis paused. 'There's just one problem. No one alive has ever seen this stone. No one knows if it ever existed. But every book about Oak Island, and there are many, mentions it.'

Davis explained the provenance.

The slab was apparently found by one of the treasure consortiums digging on the island around 1805. A local resident named John Smith subsequently used it in his fireplace for decoration. There it stayed for nearly fifty years, until Smith died. Then it disappeared.

'So how do we know what it looks like?' Daniels asked.

'An excellent question. One to which there is no good answer. That image you have is the one that's in all the books.'

'Who deciphered it?'

'No one knows that, either. There are multiple stories.'

Daniels sat back in the chair, holding the two pages. 'A stone no one has ever seen, translated by no one we know, yet Andrew Jackson uses nearly identical symbols to hide two missing congressional journal pages?'

'It's possible,' Davis said, 'Jackson could have heard tales of Oak Island. By 1835 treasure hunters had been digging there for years. Mahone Bay was also a pirate den. Perhaps he intended a touch of irony in the selection of his hiding place.'

'You're awfully quiet,' Daniels said to her.

'We need to speak to your wife.'

'You anxious to use that phone tap?'

'I'm anxious about Stephanie.'

'We have Kaiser's house video monitored now,' Davis said. 'We snuck two agents in before dawn and installed a camera.'

'We have to send Hale a message,' she said. 'Enough to flush him from the field, too.'

The president understood the importance. 'I know. But I wonder. Did those damn pirates really try to kill me?'

'It's possible,' Davis said.

'I meant what I told those people a few minutes ago,' Daniels said. 'We're going to take the whole bunch of 'em down.'

But she knew Daniels' dilemma. There was no way this could escalate into a public fight. That would not be good for the White House, the intelligence community, or the country. Whatever he did had to be done in private. Which, she assumed, was where she and Cotton came in. Of course, only she and Davis were privy to what Quentin Hale really knew. But she agreed with Davis: Now was not the time to bring any of that up.

'Cotton needs to find those two missing pages,' Daniels said.

'It may not matter,' she said. 'We can telegraph anything we want to Hale through that phone tap. We could lead him to believe that we already have them.'

'Which would help Stephanie,' Daniels said. 'If the pirates have her.'

'You realize,' Cassiopeia said, 'that Carbonell could have Stephanie—'

Daniels held up a hand. 'I know. But I just made it clear that Stephanie's life is important. And if Carbonell and the pirates are as close as everyone seems to think, then they'll get that message, too. Let's hope they all understand.'

She agreed.

'Pauline is in her office,' Daniels said. 'She has to leave soon for an engagement. I asked her to wait and speak with you.'

Davis stood. So did she.

The president kept his eyes to the floor, his face solemn.

'Find Stephanie,' he said. 'Do whatever you have to do. Lie, cheat, steal. I don't care. Just find her.'

Cassiopeia and Edwin Davis entered the First Lady's office. Pauline Daniels waited behind her desk and rose to greet them in a cordial tone. They sat at a grouping of chairs before an ornate French-style desk, the office door closed.

Cassiopeia felt like the odd person out but took charge and said, 'We're going to stage a conversation tonight on your phone. I'm told Ms. Kaiser's out at an event until eight thirty. By the time she returns, I'll have a script for you. Memorize the gist of it, then say it in your own words. Edwin will be here with you. I'll be on the other end.'

The First Lady glanced at Davis. 'I'm so sorry. I had no idea any of this would happen.'

'It's not your fault.'

'Danny thinks I betrayed him.'

'He said that?' Davis asked her.

'No. In fact, he didn't say a word. And that was what said it all.' She shook her head. 'I almost killed him.'

'We don't have time for this,' Cassiopeia said in a curt tone.

'You have no sympathy for us, do you?'

'A woman's life is at stake.'

The First Lady nodded. 'So I've been told. Stephanie Nelle. Do you know her?'

'She's my friend.'

'I can't believe this is happening. Shirley and I have discussed many things. But I'm not privy to a great deal that goes on around here. As you may have gathered, the president and I exist in separate lives. I was only made aware of the New York trip in a passing remark. Honestly, I thought nothing about it. Just a quick trip up and back that would be kept quiet until the day of it.'

She heard the plea in her voice.

'I've been a fool,' the older woman said.

Cassiopeia didn't disagree, but kept her mouth shut, as did Davis.

'I'm sure Edwin has made clear that nothing improper has occurred between us.'

'More than once.'

Pauline cast a weak smile. 'I don't know about you, Ms. Vitt, but this is a new experience for me. I'm unsure what to do.'

'Tell the truth. About everything.'

She waited to see if they both caught her message.

'I suppose it is time Danny and I discuss Mary. We haven't in a long while.'

'I agree. But right now two people I care a great deal about are in danger, and we need your help.' She stood. 'I'm headed back to Fredericksburg. I'll call Edwin about seven and provide the script.'

She stepped toward the door but stopped and turned back. There was one other matter that the First Lady and Davis had ignored.

'Your husband said something to me once. "Don't cut the dog's tail off one inch at a time. If he's going to howl, get it over with in one slice." I'd recommend you both follow that advice.'

57

Bath, North Carolina

*H*ale listened to his father, who was speaking again of things he was hearing for the first time.

'James Garfield was the only sitting member of the U.S. House of Representatives to ever be elected president. He served eighteen years in Congress before moving to the White House.'

His father had told him about Lincoln's and McKinley's assassinations, but he'd never mentioned the one that had occurred in between.

'Garfield was a major general who resigned his military commission in the middle of the Civil War, after being elected to Congress in 1863. He was instrumental in pushing Lincoln to prosecute us. He hated the Commonwealth and everything we did. Which is strange, considering how hawkish he was.'

'But we also aided the South, didn't we?'

His father nodded. 'That we did. But how could we abandon them?'

His father started coughing. That was happening more and more of late. He was approaching eighty, and sixty years of heavy smoking and hard drinking had finally caught up with him. He was wasting away. The last will and testament was ready, all of its provisions reviewed by the lawyers and the children informed as to what was expected of them once he was gone. He'd provided for everyone with great generosity, as was expected of Hale patriarchs. Quentin, though, was the recipient of an additional private bequest, which only one Hale heir could receive.

Membership in the Commonwealth.

Which came with the house and land in Bath.

'When Lincoln died,' his father said, 'the country fell into chaos. Political factions fought one another with no room for compromise. Andrew Johnson, who succeeded Lincoln, was caught up in this fighting and impeached. Corruption and scandal marred the federal government for decades. Garfield served in the House during this time. Finally, in 1880, he was chosen by the Republicans as a compromise candidate, selected at the party's convention on the thirty-sixth ballot.'

His father shook his head.

'Just our luck. We fought against him in the general election. Spent time and money. Winfield Hancock ran for the Democrats and took every state south of the Mason Dixon line. Garfield claimed the North and Midwest. Nine million ballots were cast that November and Garfield beat Hancock by only 1,898 votes. That election remains the smallest margin of victory in all our history. They each also carried 19 states, but Garfield's brought him 59 more electoral votes than Hancock and he won.'

His father told him what happened next.

Garfield was sworn in on March 4, 1881, and immediately began an investigation of the Commonwealth. He was intent on prosecuting all four principals, who were still alive sixteen years after the Civil War. He convened a special military court and handpicked its panel. The four captains had expected no less from him and used the time between the 1880 election and the March 1881 inauguration to prepare. Charles Guiteau, a deranged lawyer from Illinois who'd convinced himself that he alone had been responsible for Garfield's election, was recruited. His personal requests for some type of government position after Garfield was sworn in had all been rejected. For months he roamed both the White House grounds and the State Department seeking his reward. He became so insidious that he was banned from those premises. Eventually, he became convinced that God had commanded him to kill the president. After money was provided he bought a .44 Webley British Bulldog revolver, with an *ivory handle, because he thought it would look better as a museum exhibit after the assassination.*

He then stalked Garfield for the month of June 1881.

'Presidents then had no protection,' his father said. 'They walked among the crowds just as anyone else. They used public transportation. Amazing, really, considering that, by then, one had already been slain. But we were still innocent.'

Finally, on July 2, 1881, Guiteau confronted Garfield at a Washington railroad station and shot him twice. Garfield's two sons, Secretary of State James Blaine, and his Secretary of War, Robert Todd Lincoln, were eyewitnesses.

One bullet grazed the shoulder, but another lodged in his spine.

'The damn fool shot him at point-blank range and didn't kill him,' his father said. 'Garfield lingered eleven weeks before he died. Nine months later Guiteau was hanged.'

Hale smiled at another of the Commonwealth's successes. Bold and brilliant.

Guiteau had been the perfect choice. At his trial he recited epic poems and sang 'John Brown's Body.' He solicited legal advice from spectators and dictated his autobiography to *The New York Herald*. Even if he implicated anyone, nobody would have believed him.

Hale's father had died three months after telling him about Garfield. The funeral had been a grand affair. The entire company had attended. Hale had been immediately inducted as captain.

Thirty years ago.

Men still spoke of his father in reverent terms. Now he was about to do what his father had never accomplished.

Find their salvation.

A knock on the study door interrupted his thoughts.

He glanced up from the chair to see his secretary, who said, 'She's on the line, sir.'

He reached for the phone, a landline, secured, checked daily.

'What is it, Andrea?'

'Wyatt is weather-delayed in Boston. His plane was returned to the terminal. I'm told he should leave within the next two hours. I assume your man is away.'

'Gone.'

'He should arrive first, even though he has a longer flight. He can make it to the fort and be waiting. You see, Quentin, I'm trying to be cooperative.'

'Something new for you?'

Carbonell chuckled.

'Knox will handle the matter,' he said. 'He's good. But I do need to know something. Do you have a second spy in this company?'

'How about I answer that question after we see how successful your quartermaster will be.'

'All right. We'll wait. That shouldn't be but a few hours from now. Then I will want an answer to my question.'

'I'm assuming, Quentin, that once you have those two missing pages and your letters of marque are fortified, you will handle that other matter we discussed.'

Killing Stephanie Nelle.

'You can't release her,' she said.

No, he couldn't. But two could play her game.

'How about I answer that question after you answer mine.'

Wyatt was growing impatient. Rain blanketed the Boston airport, and the gate attendant had informed everyone that the weather should pass within the next hour and flights would resume shortly after that. That meant it would be close to nightfall before he reached the island.

No matter. Whatever was there had waited 175 years, another few hours would not be a problem.

His cellphone vibrated in his pocket. He'd switched the unit back on once he was inside the terminal. It was a prepaid disposable bought yesterday in New York. Only one person had the number.

'I understand the weather is awful,' Carbonell said.

'Bad enough.'

'I just came from the White House. The president knows all about you.'

No surprise there, once Malone had spotted him.

'Lucky for me I'm leaving under another name,' he said in a low voice, huddled across the concourse at an empty gate.

'CIA, NSA – none of them knows a thing,' she said. 'Malone erased his copy of the solution off his email and his Danish server doesn't keep backups. But Malone doesn't have the cipher wheel.'

'You gluing it back together?'

'Why do I have to? I have you.'

'And the point of this call?'

'I thought you'd like to know where you stand, considering your weather problem. Though the White House is investigating, you still have an open-field run to the goal line.'

Like he believed her. Nothing was ever that easy.

'Anything else?' he asked.

'Be successful.'

And he ended the call.

58

Malone drove into the town of Mahone Bay – founded, the sign welcoming him proclaimed, in 1754. It nestled close to the inlet of the same name, crisscrossed by winding streets and lined with Victorian-era architecture. Three towering church spires kept watch. Yachts and sailboats rimmed the waterfront. A late-afternoon sun cast weak rays of smoky light through refreshingly cool air.

Before landing a few miles south of town, they'd overflown and he'd studied the island-strewn bay. They'd found Paw Island and reconnoitered it from the air, a mass of dark rock, tumbled grass, oaks, and spruce. Limestone cliffs dominated the shore that supported the ruined fort. He'd noted several places to beach a boat on the south shore and also saw the birds. Thousands of them scattered across the decaying walls, on the cliffs, in trees. Gannets, kittiwakes, gulls, terns, and murres massed so thick they obscured the ground in places.

He parked near a cluster of shops, art galleries, and cafés. Though it was late on a Sunday afternoon, he was glad to see that most of the businesses remained open. A bakery drew his attention and he told himself to pay it and a nearby fruit market a visit before heading out. Food would be good. He had no idea how long he'd be on the island.

Buildings backed to the bay above boulders that protected

the shore from a restless tide. Kayaks, motorboats, and sail-boats were all available for hire, and he decided that a fast and sturdy powerboat would do the trick. Paw Island was about six miles away by water.

Some local knowledge could also help.

So he decided to make a few inquires about the fort before heading for the island.

Cassiopeia stuffed her dirty clothes into the shoulder bag. She'd packed light for the New York weekend, bringing only a few items. Davis had offered her use of what he called the Blue Bedroom on the White House's second floor. It came with its own bath, so she'd been able to shower. While she bathed and rested – a lack of sleep had caught up with her – the staff had laundered her clothes. There was no rush to head back to Fredericksburg. Shirley Kaiser would not be home for another four hours. They'd told Kaiser to do nothing out of the ordinary. Stay as long as usual. Be herself.

A light knock drew her across the room.

She opened the door to see Danny Daniels standing outside.

Her guard immediately went up.

'I need to speak with you,' he said in a soft voice.

He came in and sat on one of the twin beds. 'I've always liked this room. Mary Lincoln lay in shock here following ol' Abe's assassination. She refused to enter their bedroom down the hall. Reagan used it as a gym. Other presidents had their small children live here.'

She waited for what he wanted.

'My wife betrayed me, didn't she?'

She wondered about the question. 'In what way?'

'I listened to Edwin when he told me what happened with Shirley. He's convinced that Pauline's motives were innocent.' The president paused. 'But I wonder.'

She had no idea how to respond to that comment.

'Edwin told you about Mary?'

She nodded.

'I asked him to do that. I don't speak of her. I can't. You understand that, don't you?'

'Why are telling me this?'

'Because I can't tell anyone else.'

'You should tell your wife.'

Daniels' eyes seemed distant. 'I'm afraid there's little left to say between us. Our time has come and gone.'

'Do you love her?'

'Not anymore.'

The admission shocked her.

'I haven't in a long time. It's not malice, or hate, or anger. Just nothing.'

His mellow tone unnerved her. She was accustomed to the booming voice.

'Does she know?'

'How could she not?'

'Why are you telling me this?' she asked again.

'Because the one other person I could speak to about this is in trouble and needs your help.'

'Stephanie?'

Daniels nodded. 'Last Christmas, with all that happened with Cotton's father, she and I began to talk. She's an extraordinary woman who's led a tough life.'

Cassiopeia had known Stephanie's late husband and had been there, in the Languedoc, a few years ago when the tragic events finally played out.

'She told me about her husband and son. I think she wanted me to tell her about Mary, but I couldn't.'

Pain clouded the president's face.

'Stephanie went out there because of me. Now she's gone. We have to find her. My gut wants to send a hundred FBI agents into that pirate compound at Bath. She could be there. But I know that's foolishness. What you're planning is the better way.'

'Are you and Stephanie . . . involved?'

She hoped the question would not offend him, but she had to ask. Particularly considering what she already knew.

'Not at all. I doubt she even gave our talks a thought. But I liked that she listened. Stephanie has a great respect for you. I don't know if you know that. That's why I agreed with Edwin. We need you *both* on this.'

A moment of strained silence passed between them.

'Stephanie told me that you and Cotton are an item. Is that true?'

Strange, having this conversation with the president of the United States. 'It looks that way.'

'He's a good man.'

Speaking of which, 'What do you think is going to happen in Nova Scotia?'

'Cotton and Wyatt will be there. It remains to be seen if the Commonwealth appears. If Carbonell is in league with them, that's a definite possibility. But Cotton is tough. He can handle things.' Daniels stood from the bed. 'A little advice from an old fool?'

'Of course. Not that you're a fool.'

'Actually, I'm one of the biggest. But follow your heart. It rarely leads you astray. It's thinking that gets us into trouble.'

59

Mahone Bay

Malone chose to rent a ten-foot V-hulled with a single outboard and two spare gas tanks. The time was approaching five PM. He was running behind, thanks to the weather delay back in DC, but he hoped Wyatt was, too. He'd been told that flights all along the eastern seaboard had been affected.

He'd visited the bakery and the market. The boat came equipped with a heavy-duty flashlight and spare batteries. It definitely appeared that he'd be spending the night on Paw Island. Thankfully, he was armed, the benefit of arriving on a Secret Service jet with official Canadian clearance. No questions from anybody. Wyatt would not have that luxury if he'd flown commercial, or even a charter, as customs would search both the plane and his belongings.

Before leaving town he decided to visit a bookstore that'd caught his eye. When he'd worked for Stephanie Nelle at the Justice Department, after assignments ended he'd always found one wherever he was in the world. This shop was located inside a brightly colored clapboard house with nautical touches that included maps, knots, even a ship's figurehead. The shelves lining the walls were crowded with tales about the bay, the towns, and Oak Island. Davis had explained a possible connection between the five symbols in Jackson's message and a mysterious slab found ninety feet belowground by treasure seekers on Oak Island. He located the slab in one of the books and showed it to the woman behind the counter. She was older, with brown hair streaked by waves of red.

'This drawing,' he asked her. 'The stone, with writing on it. Where is this located?'

'Not far. It's a replica of the original, on display. You into the Oak Island thing?'

'Not really. Seems like the only real treasure there is the money made from people who come to visit.'

'No reason to be so cynical. You never know. There could be something to it.'

He could not argue with that.

'The symbols are unique. Is there any explanation where they might have come from?

'You'll find them on several islands in the bay.'

That was news.

'They're common around here. Carved into rocks, trees. But, of course, nobody knows when they were put there.'

He caught her drift. Which came first, the Oak Island slab that no one had ever seen or the other symbols? Davis had told him that the stone was supposedly found in 1805 so, if the slab actually existed, symbols in other places could have appeared after. He recalled Rennes-le-Château, in France, and the mystique associated with that place, nearly all of it manufactured by a local hotel owner to generate business.

'Is Paw Island one of those places where the symbols can be found?' he asked.

She nodded. 'There are a few scattered around near the fort.'

'I flew over coming in. Quite a few birds live there.'

'You could say that, and they don't like visitors. You headed there?'

He closed the book. 'I don't know. Thought I'd just tour the bay and see what's out there.'

'Paw's restricted,' she said. 'National preserve. You have to get permission to go there.'

'Since I can't go,' he said. 'You have any books on it?'

She pointed to a shelf across the store. 'Two or three. Picture books, some stuff on the fort. What's your deal?' She apprised him with suspicious eyes. 'You're one of those bird-watchers, aren't you? We get a lot. Paw Island is like Disneyland to them.'

He smiled. 'Guilty. How much trouble will I get into if I go?'

'Plenty, and the Coast Guard Auxiliary patrol it all the time.'

'You know where I can find those symbols on the island?'

'You're going to end up in jail.'

'I'll take the chance.' He handed her three hundred-dollar bills. 'I'd like an answer to my question.'

She accepted the money and handed him a card for the shop.

'I'll tell you about the symbols. But I also know a lawyer. You're going to need one after you get to jail.'

Wyatt made his way through the trees on Paw Island, heading south from where he'd hidden his boat on the north shore.

He'd finally arrived in Halifax after several delays. He'd then rented a car and driven south to Chester, a quaint town that extended out into the northern reaches of Mahone Bay, its two natural harbors dotted with expensive sailboats and yachts. More wealth appeared in the form of brightly colored clapboard houses, meticulously maintained, that clung to a rocky shore, the streetscape right out of the 18th century.

It was after six when he arrived and most of the businesses were closed. He'd walked the empty docks and spied the moored motorboats. One, a twelve-footer with a respectable outboard, seemed right. So he'd used some of his old skills – how to start an engine without a key – and stolen transportation.

The trip across the bay had been quick, the water calm. So far he'd seen or heard nothing on the island, except birds. He was hoping that whatever there was to find could be located quickly. True, it had stayed hidden a long time, but he was the first person to look with the right information.

The oak forest ended and a grassy meadow stretched before him.

On the far side, a hundred yards away, stood Fort Dominion in all of its solitary neglect. Birds stood guard. He spotted what was its main gate, surrounded by decaying walls, and tightened the backpack on his shoulders.

He wondered.

Who else would be here?

Hale drove across the estate, enjoying another lovely late-summer evening in North Carolina. He'd decided to do a little fishing from the dock and relax for a couple of hours. Little could be accomplished until he heard from Knox. Usually, this time of day had proven lucky, when the gray-brown waters settled for the night, before the predators appeared. He'd dressed in stout boots, loose-fitting pants, a leather jacket, and a cap. He needed some bait, but there should be some on the dock.

His cellphone rang.

He stopped the cart and checked the display.

Shirley Kaiser.

He should not ignore her, so he answered and said, 'I planned to call you later. I thought you were at a fund-raiser this evening.'

'I skipped it.'

'Feeling poorly?'

'Not at all. In fact, I feel great. So much so I took a trip. I'm here, in North Carolina, parked at the gate to the estate. Do you think you could let me in?'

60

Nova Scotia

Knox was pleased.

He'd arrived on Paw Island before Wyatt and, with two associates, assumed strategic positions atop the crumbling walls of Fort Dominion. They'd stolen a boat from a private dock at an unoccupied home along the bay's north shore, specifically avoiding the town of Chester, where Wyatt might appear. The craft came with flashlights and he'd smuggled in three weapons aboard the corporate jet – Canadian customs asking few questions on his arrival.

The island locale was both isolated and deserted, save for thousands of stinking birds. Night's ever-hastening arrival should provide them with more than enough privacy. All in all, this should be an easy kill. Hopefully, finding the missing pages would not take long, though the information Carbonell provided to Hale was obscure at best. Five symbols. She'd said that was all she possessed and, hopefully, their significance would become evident once he was on the ground. He'd be glad when this nightmare was over. He was actually looking forward to spending next weekend with his wife at the beach. A little relaxation would be a good thing.

He'd brought a pair of binoculars and used them to survey where the forest ended and a grassy meadow began. About a hundred yards of open terrain stretched from the trees to the fort's main gate, none of it fenced or restricted. Their arrival inside earlier had caused an uproar from the residents, but all was calm once again in bird land.

He caught movement in the dimming light.

Through the binoculars he spotted a man emerging from the trees.

He focused on the face.

Jonathan Wyatt.

He grabbed the attention of one of his men, stationed on another rampart, and tossed him a signal.

Their target had arrived.

Hale welcomed Shirley Kaiser into his home. She'd visited twice before, and each time he'd ensured that nothing unusual occurred on the grounds. They called it *visitor mode*. Of course, guests were never taken to certain areas, like the prison building, whose exterior looked like nothing more than a two-story barn, and were not encouraged to roam at will.

He wondered what she was doing here.

'To what do I owe the pleasure of this surprise?' he asked her.

She looked great. Though pushing sixty – or maybe even sixty-five, he really wasn't sure – she cast the appearance of a woman in her midfifties. He'd enjoyed seducing her and she'd seemed to enjoy it, too. Their relationship, though cultivated by him for an ulterior motive, had not been unpleasant. Passion stirred within her, and she was surprisingly uninhibited for a woman of her generation. She was also a wealth of information on the First Family and liked the fact that he seemed sincerely interested in her life. That was the key to women, his father had always said. Make them think you care.

'I missed you,' she said to him.

'We were planning on seeing each other in a few days.'

'I couldn't wait, so I chartered a flight and flew down.'

He smiled. Her timing was not all bad. The evening was quiet. He'd already checked on the other three captains. Each had returned to his home, enough excitement for one day.

'As you can see,' he said, 'I was going fishing. I assume you don't want to join me.'

'Hardly.' She motioned to a small overnight bag. 'I brought some special garments.'

He'd seen a sampling of those before.

'Wouldn't they be more interesting than fishing?'

Wyatt thought Fort Dominion looked better suited to Scotland or Ireland, its limestone walls splayed at the base and once reinforced by towers, its bastions decaying but still relatively intact. Eroded earthworks and a dry moat barred any approach from the north, west, or east, and the ocean guarded the south. The setting sun cast the gray stone in a rose-colored hue, but any impression of invincibility was betrayed by the rubble. From what he'd read, this had once been a theater of important events, its mission to hold Mahone Bay for King George, but now it was only a ruin.

Puffins lined the wall crests. Hundreds more fluttered in the evening sky. He'd heard the murmur of murres, gulls, gannets, and kittiwakes on his approach – rich, sensuous, hypnotic, swelling like thunder. Thousands of birds stained the rubble, their cries pitching then fading in a haunting harmony, the walls alive with a riotous motion.

He crossed a grassy field toward the main gate.

Dead birds lay everywhere.

Apparently, there were no native scavengers here besides bacteria. The waft, faint back at the cove, now become overpowering. A choking smell of countless creatures packed together, the air clotted with the sickening scent of life, death, and excrement.

He approached the main gate.

A wooden bridge spanned a washed-out moat, its boards newer and fitted with galvanized nails.

A rising roar from the residents protested his arrival.

He passed through the gate, beneath a row of parallel stone arches.

Sunlight dimmed.

He entered an inner ward where it was downright dark, save for dusty shafts of blue light that filtered in through gaps in the walls. More weathered stone rose three stories around him. A variety of buildings hugged the outer curtain, the inner walls broken by windows that no longer held anything save for vines.

Definitely a feeling of security here, but also one of being trapped.

He should look around.

So he plunged ahead.

Malone beached the boat on the south side of Paw Island. The evening air carried an aroma of salt and trees, along with something else – acidic and astringent. The sky had turned the color of slate, the forest casting violet shadows over the sandy inlet. Herring gulls decorated the trees.

His rubber soles crunched crab shells and dried urchins. The temperature had dropped and he was glad for a lined jacket. Thick stands of oak lay ahead, the woods bedded with ferns and heather. He turned back and studied the bay for boats. Crimson patches of fading sun colored the surface. The horizon remained empty.

The bookstore owner had told him where in the fort symbols could be found. Were they decoration? Graffiti? Old? New? During the summer months when visits were allowed fifty-plus people a day roamed the island, which meant, as she'd told him, *the symbols could have come from anywhere*. Except that he knew Andrew Jackson was aware of their presence in 1835.

Perhaps the president himself had them placed there?

Who knew?

Cassiopeia parked the motorcycle at a Comfort Inn just inside the Fredericksburg city limits. She'd thought about the call to Quentin Hale on the ride down. The conversation had to be subtle and clever, telegraphing just enough for Hale to know that the White House may indeed have what he sought.

The Secret Service had taken a room here earlier, about three kilometers from Kaiser's residence, where they could remotely monitor the TV camera that had been installed inside one of the second-floor bedrooms, facing the garage.

She knocked and was allowed inside.

Two agents were on duty, one male, the other female.

'Kaiser left about three hours ago,' the female agent said. 'She took a small case and a garment bag with her.'

They knew Kaiser was due at some sort of fund-raising event in Richmond. No tail or escort had been provided. Better to do nothing that might alert Hale. A big enough risk had been taken installing the camera, but they had to ensure that the site remained under surveillance. A small LCD screen displayed, from an elevated angle, Kaiser's garage and the hedgerow that guarded its outer wall. Sunlight was fading and she watched as the male agent switched the camera over to night vision, the image transforming to a greenish hue, still displaying the building and hedge line.

Cassiopeia would pay Kaiser an innocent woman-to-woman visit when she returned home that should draw no attention. Her talk with Danny Daniels still disturbed her. Clearly, the Daniels' marriage was over and the president had spoken of Stephanie in an odd way. She wondered what had transpired between them. Easy to see how he might find solace with her. Stephanie's life also had been marred by tragedy – the suicide of her husband, the disappearance of her son, an eventual coming to grips with harsh past realities.

Interesting how presidents were people, too. They had wants, needs, and fears, just like everyone else. They carried emotional baggage and, worse, were forced to conceal it.

Unfortunately for Danny and Pauline Daniels, their baggage had been revealed through careless comments and misplaced trust.

'Look there,' the female agent said, pointing to the screen.

Her mind refocused on the moment.

Two men could be seen near Shirley Kaiser's garage, studying the surroundings, slipping into the space between the hedge and the building.

'Seems we have visitors,' the male agent said. 'I'll call for backup.'

'No,' Cassiopeia said.

'That's not procedure,' he said to her.

'Which seems to be standard for this entire operation.' She pointed to the woman. 'What's your name?'

'Jessica.'

'Me and you. We'll handle it.'

61

Wyatt stroked the blackened stones and visualized men-at-arms clambering to the walls, cannons readied for firing. He could hear bells tolling and smell fish turning on a spit. Life on this lonely outpost 230 years ago would have been tough. Easy to see how seventy-four men could have lost their lives.

He noticed a staircase that right-angled upward.

Higher ground would be good, so he climbed the steep steps and entered what had once been a large hall. Windows ran the length of each side, the grilles and glass long gone. No ceiling existed, the room exposed to the elements, a wall walk wrapping the outer curtain high above. Puddles of stagnant water nourished brown grass that grew like stubble. The air remained clotted with the stench of birds, many of which flitted around.

His gaze was drawn to the fireplace and he wove a path around loose blocks. The hearth would hold half a dozen men standing side by side. He noticed places where planks covered the stone floor, some milled and clearly of a more recent vintage, others rotting and dangerous.

Beyond a darkened passageway, he spied another room. He negotiated a short hall and entered that empty space. A second staircase led up. Probably to the walk he'd spotted encircling the battlements.

Something to his right, near a pile of grass-infected rubble, caught his attention.

Smears on the rock floor.

Footsteps. Toward the second staircase.

More stains colored the risers. Fresh, moist.

Somebody was above him.

Knox waited on the battlements for Wyatt to emerge from the cluster of decaying buildings. Though the ceilings were gone, as were most of the walls, there remained many places to hide. He'd watched as Wyatt entered the fort. Before he killed him he hoped perhaps Wyatt might point the way to where the missing pages waited. He had the full text of Jackson's message with him, including the five curious symbols. Instead of spending all night searching, he could let Wyatt lead him straight there.

But his adversary was wandering, as if lost.

Apparently, he did not know where to find whatever Andrew Jackson had hidden.

So kill him and be done with it.

Wyatt had learned long ago that when your opponent was expecting the expected, it was best not to disappoint. That was why he'd boldly entered the Garver Institute through the front door. Near the base of the staircase, where more footprints in the mud and excrement led upward, a bare window opened through the outer wall facing the sea. He crept over and carefully poked his head out, checking above.

Maybe a ten-foot climb to the top, with plenty of handholds in the withering stone.

He glanced down at the hundred-foot drop to a rocky shoreline being assaulted by the sea. Birds leaped from the cliff-like walls and hung in the breeze. The half-choked cries of gulls accompanied their waltz. He retreated inside and found a stone the size of a softball. The battlements above were certainly populated by birds, too. Carefully, he crept up one flight of risers and peered up into an ever-dimming sky.

He lobbed the rock up through the opening, but did not wait for it to land.

Instead he retreated down to the window.

Knox was positioned across from Wyatt, on the fort's north wall. One of his men waited on the south battlement with Wyatt, the other man on the west wall. The oppressive silence was broken only by surf and a steady wind that masked all noise.

Birds suddenly took flight from the south wall in a thick layer, sweeping upward, their wings colliding in midair.

What had panicked them?

His gaze locked on the battlement.

Wyatt grabbed hold of the gray limestone, using the crevices as holds. The stone he'd tossed upward had flushed the birds and caused enough of a distraction to cover him. He was suspended in the air, nothing but ocean to his back. Night was rapidly grabbing hold. His shoes were planted firmly in a deep scar in the wall. One hand gripped the top. He reached up with his other hand and peered over the edge.

A man stood eight feet away, his back to him, near where the stairway he'd avoided emptied down from the battlements.

He held a gun in one hand.

Exactly as he'd thought.

They were waiting for him.

Cassiopeia and her new partner, Jessica, approached Shirley Kaiser's house. They'd driven over in a Secret Service car, parked down the street, and trotted to the wrought-iron fence that encircled the property, an easy matter to leap over.

They made their way toward the garage.

'Have you done this before?' she whispered.

'Not outside the training academy.'

'Stay calm. Think. And don't do anything stupid.'

'Yes, ma'am. Any other words of wisdom?'

'Don't get shot.'

No smart remarks came in reply to that one.

Jessica hesitated, listening to something through her ear fob. They were in radio contact with the agent back at the Comfort Inn.

'The two guys are still there.'

Because, Cassiopeia thought, they knew they would not be interrupted. Hale apparently was aware Kaiser was gone, but she wondered why he'd decided to remove the device. Did he know that they knew? If he did, he would not have gone anywhere near Kaiser's house. No physical evidence tied him to the device. No, he was covering his tracks. Maybe readying himself for something.

She signaled for Jessica to swing around to the rear of the garage. She would approach from the front and flush them out.

Surprise should work in their favor.

Or at least she hoped it would.

Knox stared across to where his man on the south wall waited. The birds had settled down, some returning to their perch, others flying off into an ever-darkening sky. A man suddenly appeared from the outer portion of the wall, facing the ocean, balanced atop the battlement.

No question as to his identity.

Wyatt rushed forward and attacked. The fight was brief and silent thanks to the distance and the wind.

A gun appeared in Wyatt's hand.

One shot, the retort muffled to a sound like hands clapping, and one man was down for good.

Knox raised his weapon, aimed, and fired.

62

Malone caught the sudden flight of birds from the crest of the fort. He was just outside the main gate, using the enveloping darkness for cover, unsure if there was anyone else around.

He heard a pop, then another, and knew he was not alone.

He needed to enter the fort, but to do that meant crossing an open fifty feet. The only cover was a pile of rubble ten feet away. He rushed the mound, leaping over to its protected side.

Two bullets pinged the limestone wall behind him.

From the battlements.

He kept his head down and peered through an opening in the rocks. Movement came high on the wall walk, to the left of the doorway he wanted to negotiate. Waiting would do nothing but allow his attacker time to prepare. So he aimed at the spot on the wall where he'd last spied anything and laid down two rounds, then took advantage of the moment and dashed through the doorway.

No bullets followed him.

The base of a stairway rested to the left, a passageway deeper into the fort straight ahead. But an open space loomed directly ahead. A decayed tower.

He glanced upward.

The wall walks above were exposed.

A bad feeling swept over him.

One that signaled he'd made it here far too easily.

* * *

Wyatt lunged forward, diving just before the man across the fort fired at him. He'd caught sight of the second assailant an instant before he'd killed the first – and recognized the face.

Clifford Knox.

Carbonell had sold him out to the Commonwealth.

But he told himself to stay calm and handle that later.

Puffs of stone erupted inches away as bullets penetrated the semi-darkness, searching for him. Thankfully, the battlements offered ample protection and he was now armed with the dead man's gun.

But that wasn't discouraging Knox.

Who kept firing.

Cassiopeia swept across the driveway's pavers. If they timed their approach properly they should be able to catch the two interlopers off guard and snag an easy capture. Hale's decision to make this move had changed her thinking. Living, breathing proof of a crime would finally give the White House some immediate bargaining power, and Hale would surely then be in a panic. Maybe enough to guarantee Stephanie's safety. True, there was no tangible proof, as yet, of the Commonwealth being involved with the assassination attempt or Stephanie's disappearance. But there would be a direct link to a burglary and violations of various wiretapping laws, and no letters of marque, valid or not, would protect them since Shirley Kaiser was not an enemy of the United States.

Something metallic clattered to a hard surface.

Movement on the other side of the garage signaled that the two men had taken notice of the sound, too.

'Freeze,' she heard Jessica yell.

A shot rang out.

Malone studied the tower. An exposed staircase wound only halfway up to the summit, the remainder having decayed long ago. Wooden planks that once separated the various levels were gone, as were the roof timbers. A night sky loomed overhead. Moonlight had begun to spill down like smoke through the ruins.

On the wall walk above a shadow appeared. The tower's shell stretched about thirty feet across, its lichen-encrusted walls eroded from wind and rain. Its height created a protective angle that shielded him from any bullets, so long as he stayed beyond the doorway.

He quickly summarized his situation.

If he retreated, the only way out was the way he'd come, which the man above had covered. Forward was through the open tower, and that clearly would be a problem. He noticed he was standing on a wooden plank, about three feet wide and five feet long.

He bent down and lightly caressed the surface.

Hard, like stone.

He curled his fingers between the wood and the earthen floor and lifted. Heavy, but he could handle it. He only hoped the caliber of bullet being used up above was low.

He stuffed his gun into his jacket pocket, raised the plank above his head, then balanced the length on his open palms. He swung around so that he faced the archway and the tower beyond his shield angled downward, which he hoped would provide enough protection from any ricocheting rounds.

He gritted his teeth, drew a breath, then bolted through the archway, careful to keep the planks balanced.

Ten yards or so was all he had to negotiate.

Shots erupted immediately and a steady crack of timber sounded as lead knocked off the upper surface. He found the doorway, but immediately noticed that the plank's width was too great. It would not pass through.

A steady tap-tap-tap continued on the wood above his head. Any bullet might signal disaster if a soft spot was found.

No choice.

He allowed the wood to slide off his palms as he pushed upward and vaulted into the doorway.

The board crashed to the ground.

He gripped his gun.

Cassiopeia bolted forward, using the side of the garage nearest to her for cover. A man appeared, rushing her way, his attention more on what was behind him than what was ahead. She wanted to know if Jessica was okay, but realized that the first order of business was taking down this problem. She waited, then stretched out her leg and tripped him to the grass.

She aimed her gun down and whispered, 'Quiet and still.'

His eyes seemed to say, *No way.*

So she made her point clearer, swiping the gun into his left temple, stealing his consciousness.

She then turned and advanced to the garage's corner. Jessica stood with her gun aimed downward, both hands on the trigger. The other man lay on the grass, writhing from a wound in his thigh.

'I had no choice.' Jessica lowered her weapon. 'I hit a shovel back there and tipped them off. I told him to stop, but he kept coming. I think he thought I wouldn't shoot him.'

'The other one's down, too. Call for medical help.'

63

Knox laid down a few rounds, trying to flush Wyatt from his hiding place on the far wall.

'Where are you?' he said into his lapel mike, talking to his second associate.

'There's another man here,' the voice said in his ear. 'He's armed, but I have him pinned down below.'

Two men?

He hadn't expected anyone other than Wyatt. No mention had been made of any assistance.

'Take him out,' he ordered.

Malone started to climb the stone stairs that right-angled upward. Obviously, there were others inside the fort, as gunfire had echoed from more spots above, to his right and left. Night had taken a firm hold, and darkness was now his ally. He still carried the flashlight, stuffed into his back pocket, but there was no way to use it.

He came to the top and watched for movement.

Emerging from the stairwell meant exposure, and though he was known to occasionally do dumb things this was not going to be one of them.

He studied his surroundings.

One side of the stairwell, which formed the fort's outer wall, was gone. Through the darkness he spotted a series of arches that supported the battlements above. If he was careful, he could negotiate them and make an end run. He stuffed the gun inside his belt and climbed out. Fifty feet below, surf pounded rock. A musky smell of the birds mixed with the salt air. Below him cries mingled with a clash of wings. He balanced on the first arch and shifted to the second, hands and arms grasping the moist, gritty supports.

He shifted to the next arch, then another.

One more and he should be sufficiently beyond the stairwell's entrance above that he could surprise his attacker.

He reached up and grasped the top of the wall.

One chin-up and he peered over the top.

A dark form huddled twenty feet away, his back to him, facing the stairwell. To climb up fully would draw attention. So he settled back on the arch and found his gun. He searched the wall above him and discovered more indentations. One hand stretched back to the top and he maneuvered himself upward, his right shoe finding a foothold, enough that he could pivot upward, aim, and fire one time.

Wyatt heard a retort from across the fort, this one not from Knox's direction. That meant somebody else was here whom Knox's men did not appreciate. He decided to take advantage of the situation and belly-crawled back to the man he'd shot. A quick search revealed two spare magazines of ammunition.

Just what he needed.

Another bullet came his way, pinging off the stone a few feet away.

The birds had all fled with the first commotion, but their stench remained, the stones slippery from their excrement.

He found an opening that led down. No stairs, just a hole in the rampart. He gripped the coarse limestone edge and dropped the few feet to another level, protected for the moment.

He freed the backpack from his shoulders.

*   *   *

Malone swung his body upward, his sole brushing the prickly stone then catching a grip. His target whirled, a gun leading the way. Before the man could level the weapon, Malone fired a shot to the chest. He dropped off the wall and hustled over, gun aimed, ready.

He rolled the body over, the face unfamiliar. He checked for a pulse. None. He retrieved the man's pistol and pocketed the weapon. A quick frisk revealed spare magazines and a wallet. He pocketed them, too, then grabbed his bearings.

He was atop the fort's west façade.

Gunfire erupted from the south wall.

Knox had not expected an attack.

Wyatt had reappeared fifty feet away, on another wall, and started shooting, the bullets arriving around him with precision.

Too precise, considering the darkness.

Wyatt had come prepared. Carbonell had provided him a pair of night-vision goggles, which allowed him to see Clifford Knox huddled within the rubble. Unfortunately, his target had not ventured far enough from his cover for a kill shot. He caught movement atop another wall and heard a shot. He quickly scanned the battlements and spotted an armed man frisking another who lay prone. Size, shape, and movement confirmed the identity.

Malone.

How could that be?

He returned his attention to his own problem.

'Knox,' he called out. 'I know Andrea Carbonell provided you this location. She's the only person who could have. She wants you to kill me, right?'

Knox listened to the question and realized that his situation was bad. He'd lost one man for sure and could not raise the other on the radio. More gunfire from other parts of the fort signaled trouble. This easy kill had turned into anything but. He hadn't risked everything just to die in this godforsaken place for Quentin Hale or any of the other captains.

'There's another man here,' Wyatt called out. 'It's Cotton Malone. And he's not your friend.'

Malone listened to the exchange. Typical Wyatt.

Grandiose.

One thing was certain – he wasn't going to enter the conversation.

Not yet anyway.

Wyatt smiled. 'No, I guess Malone is not going to show himself. Knox, I want you to know that I don't have any beef with you.'

'I do with you.'

'That stupid assassination attempt? You should thank me for stopping it. Carbonell set us both up here. So I'm going to give you a chance to leave. I want you to take a message to Quentin Hale. Tell him I plan to get what he wants and he can have it. Of course, it will cost, but it's not a price he can't afford. Tell him I'll be in touch.'

He waited for a reply.

'She said you wouldn't bring those pages back to her,' Knox yelled.

'That all depended on her keeping her word. Which she didn't. So she called on you and hoped you'd kill me for her. It's two against one, Knox. Cotton Malone wants those pages, too. They'll be of no use to you if he finds them. He works only for God and country.'

'And you'll be the one to find them?'

'Malone and I have some unfinished business. Once it's completed, I'll get what you want.'

'And if I stay?'

'Then you're going to die. Guaranteed. One of us will get you.'

Knox weighed his options. He was alone with two pursuers. One appeared to be friendly, the other unknown.

Who was this Cotton Malone?

And the crew.

There'd been casualties.

Not something that happened often.

It had been years since they'd lost anyone. He'd come here because it seemed the only play. Hale was happy, the other three captains were content. Carbonell had provided the information, seemingly wanting Knox to be here.

But enough was enough.

He was risking his life for nothing.

'I'm leaving,' he called out.

Malone crouched low and studied the blackness. The nearest light source was miles away on a neighboring island. The surf continued its relentless attack on the rock below. Wyatt was out there, waiting. It was impossible to go after the third man. Knox. Wyatt would be ready for that.

Just sit tight.

'Okay, Malone,' Wyatt called out. 'Obviously you're privy to the same information I am. One of us is going to win this fight. Time to find out who.'

64

Bath, North Carolina

A gale pounded the deck, strong enough to shift the cannons. He held the wheel tight, keeping the bow pointed northeast. He was running at the edge of the sand that extended from shore, a narrow gap that required a tight course. Close-reefed topsails billowed outward, driving them along.

A ship appeared.

On a parallel course, its masts thrusting dangerously close to his sails. What was it doing here? They'd dodged it for most of the day, and he'd hoped the storm would be his shield.

He sounded the alarm.

The tumult increased as crewmen flooded out from below into the squall. Danger was quickly realized and weapons were burnished, ready for an attack. Men who found their cannons waited for no order and poured the newcomer's broadside with salvos. He kept the helm steady, proud of his ship, which belonged to the house of Hale, in North Carolina.

It would not be taken or sunk from under him.

A fresh wind tested the rudder.

He fought for control.

Men were swinging across from the other ship, boarding his. Pirates. Like him. And he knew where they came from. The house of Bolton. It, too, of North Carolina. Come for a fight on the open sea, during a squall, when his guard would be down.

Or so they thought.

This kind of attack was foolhardy. It violated every principle under which they lived. But Boltons were fools, and always had been.

'Quentin.'

His name on the wind.

A female voice.

More men appeared on deck, armed with swords. One leaped through the air and landed a few feet away.

A woman.

Strikingly beautiful, her hair blond, skin pale, eyes alight with interest.

She sprang upon him and tore away his grip on the wheel. The ship slipped from its course, and he felt ungoverned motion.

'Quentin. Quentin.'

Hale opened his eyes.

He lay in his bedroom.

A storm raged outside. Rain assaulted the windows, and a howling wind molested the trees.

Now he remembered.

He and Shirley Kaiser had retreated here on the promise of some special garments she'd brought.

And special they had been.

Lavender lace, draping her petite frame, sheer enough to fully distract his attention for a little while. She'd come to his bed and undressed him. After nearly an hour of fun he'd dozed off, satisfied, glad she'd appeared without an invitation. She was just what he'd needed after dealing with the other three captains.

'Quentin.'

He blinked sleep from his eyes and focused on the familiar coffered ceiling of his bedroom, its wood from the hull of an 18th-century sloop that had once plied the Pamlico. He felt the comfort of fine sheets and the firmness of his king-sized mattress. His bed was a four-poster, stout and tall, requiring a stool for ingress and egress. He'd twisted his ankle once years ago when he stepped off too quick.

'Quentin.'

Shirley's voice.

Of course. She was here, in the bed. Perhaps she was ready for more? That would be okay. He was ready, too.

He rolled over.

She stared at him with an expression not broken by a smile or desire. Instead, the eyes were hard and angry.

Then he saw the gun.

Its barrel only inches from his face.

Cassiopeia watched as the rescue vehicle removed the wounded burglar. The remaining intruder, the one she'd taken down with a swipe of her gun, remained in custody, using an ice pack to nurse a lump the size of an egg. No identification had been found on either one, and neither was talking.

'Every minute we're stalled,' Danny Daniels had said, 'is another minute Stephanie stays in trouble.'

He stood at the door leading out of the Blue Room.

'I know the symptoms, Mr. President. Caring for someone is hell.'

He seemed to understand. 'You and Cotton?'

She nodded. 'It's both good and bad. Like right now. Is he okay? Does he need help? I didn't have that problem until a few months ago.'

'I've been alone a long time,' Daniels said.

His somber tone made clear he regretted every moment.

'Pauline and I should come to terms. This needs to be over.'

'Careful. Make those decisions slowly. There's a lot at stake.'

His gaze agreed with her. 'I've served my country. For forty years politics has been my life. I've been a good boy the whole time. Never once took a dime from anyone contrary to the law. Never once sold myself out. No scandal. I stayed to my conscience and principles, though it cost me sometimes. I've served as best I could. And I have few regrets. But I'd like to serve myself now. Just for a while.'

'Does Stephanie know how you feel?'

He did not immediately answer her, which made her wonder if he even knew the answer. But what he finally said surprised her.

'I believe she does.'

A car wheeled into Kaiser's drive, and Edwin Davis emerged from the passenger side. Fingerprints from both intruders had been taken more than an hour ago and she'd been promised an identification. Davis had then been only a voice on the phone, but apparently he was on the move. The neighborhood had come alive with people, police cars filling the street.

No way to keep this a secret.

'The car they used was found a few blocks over,' Davis said to her as he approached. 'It carried stolen North Carolina plates, and the car was stolen, too. Registered to a woman in West Virginia. We're still waiting for the prints to run. But that assumes these guys have either been in trouble, registered to buy a gun, taught school, or any of the other thousand things that requires fingerprinting. The one I'm hoping for is military service. That would provide a wealth of info.'

He looked and sounded tired.

'How are the president and First Lady?' she asked.

'I heard he paid you a visit before you left.'

She had no intention of violating Daniels' confidence. 'He's upset over Stephanie. He feels responsible.'

'Don't we all.'

'Anything from Cotton?'

'Nothing from him personally.'

She caught what he hadn't voiced. 'Who have you heard from?'

'Cotton wanted no backup on the scene.'

'And you went along with that?'

'Not exactly.'

Hale realized this was the first time he'd ever had a weapon pointed at him. A strange sight, particularly given that he was lying naked in his bed. Kaiser held the gun like she knew what she was doing.

'I've been shooting since I was a little girl,' she said. 'My daddy taught me. You used me, Quentin. You lied to me. You've been a terribly bad boy.'

He wondered if this was some sort of game. If so, it could be particularly arousing.

'What is it you want?' he asked.

She shifted her aim from his face to his crotch, only the blanket separating his bare skin from the gun.

'To see you suffer.'

65

M alone studied the crenellations on the crumbling walls for movement. A knot formed in the pit of his stomach. His heart raced.

Just like the old days.

He retreated to a stairway and quickly found the ground. Leading with the automatic, he crept forward into the darkness of the inner ward. He stopped in the shadows and allowed his eyes to adjust.

A deathly chill crept into his body.

One that primed every nerve to be ready.

The fort was like a maze on three levels, rooms leading one into another. He recalled what he'd read about its lowest levels and the 74 British prisoners who'd drowned. The courts-martial had revealed that the fort's foundations rested on a tangle of tunnels, cut from rock, high tide filling them, low tide offering a respite. The colonial officers claimed that they had no knowledge of the fact and simply chose the underground locale as the securest place to hold their prisoners. Of course, none of the Brits survived to contradict that testimony and none of the hundred or so colonial soldiers refuted the account.

He heard movement above.

Footsteps.

His gaze shot to the ceiling.

* * *

Cassiopeia waited for Edwin Davis to explain.

'Cotton was insistent that no one be there except him,' Davis said. 'But I thought that foolish.'

She agreed.

'So I had the two Secret Service pilots who flew him there keep an eye on things from shore.'

'What is it you're not saying?'

'I got a call just before I arrived. There's a lot of gunfire coming from Paw Island.'

She didn't want to hear that.

'I'm waiting for an update before deciding what to do.'

She checked her watch. 9:20 PM. 'Kaiser should be home by now. She told us eight thirty at the latest.'

'Has anyone been inside the house?'

She nodded. 'They went in a little while ago.'

'The prisoner? Still quiet?'

'Not a word.'

'Some lawyer, expensive and connected, will appear tomorrow and demand bail. He'll get it, too. The Commonwealth takes care of its own.'

A soft chime came from Davis' coat pocket. He withdrew his cellphone and retreated from her.

An agent exited Kaiser's front door and stepped over to her, saying, 'I think you should see this.'

Hale had been caught off guard. He'd allowed this woman to seduce him, thinking all the while that he possessed the upper hand.

'How long have you been listening to my phone calls?' she asked.

The gun aimed at his midsection made clear that lying would not be a good idea. 'Several months.'

'Is that why you've been involved with me? To find out about the president?'

'At first. But that changed over time. I have to say, it's been a joyous union between the two of us.'

'Charm doesn't work anymore.'

'Shirley. You're a big girl. You've never used anyone to get what you want?'

'What is it you want, Quentin?'

The storm continued unabated outside.

'For my family to keep what it has worked three hundred years to achieve.'

Malone entered what appeared to have once been a large hall, most of the walls and the ceiling gone. Above him, on an exposed walk, he caught no sign of anyone. The sky above glowed from an ever-brightening moon, a cool wind swirling from east to west.

His mouth was dry from anticipation and a light sweat prickled his chest.

He crept to the far end toward a massive hearth framed by a crumbling stone mantel. A rectangular chasm, maybe ten feet wide and eight tall, opened in the center beneath a flue. He knew the hole was for hot embers, swept below for easier removal. The vertical shaft above vented smoke to the roof. He stepped into the hearth and stared into the opening below. Nothing but blackness could be seen, though the sound of surf was louder. He could use his flashlight and learn more, but that would not be smart.

The flue above might provide a concealed way for him to climb toward the roof.

He turned his head to gaze upward.

The sole of a shoe slammed his forehead.

He staggered back, but retained a grip on his gun.

The scene before him winked in and out, but he managed to see a black form drop from the flue into the hearth.

The form rushed him and they pounded onto a pile of rubble.

Pain seared through his right arm, which caused his fingers to release their grip on the gun.

Cassiopeia entered Shirley Kaiser's brightly lit home and followed the agent through the entrance hall, to the kitchen and a small work area that opened off it, leading toward a laundry room and the garage. A granite-topped built-in desk supported a computer, printer, and wireless modem along with stationery, pens, pencils, and other office accessories, all in a matching flowery print.

'We decided to remove the camera upstairs,' the agent told her, 'so we came inside. Our transmission line was through the house's Internet connection. That's when we saw this.'

He pointed to the computer.

She focused on the screen and read GAULDIN CHARTERS.

A closer examination revealed that the company operated private air flights out of Richmond to various locales along the eastern seaboard.

'We checked,' the agent said. 'Kaiser booked a charter flight earlier today and left several hours ago.'

'Where did she go?'

'Pitt Greenville Airport. In North Carolina.'

Fear surged through her.

Though she had no idea how far away Bath lay from Greenville, she knew it was nearby.

Wyatt finally had Cotton Malone within his grasp. He'd watched Malone's progress through the ruins, the night-vision goggles granting him a clear advantage. When he'd spotted his target entering the hall, he'd made his way down the flue in an easy climb. Malone's appearance within the hearth itself just made things easier.

His hands went for the throat and clamped tight.

They rolled off the rock onto the rough floor and kept rolling until they collided into another pile.

He slammed a fist into Malone's ribs, working the kidneys. Malone reeled but did not let go.

He punched again, harder.

Malone pivoted onto his side and sprang to his feet.

So did he.

They circled each other, hands empty, arms ready.

'Just you and me,' he said.

Cassiopeia waited in the kitchen for Edwin Davis. The Secret Service agent had volunteered to get him. What Shirley Kaiser had done may well have jeopardized everything. What was she thinking? The man she was dealing with was every bit a pirate, his only goal to survive, and killing a scorned woman would not be a problem.

Davis entered, concern on his face. He, too, apparently realized the implications. 'That airport in Greenville is the closet one to Bath. She's nuts to have done this.'

'I'm going,' she told him.

'I don't know if I can allow that.'

'So it's okay to drag me into that mess at the White House, but not okay for me to do any more?'

'That was private. This isn't. You're not on the payroll.'

'Exactly why I'm the one to go. And by the way, me not being on the payroll wasn't a problem the last time Daniels was in a mess.' He seemed to get her message, so she added, 'Give me a few hours, and if you don't hear from me, then send in the Secret Service.'

He considered for a moment then nodded. 'You're right. It's the best move.'

'What about Cotton? That call you took outside was about him, wasn't it?'

'The agents reported in. They're a few miles away, on shore, but they have telescopic night-vision equipment. One boat left the north shore a short while ago. Lone occupant, heading north, toward shore, away from their location. Lots of gunfire has been occurring, though it's subsided some now.'

'What are you going to do?'

'Nothing,' he said. 'I have to give Cotton the time he asked for to play things out.'

66

Malone tackled Wyatt who, with great agility, reversed the situation and pounded the back of Malone's head into stone.

Everything winked in and out.

Nausea swelled in his throat.

Wyatt slipped off him and he caught the blurred image of a gun in his opponent's right hand.

He struggled to one knee.

His head throbbed with every beat of his heart. He rubbed his scalp and tried to stand. 'You do realize there are people high on the food chain who know you and I are here.'

Wyatt tossed the weapon aside. 'Let's finish this.'

'Is there an actual purpose here?' The question gave his stomach the few moments it needed to calm. 'And what did you want, those New York cops to kill me? Or a Secret Service agent?'

'Something like that.'

His eyes surveyed the darkness, but he could not determine much beyond the stacks of collapsed walls and old timbers. The bird stench remained, which didn't help his queasiness.

'I have a friend in trouble,' he said to Wyatt. 'Stephanie Nelle. The guy you just let walk out of here works for the people who probably have her captive.'

'That's not my problem.'

Anger swelled inside him. He sprang forward, wrapping

his arms around Wyatt's body and allowing momentum to propel them both onto the floor.

But instead of finding hard stone, a crack signaled that they'd landed on wood, the timbers offering little resistance, their combined weight sending them crashing downward.

And they kept falling.

Hale was buying time, trying to find a way into Shirley Kaiser's psyche. He hoped compassion might be the way.

'My family,' he said, 'has served this nation since before it was formed. Yet now the government wants to prosecute me and my associates as criminals.'

'Why?'

The gun continued to be pointed at his crotch, but he told himself to show no fear.

'My family were first pirates, then privateers. We have lived on this land for nearly three hundred years. We became for the fledgling colonial forces its navy, destroying British shipping during the American Revolution. Without us, there would have been no United States. We've performed similar services for many administrations since that time. We are patriots, Shirley. Serving our country.'

'What does that have to do with me? Tell me why you used me to try to kill Danny Daniels.'

'Not me,' he made clear. 'That was my associates, unbeknownst to me. I was furious when I learned what they did.'

'So *they* tapped my phones?'

Careful. This woman was no dummy. 'No. I did that. I was looking for anything I could learn that might help our situation. I knew of your relationship with the First Lady before I made contact with you.'

'So give me a good reason why I shouldn't make you a soprano.'

'You'd miss me as a baritone.'

'More of that charm. You don't quit, I'll give you that.'

He shifted in the bed.

Her grip on the gun stiffened.

'Calm down,' he said. 'Just lightening the load on some old muscles.'

'What did you do with what you heard on the phone?'

'Most of it? Nothing. But when I heard of the New York trip, I did inform my associates. With the White House not announcing the trip, we thought an opportunity might have opened. We discussed the matter, but decided not to act. Unfortunately, they changed their minds and did not bother to inform me.'

'Have you always been such a good liar?'

'I'm not lying.'

'You used me, Quentin.' Her voice carried no anger, no contempt.

'So you come here, lure me to bed, simply to shoot me?'

'I decided to use you a little.'

'Shirley, my wife and I have been apart a long time. You know that. You and I have enjoyed quite the healthy relationship. As we are speaking, right now, men are at your house removing the listening device. That's over. Can't we let it be? We can enjoy an even healthier relationship now—'

'That we know what a liar and cheat you truly are.'

'Shirley,' he said in gentle voice. 'You are not naïve. The world is a difficult place, and we all have to do what we can to survive. Suffice it to say that my situation borders on desperate, so I chose the means I thought might achieve results. I did lie to you. At first. But once we came to know each other that changed. You know that I could not fake everything – if only from what just happened. You are an exciting, vibrant woman.'

The gun stayed aimed. 'You destroyed my relationship with the First Lady.'

'She needs professional help. You know that. Or better yet, allow Mr. Davis to be her confidant. She seems to like him.'

'It's not a dirty thing.'

'I'm sure it is not. But it is still a *thing*. One they would not want public.'

'What were you going to do? Blackmail them?'

'The thought had occurred to me. Luckily, better solutions to the problem may have come along. So their secret is safe.'

'How comforting.'

'Why not lower that gun and you and I consummate our new relationship. One built on *mutual* trust and respect.'

He liked her eyes, so blue they could at times seem purple. Her angular features barely reflected her age. She possessed the lissome grace of a dancer – curvy, slender-waisted, full-bosomed. And she always wore a peculiar scent of perfume with a citrus aroma that lingered long after they parted.

'I don't think any relationship between us is possible,' she finally said.

And she pulled the trigger.

Knox ditched the boat on shore and hustled back to the vehicle he'd left parked near a small strip of closed shops. He was glad to be away from Paw Island.

Him dying there was not part of any equation.

No one was around. He needed to leave Canada, and fast. The stolen boat would be discovered tomorrow by whoever. His two associates would also be found inside Fort Dominion. One was clearly dead, the other most likely. None of them carried identification, though they both lived toward Nags Head, on the Atlantic shore. He'd long ago encouraged many of the crew to move out from Bath into the surrounding communities, the farther away the better, though close enough to be on site within two hours. Many were single, like these two, with few attachments. Once the bodies were identified and it was determined that they worked at the estate, law enforcement would appear. There'd be inquiries. But then that was why the Commonwealth employed a bevy of lawyers. It should not be a problem.

Andrea Carbonell, on the other hand.

She was a problem.

He was tired of being scared. Tired of watching his back. Tired of worrying. A good quartermaster would never have placed himself in such jeopardy.

Yet he had.

A year ago he might have stayed at Fort Dominion and fought it out with Jonathan Wyatt. But he'd already chosen another course, one that paid no heed to either duty or heritage. He just wanted to get out and not be killed by either the government or the Commonwealth.

He was a survivor.

And Jonathan Wyatt was not his enemy. Nor was Quentin Hale, really, or the other three captains.

They knew nothing.

Only Andrea Carbonell knew it all.

67

Bath, North Carolina

Hale heard the trigger click but no retort.

Kaiser smiled. 'The next one will be live.'

He did not doubt her prediction.

'Do you have any idea the situation you've placed me in,' she said to him. 'Pauline Daniels will probably never speak to me again.'

'Are they aware of my listening in on your calls?'

'They found your little device in my backyard.'

Panic surged through him as he thought about the two men sent to retrieve the equipment. Were agents waiting for them?

'Shirley, you must listen to me. There is more at stake here than your pride. The entire weight of the U.S. government has been brought to bear on me and my associates. I need allies, not more enemies. It's long past time for me to divorce my wife. Having you here full time would be most pleasant.' He paused. 'For us both, I hope.'

He had to contact Knox and deal with the situation in Virginia. That had now become even more critical than what was happening in Nova Scotia.

'You honestly think that would sway me?' she said. 'A promise of marriage? I don't need a husband, Quentin.'

'What do you need?'

'How about an answer to a question. Are you holding a woman prisoner here named Stephanie Nelle?'

He considered lying, but again decided against it. 'She is part of that enemy. Sent here to destroy us. I captured her in self-defense.'

'I'm not asking you to justify it, Quentin. I simply want to know if she's here.'

Alarm bells rang in his brain.

How would she know to ask that question?

Only one way. Someone told her. Someone in the know. If she wasn't naked he'd be worried she was wired. Her clothing and overnight bag were not a concern either since they were in the next room, a closed door between here and there.

'Shirley, you must understand that these are extraordinary times. I did what I had to do. You would have done the same. In fact, is that not what you are doing now? Defending yourself, however you can.'

Cassiopeia wanted to argue with Edwin Davis but knew that she had to trust both his and Cotton's instincts.

But there was still a problem.

'We need to contact Kaiser,' she said to Davis.

'I'm not sure that's possible. What are we going to do? Call her?'

'Not us. But there's someone who could make the call.'

She saw that he understood.

Davis found his phone and dialed.

Hale waited for Shirley to answer him. She seemed to be considering his inquiry.

'You used me,' she finally said.

A fresh burst of wind and rain pounded the house.

Which startled her.

He used the moment to slam his fist into her face.

★ ★ ★

Cassiopeia listened as Davis informed Pauline Daniels what Shirley Kaiser had done.

'I can't believe she went there,' the First Lady said.

They'd retreated into the dining room to make the call, clearing the house of agents.

'She feels horrible about this,' the First Lady said. 'She was so angry at being used. Still, she should have never gone there.'

But there was something even more serious to consider. The shooting that had just happened would make the local news. Once Hale learned of the fate of his two men he would know Kaiser had been compromised. Which meant she just became a problem.

'Pauline,' Davis said. 'Call her. Now. See if she answers.'

'Hold on.'

'There's no way to keep what happened here quiet,' Cassiopeia whispered to Davis.

'I know. The clock's ticking for Shirley Kaiser.'

'Edwin,' Pauline said through the speaker. 'No answer. It went to her voice mail. I didn't think you'd want me to leave a message.'

'We have to go,' Davis said to the phone.

Cassiopeia caught the frustration in his voice.

'Edwin, I didn't—'

Davis ended the call.

'That was rude,' she said.

'She wouldn't have liked what I would have said next. At some point everyone is going to have stop making stupid mistakes.' He paused. 'Myself included.'

'That woman's life is in jeopardy,' she said. 'Get me down there fast.'

And he didn't argue.

Hale stood from the bed.

Kaiser lay unconscious from the blow to her face.

His hand hurt. Had he broken her cheekbone? He retrieved the gun and checked. Indeed, the next round would have caused much damage.

His mind reeled.

Had his men been caught at Kaiser's residence? He had to know. Knox remained inaccessible, most likely still on Paw Island.

He found his robe and slipped it on.

He glanced at the bedside clock. 9:35 PM. He reached for the phone and punched the house intercom. His secretary answered after the second buzz in his ear.

'Have two men come to my bedroom immediately. I have a new guest for our prison.'

68

Malone opened his eyes. His body ached. Pain radiated throughout his legs. He was lying on his back, his gaze shooting upward back through the gaping hole of rotting wood that he and Wyatt had plunged through.

He tested his limbs and discovered that nothing seemed broken.

Shafts of moonlight spilled down from above, enough for him to see that they'd fallen about thirty feet. The spongy wood had cushioned the landing. Rock lay beneath him.

Along with chilly water.

The walls around him glistened a silvery sheen in the faint light, signaling that they were damp.

He heard surf and smelled the birds again.

Where was Wyatt?

He pushed himself up. A light switched on. Bright, singular, a few feet away. He shielded his eyes with an arm.

The light moved away from his face.

In the ambient glow he saw Wyatt holding the flashlight.

Knox arrived at the private airstrip where he'd landed the Hale Enterprises corporate jet, just south of Halifax, the facility catering to tourists who could afford the luxury of owning their own planes.

He'd made it out of Mahone Bay and back north without incident.

His phone vibrated in his pocket. He checked the display. Hale. Might as well deal with this now.

He answered, told the captain what had happened, then said, 'Carbonell lied to you. Again. There was another person here. Wyatt called him Cotton Malone. He was definitely not on our team. From what Wyatt implied, he was from the government. I can't be responsible for all of this—'

'I understand,' Hale said.

Which surprised him. Hale generally comprehended nothing other than success.

'Carbonell is a liar,' Hale said, bitterness in his tone. 'She's playing us all. You were right, and I have to now wonder if the information she provided about the cipher was even real.'

'It still could be true. Wyatt said to tell you that once he had those two pages, he'll sell them to you. He specifically wanted that message brought back.'

'So we have to hope that this renegade, whom Carbonell obviously dislikes and distrusts, is right and will cooperate.'

'We've also got two dead crewmen here,' he made clear.

'And we have an even worse problem.'

He listened as Hale told him about Shirley Kaiser and what may have gone wrong at her residence.

He decided to take a chance and said, 'Captain Hale, Carbonell is using us. She's complicating an already complicated problem. She said only she and Wyatt knew about this location, yet this Cotton Malone was there. Did she send him, too? If not, then who the hell else knows about this? How much more risk are we going to take? How much do we gamble?'

Silence on the other end of the phone signaled that Hale was thinking about that question.

'I agree,' Hale finally said. 'She needs to pay.'

Excellent. Her death would right all his mistakes. He'd be right back where he started.

'First,' Hale said. 'Find out if we have a problem in Virginia. I need to know. Then, you have my permission to deal with NIA as you see fit.'

Finally.

Freedom to act.

He ended the call and trotted toward the plane. He'd check the weather and receive clearance for takeoff once on board. No tower existed here, Halifax controlled ingress and egress. He popped the hatch on the jet and climbed into its spacious cabin.

'Leave the light off,' a female voice said.

He froze.

His gaze raked the blackened scene. In the glow from the outside tarmac lights he caught three forms sitting in the leather seats.

The voice was instantly recognizable.

Andrea Carbonell.

'As you can see,' she said, 'I didn't come alone. So be a good boy and close the cabin door.'

Cassiopeia sat in the passenger compartment of an air force transport chopper, flying south from Virginia to the North Carolina coast. Edwin Davis sat beside her. Weeks ago he'd reconnoitered the Commonwealth's compound and was able to provide her with a detailed satellite image of the acreage. The Secret Service had arranged through the North Carolina State Bureau of Investigation for a boat to be waiting on the Pamlico's south shore. From there, she'd motor across to the north bank and Hale's land. Avoiding local law enforcement seemed the safest course for now, as there was no way to determine how far the Commonwealth's reach stretched.

It was approaching midnight. Local news outlets in Fredericksburg would be reporting the shooting at Kaiser's residence early tomorrow. Assuming that no one else had been around to report back the disaster, she should have a few hours in which to operate.

Surely the Commonwealth compound was monitored electronically, as cameras would offer a far better line of defense than guards. Unfortunately, Davis had little intel on what awaited her on the ground. She'd been told of a nasty storm engulfing the entire coastal region, which should offer cover.

The Secret Service agents watching Paw Island had reported all quiet there for the past hour.

And Cotton?

She couldn't shake the thought that he was in trouble.

Wyatt stared down at Malone, who was slowly coming to his feet. Thankfully, he'd awakened first and managed to find a flashlight that Malone had apparently been carrying, which survived the fall.

'You happy now?' Malone said.

He said nothing.

'Oh, I forgot. You don't speak much. What was it they called you? The Sphinx? You hated that nickname.'

'I still do.'

Malone stood in ankle-deep water and worked out some kinks in his shoulder, stretching his back. Wyatt had already studied their surroundings. The chamber was about thirty feet high and half that wide. The walls were wet limestone, the rock floor engulfed by water, agate and jasper pebbles glistening in his beam.

'It's from the bay,' he said, motioning to the water.

'Where the hell else would it come from?'

But Wyatt watched as Malone comprehended the significance of his comment. He'd apparently read the history on this place, too. Seventy-four British soldiers died at Fort Dominion in a subterranean chamber subject to the tides.

'That's right,' he said. 'We're trapped in here, too.'

69

Bath, North Carolina

Hale watched as two crewmen yanked Shirley Kaiser from an electric cart and dragged her through the rain into the prison. He'd called ahead and told them to be ready for another occupant. She remained groggy from his blow to her face, a nasty bruise on her left cheek.

She tugged at the grip of her two minders as they forced her inside.

He entered and slammed the door shut.

He'd ordered Stephanie Nelle roused from her sleep and brought downstairs to new accommodations. He intended on placing these two women together since you never know what they might say to each other. Electronic monitoring would not miss a word.

Nelle stood in the cell, watching as they approached. The door was unlocked and Kaiser shoved inside.

'Your new roommate,' he told Nelle.

The older woman was examining the bruise on Kaiser's face.

'Your doing?' Nelle asked.

'She was being most disagreeable. She had a gun pointed at me.'

'I should have shot you,' Kaiser spit out.

'You had your chance,' he said. 'And you were wondering about Stephanie Nelle. Here she is.' He faced Nelle. 'Do you know a man named Cotton Malone?'

'Why?'

'No reason, other than he appeared somewhere he was not expected.'

'If Malone's there,' Nelle said, 'you've got a problem.'

He shrugged. 'I doubt that.'

'You think you could get this woman an ice pack?' Nelle asked. 'She has a nasty knot.'

Not an unreasonable request, so he ordered it done. 'After all, she must look her best.'

'What does that mean?' Nelle asked.

'As soon as the storm passes, the two of you are taking a sail. Your last voyage. Out to sea, where you will stay.'

Cassiopeia navigated the churning black waters of the Pamlico River. She'd arrived from the west, deposited by helicopter a kilometer or two from the south shore. The State Bureau of Investigation agents who'd waited for her and Davis had pointed across the nearly three-kilometer black expanse. Though she could see nothing, she'd been told about a dock that extended into the river, at the end of which should be moored a sixty-meter sailing yacht, *Adventure,* that belonged to Hale. If she wanted to gain entrance to the property, that was the place. Just maintain the right heading, which they'd provided – but it was proving difficult. A gale had blown in off the Atlantic. Not quite a tropical storm, but strong enough with high winds and sheeting rain. The last few minutes of her helicopter ride had not been pleasant. Davis would be nearby, waiting either for her signal or dawn, whichever came first. Then he'd move in with Secret Service agents who were amassing north of Bath.

Rain pelted her.

She cut the motor and allowed the boat to drift closer to Hale's dock. She'd found it exactly where they'd predicted. Swells rose in the meter-plus range, and she had to be careful not to crash into anything. The yacht tied to the dock was indeed impressive. Three masts, their stout size and shape indicating that they housed one of those automated sail systems she'd seen before. No lights burned anywhere, which was unusual. But it could be the storm. Power may have been affected.

Through the rain she caught movement on the deck.

And on the dock.

Men.

Running toward shore.

Malone asked Wyatt, 'Why is all this necessary? What happened between us was a long time ago.'

'I thought I owed you.'

'So you involved me in an assassination attempt? What if I hadn't stopped the guns?'

'I knew you'd do something. Then maybe you'd either get the blame or get shot.'

He wanted to smack the SOB in the jaw but realized that would be fruitless. He stared around at their confines. The water level on the floor remained at ankle level.

'So why not just kill me? Why all the drama?'

'It doesn't matter anymore.'

'Which means you now owe somebody else more.'

'It means it doesn't matter anymore.'

He shook his head. 'You're a strange bird. You always have been.'

'There's something you should see,' Wyatt said. 'I found it while you were sleeping.'

Wyatt angled the beam down the rock corridor. Twenty feet away, carved into the stone, gleaming from moisture and encrusted with algae, was a symbol.

Θ

Malone instantly recognized it as one from Jackson's message. 'Any more?'

'We can find out.'

He glanced upward from where they'd fallen. No way to climb back up. A good thirty feet of air stretched overhead, the walls a slick mass of slime. Not a handhold anywhere.

So why not. What the hell else was he going to do?

'Lead the way,' he said.

Hale decided to grab a few hours of sleep. There was no way they could make it to sea in this weather. *Adventure* was good, but every ship had its limits. He'd already ordered Kaiser's rental car locked away, off premises, where it could not be found. He still hadn't heard from the two men sent to Kaiser's residence and he had to assume that they were either dead or captured. But if they had been captured, why hadn't law enforcement already descended on him?

He left the prison and headed for his cart.

An alarm sounded.

His gaze shot to the darkened trees surrounding him, in the direction of his house. No lights could be seen.

A man burst from the prison and sloshed through the standing water, running his way.

'Captain Hale, there are intruders on the premises.'

Cassiopeia heard the alarm, then the steady *rat-tat-tat* of automatic weapons fire.

What was happening?

She leaped from the boat, taking a line with her, which she tied to a piling.

At the top of the ladder she found her weapon and turned for shore.

* * *

Hale rushed back into the prison. He'd heard the distant gunfire. A disturbing sound within his fortress of solitude. He found a phone and called the security center.

'Ten men entered the estate from the north perimeter,' he was told. 'They tripped motion sensors and we spotted them on camera.'

'Police? FBI? Who are they?'

'We don't know. But they're here, shooting, and they don't act like police. They've cut power to the main house and dock.'

He knew who they were.

NIA.

Andrea Carbonell.

Who else?

Knox wanted to leave Nova Scotia, but Carbonell and her two companions seemed in no hurry. He decided not to try their patience, at least not yet, and sat in the plane.

'Did you find what you came for?' she asked him.

He wasn't going to answer her. 'Two of my men are dead in that fort. Your man Wyatt is battling it out with someone named Cotton Malone. You send him, too?'

'Malone is there? Interesting. He's from the White House.'

He then realized why she was here. 'You were going to take back whatever I found. You had no intention of letting the captains have the solution.'

'I need those two missing pages in my possession.'

'You still don't get it, do you? The Commonwealth is not your enemy. But you've gone out of your way to make it one.'

'Your Commonwealth is radioactive. CIA, NSA, the White House, they're all closing in.'

He did not like the sound of that.

'We have to go back to Paw Island,' she said.

'I'm leaving.'

'There's nowhere for you to go.'

What did that mean?

'Your precious Commonwealth is being attacked, as we speak.'

'By you?'

She nodded. 'I decided Stephanie Nelle needs rescuing. And if Hale or one or two of the captains is killed in the process? That would be good for us all, wouldn't it?'

Her right arm moved and he caught the silhouette of a weapon in her hand. 'Which brings me to the other reason why we're here.'

He heard a pop, then felt something pierce his chest.

Sharp.

Painful.

A second later, the world vanished.

70

Nova Scotia

Malone recalled what the bookstore owner had told him about the symbols. That they could be found at various points inside the fort and on stones and markers around the island, but she'd said nothing about them appearing beneath. Understandable, considering that this was surely off limits.

The passage they were trapped in seemed to span from one end of the fort to the other. Dark yawns dotted the walls at varying heights. None of it was natural, the cut stones all man-made. He examined one of the yawns and noted that the rectangular chute, which extended into blackness, had also been crafted by hand. Positioned at points about three and six feet high, each dripped with remnants of the last high tide. He knew what these were.

Faucets and drains.

'Whoever built this place made sure it would flood completely,' he said to Wyatt. 'These openings are the only way out.'

He began to feel what those 74 British soldiers must have felt. Underground spaces were not his favorite. Especially confined ones.

'I didn't sacrifice those two agents,' Wyatt said to him.

'I never thought you did. I simply thought you were reckless.'

'We had a job to do. I just did it.'

'Why does that matter right now?'

'It just does.'

And then he realized. Wyatt truly regretted those deaths. He hadn't thought so at the time, but now he saw different. 'It bothers you they died.'

'It always did.'

'You should have said that.'

'It's not my way.'

No, he supposed not.

'What happened up there?' he asked. 'The Commonwealth came to kill you?'

'NIA sent the Commonwealth to kill me.'

'Carbonell?'

'An act she will regret.'

They came to a point where two more tunnels opened into the rock, forming a Y-shaped junction. With the flashlight Wyatt examined another of the chutes that opened from the wall, this one about shoulder-high. 'I hear water at the other end.'

'Can you see anything?'

Wyatt shook his head. 'I'm not staying here and waiting for high tide. These have to lead out to the sea. Now's the time to find out – before they start filling.'

He agreed.

Wyatt laid down the flashlight and removed his jacket. Malone grabbed the light and shone it around the junction point. As long as they were here they might as well make a full reconnoiter.

Something caught his attention.

Another symbol, chiseled into the stone to the left of where the main passage broke into two.

φ

He recalled it from Jackson's message. He studied the remaining walls and spotted a second symbol opposite the first.

:

Then directly across from those, on the far wall of the first passage, two more, about eight feet apart.

X Θ

That made four of the five Jackson had included in his message. And something else. They were positioned in relation to one another.

Wyatt noticed his interest. 'They're all here.'

Not quite.

He sloshed through the water to the center of the intersection of the three tunnels. Four markers surrounded him. The fifth? Down? He doubted it. Instead, he glanced up and shone the light at the ceiling.

Δ

'Triangle marks the spot,' he said.

Water burst from the lower chutes, surging through the chamber, swamping the floor in a cold wave.

He walked back to Wyatt, switching the flashlight from his right to his left hand.

He whirled his right arm up and smashed a fist across Wyatt's jaw.

Wyatt staggered back, splashing into the water on the floor.

'Are we done now?' he asked.

But Wyatt said nothing. He simply came to his feet, hopped into the closest chute, and disappeared into the blackness.

Cassiopeia sought cover in a stand of trees, watching the house that stood fifty meters away. Wind chimes performed a symphony of high-pitched tones. She glimpsed dark forms scurrying from one side of the house to the other, and more shots were fired. She decided to take a chance and found her phone, dialing Davis' number.

'What's happening there?' he immediately asked her.

'This place is under siege.'

'We can hear the gunfire. I've already checked with Washington. It's nobody that I can identify.'

'It's good cover,' she said. 'Just sit tight and stick to the plan.'

She sounded like Cotton. He was rubbing off on her.

'I don't like it,' Davis said.

'Neither do I. But I'm already here.'

She ended the call.

Wyatt wiggled down the tight tunnel, no more than three feet high and a little more than that wide. Cold water continued to drain from outside toward him with an ever-increasing intensity, the rush from its source growing more distinct.

He was coming to the end.

In more ways than one.

He'd allowed Malone the violation. He would have done the same, or worse, if the roles were reversed. Malone remained too self-important for his taste, but the cocksure SOB had never lied to him.

And there was something to be said for that.

Andrea Carbonell had sent him to Canada, assuring him repeatedly that the journey was between the two of them. Then she promptly informed the Commonwealth.

He could imagine the deal she'd made.

Kill Jonathan Wyatt and you get to keep whatever there was to find.

And that rattled him more than Cotton Malone.

He'd done okay the past few days, stopping the assassination of the president of the United States and managing to come as close as anyone to solving the puzzle Andrew Jackson had created long ago. He would have saved Gary Voccio's life, too, if the man had not panicked. His physical confrontation with Malone seemed to quell whatever anger had lingered inside him from eight years ago.

Instead, a new fury raged.

Faint rays of light appeared ahead.

In the absolute darkness, any glow, however minor, was welcome. The chilly water now rose to his elbows. He continued to crawl on all fours. The end of the shaft appeared and he saw a pool inside a rocky cavern. Surf lapped its sides as water rose to the chute. Beyond the cavern entrance he spotted open sea, bright streaks of moonlight glimmering off the restless surface.

He began to understand the engineering. The shafts had been cut into the rock at varying heights, emptying beneath the fort. As the tide rose so would the pool, flooding each of the tunnels in turn, forcing water into the chambers. When the tide receded, so would the water. A simple mechanism utilizing gravity and nature, but he wondered what its purpose had been in the first place.

Who cared?

He was free.

71

Knox Awoke.

Cool air rushed across his body. His head hurt and his vision was blurred. He heard the monotonous drone of an engine and felt himself jostled up and down. Then he realized. He was back on Mahone Bay. In a boat. With three people on board.

Two men and Carbonell.

He pushed himself up on his feet.

'My little dart works, doesn't it?' Carbonell called out.

He recalled the weapon in her hand, the pop, then the sting to his chest. She'd tranquilized him. He didn't have to ask where they were headed. He knew. Paw Island.

'It's the same boat you stole earlier,' she said.

He rubbed his aching head and longed for a shot of bourbon. 'Why are we going back?'

'To finish what you started.'

He steadied himself. Everything tossed and turned, and not from the boat. 'You understand that Wyatt is not going to be happy to see you.'

'Actually, I'm counting on that.'

Cassiopeia watched the attack on Hale's residence. Whoever these assailants were, they weren't being subtle. The shooting had subsided, but there was still plenty of movement, both sides seemingly jockeying for a better position. She blinked rain from her eyes and tried to focus on the black house, every window devoid of light. In fact, there were no lights burning anywhere she could see.

From a side door, someone slipped outside.

A man, who immediately crouched low and crept to the veranda steps, where he slowly descended, staying down. Open hands signaled that he held no gun. Was this Hale? She watched as the figure hustled into the rain, toward the trees, using the wind and thick trunks for cover, advancing away, toward the dock from where she'd come.

More crackling gunfire raged in the distance.

She headed toward where the man had gone, keeping her steps light. Wet leaves, roots, and fallen branches challenged her balance. Thankfully the soil was more sand than dirt and seemed to drain fast. No mud. She found the graveled road that led to the dock, the one she'd just paralleled to the house, and spotted her quarry, maybe twenty meters away, trotting down the right side of the road.

She ran and came within ten meters of him before he realized she was approaching. As his head whirled around, she stopped, leveled her gun, and said, 'Stay right where you are.'

The man froze. 'Who are you?' he asked.

The voice was not of the age she knew Hale to be. So instead of answering his question, she asked one of her own. 'Who are you?'

'Mr. Hale's secretary. I'm not a pirate or a privateer. I don't like guns and I don't want to be shot.'

'Then you'd better answer my questions, or you're going to find out what a bullet wound feels like.'

Malone swam out of the cavern and into Mahone Bay. The sea was cold. He shook water from his eyes and stared up at Fort Dominion. The shaft he'd negotiated had emptied into a rocky cleft. He wondered about Wyatt. He hadn't seen or heard any more from him. The shaft Wyatt had chosen apparently opened into another cavern. If he made it, Wyatt should be out here somewhere swimming, but Malone could not see or hear much beyond where he floated. He should be a hell of a lot angrier at Wyatt. But there was one thing. If Wyatt had not involved him, he wouldn't be in a position to help Stephanie.

Strange, but for that he was grateful.

He had to get out of the water, so he started swimming toward a flat part of the island, south of the fort. He found a small beach and emerged from the bay. Night air chilled his bones. His jacket was back in the chamber, left there as Wyatt had done, since it would have been little more than an anchor. Thank goodness he'd come prepared with a change of clothes.

The stench of the birds returned as he plunged inland, turning toward where he'd beached his boat. He recalled a coil of nylon rope that he could use to reenter the underground chamber. He'd wait for low tide, which should provide a few hours to safely explore. Surely, Andrew Jackson had known of Fort Dominion and what had happened here during the Revolutionary War. Why else would he have selected such an out-of-the-way locale? Perhaps because, even if Jefferson's cipher had been cracked and the cipher wheel found, nature would stand guard, ready to thwart all but the cleverest of hunters.

He pushed through the last of the foliage and found his boat. An easterly breeze stirred up tiny funnel clouds of sand near the water. He yanked off his wet shirt. Before changing he checked his cellphone. Edwin Davis had called four times. He hit REDIAL.

'How are things there?' Davis asked.

He reported the disaster, but also the success.

'We have a problem here,' Davis said.

He listened to what Cassiopeia had done, then said, 'And you let her go?'

'It seemed the only course. The storm is excellent cover. Apparently, though, we're not the only ones who think that.'

'I'm coming down there.'

'Shouldn't you get those pages?'

'I'm not going to sit around here with my head up my ass and wait for low tide while Stephanie *and* Cassiopeia are now in trouble.'

'You don't know that. Cassiopeia can handle herself.'

'Too much can go wrong. I'll contact you from the air. Keep me posted.'

He ended the call and stripped off the remaining wet clothes, replacing them with the dry ones from the boat. Before pushing off from the beach, he called the Secret Service pilots and told them to stand by to leave, he was on his way.

Wyatt found his boat on the island's north shore. His body was chilled, his clothes soaked from the cold swim. He'd anticipated spending the night on the island and, not knowing what to expect, had brought an extra shirt and pants. He'd also packed a knapsack with supplies, including matches, which he used to start a fire just beyond the beach.

What had happened to Malone?

He had no idea, not seeing or hearing anything while in the choppy bay. He was tired from the fully clothed swim, his muscles unaccustomed to such a workout. He huddled close to the flames and increased the warmth with more brush and sticks. He hoped Knox had made it back to shore and delivered his message to the captains. He hadn't meant a word of what he'd said about selling them the missing two pages.

He was concerned with only one thing.

Killing Andrea Carbonell.

He changed into the spare clothing and wished for another jacket like the one he'd left underground. The ride back across the bay would be brisk. He was hungry, and found a couple of energy bars along with a container of water. He would return the stolen boat to shore and leave it where it would not be found for a couple of days.

He checked his watch.

11:50 PM.

Lights on the bay caught his attention. He spotted a boat speeding toward the island from the direction of Chester. This late? He wondered if it was law enforcement, alerted by the gunfire.

He quickly extinguished the fire and hid among the foliage.

The boat changed course and headed his way.

Knox sat at the stern and tried to clear his head.

'What do you hope to gain by going back?' he called out to Carbonell.

She stepped close to him. 'First, we have to clean up your mess. Aren't the bodies of two of your men still there? You apparently weren't concerned with that. Or were you so intent on killing me you didn't care?'

How did this woman read his mind?

'That's right, Clifford. I heard what Wyatt said to you. I had a man on site, watching everything. You decided the smart play was to do as Wyatt asked and leave. Take me out. Once I'm dead, you're in the clear since no one else knows of our . . . arrangement. Am I wrong?'

'Why are you attacking the Commonwealth?' he asked.

'Let's just say that Stephanie Nelle's dying would no longer be good for any of us. And if I manage to find those two missing pages in the process, my stock rises even higher. If you're a good boy and behave, you can keep breathing. I might even give you that job I mentioned. And the captains?' She paused. 'They still go to prison.'

He had to point out, 'You don't have those two missing pages.'

'But either Wyatt or Malone does, or will. I know them both. Our task is to figure out which, then kill them both.'

One of the men signaled to Carbonell, pointing toward the middle of the island's flat topography. Knox looked, too. For a moment there was light, like a fire burning, then it was gone.

'You see,' Carbonell said. 'There's one of them now.'

72

North Carolina

Hale had command of the situation. He kept about a dozen crewmen on the estate at all times, each more than capable of defending himself. He'd ordered the armory opened, and everyone had been provided weapons. The thrust of the attack seemed to be centered on the main house and the prison. But at least four armed men were outside, in the trees, firing on the prison. Power had been cut, as at the main house, but this building was equipped with a backup generator.

'Shackle both prisoners,' he ordered. 'And gag them.'

His crewman hustled off.

He was in constant radio communication with the security center. More crewmen had been summoned to the estate, and he'd decided a relocation of the prisoners to *Adventure* was the prudent course. He turned to the other jailer. 'I want those men out front occupied. Pin them down.'

The man nodded.

He headed toward the ground-floor rear and a secondary entrance used to service the prison. It was built into the outer wall façade, invisible to anyone who did not know it existed. A man he'd stationed there half an hour ago reported all was quiet out back. With no windows and no visible entrance on that side of the building, he wasn't surprised. Apparently, Carbonell had decided to deal with Stephanie Nelle herself. But he had to wonder. Was this a rescue mission? It was the only thing that made sense. Never would she draw this much attention to killing Nelle.

Things had changed.

Again.

Fine. He could adapt.

Nelle and Kaiser were carried from the cell, their hands and feet secured with tape, their mouths gagged. Both were trying to resist.

He raised a hand and halted their removal.

He stepped close to a writhing Stephanie Nelle and nestled the barrel of his pistol to her skull. 'Stay still or I'll shoot you both and be done with it.'

Nelle stopped moving, her eyes alight with hate.

'Look at it this way. The longer you breathe, the more chances you have to live. A bullet to the head ends things completely.'

Nelle nodded in understanding, caught Kaiser's gaze with her own and shook her head. *No more.*

'Good,' he said. 'I knew you would be reasonable.'

He motioned for them both to be hauled outside. One of the electric carts waited in the rain. Both woman were laid onto its wet cargo bed. Two men with rifles stood guard, watching the trees, alert to the storm.

All seemed clear.

The two armed men hopped into the cart.

He'd already told them to avoid the main road to the dock and use the secondary path, which was primarily for the farm equipment that tended the fields.

And to hurry.

The cart sped off.

He rushed back inside the prison. As captain, it was his duty to stand with his men.

And stand he would.

★ ★ ★

Cassiopeia approached the building that Hale's secretary had identified as the prison. She'd learned from the terrified man that both Stephanie Nelle and Shirley Kaiser were being held there. She'd also learned that the building was under attack, so she'd approached from its rear, eastern side, staying in the trees, seeing no one so far. But that didn't mean much. The storm provided excellent cover for both her and everyone else.

A door opened in the rear of the building. In the wedge of light that escaped she watched two women being carried out.

Her heart sank.

Then she realized the hands and feet were bound. No need to tie up a corpse.

Two men with rifles stood guard and another man seemed in charge. Both prisoners were laid across the back of a vehicle not much larger than a golf cart. The two men with rifles climbed into the front seats.

The rest retreated inside.

The cart headed off into the dark.

Finally, a break.

Wyatt retreated farther into the trees that dominated the north shore of Paw Island and watched as the boat drew close to shore.

Who was this? The fire had clearly drawn them. He spotted four people in the small craft. One with long hair, thinner. A woman.

The boat's bow beached.

The woman and one man leaped out, both holding guns. Another man, standing at the wheel, also brandished a weapon. They examined his stolen boat using a flashlight. Then they cautiously advanced inland, toward where he'd doused the fire.

'He's here,' he heard the woman say.

Carbonell.

Good fortune had finally turned his way. But he didn't like the odds. Four to one, and his ammunition was limited. Only five shots remained in the magazine.

So he stayed still.

'Okay, Jonathan,' Carbonell called out. 'We're going to the fort to clean up your mess. I'm sure you can get there before we can. If you want to play, that's where you'll find me.'

Knox did not want to be here. This was insane. Carbonell was deliberately challenging Wyatt. And what about this Cotton Malone? Was he still around, too? He watched as Carbonell found her cellphone and pressed one of the buttons. She listened for a moment then ended the call.

'Jonathan,' she called out. 'I'm told Malone has left the island. Now it's just us.'

He checked his watch. Nearly midnight.

Dawn was only a few hours away.

They needed to get out of here.

Carbonell returned to the boat and seemed to sense his edginess.

'Relax, Clifford. How many times do you get to do battle with an accomplished pro? And that's exactly what Jonathan is. A pro.'

Wyatt heard her compliment, which he took as anything but. She was goading him. But that was okay. He was going to kill her, tonight, inside Fort Dominion.

Yet there was something else.

Carbonell had come here to announce her intentions.

She was leading him. Pushing him forward.

Toward the fort.

He smiled.

★ ★ ★

Cassiopeia hustled through a forest of cypress laden with dripping moss beards. The cart with Stephanie and Shirley made its way toward a graveled path that cut a swath back toward Hale's house and the river. Not the main road she'd followed to get here, but a secondary route, most likely being used to avoid whomever had decided to pay the estate a visit on this stormy night.

The cart sloshed its way ahead through the rain, its electric motor whining as it turned left onto a straightaway into the trees. She timed her approach carefully, both hands empty, swiping the soaked foliage aside, shaking her head to keep her eyes clear, building momentum.

She caught sight of the cart to her left, winking in and out beyond the branches, coming her way.

She waited until it was perpendicular to her path, then burst from hiding, her body slamming into the man sitting on the front passenger side.

73

Hale received the news he was waiting for – reinforcements had arrived outside the prison and were in position. Now they had their attackers in a vise. Similar to when privateers swarmed their prey, circling, the noose ever tightening, each watching out for the other until together they captured the target.

He faced the six crewmen inside the prison. 'We strike them hard, flushing them back. Our men are waiting for them.'

The others nodded.

He knew none of their names, but they knew him and that was all that mattered. Earlier, they'd witnessed the vengeance he and the other three captains could mete out, so each one of them seemed eager to please.

But he wasn't asking them to do anything he wasn't planning on doing, too.

He'd already decided that he'd had enough of pacification.

Time to personally deliver a blow that his opponents would understand.

'I want only one of them alive,' he made clear.

Cassiopeia watched as the cart driver was flung onto the wet roadbed. The man from the passenger side had been driven across the front seat, his hands now clinging to the steering wheel. A right cross sent him reeling out of the cart. She righted herself as the wheels rolled to a stop.

Gun in hand, she took aim behind her.

The two men were recovering, grabbing for their rifles.

She dropped each with a shot to the midsection.

She advanced toward the still forms lying in the road, two hands steadying her aim, and kicked the rifles away.

Neither man moved.

One lay faceup, his lips open, mouth filling with rain. The other was on his side, legs at an odd angle.

She ran back to the cart.

Knox reentered Fort Dominion, this time the prisoner of Andrea Carbonell.

'How many men do you have here?' he asked her.

'Just these two now. I ordered the others to leave.'

But why should he believe her? Of course, the fewer witnesses to what she was about to do the better, but he had no illusions. Not only was Jonathan Wyatt on her hit list, so was he. She'd made him think they were still allies, that their interests remained aligned—

I might even give you a job – but he knew better.

She was also doing something he'd never seen her do before.

Carrying a weapon.

She stopped within the inner bowels of the fort, crumpled buildings and collapsed walls all around them, the stench of birds heavy once again in the chilly air. He recalled the fort's geography from his first visit and wondered how much Carbonell knew of this place.

Would that knowledge give him a slight advantage?

His two men lay dead about fifty feet above him. They'd carried guns. He had to make a move.

But he'd only get one chance.

Make it count.

Malone was flying south, out of Canadian airspace, back to the United States. He was worried about Cassiopeia, wishing she hadn't gone in there alone. Okay, she was brave, and he knew how she felt about Stephanie. And yes, they were all frustrated and wanted to do something. But going solo? Why not? He'd probably have done the same thing himself, but that didn't mean he liked it.

The plane's phone buzzed.

'We have quite a storm here,' Edwin Davis said from North Carolina. 'It's creating a mess. You might have a problem landing.'

'We'll worry about that in three hours. What's happening across the river?'

'Gunfire has resumed.'

Cassiopeia ripped the tape from Stephanie's mouth, and the older woman immediately said, 'Damn, I'm glad to see you.'

'You look pretty good, too.'

She peeled tape from Shirley Kaiser's face and asked, 'You okay?'

'I'll live. Get this crap off my hands and feet.'

When both women were free, Stephanie rushed back and retrieved the two rifles. She returned and handed one to Shirley. 'Can you use it?'

'You bet your sweet ass I can.'

Cassiopeia smiled and asked them both, 'You ready?'

Rain continued to pour.

'We have to make it to the dock,' she told them. 'I have a boat there. Edwin is waiting across the river, and there are Secret Service agents on this side in Bath.'

'Lead the way,' Stephanie said.

'I want to kill Hale,' Shirley said.

'Take a number,' Stephanie said to her. 'But that's going to have to wait. Cassiopeia, are you saying that all that gunfire we heard has nothing to do with you?'

'Not a thing. They showed up just as I did.'

'What's going on?'

'I wish I knew.'

Hale directed his men as they fled the prison through the concealed rear door and advanced around toward the front, where their attackers waited. Many of the building's windows had been shot through but the old timbers had withstood the barrage. He was still in radio communication with his men who were flanking the attackers. They were awaiting his order before revealing their presence.

He came to the edge of the building and stayed low.

The storm had hardly abated during the past hour. His eyes were blurry with water. He used the upper eave for protection and focused out at the tree line. The yard, where the prisoner had died earlier, was acting as their salvation, as the intruders were hesitant to advance across its open expanse.

A blast of lead peppered the building.

He heard something thud to the ground and saw a splash. Then another.

'Captain, get down,' one of his men yelled.

Cassiopeia whirled at the sound of two explosions coming from the direction of the prison.

'Whoever they are,' Stephanie said, 'I'm glad they're here.'

She agreed. 'But we need to stay in the trees. There are men everywhere, and it's a good twenty-minute trek back to the dock.'

★ ★ ★

Hale pushed himself up from the wet ground and surveyed the damage. Two grenades had destroyed the prison's front door and taken out the remaining windows.

But the walls had continued to hold.

He found the radio and gave the command. 'Kill them, but make sure I have one prisoner.'

The men with him already knew what to do and started firing, drawing the intruders' attention.

Shots were returned.

He sought cover behind the trunk of a hefty oak.

Shouts were heard.

Automatic weapons fire came steadily, then lapsed, the clicks gradually slowing until only the wind and rain could be heard.

'We have them,' came the voice over the radio. 'All dead, except one.'

'Bring him to me.'

74

Wyatt beat Carbonell and her contingent back to Fort Dominion. He felt a little like he had that night years ago, trapped with Malone in the warehouse. Except he was now the fox, instead of the hare. He'd assumed a position similar to what the Commonwealth had taken on his arrival, utilizing the wall walks to maximum advantage. He'd also found his backpack, ditched earlier before his confrontation with Malone, and re-donned his night-vision goggles. He wished he had a supply of flash bombs. They'd come in handy right about now.

Below, he spotted Carbonell with three men. Two were armed. The third was Clifford Knox and he was unarmed.

He decided to strike the first blow.

So he aimed for one of the armed men, the night-vision goggles providing excellent visibility, and fired.

Knox heard a shot crack through the night.

The man standing five feet away from him cried out in agony then collapsed.

The other armed man reacted, diving for cover.

So did Carbonell.

He fled.

Disappearing into a doorway a few feet away and climbing toward the roof.

★ ★ ★

Cassiopeia led the way, trying to stay as far away from Hale's house as possible. There'd been no more explosions, and the gunfire had subsided.

'You're telling me,' Stephanie whispered, 'that Edwin has no idea who's attacking this place?'

'That's what he said. But it's most likely NIA. We suspect its director is deep into this.'

'You can't trust a thing Andrea Carbonell says or does.'

'Right now, I'm glad for whatever she's doing. That attack made my job a thousand percent easier.'

They kept moving, guns ready, keeping a watchful eye on the forest around them. Something caught Cassiopeia's attention off to the right. She grabbed Stephanie's arm and signaled for Kaiser to stop. Sprawled on the wet soil was a man, not moving. She crept over and saw that half of his skull was gone.

The other two women came, too.

Stephanie bent down and examined the corpse. 'Body armor. Night goggles.'

A radio lay to one side.

Stephanie lifted it and tried, 'Is anyone listening on this channel?'

Silence.

'This is Stephanie Nelle, head of the Magellan Billet. I ask again, is anyone on this channel?'

Hale surveyed the dead men, all equipped with body armor, night-vision goggles, grenades, and automatic weapons. They lay in the trees, rain drenching their corpses. They each carried a radio with an ear fob, one of which he now held.

'Where is my prisoner?' he asked his crewman.

'We took him inside. He's waiting for you.'

He still held his weapon. Reports from the main house confirmed that more intruders were dead there. Nine all told.

None of his men had sustained any injuries. Had Carbonell thought him that incapable? The security center confirmed that the estate was again secure, and the two vehicles the men had arrived in had been found about half a mile from the north perimeter. The storm had effectively masked the gunfire and the estate's isolation would aid in the cleanup. His men had also checked with the other captains. No one had been attacked save for him, and none of the three had dispatched any men to assist.

'Is anyone listening on this channel?'

The words startled him. A female voice. Coming through the radio's ear fob, which he'd inserted a few minutes ago on the off chance that there might be some chatter.

'This is Stephanie Nelle, head of the Magellan Billet, I ask again, is anyone on this channel?'

Knox found the upper wall walk but kept low. He made his way to one of his dead men and discovered no weapons. Either Wyatt or Malone had made sure there was nothing to find. The only other gun he might retrieve was from the man Wyatt had just taken down. But that would be difficult.

Two shots rang out from below.

One sent a round off into the night.

The other a bullet his way.

Cassiopeia watched as Stephanie tossed the radio to the ground and said, 'Useless.'

'Shouldn't we get out of here?' Kaiser asked.

Cassiopeia agreed. 'We're only about halfway and it sounds like things have calmed down. It won't be long before they know you're gone.'

Stephanie gestured with her weapon. 'We're leaving, but I'll back for these bastards.'

* * *

Hale ran to the prison building, found an estate phone, and called *Adventure*.

'Has a cart arrived with two prisoners?' he asked the man on the other end.

'Nothing, Captain. Just a lot of wind and rain.'

He hung up the phone and pointed at two crewmen.

'Come with me.'

Wyatt was pleased.

One down. Three to go.

On his run over from the boat he'd realized that Carbonell would not just parade into the fort. She knew he'd come and she knew he'd want her dead. She'd have a plan with contingencies. So when he'd reentered he'd stayed hidden, intentionally avoiding the main gate, slipping inside through a collapsed portion of the exterior wall.

'Come on,' he whispered to her. 'Don't disappoint me now. Be your usual cocky self.'

Hale found the empty cart and his two dead crewmen about a hundred yards from the prison.

Dammit.

He'd been told that they'd stopped all of the intruders, but that apparently was not the case. Where were Nelle and Kaiser? They could not have gone far. It was more than a mile to the nearest fence, and depending on which direction they chose, that would take them either onto another captain's land or to the water.

The river.

Exactly.

It had always been their greatest security threat, its wooded shoreline nearly impossible to patrol.

His cellphone vibrated in his pocket.

Security center.

'Captain,' the man said as he answered. 'We've reviewed the recordings and noticed that a single intruder gained access to the dock by boat about ninety minutes ago. Resolution was poor because of the storm, but it appears to be a woman.'

'Any sign of her?'

'We've had trouble with the cameras everywhere tonight, but no, no other sign of her.'

'Is her boat still there?'

'Tied to a piling. Do you want it released?'

He thought a moment.

'No. I have a better idea.'

75

Malone was anxious to be on the ground. They were back in American airspace, racing down the northeastern seaboard, headed for North Carolina. The pilots had informed him that they were about two hours from landing and the last thirty minutes would be extremely bumpy thanks to a late-season gale that had blown in from the Atlantic. In the meantime, there was nothing he could do but sit and worry.

His relationship with Cassiopeia had certainly added a new dimension to his life. He'd been married to Pam, his ex-wife, a long time. They'd gone from the navy, to law school, to the Magellan Billet. Together they'd birthed and raised Gary. Pam had even become a lawyer, too, something they should have shared but actually drove them apart.

Neither one of them had been a saint.

His indiscretions were known by her from their start. Hers only came to light years later. Thankfully, they'd made their peace, but that had taken more than either of them had ever bargained for to accomplish. Now another woman had entered his life. Different. Exciting. Unpredictable. Where Pam had been the picture of patience, Cassiopeia was like a moth, fleeting from one thing to the next, all with a grace and agility that he'd come to appreciate. Her faults were there, but nothing he could not lay claim to himself. From the first moment they'd encountered each other in France he'd been drawn to her. Now she might be in trouble, single-handedly trying to challenge a company of pirates.

Damn he wished they would land.

The cabin phone rang.

'Cotton, I thought you'd like to know that it's gone dead quiet at the compound.'

The deep voice on the other end of the line was unmistakable.

'Go get them,' he told the president of the United States. 'Cassiopeia should not have been allowed to go in there.'

'She was right, and you know it. Somebody had to go. But I understand where you're coming from. I feel awful about Stephanie. And Shirley Kaiser. The crazy fool. She's placed herself right in the middle of this.'

'How much longer do you wait?'

'She said till dawn. We'll give her that. Men have been arriving at the compound constantly. Beyond that, we don't know what's happening. She could be making progress.'

'I'll be there in less than two hours,' he said.

'Did you find those pages?'

'I think so, but I'll have to go back to get them.'

'Wyatt is still there. Carbonell is, too. She came after you left.'

'I figured Edwin had some eyes and ears on the ground.'

'I insisted. One of the Secret Service pilots who flew you there stayed behind. He's watching.'

That wasn't his main concern. 'I want to know what's happening in Bath, as it happens.'

'We'll act the instant we have cause. Otherwise, it's all yours in two hours.'

Cassiopeia studied the Hale house. Lights had been restored and armed men patrolled the covered verandas.

'Stay low and in the trees,' she whispered. 'Once we're around the house, it's not far to the dock.'

The storm continued to rage with little sign of slowing. The trip back across the river would be a challenge.

'I wish I could go in there and kill that son of a bitch,' Shirley muttered.

'How about you just testify against him,' she whispered. 'That should do it.' She motioned ahead. 'That way.'

They headed off.

Fifty meters past the house she heard shouts.

She turned back and, through the foliage, spotted men bursting out of doors and off the porches. Something had spooked them. None headed directly toward them. Most rounded toward the front, away from the river.

'We need to hurry,' she breathed.

Wyatt watched as Knox dove for cover. The shots had come from the direction of Carbonell and her man. Through the night goggles he saw a man emerge from the stairwell Knox had just used to climb onto the wall walk.

One of the men who'd come with Carbonell, come to finish Knox off.

He decided to help out.

He aimed and fired, dropping the man to the stones.

Knox seemed to sense an opportunity and belly-crawled to the body, finding the man's gun. He imagined what Carbonell was doing. She knew he was armed. His killing of her man had revealed his location. Now she was probably on her radio, trying to contact the two other men she'd previously stationed here.

Her aces in the hole.

Her plan with contingencies.

While she and the others occupied his attention, those two would take him out. She'd apparently captured Knox and brought him back, intent on cleaning up that loose end, too.

Poor Andrea.

Not this time.

★ ★ ★

Cassiopeia emerged from the oaks near the dock. The long wooden expanse remained unlit, Hale's sloop still tied at the end. There had to be men stationed on the boat. Unlikely that they would leave a yacht that large unattended in a storm. She motioned and they raced toward the ladder where she'd first gained ingress. Her boat waited at the bottom, tossing on the swells. They climbed down and she untied the lines.

So far so good.

She'd have to crank the engine, but not until the wind and current drove them out into the river.

A light appeared from the dock.

Bright, like the sun. Blinding her.

She raised an arm to shield her burning pupils.

She reached for her weapon and saw that Stephanie and Shirley were already raising theirs.

'That would be foolish,' a male voice said over the wind, through a loudspeaker. 'We have guns trained. Your engine has been disabled and the boat is tied from beneath to the dock. You can die there, if you like. Or—'

'It's Hale,' Shirley said.

'You can come ashore.'

'Let's swim for it,' Cassiopeia said.

But another light appeared out on the river, coming their way.

Anxiety turned to fear.

'My men are quite the seamen,' Hale said. 'They can handle this storm. There is no place for you to go.'

Knox scrambled over to the dead man and found a gun, along with a spare magazine in a jacket pocket.

Good to be armed.

He descended back into the fort, but avoided the ground, exiting one level above into a darkened passageway. He negotiated a short hall and entered a tight space where the outer wall, facing the sea, had collapsed. For a moment he allowed the breeze to alleviate some of his apprehension. Only the stench of guano disturbed the tranquility. He was just about to leave when something to his right, beyond a pile of rubble, caught his attention.

A leg.

He crept forward.

A mutter of concern growled among some nearby restless birds.

The darkened image sharpened.

Two legs, prone. A pair of rubber-soled shoes.

He glanced over the pile.

Two men lay sprawled. Their necks were broken, heads drooped at odd angles, mouths agape. A flashlight lay beside them. Now he knew why Wyatt was so bold.

He'd eliminated Carbonell's safety valves.

Now it was just the three of them.

76

North Carolina

Hale's trap for the fugitives had worked and now he had them all in custody at the prison. The rain outside had slackened but was still falling, a stiff breeze from the southeast hurling droplets through the destroyed windows. Crewmen were busy nailing plywood across the open frames. Another sheet already had been rigged as a makeshift door. The estate was on full alert. Nearly a hundred men had answered the late-night call. While patrols began on the grounds, he'd ordered the captive man prepared for questioning. He'd housed his three female prisoners in a nearby cell so they could watch.

He entered the prisoner's cell, two of his men following. 'I want to know the answer to a simple question. Who sent you?' The man, on the stout side, with wet, stringy black hair and a mustache, stared back at him.

'Your comrades are dead. Do you want to join them?'

No reply.

He'd almost hoped this fool would be difficult.

'Centuries ago, when my ancestors took prisoners, they had a simple way of extracting the truth. Would you like me to explain the method?'

Cassiopeia watched Quentin Hale, his eyes aglow with fire. He carried a gun in one hand, brandishing it toward the prisoner as if it were a cutlass.

'He takes this pirate crap seriously,' Stephanie mouthed. 'I watched him torture another one.'

Hale turned toward them. 'Whispering over there? Why not speak up so we can all hear?'

'I said I watched you mutilate another man, then shoot him in the head.'

'That is what we do to traitors. Do you perhaps know the answer to the question of what my ancestors once did to their prisoners?'

'My knowledge of your family tree is limited to *Pirates of the Caribbean,* so why don't you enlighten us.'

Shirley Kaiser stood silent but Cassiopeia spied the hate in her eyes. This woman had, so far, shown not the slightest hint of fear. Surprising. She hadn't expected such courage.

Hale faced them. 'There's a book that I particularly don't like, written long ago. *A General History of the Pyrates.* Mainly garbage – fiction – but there is one thing in it I agree with. *Like their patron, the devil, pirates must make mischief their sport, cruelty their delight, and damning of souls their constant employment.*'

'I thought you were some virtuous privateer,' Shirley said. 'Who saved America.'

He glared at her. 'I am what I am. What I am not, is ashamed of my heritage.' He motioned with the gun toward the man in the cell with him. 'He is the enemy, employed by the government. Torturing government officials was acceptable then and remains so today.' He turned back to the prisoner. 'I'm waiting for an answer to my question.'

Still nothing.

'Then I owe you an explanation. Bring him.'

The two men with Hale dragged the prisoner out into an open area before the cells. Three stout timbers rose about ten meters apart and supported the upper story. Candles wrapped the center post, held aloft in iron brackets.

The plywood shielding the front door was pushed open and seven men entered. Among six of them, in both hands, they carried knives, pitchforks, and shovels. A seventh held a fiddle. The prisoner was shoved toward the center post wrapped with the burning candles. The six men encircled him, standing a meter or so away, making it impossible for him to flee.

Hale said, 'It is called the sweat. In the glory days, the candles would encircle the mizzenmast. Men would surround it with points of sword, penknives, forks, anything sharp in each hand. The culprit enters the circle. The fiddler plays a merry jig and the culprit must run around the circle while each man jabs him. The heat from the candles works on the culprit. Hence, the sweat. Exhaustion becomes an issue as the men gain the upper hand, thrusting the points ever deeper. Eventually—'

'I'm not watching this,' Stephanie said.

'You shall watch,' Hale made clear. 'Or you will be next to experience it.'

Wyatt waited for Carbonell to communicate with the two men she'd stationed within the fort. Maybe they already had their orders and knew what to do? They'd both carried guns and radios, and he'd relieved the corpses of both just after breaking the men's necks. He now held a radio and heard nothing through its earpiece. He hadn't killed anyone so directly in a long while. Unfortunately, it had been necessary. He'd hidden the bodies near where Knox had disappeared back into the fort. Perhaps he'd found them.

The enemy of my enemy is my friend.

Cliché as hell, but appropriate here.

Carbonell had yet to leave her hiding spot. He had a clear view of where she'd ducked for cover. She was probably waiting for some sort of radio confirmation from her men.

Since none would ever come, he decided to move things along.

'Andrea,' he called out.

No reply.

'You can hear me.'

'Let's talk this through,' she said in her usual calm voice. 'Come out. Face-to-face. You and me.'

He wanted to chuckle.

She didn't know a damn thing.

'Okay. I'll come out.'

Hale watched as the culprit tried to avoid the pokes and prods from the six men encircling him. The prisoner rounded the timber post, the flames on the candles dancing, like him, to the fiddler's tune. He hugged the timber, drawing close, but his men showed no mercy. Nor should they. This man had attacked their sanctuary. He was part of the enemy trying to imprison them all. He'd made that clear to each one of them earlier, and they'd understood their duty.

One of the men jabbed his shovel, a sucking sound indicating that the sharpened blade had penetrated deep. The culprit lurched forward and grabbed for his left thigh, staggering around the post, trying to avoid the others. He'd cautioned them against finishing him too soon. That was the thing about the sweat. It could last as long as the captain desired.

Blood stained the man's pants, oozing from fingers that tried to keep the wound contained.

Wax dripped from the candles. Perspiration beaded on the victim's brow. He raised a halting hand.

The music stopped.

His men ceased their prodding.

'Are you ready to answer my question?' he asked.

The culprit panted, trying to grab his breath. 'NIA,' the man finally said.

Just as he suspected.

He motioned to one of the men holding a knife. Two of the others dropped their tools and grabbed the wounded man by the shoulders and arms, forcing him down to his knees. A third locked his fingers onto a handful of hair and angled the head back. The man with the knife approached and, with one slice, removed the prisoner's right ear.

A howl filled the prison.

Hale stepped over, retrieved the ear, and ordered, 'Open his mouth.'

They did.

He stuffed the ear past the man's front teeth and protesting tongue.

'Eat it,' he said, 'or I'll cut the other one off.'

The man's eyes went wild at the thought.

'Chew it,' he screamed.

The man shook his head and gurgled as he fought for breath.

Hale motioned and his men released their grip.

He raised the gun he was holding and shot the man in the face.

Cassiopeia had seen people die before, but it sickened her still. Stephanie, too, was surely hardened. But Shirley Kaiser apparently had never witnessed a murder. She heard Kaiser's gasp and watched as the older woman turned away.

Stephanie offered comfort.

Cassiopeia kept her gaze on Hale. He stared over at her, past the bars, and pointed with the gun.

'Now, little lady. It's your turn to answer questions.'

77

*H*e was a tall, spare man with a black beard, which he wore long and tied with ribbons. A sling draped his broad shoulders and held a brace of pistols. Smart, politically astute, and bold beyond measure. No one knew his real name. Thatch? Tache? He chose Edward Teach, but his nickname was the one that everyone remembered.

Black Beard.

Born in Bristol but raised in the West Indies he'd served with Jamaican-based privateers during the War of Spanish Succession. After, he arrived in the Bahamas and signed on with the pirate Hornigold, learning the trade, and eventually acquiring his own ship. In January 1718 he came to Bath Town and established a base at the mouth of the Pamlico River, on Ocracoke Island. From there he pillaged ships and bribed the local governor for protection. He cruised the Caribbean and blockaded Charles Town harbor. Then he retired, sold his plunder, bought a house in Bath, and secured a pardon for all his past acts. He even managed to gain title to the vessels he'd captured. All of which made the adjacent colony of Virginia both angry and nervous. So much so that its governor vowed to flush out the pirate's nest that was Bath Town.

Two armed sloops arrived at sundown on November 21, 1718, stopping just outside Ocracoke Inlet, far enough away so that the unfamiliar shoals and channels would not pose a danger. Royal Navy fighting men crewed the boats and Lieutenant Robert Maynard commanded them, an experienced officer of great bravery and resolution.

Black Beard, aboard his anchored ship Adventure, *paid the vessels little mind. He was through with fighting. For six months he'd plied the local waters unmolested. His crew was greatly reduced, as there was no profit associating with a man who no longer looted vessels. Most of his experienced shipmates were either long gone or ashore in Bath. All that remained on board were twenty or so, a third of whom were Negroes.*

Some precautions, though, were taken.

Powder, balls, and scrap were stacked near the eight mounted guns. Blankets were soaked and hung around the magazine, there for any deck fires that might occur. Pistols and cutlasses were piled near battle stations. All routine. Just in case. But they would not dare attack him, Black Beard was heard to say.

The assault began in the early gray light of dawn.

Maynard's force outnumbered Black Beard's three to one. But in their haste to gain an advantage, Maynard's sloops ran aground in the shallow water. Black Beard could have easily fled northward, but he was no coward. Instead he hoisted a mug of liquor and yelled across the water, 'Damnation seize my soul if I give you quarter or take any from you.'

Maynard hollered back, 'I expect no quarter from you, nor shall I give any.'

They both knew. This would be a fight to the death.

Black Beard aimed his eight cannons at the two sloops and barraged them with mortars. One sloop was disabled, the other badly damaged. But the effort caused Adventure *to ground on a shoal, too. Maynard, seeing his adversaries' predicament, ordered all water barrels staved and ballast jettisoned. Then, like a hand from providence, a stiff breeze blew in from the sea and pushed him free of the sandbar, sending him straight for* Adventure.

Maynard ordered all his men belowdecks, their pistols and swords ready for close fighting. He himself hid belowdecks with them, a midshipman at the helm. The idea was to draw his adversary into boarding.

Black Beard alerted his men to ready their grappling irons and weapons. He also produced an invention of his own. Bottles filled with powder, shot, and pieces of iron and lead, ignited by fuses worked into the center. Later generations would call them hand grenades. He used them to create havoc and pandemonium.

The explosives landed on Maynard's sloop and enveloped the deck in dense smoke. But since most of the men were below, they had little effect. Seeing so few hands on board, Black Beard shouted, 'They are all knocked on the head but three or four. Board her and cut them to pieces.'

The ships touched. Grappling irons clanked across the bulwarks.

Black Beard was the first to board.

Ten of his men followed.

Shots were fired at anything that moved.

Maynard timed his response with precision, waiting until nearly all of his opponent's men were aboard, then allowing his forces to burst from the hold.

Confusion reigned.

The surprise worked.

Black Beard immediately grasped the problem and rallied his men. Each fight became hand-to-hand. Blood slicked the deck. Maynard fought his quarry directly and leveled a pistol. Black Beard did the same. The pirate missed, but the lieutenant found his mark.

The bullet, though, did not stop the renegade.

Both men engaged the other with cutlasses.

A powerful blow snapped Maynard's blade. He hurled the hilt and stepped back to cock another pistol. Black Beard advanced for a finishing blow, but at the moment he swung his blade aloft another seaman slashed his throat.

Blood spurted from the neck.

The Brits, who'd steered clear of him, sensed his vulnerability and pounced.

Edward Teach died a violent death.

Five pistol wounds. Twenty cuts to his body.

Maynard ordered the head removed and suspended from the bowsprit of his sloop. The rest of the corpse was thrown in the sea. Legend holds that the headless body defiantly swam around the ship several times before it sank.

Malone stopped reading.

He'd tried to take his mind off the situation by surfing the Internet, reading about pirates, a subject he'd always found fascinating, and the fate of Black Beard had caught his attention.

The pirate's skull dangled from a pole on the west side of the Hampton River in Virginia for several years. That spot today is still known as Blackbeard's Point. Someone eventually fashioned it into the base of a punch bowl, which was used for drinking at a Williamsburg tavern. Eventually it was enlarged with silver plate, but disappeared over time. He wondered if the Commonwealth had anything to do with that. After all, he assumed it was no coincidence that Hale had named his own sloop *Adventure*.

He checked his watch. Less than an hour till they landed.

He'd made a mistake reading about pirates. It only made him more anxious. For all of the romanticism associated with them, they were cruel and vicious. Human life meant little to them. Theirs was an existence based on profit and survival, and he had no reason to assume that the modern version was any different. These were desperate men, faced with a desperate situation. Their only goal was success, and who they hurt in the process meant nothing.

He felt a little like Robert Maynard on his way to confront Black Beard.

A lot had been at stake then, and was now.

'What have you done?' he whispered, thinking of Cassiopeia.

★ ★ ★

Knox shifted his position, staying one level aboveground, keeping close to the outer wall, using the rubble for cover. Gaping holes stretched everywhere in the outer curtain, exposing a moonlit bay. A stiff breeze chapped his lips, but at least it flushed most of the bird pall away. He'd listened to the exchange between Carbonell and Wyatt and was trying to find a vantage point from which he could more closely observe their confrontation. Perhaps, if he was lucky, he could take them both out?

'Knox.'

He stopped. Wyatt was calling to him.

'I know where those two pages are hidden.'

A message. Loud and clear. *If you're thinking about killing me, think again.*

'Be smart,' Wyatt yelled.

He realized what that meant.

We have a common enemy. Let's deal with that. Why do you think I allowed you to have a gun?

Okay. He'd go along with that.

For now.

Hale stepped toward the cell that held his three female prisoners. Kaiser's hair lay matted to her head, her clothes soaked, but there was still something about her – a beauty that came from age and experience – that he would miss.

Along with her special garments.

'So you came to learn what you could? To find Ms. Nelle?'

'I came to try and right my own screwup.'

'Admirable. But quite stupid.'

He listened outside and was pleased to hear the rain and wind abating. Finally. Perhaps the worst of the storm had gone. His immediate problem, though, was more pressing.

He faced the woman he did not know.

Slim, toned, with dark hair and swarthy skin. Quite a

beauty. Gutsy, too. She reminded him of Andrea Carbonell, which wasn't a good thing.

'Who are you?' he asked.

'Cassiopeia Vitt.'

'You were to be their rescuer?'

'One of many.'

He caught her point.

'It's over,' Stephanie Nelle said to him. 'You're done.'

'Is that what you think?'

He reached into his pocket and removed the cellphone that his men had found on Vitt. Interesting device. It contained no phone log, contacts, or saved numbers. Apparently its only use was to send and receive one call at a time. He assumed it was something the intelligence community utilized.

Which made Vitt part of the enemy.

He'd already surmised that the other men had been sent to draw his attention while she made the extraction.

And the plan had almost worked.

'Do you work for NIA, too?' he asked her.

'I work for me.'

He gauged the response and decided that his initial assessment was correct. This woman would tell him nothing without prodding.

'You just saw what I do when someone refuses my questions.'

'I answered your question,' Vitt said.

'But I have another one. A much more important one.' He displayed the phone. 'Who do you report to?'

Vitt did not reply.

He said, 'I know Andrea Carbonell is waiting for you to report in. I want you to tell her that Stephanie Nelle isn't here. That you failed.'

'There's nothing you can do to me that would make me do that.'

He realized that was true. He'd already sized up Cassiopeia Vitt and decided she would play the odds. If he was right, and there were others monitoring her progress, when she failed to report, they would act. All she had to do was hold out until enough time passed.

'I don't plan to do anything to you,' he made clear.

He pointed at Kaiser.

'I intend to do it to her.'

78

Nova Scotia

Wyatt hoped Knox heeded his warning. He required a few uninterrupted minutes with Carbonell. Then he and Knox could play between themselves. And play they would, since he doubted Knox was simply going to walk away once he realized the odds had now evened. Had Knox found the two bodies? Probably. But even if he hadn't, there was no reason for him to assume anyone else remained in the fort besides the three of them.

He descended to ground level, caution lacing each step, the night-vision goggles helping within the dark recesses. He found the base of the stairway, then a doorway that opened to the inner courtyard where Carbonell waited.

He checked his watch.

Nearly three hours had passed since he and Malone were underground. Every six hours. That was the rhythm – low tide to high.

'I'm here, Andrea,' he said.

'I know.'

Both of them remained concealed.

'You lied to me,' he said.

'Did you expect that I wouldn't?'

'You don't know when to quit, do you?'

He heard her chuckle. 'Come on, Jonathan. You're not

some rookie agent. You've been around. You know how this is played.'

He did. Duplicity was a way of life in intelligence. But this woman had gone beyond the norm. She was using him. Nothing more, nor less. He had little or nothing to do with her goal. He was simply a means to that end. And though he was being paid well, that did not offer her immunity to do with him as she pleased. Besides, she'd come here to kill him, never intending for him to enjoy her money.

'What's the problem?' he asked her. 'You can't have me talking to anyone? I know too much?'

'I doubt you'd say anything. But it pays to be one hundred percent sure. Did you really find those pages?'

'I did.' Not exactly true, but close enough.

'And why would I believe you?'

'No reason I can think of.'

He knew the idea was to keep him talking so her men could zero in and finish him off.

'There's no need for this hostility,' she said.

'Then come out and face me.'

He removed the goggles.

Knox was nearby, and armed. He could feel him. Hopefully, he'd do more listening than acting, since he wanted what Andrew Jackson had hidden here, too.

Cassiopeia could do nothing. Two of the crewmen had yanked a screaming Shirley Kaiser from the cell while three more trained guns on her and Stephanie. Shirley was dragged into another cell, two down, a clear view of her through the open bars. Her wrists and ankles were taped to a heavy oak chair, her mouth gagged, her head shaking in protest.

The two men with guns had withdrawn from their cell.

She and Stephanie stood alone.

'What do we do?' Stephanie whispered.

'If I don't make the call, the cavalry is coming.'

'But there's no telling what's about to happen to her. How much time do we have?'

'An hour or so till dawn.'

Another man appeared, carrying a black leather bag.

'This is our company surgeon,' Hale said. 'He tends to our wounds.'

The doctor was a solid, bland-faced man with closely cropped hair. His clothes were soaking wet. He laid the bag on a wooden table in front of Shirley. From within, he withdrew a set of stainless-steel bone shears.

'A doctor is an important member of any crew,' Hale said. 'Though he didn't fight or defend the ship, he always received a higher portion of the booty than a regular crewman, which everyone gladly paid. That remains true today.'

The doctor stood beside Shirley, holding the cutters.

'Ms. Vitt? Ms. Nelle?' Hale said. 'I have no patience left. I've dealt with deceit until I'm sick of it. I want to be left alone, but the U.S. government will not do that. Now my home has been attacked—'

The plywood covering the prison door burst open and three men entered, shaking rain from their coats.

They were about the same age as Hale.

'The other captains,' Stephanie whispered.

Knox eased his way closer to where Wyatt and Carbonell were confronting each other. He wondered if Carbonell realized Wyatt was drawing her close, allowing her to think that she retained the upper hand. He could hear snippets of their conversation as he maneuvered to a point directly above them. Rocks and rubble made the going slow, the loitering birds an aggravation as he had to be careful not to disturb them, a change in their rhythmic cooing a clear alert to his presence.

Wyatt had said that he'd found the pages. Was that true? And did it even matter anymore?

Maybe.

If he could return to Bath with Wyatt *and* Carbonell dead and the two missing pages in his hands, his worth with the captains would multiply a hundredfold. Not only would they be legally protected, but he would have saved them all.

That prospect was appealing.

He held the gun tight.

His targets were now just below him.

'All right, Jonathan,' he heard Carbonell say. 'I'll face you.'

Hale did not appreciate the interruption from his colleagues. What were they doing here? This did not concern them. His house, not theirs, had been attacked, and they hadn't lifted a hand to help. He watched as they spotted the body on the floor, one ear missing, a hole in the head.

'What are you doing?' Bolton asked him.

He was not going to be reprimanded by these fools, especially in front of his men and prisoners. 'I'm doing what none of you has the courage to do.'

'You're out of control,' Surcouf made clear. 'We've been told that there are nine dead men outside.'

'Nine men who attacked this compound. I have the right to defend myself.'

Cogburn pointed to Shirley Kaiser. 'What did she do to you?'

None of the three had ever met her. He'd made sure of that.

'She is part of the enemy.'

Though the prison building sat on Hale land, the Articles expressly made it neutral ground where they shared jurisdiction. But he was not going to tolerate any interference.

'That woman there.' He pointed at Vitt. 'Came with the

others and attempted to free my prisoner. She killed two of our crew.'

'Quentin,' Surcouf said. 'This is not the way to solve anything.'

He wasn't going to listen to their cowardice. Not anymore. 'The quartermaster is, at this moment, retrieving the two lost pages. They've been found.'

He saw the shock on their faces.

'That's right,' he said. 'While you three slept, I saved us all.'

'What are you about to do?' Bolton asked, pointing at Kaiser.

He held up the phone. 'I need a call made. Ms. Vitt will not cooperate. I'm simply going to motivate her. I assure you that if I don't act we will all be visited shortly by a contingent of federal agents, this time with warrants.'

He watched as that realization took hold. The attack tonight had been a rogue action designed to catch him off guard. The next round could be different. More official. He still did not know what had happened in Virginia. For all he knew the authorities already possessed the requisite probable cause to act.

'Quentin,' Cogburn said. 'We're asking you to stop. We understand you were attacked—'

'Where were your men?' he asked them.

Cogburn said nothing.

'And yours, Edward? John? I'm told that not a one of your people came to our defense.'

'Are you implying we had something to do with this?' Surcouf asked.

'It's not beyond the realm of possibility.'

'You're insane,' Bolton said.

He gestured for his men to train their weapons on the captains. 'If any of them makes a move, shoot him.'

Guns were leveled.

He motioned, and the doctor nestled the shears to the base of Kaiser's middle finger. Kaiser's eyes went wide.

He turned to Vitt.

'Your last chance to make the call. If not, I'll start snipping off fingers until you do.'

79

Nova Scotia

Wyatt watched as Andrea Carbonell stepped from the shadows and into the moonlight. He'd just checked his watch and noted that time was running short. He caught her shapely silhouette and saw the outline of a weapon in her left hand, the barrel pointing toward the ground.

He, too, stepped out, a gun in his right hand, pointing down.

'It shouldn't have to come to this,' she said. 'You should have just died.'

'Why even involve me?' he asked.

'Because you're good. Because I knew you'd be tough when others weren't. Because nobody would give a damn if you disappeared.'

He smiled.

She was still buying time for her men to act.

'Do you care about anything beyond yourself?' he asked.

'Oh, my. Jonathan Wyatt going soft? Do *you* actually care about anything other than *your*self?'

Actually, he did. There wasn't a day that went by he didn't think about those two dead agents. He was alive thanks to them. They'd done their job, drawn fire, and the mission had been a success because of their sacrifice. Even the admin board had voiced that finding.

But he'd never sacrificed *them* to save *himself*.

Not like this woman.

The only human life that meant anything to her was her own. *That was the worst part. You were a good agent.* Malone's comment to him after the board's verdict, when they confronted each other, his hand at Malone's throat.

Yes, he was.

He wanted to know, 'Did you send those men into the Garver Institute?'

'Of course. Who else would have done it? I thought it a good opportunity to eliminate you, Malone, and the man who broke the cipher. But you were lucky there. So was Malone. Come now, Jonathan, you knew all along I was using you. But you wanted the money.'

Maybe so. And he'd also made it this far, covertly shifted his position from defense to offense.

A fact Carbonell did not, as yet, understand.

'The spring gun yours, too?' he asked.

She nodded. 'I thought it a good way to divert attention from me. If your foot had not stopped the door, I would have flung it open and stepped out of the way, barely escaping harm.'

'Sorry to interrupt your plan.'

She shrugged. 'As it is, things have turned out even better. Lots of possibilities here. Where are the two pages?'

That was the one thing holding her back. She could not make a move on him until that question was answered. Her orders to her minions had certainly included a proviso that their location was vital before they acted.

'I can show you,' he said. 'I haven't had an opportunity to retrieve them.'

'Please do.'

He knew she could not resist, so he gestured toward his right and, together, they reentered the great hall where he and Malone had fought. He found the hole with the rotted timbers and pointed. 'Down there.'

'And how do we get there?'

He'd already thought about that. The upper wall walk was lined on its inner edge with a rope barrier that stretched through iron holders. Not much protection, but enough for someone to be aware of the danger. After eliminating Carbonell's two men, he'd removed the nylon hemp and coiled about fifty feet into his backpack.

He slid the pack off his shoulders and said, 'I came prepared.'

Cassiopeia considered Hale's question. He'd chosen the right victim. If either she or Stephanie had been strapped to that chair, neither would have spoken, since the only bargaining power they possessed was holding out.

But Shirley Kaiser would not understand that.

The woman's eyes were bright with fear as she stared at the steel shears centered on her middle finger. Shirley shook her head, signaling *No, please no*. But she could do little to resist.

'You know you can't call,' Stephanie whispered.

'I have no choice.'

'Yes,' Hale said, noticing but not hearing their conversation. 'Talk it through. Make the right choice. Shirley is counting on it.'

The three other captains stood and watched.

Guns remained aimed at them.

Cassiopeia could not allow this to happen, so she said, 'Give me the damn phone.'

Malone tightened his seat belt and prepared for landing. The descent from thirty thousand feet had been rough. The pilot had informed him that the storm was moving north and that they were skirting its trailing southern edge. Edwin Davis had called twice to say that nothing had been heard from Cassiopeia, but no further gunfire had been heard, either.

Which did not comfort him.

He'd already reloaded his weapon and stuffed two spare magazines into his jacket pockets.

He was ready to move.

Just get me on the ground.

Knox stood above the decayed hall and stared down from the wall walk at Wyatt and Carbonell. He'd heard Wyatt when he told her that the lost pages waited below, in the dark chasm through the floor. He watched as Wyatt secured a rope to one of the pillars that had once supported the roof. Wyatt had descended first, then Carbonell. A light had switched on below, then faded. Should he follow, or just wait for them to return? What if there was another way in or out?

He thought of his father, the legendary quartermaster.

A wave of shame swept over him. He'd sold out. Done the one thing his father never would have done.

His father had, in fact, accomplished the impossible.

He'd killed a president.

John Kennedy acquired the White House thanks to a coalition that his own father, Joe, secretly forged. It involved political bosses, labor unions, and organized crime. Quentin Hale's father had been close with Joe and made a deal with the Kennedys. *Agree to honor the letters of marque once you're in the White House, and the Commonwealth will deliver money and votes.*

Which it did.

But all of that camaraderie was forgotten after the election.

The Kennedys turned on everyone, including the Commonwealth. Labor and the mob were at a loss as to what to do.

Not so the captains.

They recruited an inept Russian defector named Lee

Harvey Oswald to assassinate Kennedy, then had the terrific good fortune of Jack Ruby murdering Oswald.

No trail led anywhere.

Conspiratorialists had theorized for decades as to what really happened, and they would for decades more. But no one would ever know the truth. His father had been a true quartermaster.

Loyal to the end.

Maybe it was time he acted like one again, too.

He'd need a light.

He carried no flashlight, but one was upstairs, lying beside the two corpses.

He headed that way.

Cassiopeia accepted the phone from Hale through the bars.

'Make this short and convincing,' he said to her. 'Just a nod of my head and she loses a finger.'

She snatched the unit from his grasp and dialed the number she'd memorized. Edwin Davis answered on the second ring.

'What's happening there?' he asked.

'All is good. But I haven't located Stephanie or Kaiser. This is a big place.'

'The shooting we heard?'

Hale clearly thought that the men who'd come were connected to her. After all, they'd arrived at the same time. Of course that was false, but on hearing that connection Davis might get the message.

'Our men made a mess of things,' she said. 'They shot up the place, but ended up dead. The tactic didn't work. I'm okay. Looking around, but the place is full of activity.'

'Get out.'

'I will. Shortly. Right now, I want a little more time. Sit tight.'

'I don't like it.'

'You're not here and I am. We'll do this my way.'

A pause. Then, Davis said, 'All right. Your way. For a little while longer.'

She ended the call.

'Excellent,' Hale said. 'Even I believed you. Who was that?'

She kept silent.

Hale raised a hand, as if to say, *One drop and her finger's gone*.

'NIA special agent. He's in charge here. The men were ours, too, as you already know.'

Hale smiled. 'Where's Andrea Carbonell?'

'That I don't know. She doesn't check in with me. She gave us orders, we followed them.'

A man entered from outside armed with an automatic rifle and hustled over to Hale. He whispered something to his captain, then withdrew.

Hale relieved her of the phone. 'A slight problem. The storm is passing, but a fog has settled in. The Pamlico is infamous for its fogs. This one will delay our departure for a short while.'

'Where are we going?' Stephanie asked.

'As I mentioned to you earlier, a sail on the Atlantic.'

Cassiopeia watched the doctor. Shirley wasn't resisting as much since the call had been made and Hale seemed satisfied.

'More killing on the high seas?' one of the other captains asked Hale.

'Edward, I would not dare hope for you to understand. Soon our letters of marque will be irrefutable and all will be right with our world again. These three ladies are no longer useful toward that result.' Hale turned to Cassiopeia and Stephanie. 'You must know that?'

'We have your man in Virginia,' Cassiopeia said. 'In custody.'

She was hoping that might slow him down.

Hale shrugged. 'Tomorrow our lawyers will visit him. He knows that he will be protected so long as his lips stay sealed. Nothing will lead here.'

She'd suspected as much, as had Edwin Davis.

'What man in Virginia?' one of the other captains asked.

'A loose end that had to be plugged, thanks to you three's stupidity.'

'You're going to regret having guns pointed at me,' another of the captains said.

'Really, Charles? What do you plan to do? Grow a backbone?' He turned back toward Cassiopeia. 'So you'll know, I had nothing to do with trying to kill Danny Daniels. That was their undertaking entirely. Foolishness.'

'And this is smart?' the captain named Charles asked Hale.

'This is necessary. Two of my crew are dead.'

Hale turned toward Shirley.

'No,' Stephanie yelled.

Hale nodded.

And bone snapped.

80

Wyatt kept Carbonell ahead of him and allowed the flashlight beam to lead the way. Water in the chamber was rising, now almost shin-high, the tide definitely coming in. He and Malone had caught it at its lowest. Carbonell was her usual cocky self, oblivious to the real danger, confident that her men would follow and watch her back.

'Is this where the British prisoners died?' she asked.

'No doubt.'

'This water is cold.'

'It won't be long.'

He followed the same path he and Malone had explored, heading for the convergence of the three tunnels where the symbols awaited.

They found the Y-junction.

With his light he pointed out the four symbols ringing the walls and the fifth centered in the ceiling.

'Incredible,' she said. 'It's hidden here?'

Water poured from the chutes that opened about three feet off the floor. Salt foam formed, then dissipated, but the flow remained constant. Another set of chutes awaited at the six-foot point.

'The fifth symbol is high for a reason,' he said. 'What we're looking for is behind that top stone.'

'How do you plan to get to it?'

'I don't.'

* * *

Knox advanced with caution, careful not to slosh the nearly knee-high water, which appeared to be rising. He'd found the flashlight near the bodies in the fort's upper level and was keeping the beam down since Wyatt and Carbonell were ahead of him.

He could hear them talking, beyond a bend twenty feet away.

He switched off the light and crept forward.

Cassiopeia knelt with Stephanie beside Shirley Kaiser, who remained in shock, her wound sutured and bandaged by the doctor. He'd also given her a shot for pain.

'I don't want you to think me a barbarian,' Hale had told them.

They'd watched as Kaiser's middle finger had dropped to the floor, her eyes alight with shock, her screams muffled by the tape across her mouth. Both she and Stephanie had felt her agony. Luckily, Shirley had passed out.

'She's still dazed,' Stephanie said. 'Do you think Edwin got your message?'

She realized that Stephanie would catch the lie she'd cultivated with Davis.

'Trouble is, Edwin is a cautious soul,' Stephanie said.

Not when it came to Pauline Daniels, Cassiopeia thought. Hopefully, he'd be equally as impetuous here.

'President Daniels is concerned about you,' she told Stephanie.

'I'm okay.'

'That's not what I mean, and you know it.'

She saw that Stephanie caught the irritation in her voice.

'What did he say to you?' Stephanie asked.

'Enough.'

'I assure you, I haven't done anything wrong.'

'There are a lot of people saying the same thing. Yet we have all these problems.'

'What do you mean by that?'

She wasn't going to breach Davis' or Pauline's confidence, so she said, 'Stephanie, the Daniels' marriage is a disaster. Obviously, you and the president have been speaking about that. Enough that he feels a connection with you. He told me that he thinks you feel the same. Is that true?'

'He said that?'

'Only to me. And there were good reasons to express it.'

Shirley moaned. She was coming around.

'That hand is going to hurt when she wakes up,' Stephanie said.

She waited for an answer to her question.

Stephanie cradled Shirley's head in her lap as they sat on the cell floor. Hale and the captains were gone, as were all of the crewmen. The earless corpse had been dragged outside. They were alone, locked away, waiting for the fog to clear before they left.

'I don't know what to think,' Stephanie quietly said. 'All I know is that I think about him more than I should.'

The makeshift prison door opened and Hale entered.

'Good news. We're off.'

Malone burst from the vehicle as it stopped in the dark near a boat ramp at the end of a wet, sandy trail. Only a light misty rain fell, the sky overhead clearing to reveal scattered stars. Dawn was less than an hour away. It had been a long night and he'd caught only a short nap on the plane, his mind churning with fear over Cassiopeia and Stephanie.

'What have you heard?' he asked Davis, who waited beside an SUV.

'She called about an hour ago.'

He knew that was required in order to buy more time, but he caught the reservation in Davis' tone.

'She gave me false information. Implied that the men who were attacking the place were ours.'

'You think the call was forced?'

'Probably. We still have no probable cause for anything, except what Cassiopeia reported, which we can't use since she's there illegally.'

He knew what the Fourth Amendment provided, but screw the Constitution. 'We need to act.'

'You're our only move.'

He realized this man had more to consider than just Cassiopeia.

'There's a fog out over the water that's spread inland to the north shore. It stretches downriver a few miles, toward the sea. Not uncommon, I'm told, this time of year.'

'Great cover to use to get onto that estate.'

'I thought you might feel that way.' Davis pointed toward the darkened river and the concrete ramp.

'There's a boat waiting for you.'

Wyatt sensed that someone else was nearby. He'd caught only the faintest hint of water splashing, but instinct told him Knox had followed them.

Two birds with one stone?

Was that what the quartermaster was thinking?

Hale was both pleased and concerned. He'd contained the intruders and thwarted a prison break, but the extent of his problem in Virginia had yet to be ascertained. Vitt's statement that they had a man in custody, if true, could be troublesome. He'd already called lawyers and told them to investigate. He'd also heard no more from Knox in Nova Scotia. Thankfully, the three other captains had left. He'd severed Kaiser's finger because his men, his equals, and his enemies had to know that he was someone to fear.

He watched as Nelle and Vitt helped Kaiser into the bed of a wet pickup truck. Four armed crewmen joined them. A contingent of six more would follow in another truck.

'To the dock,' he called out.

Malone navigated the twelve-foot V-hull through the short, blunt-shaped waves of a tossing Pamlico River. Finally, he encountered the fog and kept a bearing due east toward a dock that should extend a couple of hundred feet from the north shore. The storm had subsided, the wind and rain gone, but the river continued to churn. He'd been told it was about two miles across and he estimated that he'd gone just about that distance.

He checked his watch.

5:20 AM.

A bright glow through the mist to the east signaled dawn on the horizon.

He shifted to neutral and drifted, lightly working the throttle on and off to compensate for a swift current that drew him back toward the river's center and east to the sea.

A nest of blurred lights sparked ahead.

Four arranged in a row.

He shut off the outboard and listened.

Davis had told him about *Adventure*. A two-hundred-foot-plus, state-of-the-art sailing sloop. The ship's outline appeared ahead, and he heard activity on the deck. Men shouting.

Swells drove him closer.

He could not strike the hull.

More activity seemed to be happening beyond the ship, toward shore, perhaps on the dock. Jouncing beams of light stabbed the dark. Two together, like headlights. Nothing could be seen clearly, the fog masking reality, as if he were viewing the dark world through a smoky bottle.

He gripped his gun and shifted the outboard into gear, keeping the throttle barely out of neutral, easing closer.

He found the hull and angled left, following the waterline.

An anchor chain appeared, apparently used for stabilization even while docked, which made sense given the river's strong current.

Above him stretched fifty feet of thick, wet chain.

He could do it, but he needed to know something.

He spun the wheel hard to port and shifted the throttle into neutral. Immediately the boat drifted away. Satisfied as to the current's direction, he reengaged the throttle and gave himself a gentle nudge forward. He stuffed the gun between his belt and waist, switched off the engine, then grabbed the wet links above him and climbed.

He glanced back and watched the current grab the boat as it disappeared into the night.

Only one way left to go now.

81

Nova Scotia

Wyatt waited for Andrea Carbonell to process his defiant stand. The face displaying the fifth symbol was only a few feet above his head. Wide mortar lines outlined the stone's odd shape. The builders of this foundation chamber had used many irregular stones, carefully fitting them into place with mortar. It wouldn't take much to break this one away – a hammer and chisel, or maybe a crowbar.

'What do you plan to do?' she asked him, a gun still in her hand.

'Is your entire life one scheme after another?' He truly wanted to know.

'My life is about survival. As is yours, Jonathan.'

'You've manipulated yourself all the way to this point. People have died. Do you care? Even a little?'

'I do what I have to do. Again, just like you.'

He resented the equating of herself to him. He was a lot of things, but he was not like her in anyway. He held the light down, the beam illuminating the rising seawater. He noted that the lowermost chutes were now submerged.

'What are you waiting for?' she asked.

'Our guest to arrive.'

'Did you hear them, too?' she asked.

He caught the plural *them*. 'That's not your men coming. I killed them both.'

She raised her gun.

He switched off the flashlight, plunging the chamber into total darkness.

A loud retort echoed off the stones, which pounded his eardrums.

Then another.

He'd shifted position, assuming she would fire at where he'd been the moment darkness arrived.

'Jonathan, this is madness,' she said through the blackness. 'Why don't we just make a deal? One or both of us is going to get hurt.'

He said nothing. Silence was now his weapon.

More cold water surged into the chamber, announcing itself with a roar. He rested on his knees, the unlit flashlight held above the surface, waiting.

Carbonell kept quiet, too.

She was no more than ten feet away, but with water gushing about them and the complete lack of light, her locating him was impossible.

Luckily, the reverse was not the case.

Cassiopeia and Stephanie helped Shirley Kaiser out of the pickup truck and onto the dock. She remained a little stunned, her hand bandaged tight.

'Damn, that hurts,' Shirley muttered.

'Hang in there,' Stephanie whispered. 'There's help on the way.'

Cassiopeia hoped that was true. Edwin Davis had to be suspicious. She saw that *Adventure* was now lit with activity. Hale was true to his word. They were going for a sail. She noticed fog, but also the fact that out on the river, higher in the sky, the ground mist dissipated, stars winking in and out from a misty veil.

'I'll be all right,' Shirley said.

Hale stood six meters away near the gangway.

'You think you can kill all three of us and no one will notice,' Cassiopeia called out.

He walked closer. 'I doubt anyone will raise much of a stink. That failed rescue attempt gives me bargaining power. I would say myriad laws were violated with that nonsense. Once our letters of marque are fortified, we'll be fine. Danny Daniels doesn't want a public fight on any of this.'

'You might be wrong,' Stephanie said.

And Cassiopeia agreed, recalling the fortitude with which Daniels had urged both she and Cotton to find Stephanie. He could well do whatever was required and damn the consequences. Hale was underestimating the president. As Daniels had told her, his political career was about over.

Which provided a lot of room to maneuver.

'Get them on board,' Hale said to his men.

Malone finished his climb and slipped onto the yacht's bow deck unnoticed. He'd almost lost his grip twice on the slippery chain.

He found his gun and readied himself.

Decks wrapped a path on either side of a forward cabin, its mirrored windows lit from behind, the angled front softened by rounded, tapered sides. He saw no one past the windows, but kept low.

He heard a commotion from shore.

Investigating that could prove tricky, as someone might come forward along the deck. But he decided to take the chance. He stayed low and crept to the rail. Through the darkness and mist he spotted men boarding the ship along with three women, two of them helping a third. An older man stood on the dock, watching, then followed them on board.

Cassiopeia and Stephanie he recognized.

The third had to be Shirley Kaiser.

He found his cellphone and hit a speed dial button. Davis immediately answered.

'The sloop's leaving,' he whispered. 'We're all on board. Time to bring in the troops.'

Literally. They'd talked about that before he left the south shore.

'I'll handle it. What are you going to do?'

'Whatever I have to.'

Hale stepped aboard *Adventure*, imagining himself as one of those daring men from three hundred years ago, challenging anything and everything, caring only what his men thought of him. His had to be proud of him tonight. He'd stood with them toe-to-toe. Now he would stand toe-to-toe with Andrea Carbonell to finish what she'd started. He hoped Knox would be successful in killing her and he hoped the two missing pages had been found. He'd gladly pay whatever Jonathan Wyatt wanted. Hell, he might even hire him permanently.

'Ready to sail,' he hollered. 'Cast the lines and raise anchor.'

He would personally captain this voyage.

He listened to the purr of the two 1800 horsepower, Deutz engines. State of the art. Both barely made a sound, with little to no vibration. No generators roared, either. Instead, a bank of lithium polymer batteries provided power. The DynaRig's sails were stored safely within the yards, awaiting the command from one of twenty onboard computers to unfurl and catch the wind. That would happen closer to the Oracoke Inlet, where the Atlantic waited.

He noticed that his three prisoners were being led into the main salon.

'Oh, no,' he yelled. 'Have our guests wait on the aft deck, by the pool. I have a special surprise for them.'

* * *

Wyatt re-donned the night-vision goggles that he'd brought in his backpack. Carbonell stood a few feet away, smart enough to crouch down, her head surveying the darkness, her eyes of no help. Instead she was probably listening for any change in the pitch or tone of the water rising around her.

He glanced down.

Water lapped his thighs.

The real shift would come when the six-foot-high chutes filled from their grottoes. Which gave him maybe half an hour.

Movement disturbed the otherwise stable background.

A man appeared from around one of the corners. He held an unlit flashlight in one hand and a gun in the other.

Clifford Knox.

Welcome.

And here's a gift.

He switched on his flashlight and tossed it straight toward a huddled Andrea Carbonell.

82

Malone retreated down into a forward hold that opened at the bow. Two tenders, maybe thirty-footers, were lashed to the deck on either side of the hatch. He had to admire the gigantic steel-hulled sloop, a sleek tower of smooth lines, everything perfectly aerodynamic. And tall. Fifty feet off the water, with another thirty or so on top of that in cabins and deck. Its three masts were close to two hundred feet high. Clearly, a masterpiece of technology and design.

The yacht moved.

Interesting how the engines could barely be heard. One second they were stationary, the next off they went. He glanced out past the hatch. Fog draped the deck in a protective shield.

He fled the hold and found a doorway that opened inside the upper cabins.

The companionway led aft, casting a feeling of height and depth from a bulkhead lined with lighting that reminded him of a row of clerestory windows. A scent of magnolia and green tea came from sprayers near the ceiling. The corridor ended midship where three decks united at a circular stairway that wrapped the main mast. Above, transparent floors allowed light to stream down during the day. He noted the splendid mixture of stainless steel, glass, fine woods, and stone.

Movement from above caught his attention.

He ducked into a doorway that led into a gym. No lights

burned inside. He kept close to the wall and watched as two men descended the circular stairway at a brisk pace. They did not stop, but kept going down to the bottom level.

He'd heard Hale.

The aft deck.

That's where Cassiopeia and the others were waiting.

Hale stepped onto the aft deck. Here was where he'd dealt with his traitorous accountant and here was where he would deal with these three problems. He'd said he had a special surprise for them and, under the watchful eye of two armed guards, they were already examining it as he approached.

'It's called a gibbet,' he told them. 'Made of iron and shaped to the human body.'

He felt the engines kicked up. *Adventure* could do twenty knots, and he'd ordered maximum speed. At nearly twenty-five miles per hour they would soon be offshore.

'Good men were once encased inside these,' he said, 'then hung from a pole and left to die. A horrible form of punishment.'

'Like making someone eat their own ear?' Vitt asked him.

He smiled. 'In the same vein, except these were used on us by our pursuers.'

He motioned and two of his crew grabbed Vitt by the arms. She started to resist, but he raised a warning finger and said, 'Be a good girl.'

Before appearing on the aft deck he'd instructed that Vitt's hands be bound behind her back. The other two he'd left alone. One of the crew kicked Vitt's feet out from under her and she slammed hard to the deck. They then grabbed her by the shoes and head, tossing her into the gibbet, which lay open like a cocoon. Its top was hinged shut and secured with a clamp and pin. Little room existed now for her to struggle.

He bent down.

'You killed two of my crew. Now you will experience what my ancestors felt when they died inside one of these.'

Wind rushed back from the ship's sleek contours and washed him in moist, cool air. He caught the tart smell of the ocean and knew the sea was not far away. The fog seemed to be lifting, too.

Excellent.

He'd been worried that he would not be able to see this woman die.

Knox saw a light appear in the darkness then arc ten feet to the right. He wasn't sure who it was, but it didn't matter.

He fired straight at it.

Nothing happened.

The light continued on its path, splashing into the water, the bulb now submerged. His bullet found no target, but instead ricocheted off the walls, its pings signaling trouble. He'd caught a momentary shadow to the right of where the light found the water. More movement betrayed a position as the light was lifted from the water and shut off.

That was a target.

He fired again.

Wyatt dropped back into the water, slow and silent. In the instant after he tossed the light toward Carbonell, he'd locked his fingers onto the edge of a chute and pulled himself upward. The last place he wanted to be when bullets were ricocheting was near the floor.

Gravity sent slugs directly that way.

Through the goggles he watched Knox and Carbonell. Each carried a gun and a flashlight.

Even odds.

He used the rising surge of water to ease his retreat toward the tunnel from which they'd come. He realized that neither of them would risk switching on their lights or speaking, and firing wildly in the dark was risky.

He wondered how long they'd stand there.

Did they comprehend the danger?

Escaping through the chutes, as he and Malone had done, would not be possible with the rising tide. Fighting the flow of water inside the tight confines would be like trying to swim up a fast-moving stream, no way to hold your breath long enough to make it out.

They'd each worked themselves into a corner, from which there was no escape.

Only low tide would offer a respite.

But they'd both be dead by then.

Malone crept down the middeck, cautious and quiet, using the open doorways and darkened rooms for cover. He passed a theater, dining room, and staterooms. He'd noticed no cameras, yet every nerve in his body tinged, his finger on the gun's trigger, ready to react.

The passageway ended at a grand salon, a juxtaposition of conservative appointments in wenge wood, ivory, and leather. A baby grand piano anchored one corner. Everything was sleek and polished, like the yacht itself. He had to see what was happening on the aft deck. The exterior walls were lined with elongated windows, so he crouched low and made his way toward the glass exit doors, where he spotted a deck, pool, and people.

A spiral stairway to his right led up.

He slowly climbed the steep risers, which opened onto a small sundeck overlooking the ship's stern. He noted their position. Center of the river, both banks visible in the distance, a sun rising ahead, toward the east, the fog all but gone. He glanced toward the bow and spotted open water. They were entering the sound, which meant the ocean was not far away.

He stayed low and made his way to the aft railing.

Staring down, he spotted Stephanie and Shirely Kaiser, two men with guns, four more standing nearby, Quentin Hale—

And Cassiopeia.

Sealed inside an iron gibbet.

83

Cassiopeia was nearing panic. Her hands were bound, her body encased in iron straps. Hale's men were busy tying a line to the top of the gibbet. She stared at Stephanie, whose eyes signaled that there was little she could do, either.

'What's the point of this,' Shirley screamed out. 'Why do this, Quentin?'

Hale faced Kaiser. 'This is what pirates do.'

'Killing unarmed women?' Stephanie asked.

'Teaching enemies a lesson.'

The men securing the line stood.

Hale drew close. 'Kings and governors loved to use the gibbet on us, so occasionally we reciprocated. But instead of hanging them up to die, we dragged them until they drowned. After, we cut the rope, and down to the bottom they went.'

Hale signaled and his men lifted the iron cage from the deck.

Malone could delay no longer. Tumultuous emotions churned inside him. He raised his gun and prepared to fire – but before he could snap the trigger a pair of strong hands locked onto his shoulders and whirled him back from the railing.

One of the crew.

A swift kick to his right arm jarred the gun from his grip.

Fury welled inside him.

No time for this.

He planted a kick to the gut, which doubled his opponent

forward. He brought his knee upward into the face, righting the man's spine. He then jammed his elbow into the bridge of the nose, snapping the neck backward. Two swipes from his fists and the man spilled over the railing, falling the fifteen or so feet to the deck below.

The men hoisting Cassiopeia heard the thud and momentarily stopped. Hale heard it, too, and whirled, then glanced upward and spotted the source of the problem.

Malone searched for the gun.

'Toss her,' he heard Hale scream.

He found the gun, snatched it up, then leaped over the railing, dropping to the deck below. He hit, rolled, and fired at the two men with guns, dropping both.

He sprang to his feet and raced ahead.

Hale tried to cut him off, a gun in his hand, but he shot the older man once, the bullet tearing into the chest and hurling the body backward to the deck.

He kept moving.

'Go,' Stephanie yelled. 'Help her.'

The four men reached the railing with the gibbet.

Too late for him to use the gun to stop them.

They tossed Cassiopeia into the sea.

Wyatt retraced his route to where the rope waited.

The water had risen to waist-high. Shortly, the upper chutes would complete the flooding. Only fitting that these two meet their end here, both of them so smug. Carbonell counting on her backup to save her, Knox thinking he had an easy opportunity to eliminate two problems. Even more fitting that they were both armed with lights and weapons, neither of them any good to them.

Carbonell was responsible for the needless deaths of several agents. Knox had personally killed a few, too.

For that, they both had to pay.

Knox had also tried to kill the president. And though Wyatt wasn't a big fan of the U.S. government, he was an American.

And always would be.

These two problems would end here. By the time they realized their dire predicament and decided to save their hides, it would be too late.

Only a few more minutes remained.

High tide had arrived.

Through the night-vision goggles, he spotted the rope.

He grabbed hold and hauled himself up.

Once there, he yanked the line from the hole and walked away.

Cassiopeia was falling. She tried to brace herself with her feet, anticipating the water's impact. Her hands were of no use and she reminded herself to grab a breath and keep sucking air for as long as she could. Unfortunately, the tight confines offered her no opportunity to use her legs, each of which was encased separately. The gibbet was snug, and the latch mechanism was nowhere close to where she could reach it. Besides, it operated from the outside.

Just before they'd tossed her overboard she'd heard what sounded like gunfire and Stephanie yelling *Go. Help her.*

What was happening back there?

Malone fired two shots at the four men, scattering them. He then tossed the gun aside and leaped from the railing, hurling his body outward and bear-hugging the falling gibbet.

His added weight increased momentum and, together, he and Cassiopeia smacked the sea.

Something had slammed into the gibbet, startling Cassiopeia. A body. Male. Together they hit the water.

Then she saw the face and relief poured through her. Cotton.

Malone held tight. No way he was letting go. They teetered on the surface, tossing in the surf, as the line's slack played out behind the yacht.

'Glad you finally made it,' she said.

His gaze found the latch mechanism.

The gibbet was starting to sink.

He reached out but the line went taut.

And they were dragged through the water.

Hale was stunned. The intruder had shot him, but thankfully in the chest. The body armor he'd donned earlier before leading the defense of the prison had saved him, though his ribs throbbed. He'd dropped to the deck, but not before seeing the man leap from the railing toward the gibbet.

He brought himself to his knees and sucked a few deep breaths.

He turned for his men, who were nowhere to be seen.

Instead Stephanie Nelle stood with a gun aimed straight at him.

'I told you Cotton Malone was trouble,' she said.

Malone kept a death grip on the gibbet, his right hand finding one of the rounded vertical supports to which the flat iron was welded. A shower of color burst before his eyes. They were skimming in and out of the water about a hundred feet behind *Adventure,* in the center portion of the sloop's long wake.

He gulped another breath and yelled to Cassiopeia, 'Breathe.'

'Like I'm not trying.'

He had more room to maneuver than she did. The sloop's

speed allowed them to hydroplane for a few precious seconds. He realized that once the speed was reduced they would sink and be dragged

underwater.

His heart rocketed in his chest.

He had to find the latch.

Cassiopeia was sucking in as much water as air, trying to spit it out and keep her lungs dry. She was rotating her upper body inside the gibbet as they rocketed in and out of the surf. A sharp pain pierced her cramped calves and she told herself to relax. She longed for speed, since slowing down meant sinking. Hale was toying with them. Enjoying their predicament.

'I'm . . . going to . . . get you . . . out,' Cotton told her as they surfaced one more time, his voice coming in staccato gasps.

'My hands,' she managed to say.

She couldn't swim long if she were bound.

Hale stared at Stephanie Nelle.

'Are you going to shoot me?' he asked her.

'I don't have to.'

A strange reply.

She motioned with the gun and he turned.

Shirley Kaiser held another of the automatic rifles his men had toted. Her bandaged hand supported the heavy weapon, the other was placed firmly on the trigger.

Men appeared from the main salon.

Some with guns.

Finally.

Malone's hand found the latch. He twisted, then yanked. Nothing gave. He yanked again, freeing the locking pin.

The gibbet opened and Cassiopeia flew out.

He released his hold and joined her in the water.

The gibbet disappeared ahead, bucking across the surface.

He snatched a breath and plunged downward, his eyes searching for movement. He saw her and wrapped an arm around her chest and, together, they kicked upward.

Both of them coughed water.

He kept them afloat with strong kicks and a sweep of his right arm.

'Grab a breath and I'll get your hands free,' he told her.

They dropped below the surface long enough for him to peel off the thick tape that bound her wrists, then they surfaced and treaded water. *Adventure* was two hundred yards away, its sails unfurled to the morning air. All was quiet except for the wind and the sea swirling around them.

Then a new sound.

Low and rhythmic.

A deep bass growing in intensity.

He turned to see four helicopter gunships powering their way.

About time.

They swept across in formation, one lingering above, the other three circling the yacht.

'You okay?'

Edwin Davis's voice through a loudspeaker.

They both gave him a thumbs-up.

'Hold tight,' Davis said.

Hale heard helicopter rotors and looked up to see three U.S. Army gunships above *Adventure*'s masts, circling like wolves.

The sight enraged him.

This ungrateful government, which his family had duti-fully served, would not leave him alone. What had happened with Knox? Or the man named Wyatt? Did they have what he needed to fortify his letter of marque? And why weren't Bolton, Surcouf, and Cogburn here to fight the battle with him? Probably because the three cowards had sold him out.

Stephanie Nelle laid down a barrage of fire at the main salon, obliterating the windscreens, ripping through the fiberglass sheathing.

His men disappeared back inside.

He faced Kaiser and her gun. 'It's not that easy, Shirley.'

He imagined himself Black Beard, facing Lieutenant Maynard on the deck of another ship named *Adventure*. That fight had also been close-quartered and to the death. But Black Beard had been armed. Hale's gun lay on the deck four feet away. He had to get to it. His gaze darted between Shirley to his right and Nelle to his left.

Just one opportunity, that's all he needed.

Shirley's gun exploded.

Bullets tore into his protective vest. The next salvo shredded his legs. Blood poured up his throat and out his mouth. He tumbled to the ground, each nerve in his body bursting into a hot flame of burning pain.

His face betrayed the agony.

The last thing he saw was Shirley Kaiser pointing the gun at his head and saying, 'Killing you was easy, Quentin.'

Cassiopeia heard the distance tap of gunfire. She then saw two people leap from the aft deck of *Adventure*.

'Stephanie and Shirley just made their escape,' Davis said from above, through the helicopter's PA system.

They kept treading water.

Adventure's sails had caught the wind. No gaps existed between them. They worked as a single airfoil, propelling the striking green hull through the choppy waves. She was like the buccaneer of old, sailing away to fight another day. But this wasn't the 17th or 18th century, and Danny Daniels was one pissed-off president. These four army gunships were not here to escort the ship back to port.

More people leaped off the yacht.

'The crew,' Cotton said. 'You know why they're doing that.'

She did.

The choppers drifted back.

Flames erupted from the sides of two of the aircraft. Four missiles rocketed from their launchers. Seconds later they pierced *Adventure*, exploding their ordnance. Black, acrid smoke rose skyward. Like a wounded animal, the sloop canted to one side, then another, its sails unfurling and losing their strength.

A final rocket from the third chopper ended its misery.

The yacht erupted into flames, then sank, the Atlantic Ocean swallowing the offering in a single gulp.

84

Wyatt climbed back into the chasm beneath Fort Dominion. Five hours ago he'd left the island and returned to shore, ditching the stolen boat near Chester and renting another. He'd also purchased a few tools to go into his knapsack and waited until the tide changed.

One last thing to do.

He dropped to the rocky floor.

As when he and Malone had visited, only a few inches of water remained. He switched on a flashlight and started for the junction point. Halfway, he encountered the first bloated corpse.

Maybe late thirties, early forties, dark hair, plain face, one he recognized.

The quartermaster.

Clifford Knox.

Lying spine-first on the rocky floor, eyes closed.

He continued on and found the five symbols. No sign, as yet, of Carbonell, but there were two other tunnels and no way out. Her body could be anywhere. It could even have been drawn out to sea through one of the chutes.

He stared up at the symbol in the ceiling.

Δ

He hoped Malone had been right and that the triangle did indeed mark the spot. He rolled one of the larger rocks close. The ceiling was low, maybe eight feet up, so not much of a boost would be needed. He removed the hammer and chisel he'd brought with him and chipped the joint that outlined the irregular-shaped block. Nearly two centuries of tidal action had hardened the mortar, but finally it gave way. He stepped back as the rock slammed to the floor, splashing water, cracking into several pieces.

He angled the flashlight upward into the niche.

A foot up from the ceiling line a shelf had been carved into the stone. Something gleamed back from the probe of his beam. Shiny. Reflective. Green-tinted. He laid the light down, angling it upward and grabbed hold of what he'd discovered.

Slick.

Then he realized.

Glass.

He slid it from its perch.

Not heavy, maybe three or four pounds. A solid chunk, perhaps a foot square, its surface and edges rounded smooth. He bent down closer to the flashlight and splashed water onto its surface, rinsing away a layer of filth.

Something was sealed inside.

Though blurred, the image was unmistakable.

Two sheets of browned paper.

He laid the container on top of the stone that had acted as his step. He found another smaller rock and, with two blows, shattered the glass.

For the first time in more than 175 years, the paper met fresh air.

Two columns of printing appeared on each page along with a header.

OF DEBATES IN CONGRESS

And a date.

February 9, 1793

He scanned one of the pages until he found

Mr. Madison. The subject of the proposition laid before the House will now, I presume, Mr. Chairman, recur for our deliberation. I imagine it to be of the greatest magnitude, a subject, sir, that requires our first attention and our united exertion. In drafting our Constitution this Congress was bestowed the specific power to grant letters of marque, as the current policy of nations so sanctions throughout the world. Indeed, our victory over England would not have occurred but for the courageous efforts of entrepreneurs possessed of both ships and the ability to make appropriate use of them. Happy it is for us that such a grant was, and remains, within our power. We are all painfully aware that we do not, as yet, possess sufficient men and ships to float an adequate navy in our common defense, so I concur in the proposal for the grant of these letters of marque to Archibald Hale, Richard Surcouf, Henry Cogburn, and Samuel Bolton, in perpetuity, so that they might continue a robust and continuous attack on our enemies.

The motion was put by the Chairman, and was agreed upon by all in attendance. The said letters of marque were directed to be forwarded to the Senate for action. The House adjourned.

He examined the other sheet and saw that its wording was similar, only from the Senate journal where the letters were also unanimously approved, the last line of that entry making clear 'that the said enactment be forwarded to Mr. Washington for signature.'

Here was what the Commonwealth had sought. What men had died for. These two documents meant nothing but trouble. Their reemergence would cause only problems.

Good agents solved problems.

He tore both sheets into confetti and scattered the pieces across the water on the floor. He watched as they dissolved away.

Done.

He retreated to the rope, passing Knox one last time.

'You died for nothing,' he told the corpse.

He climbed back to ground level. Time to leave this lonely outpost. Birds cooed all around him, their movement constant on the wall walks.

He retrieved the rope from the hole and decided, *enough*. He called out, 'Why don't you come out and let's talk?'

He'd sensed from the moment he returned to the fort that he was not alone. At the far end of the collapsed hall, Cotton Malone appeared.

'I thought you were gone,' Wyatt said.

'I came back to retrieve the pages, but then I was told you were coming for them, too.'

'I assumed the Canadian authorities would be involved at some point.'

'We waited as long as we could. What happened down there?'

'The Commonwealth is minus a quartermaster.'

He noticed Malone carried no weapon, but there was no need. Six armed men appeared on the wall walks above him.

There'd be no fighting today.

'And the pages?' Malone asked.

He shook his head. 'An empty receptacle.'

Malone apprized him with a tight gaze. 'I guess that ends the Commonwealth.'

'And no president will have to deal with it again.'

'Lucky them.'

'Whether you believe it or not, I would have never sold those pages to Hale.'

'Actually, I do believe it.'

He chuckled and shook his head. 'Still the self-righteous ass?'

'Old habit. The president says this is your one freebie, as thanks for what you did in New York, and what you did here with Carbonell.' Malone paused. 'I guess he owes you one more thanks now, too.'

The silence between them confirmed what he'd done.

'And you can keep NIA's money.'

'I planned to anyway.'

'Still defiant to authority?'

'At least neither one of us will ever change.'

Malone motioned to the gaping hole in the floor. 'Both bodies down there?'

'No sign of the she-devil.'

'You think she swam out?'

He shrugged. 'Those chutes weren't like when you and I went through them. She'd better have good lungs.'

'As I recall, she did.'

Wyatt smiled. 'That she did.'

Malone stepped aside. Wyatt asked, 'Does my free pass extend to leaving Canada unmolested?'

'All the way home to Florida. I'd offer you a ride, but that would be too much togetherness for us both.'

Probably so, he thought.

He started to leave.

'You never answered me last night,' Malone said. 'We even?'

He stopped but did not turn back. 'For now.'

And he left.

85

Cassiopeia waited inside the Blue Room, the same bedroom she'd occupied yesterday to change, the same one where she and Danny Daniels had talked. Shirley Kaiser was with her.

'How's the finger?' she asked.

'Hurts like hell.'

Once plucked from the Atlantic, she, Cotton, Stephanie, and Shirley had been brought to Washington. Shirley had received medical attention for the amputation, but the Commonwealth's doctor had done an admirable job of suturing her wound. Some medication for pain and a shot for infection was all she'd needed.

'That swim hurt worse,' Shirley said. 'Salt water. But it beat the hell out of staying on board.'

Adventure's crew had also been retrieved by a Coast Guard cutter, which arrived at the scene within minutes of the sloop's destruction. The crew had been advised by radio to abandon ship or go down with it. All of them chose to leave. Only Quentin Hale sank with her. But he was long dead by then. Stephanie had told her about what Cotton had started and Shirley had finished.

'You okay?' she asked.

They were both worn out, their bodies sore.

'I'm glad I got to shoot him. It cost me a finger, but I think it was worth it.'

She had to say, 'You shouldn't have gone there.'

'Really? If I hadn't, you wouldn't have come. And then who knows where we, or Stephanie, would be right now.'

The cocky attitude had returned.

'At least it's over,' Shirley said.

That it was.

Secret Service and FBI had raided the Commonwealth compound and arrested the other three captains and all of the crew. They were busy now searching every square centimeter of all four estates.

A soft knock came at the door, then it opened and in walked Danny Daniels. She knew it had been a tough afternoon for him, too. On their return, Edwin Davis had told the president everything. Their talk had been private, then had included Pauline Daniels, the three of them, for the past hour, together behind closed doors a few rooms down the hall.

'Pauline would like to see you,' Daniels said to Shirley.

She rose to leave, but stopped in front of the president and asked him, 'You okay?'

He smiled. 'Coming from a woman with nine fingers? I'm fine.'

They all knew what had been discussed behind those closed doors. No sense pretending anymore.

'It's okay, Danny,' Shirley said. 'You're going to be a man long after being president.'

'I thought you hated me?'

Shirley touched his shoulder. 'I do. But thanks for what you did for us out there.'

Daniels had been the one to order the choppers dispatched. He hadn't wanted to trust any local law enforcement so, when Davis radioed the problem, he'd given the army at Fort Bragg a direct command. He'd also been on the line, directing the pilots as to what to do, personally taking responsibility for the ship's sinking.

'We simply stopped some presidential assassins from fleeing the country,' he said.

'You did good, Danny.'

'That's quite a compliment. Coming from you.'

And Shirley left.

Daniels closed the door.

'You stopped more than some fleeing assassins today,' she said to him.

He sat on the bed opposite her. 'Tell me about it. Who would have thought? Edwin and Pauline.'

She knew that had to be tough.

'But I'm glad,' he said. 'I really am. I don't think either one of us knew how to end this marriage.'

The attitude surprised her.

'Pauline and I have been together a long time,' he said in a low voice. 'But we haven't been happy in years. We both miss Mary. Her death drove a wedge between us that could never be removed.'

She caught the break in his voice as he said his daughter's name.

'There's not a day that goes by I don't think of her. I wake up at night and hear her calling for me through that fire. It's haunted me in ways I never understood.' He paused. 'Until today.'

She saw the pain in his eyes. Clear. Deep. Unmistakable. She could only imagine the anguish.

'If Pauline can find peace, and some happiness with Edwin, then I wish her well. I truly do.'

He stared at her with a withdrawn look of fatigue.

'Edwin told me through the radio that Shirley and Stephanie had jumped off. Once I knew she was okay, I have to say, my anger took over. I gave the crew a chance to leave, but I didn't know Hale was already dead.'

'And what do you plan to do about Stephanie?'

Daniels stayed silent a moment, then said, 'I don't know. Pauline said to me the same thing I just said to you. She wants me to be happy. I think we can both move on if we know the other is going to be okay.'

They sat quietly for a few more moments.

'Thank you,' the president finally said. 'For all that you've done.'

She knew what he meant. He'd needed someone to open up to – someone not too close, but someone he could trust.

'I heard about how Cotton saved you. Diving off that yacht. That's pretty special. Having a man who'll lay down his life for you.'

She agreed.

'I hope I can find a woman like that.'

'You will.'

'That remains to be seen.' He stood from the bed. 'Time for me to start acting like a president again.'

She was curious. 'Have we heard from Cotton?'

He'd left North Carolina and flown straight back to Nova Scotia, but that had been early this morning.

'He should be downstairs waiting for you.'

He studied her with eyes that had softened. 'Take care.'

'You too, Mr. President.'

Malone spotted Cassiopeia descending the stairway from the White House's upper floors. He'd arrived back from Canada half an hour ago and had been driven straight here by the Secret Service, talking to the president by phone on the way, reporting what happened at Fort Dominion. Stephanie had greeted him outside and now stood with him.

'I was told about New York,' Stephanie said to him. 'Do you always come running when I call?'

'Only when you say it's important.'

'I'm glad you did. I was beginning to wonder if I was going to make it out of that cell. And nice move on the boat with that gibbet.'

'There didn't seem to be many options.'

Stephanie smiled and pointed toward Cassiopeia. 'I'd say she owes you one.'

His gaze had not left the stairs. No, they were even.

He faced Stephanie. 'Any word on Andrea Carbonell?'

She shook her head. 'We're watching. But, so far, nothing.'

He and several Royal Canadian Mounted Police had searched the caverns beneath the fort until the tide changed, but no trace of Carbonell had been found. Both the bay and open Atlantic were also scoured on the chance that she'd been sucked from the caverns.

Nothing there, either.

'We'll keep looking,' Stephanie said. 'The body has to be somewhere. You don't think she got out?'

'I don't see how. It was hard enough when the chutes were empty.'

Cassiopeia approached.

'Meeting privately with the president?' he asked her.

'Some loose ends that needed tying up.'

Across the foyer, a woman gestured toward them.

'I think it's my turn to speak with the man,' Stephanie said. 'You two try and stay out of trouble.'

He caught the look between the two women. He'd seen it before on Cassiopeia's face. In Virginia. When they spoke to Edwin Davis, then again at Monticello when she insisted that she and Davis talk alone. As Stephanie departed, he said to Cassiopeia, 'I assume, at some point, you're going to tell me what it is you know.'

'At some point.'

'And what were you thinking, going into that compound alone? Crazy as hell, wasn't it?'

She shrugged. 'What would you have done?'

'That doesn't matter.'

'Lucky for me you finally came along.'

He shook his head, then drew her attention to their luggage, which lay near the exit doors. 'We're packed and ready to go.'

'Home?' she asked.

'No way. We still have a date in New York that never happened. A show, then dinner. And there was the matter of a dress you went to buy that I never saw.'

'A black one. Backless. You'll like it.'

That he would. But he had something else on his mind.

'Before we fly home, I'd like to detour to Atlanta and see Gary. Maybe a couple of days.'

He'd not seen his son since the summer, when Gary had spent several weeks with him in Copenhagen.

She nodded. 'I think you should.'

He cleared his throat. 'I think *we* should. He thinks you're hot, you know.'

She smiled and grasped his hand. 'You saved my life out there,' she said. 'How about I properly thank you in New York. I'll get our room back at the St. Regis?'

'Already done. It's waiting for us, as is a Secret Service jet. They offered a free lift.'

'You think of everything, Mr. Malone.'

'Not everything. But I'm sure you can fill in the gaps.'

Writer's Note

This book is a departure from the six previous Cotton Malone adventures, as it's set primarily in the United States. Elizabeth and I explored Washington, DC; New York City; Richmond, Virginia; Bath, North Carolina; and Monticello.

Now it's time to separate fact from fiction.

The assassination attempt on Andrew Jackson (prologue and chapter 13) occurred as depicted, including the presence of Davy Crockett, who helped subdue the assailant and supposedly uttered the precise words quoted in the text. Jackson did publicly blame Senator George Poindexter of Mississippi (chapters 13, 19), alleging a conspiracy, but Poindexter was exonerated by a congressional inquiry. I decided to keep the conspiracy theory alive, only involving my fictional Commonwealth.

A great many actual locales are utilized. The Grand Hyatt (chapters 1, 3, 5, 6), Plaza (chapter 24), St. Regis (chapter 9), and Helmsley Park (chapter 21) hotels in New York are all superb places to stay. The Strand is an outstanding used-book store (chapter 11), which I've been known to roam for research. All particulars of the White House and the Oval Office (chapter 56) are accurate. Grand Central Station is likewise described correctly (chapter 8), including the pedestrian bridge leading to the East 42nd Street exit and the narrow ledge that descends from it to ground level. The Jefferson (chapter 35) stands in Richmond, Virginia, a historic hotel straight out of *Gone with the Wind*.

The Pamlico River and North Carolina coast are lovely (chapters 2, 5, 13), as is Bath (chapter 15), which was once a hotbed of colonial politics and a haven for pirates. Now it's a sleepy village of fewer than 300 residents. The Commonwealth's compound would occupy the woods that stand west of town. The regional airport located in nearby Greenville (chapter 29) exists.

The mention of how Black Beard died (chapter 77) at Ocracoke Inlet is true, as is what happened to his skull after. *A General History of the Robberies and Murders of the Most Notorious Pyrates,* by Charles Johnson (chapters 18, 76), remains a vital sourcebook on pirate history, though no one knows who Charles Johnson actually was. Woodling (chapters 40, 42), dismemberment, forcing prisoners to eat their own ears (chapter 76), and the sweat (chapter 76) were tortures routinely utilized on pirate captives. The gibbet (chapters 2, 82, 83), though, was something pirates endured, once convicted of their crimes.

Jefferson's cipher (chapters 10, 22) existed and was created by Robert Patterson. Jefferson himself considered it unsolvable, and it remained so from 1804 until 2009 when it was finally cracked by Lawren Smithline, a New Jersey mathematician. How the cipher was solved in this story (chapter 36) mirrors Smithline's efforts. Patterson's son, also named Robert (chapter 23), was indeed appointed by Andrew Jackson as director of the U.S. Mint. This fortuitous coincidence seemed tailor-made for this tale. Jackson's letter to Abner Hale, quoted in chapter 5, is my concoction, though it is written using many of Jackson's words. The coded message, of course, is fiction.

Mahone Bay is real (chapters 53, 55, 56, 58), as is the mysterious Oak Island. Paw Island is my creation, as is Fort Dominion, though the invasion of Nova Scotia during the Revolutionary War happened. The Oak Island slab with its strange markings (chapter 56) is part of the island's legend, though no known person has ever seen this slab. Its translation is likewise real, though, again, no one knows who accomplished the feat.

Ybor City exists (chapter 41). The financial crisis in Dubai (chapter 18) happened, though I added a few elements. *Adventure* is based on several yachts of the same size and type, all amazing oceangoing vessels.

There are, of course, no missing pages from the early House and Senate journals (chapter 19). The excerpt from *Of Debates in Congress* (chapter 84) is a composite of several entries from that time. The troubles and statistics quoted by Danny Daniels concerning the U.S. intelligence community (chapter 54) came from a 2010 *Washington Post* exposé.

Monticello is an amazing place. It is accurately described, as is its visitor center (chapters 43, 44, 45, 47, 49). The cipher wheel is real, too, and located on-site (chapters 44, 49) though not inside the house itself. A resin replica exists in the visitor center (chapter 52), but whether it is an exact copy of the original is unknown. Jefferson's library (chapter 44) was sold to the United States after the War of 1812 and formed the basis of the modern Library of Congress. Many of Jefferson's original volumes remain on display in Washington, at the library, in a special exhibit.

Assassination plays a pivotal role in this story. Four U.S. presidents were murdered in office: Lincoln (1865), Garfield (1881), McKinley (1901), and Kennedy (1963). Linking those proved a challenge, but it was interesting to discover that all of the assassins were deranged zealots and none lived long after his act. Booth and Oswald died within hours, and the remaining two were executed within weeks after hasty trials. What Danny Daniels says in chapter 16 about mistakes in presidential protection leading to disaster is true. Daniels' jaunt to New York (chapter 16) is based on Barack Obama's unannounced visit to see a Broadway play with the First Lady, which occurred early in his presidency.

Andrew Jackson was indeed the first president to face an assassin. The threatening letter sent by Junius Brutus Booth, father of John Wilkes Booth, to Jackson is a historic fact (chapter 38). Even more amazing, Booth was upset over Jackson's refusal to pardon some convicted pirates. The four actual presidential assassinations are accurately described throughout, but the Commonwealth's involvement sprang entirely from my imagination.

All of the information about pirates and their unique, short-lived society is correct to history. Fiction and Hollywood have done them a great disservice. Reality is far removed from the stereotypes presented through the years. A pirate's world, though raucous, stayed orderly thanks to agreed-upon articles that governed key ventures. A pirate ship is one of the earliest examples of a working democracy. The Commonwealth, though obviously fictitious, is inspired by accounts of pirate ships joining together in collective efforts. The language quoted throughout from the Commonwealth's articles was taken from actual articles drafted in the 17th and 18th centuries.

Privateers are a historical fact, as is their contribution to both the American Revolution and the War of 1812 (chapters 18, 25). What Quentin Hale tells Edwin Davis in chapter 18 is true: Both the Revolutionary War and War of 1812 were won thanks to their efforts. The roots of the U.S. Navy lie squarely with privateers. George Washington himself acknowledged our great debt to them. Of course, the granting of letters of marque, in perpetuity, to any group of those privateers was my addition.

Article I, Section 8, of the Constitution does indeed allow Congress to bestow letters of marque. The letter quoted in chapter 18 is based on an actual one. Also, any and all history relative to letters of marque detailed throughout the story is true. Privateering was a common weapon utilized for centuries by warring states. The 1856 Declaration of Paris finally outlawed the practice for its signees, but the United States and Spain (chapter 19) were not a party to that agreement. A congressional act in 1899 forbade the practice here (chapter 19), though it's unclear whether that law would withstand constitutional scrutiny considering the express language of Article I, Section 8. During the first 40 years of our republic, letters of marque were commonly issued by Congress. Since 1814 that constitutional clause has remained dormant, though there was an attempt to invoke it after 9/11.

But for all their beneficial contributions to this nation during wartime, a grim reality remains.

Privateers are the nursery for pirates.

About Cotton Malone

Cotton Malone was born in Copenhagen while Steve Berry was sitting at a café in Højbro Plads, a popular Danish square. That's why Cotton owns a bookshop there. Steve wanted a character with government ties and a background that would make Malone, if threatened, formidable. But he also wanted him to be human, with flaws. Since Steve also loves rare books, it was natural that Cotton would too, so Malone became a Justice Department operative, turned bookseller, who manages, from time to time, to find trouble. Steve also gave him an eidetic memory, since, well, who wouldn't like one of those? At the same time, Cotton is clearly a man in conflict. His marriage has failed; he maintains a difficult relationship with his teenage son; and he's lousy with women.

The Jefferson Key is the first Cotton Malone thriller to be set on American soil.

Turn the page now to find out more about Cotton's earlier adventures, all available in Hodder paperback and as eBooks.

HODDER

The Charlemagne Pursuit

'Action-packed, fast paced and engaging'
Sunday Express

'Pure intrigue. Pure fun'
Clive Cussler

Ex-agent Cotton Malone wants to know what really
happened to his father, officially lost at sea when his
submarine went down in the North Atlantic. But having
used his government contacts to provide the answers,
he soon finds out he isn't the only one after the truth.
Stuck in a lethal power struggle between two mysterious
twin sisters, Malone embarks on a dangerous adventure
involving Nazi explorations in Antarctica, US government
conspiracies and the legend of Charlemagne. Forced to
choose a side where neither can win, Malone must
uncover the truth behind his father's death – but can
he escape his own?

'Plenty of classic touch points are in this cliff-hanger:
Nazis, secret missions, shootouts, and cryptic journals . . .
In Malone, Berry has created a classic, complex hero.'
USA Today

The Emperor's Tomb

'One of Berry's best.' *Globe and Mail*

The tomb of China's First Emperor has remained sealed for 2200 years. It's one of the greatest archaeological sites in the world – so why can't the public view it?

That question is at the heart of the dilemma currently faced by ex-agent Cotton Malone, especially after he receives an anonymous tip containing an unfamiliar web address. On opening the website, Malone sees one of his closest friends, Cassiopeia Vitt, being tortured by a man who demands that Malone brings him the artefact which Vitt originally asked Malone to keep safe. There is only one problem: Malone has no idea what he is talking about. And so begins one of Malone's most harrowing adventures, taking him all the way from Europe to the Far East to confront a ruthless brotherhood, an explosive secret – and a deadly battle for power over the entire world . . .

'Berry has a knack for conveying history without slowing down the page-turning suspense . . . Berry has written another winner.' *Library Journal*

'Readers will relish the cat and mouse chase as the mysterious Cassiopeia Vitt provides a delightful female counterpart to Cotton Malone. The climax is a great confrontational finish to a fabulous tale.' *Mystery Gazette*

The Paris Vendetta

'A top-notch, gripping, intelligent thriller in the
very finest traditions of the genre.'
Peter James

Ex-agent Cotton Malone's closest friend, Henrik
Thorvaldsen, is in perilous danger – and the men who
want to kill him are on Malone's doorstep.

Dragged into his friend's dangerous schemes and secretly
put under pressure by the US government to stop both
Thorvaldsen and a sinister group known only as the
Paris Club, Malone soon discovers that the past is the
key to the answers he desperately seeks, and an
astounding treasure that Napoleon took to his grave.

'*The Paris Vendetta* is his best yet.'
Harlan Coben

'All the Steve Berry hallmarks are here: scale, scope,
sweep, history—plus breathless second-by-second
suspense. I love this guy.'
Lee Child

'You don't just read a Steve Barry novel. You *live it*.'
James Rollins